MOONLIGHT ENCOUNTER

Cage kissed my hand, his lips lingering for a moment longer than I thought propriety condoned. And my heart began to beat with a new hope. He drew me away from a group of people on the verandah and led me into the library. I could feel the warmth of his hand through the cloth of my sleeve. My knees were trembling. He shut the door.

"There's something I want to say," he whispered, looking at me, his eyes alight. I sat down on the sofa, trying to look appropriately puzzled. He came and sat beside me. My heart was beating so fast I thought I would suffocate. He took my hand, turned it palm up and kissed it. A little electric thrill ran up me . . .

FLORENCE HURD

SHADOWS OF THE HEART

AVON
PUBLISHERS OF BARD, CAMELOT AND DISCUS BOOKS

SHADOWS OF THE HEART is an original publication
of Avon Books. This work has never before appeared in
book form.

AVON BOOKS
A division of
The Hearst Corporation
959 Eighth Avenue
New York, New York 10019

First Avon Printing, November, 1980

AVON TRADEMARK REG. U.S. PAT. OFF. AND IN
OTHER COUNTRIES, MARCA REGISTRADA, HECHO EN
U.S.A.

Printed in the U.S.A.

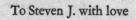

To Steven J. with love

Part I

OBSESSION

Chapter 1

THE clock on the stair chimed four.

As the last note echoed through the darkness I slipped out of bed and lit a shaded candle with trembling hands. The tiny flame flickered, a feeble nimbus of light in the black-shadowed room, and as I stared down into it, doubt twisted my heart. But only for a moment—no more. Then I was shaking it off, throwing my hair back from my shoulders, turning from the candle, rubbing my bare, goose-pimpled arms.

I tiptoed to the window and drawing the curtain aside, peered out. River mist pressed against the glass, mist thick and opaque, shutting the view completely from sight. Fog! My heart sank once more. Fog meant the river path would be shrouded, the twisting, turning lane hard to follow, let alone find.

Still—how could I give up? The fog was bad luck, something I had not anticipated, but to return to bed after waiting impatiently all the long night was unthinkable. Impossible. I had to go. I had to be there. I *had* to.

Shivering I got into my pantalets and my riding gown, hurriedly doing the buttons up with fingers now gone numb and nerveless. My hair I smoothed back and tied with a ribbon. From the wardrobe I took a warm cape and threw it about my shoulders, adjusting the hood over my head. I blew out the candle and waited a few moments for my eyes to get accustomed to the dark, then carrying my shoes I crept to the door and cracked it open.

A profound, inky silence enveloped the gallery. I drew in my breath and pushed the door wider, hesitating, fingers to my lips. Suddenly a board creaked, snapping with a pop that sent taut nerves jumping crazily. Then the silence again. I could hear the faint ticking of the tall, mahogany clock on the landing. Tick-tock, tick-tock. I strained my

3

ears—no, nothing else. Just the clock. They were all sleeping. If Papa should wake and catch me, there would be the devil to pay. And Charles, too, would be angry. "It was a mistake to have told you," he would say, his brows drawn together in a frown. "A mistake. This is a man's business, Adelaide."

I eased myself through the door and with shoulders hunched, shoes clutched in one hand, I tiptoed past Papa's bedroom door. From behind it a bed spring squeaked and the blood rushed to my face. I paused at the head of the stairs, my hand frozen on the rail. Had Papa wakened? I waited in the tense quiet expecting to hear his voice booming out at any moment. If he knew—only guessed—everything would be ruined! He would rage and rant, calling on the spirit of my dead mother. "What would she say? A disgrace! A scandal! And you hardly out of your pinafore!" he would shout and send me back to my room.

Perhaps what I was doing *was* a disgrace and for that I asked forgiveness of a mother I could not remember, but Papa erred when he thought of me as "hardly out of my pinafore." I was fourteen, going on fifteen, a young lady, not a child. And if I could possibly help it no power on earth was going to keep me from reaching Baker's Wood before first light.

At the bottom of the stairs I swallowed hard, then carefully crossed the parquet floor with a heart beating so painfully I thought I would suffocate. The heavy front door opened stiffly, its hinges squealing and groaning loudly, a sound that fairly screamed in the silence and brought the cold sweat to my brow. And then I was out on the misted verandah, drawing deeply of the chill, moist air.

I hugged the cape closer and leaning against a pillar, drew on my shoes. Next I descended the steps and walking quickly through the wet grass to the orchard where I had tethered Beau after supper the night before. He was waiting, ears up, alert. Before he could make a sound I slipped a lump of sugar between his teeth and closed his muzzle with my hands. "Nice boy, good boy." I rubbed his nose with my face. Then leading him to a tree stump I mounted and we started off.

So far, so good.

There were no lights anywhere, not a chink of shine to break the dark, only the white ghostly fog and the dim outlines of trees. The Wood was two miles north of the house, a short ride in good weather, but in this fog God alone knew how long it would take. I wanted to hurry, not to travel in a blind, slow feeling walk, but one misstep, one, and Beau and I would plunge from the embankment into the cold river below. Better to pick our way carefully, I told myself, than not to get there at all. So I kept a tight rein, my eyes straining into the fog, trusting that Beau would instinctively keep to high ground. His hooves were muffled on a thick carpet of fallen leaves, a sound that clumped irritatingly at my nerves. I wished we were there. I wished time would be swift, impossibly swift. I wished the morning were over.

The horse stumbled and my heart knocked violently against my ribs as my hands tightened convulsively on the reins. "There—Beau!—it's all right, Beau!" I soothed, bringing him to a halt. The mist was still thick but the darkness had begun to fade. I peered about trying to penetrate the gloom, looking for the crooked, leaning pine along the bank of the river which marked the turn-off point to the Wood. I could scarcely see two yards in front of my nose. The trees adrift in gossamer fog, like ghosts draped in gray shrouds, seemed all alike. Birds began to peep and twitter in hidden nests over my head. Soon it would be dawn—and now I began to worry lest someone find me on the path, someone who knew me, who would guess my destination.

I clucked at Beau, urging him into a walk. Had I missed the pine? Had I gone right by without seeing it? The next tree and the next and the next—not there or there, and then a long stretch with nothing at all. It must be behind me, I thought. I've surely passed it. I was on the verge of turning back when the pine suddenly appeared, rising out of the fog like a skeletal arm with one bony finger pointing to the sky.

I turned Beau and we went under the dripping oaks. Fortunately, the path through Baker's Wood, though narrow, was well traveled, trampled to a firm surface by the passage of countless hooves. In addition the mist here had begun to dissolve, not much but enough to allow me to see the blazed tree trunks on either side. I pressed my heel into Beau's flank and he quickened his pace, trotting now. We were almost there.

When the trees began to thin, I slid from the saddle and led Beau in from the path to a clump of tall bushes. I would be well hidden there but to make sure Beau would not give me away by whinnying at the wrong moment, I took him deeper in among the trees and tied him to a stout branch. Then I went back and creeping under low, moisture-laden foliage stationed myself where I would have a full view of the meadow beyond.

It was hard waiting there in the cold and damp, lying on the wet, pungent earth with the weeds tickling my nose, stretched out in a position that was hardly ladylike. Spying, I could hear Sissy scolding. A girl of breeding had no place, nor concern, with such matters. A real lady would remain at home and pretend that nothing was happening.

But I couldn't pretend. I couldn't bear being miles away, not knowing, wondering if the man I loved lived or died. For in an hour, perhaps less, he would be fighting a duel.

Lewis Cage Norwood.

I loved him. I loved Cage with a fierce, consuming love, a love that bewitched and tormented me. Of course, he had no idea. None. To Cage I was simply Charles Carleton's younger sister, dubbed "Little Princess," by Papa, an infantile misnomer which I loathed. "Little Princess," Cage persisted in calling me though I now wore my hair in a chignon, had added inches to my height and a small bosom to my figure. Yet truthfully, I had to admit that even if he had noticed the change in me it would have hardly mattered. I was far too plain, too shy, all elbows and stumbling feet for someone like Cage ever to consider me attractive, ever to say, "Adelaide——! What a lovely creature you've become."

And how I desperately wanted that, how I longed for a smooth, creamy skin, a small patrician nose, dimples when I smiled, how I prayed for beauty so that Cage would look at me the way he looked at the comely belles of the river plantations.

And look at them he did, the swanlike girls with rosebud mouths, cameo profiles and indolent, langorous airs, looked and flirted outrageously, bringing blushes to their cheeks and a fluttering to their hearts. How they whispered and tittered when he came into a room, how they batted their eyelashes and brandished their fans, while Cage laughed, teased and flattered in return. But the give and take was all in fun, engaged in impartially, for Cage was too much the gentleman to tarnish a lady's reputation by promises he could not keep, too much the aristocrat to compromise a planter's daughter.

But there were rumors of other women linked with his name, women who were "bad," women who lived down near the Bottoms. "Even a man of good breeding has his appetites," I once overheard Papa say. I thought the rumors vastly exaggerated. People were always talking about Cage, gossiping, saying unkind things, that he was lazy, that he squandered his papa's money, that he drank and gambled. Cage lived recklessly, that was true, but no more so than any other planter's son. My brother, for instance, always elegantly turned out in the height of fashion, had had gambling debts which Papa refused to pay. And Horton Sands, the Benton boys, the Gordons' son, all card players, a little wild, getting into one scrape after another were no better, no worse than Cage. Yet the gossips would dwell on him. There was something about his handsome face, his indifference that piqued their ire and made their tongues wag all the harder.

I did not care. I did not care about any of them or what they said. And if Cage cared, he gave no sign.

Tall, slim-hipped, broad-shouldered, fair-haired, he had the same arrogant tilt to his head as the portrait of his Cavalier ancestor hanging on the drawing room wall at Riverknoll. That full-length picture dominating the high-ceilinged room was one of the first memories I have of the Norwood family home. And I can remember as clearly as if it were only yesterday how, looking up at it one afternoon, the likeness of the Cavalier to Cage suddenly struck me. If Cage should don the same costume, the rakish plumed hat with a curling brim, the shirt with the deep ruffled collar, and long, flowing sleeves, the silk trousers and the felt boots whose wide tops flapped below the knees, one could not tell the two apart.

The Cavalier, Sir Richard Cage by name, belonged to Mrs. Norwood's side of the family. She loved to boast about Sir Richard, and I must have heard his story a thousand times; how Sir Richard had fled England during the

Cromwellian Rebellion of 1645, over 200 years ago, and came to Virginia to make his fortune. How shocked he had been at the savage wilderness, at the lack of town, commerce and civilized amenities, how nevertheless, being a man of character, Sir Richard had rolled up his fancy, billowing sleeves and gone to work wresting from the swamps and forest a paying plantation—Riverknoll, a gift as it were to his descendants who were now enjoying it in this year of our Lord, 1848.

Cage said it was all a myth. Oh, there had been a Richard, all right, but the "Sir" was gratuitous. "He was the son of an English country squire—the second son," Cage said. "A royalist, true, but not of the nobility." Cage was fond of pointing out that all the old families along the river liked to put on airs about their titled antecedents, but doubted if one bygone baronet could be found among them.

Cage had a tendency to be somewhat cynical in this matter. Like the Cavalier, he was a second son and because the English who had settled this part of the James River in colonial times had brought with them the custom of what Papa called "primogeniture"—the right of the eldest son to inherit his father's entire estate—Cage would get nothing. Thomas, his older brother, would eventually fall heir to Riverknoll, its fourteen thousand acres, its slaves, buildings, barns, everything that went with it. Who could blame Cage, the born grandee, for being irreverent, somewhat bitter?

And now he was going to fight a duel, a duel I was supposed to know nothing about. I had been kept in ignorance, not so much because duels were unlawful and held in secret, but because, according to the code, womenfolk and young children must be shielded from unpleasantness in any form. But rumor, intuition, chance and my brother Charles's overindulgence in port the preceding night had revealed time and place to me. The moment I had wormed the information out of poor Charles I made up my mind that I would be there.

Sunrise on the far edge of Baker's Wood.

The duel was to be fought over a woman, Corinne Hayley, the wife of Noah Hayley, a yeoman farmer who had accused Cage of seducing her. I had seen Corinne Hayley once at Harrison's Landing, a statuesque Juno with a mass of brown hair and a well-developed figure, dressed rather garishly, her gown cut low over a tightly laced bosom. But she was pretty, very pretty in a full blown, bold sort of way. I never spoke to her myself but someone said that she was a preacher's daughter and put on airs because of it. She had two children, they said—or was it three?—the eldest, a grown lad of eighteen.

It was obvious to me that a woman of that sort, a woman who dressed so blatantly, would have lovers. And if it were true that Cage had been one of them I felt sure that it had been Corinne Hayley who had seduced *him*, not the other way round as Noah charged. Older women of Corinne's type often fell passionately in love with younger men (or so Sue Benton, an avid reader of forbidden novels assured me), men of twenty-two like Cage. And if Corinne had thrown herself at him, he could hardly be blamed for what followed. Yet Noah claimed that Cage was at fault, and when he came up to Cage and spat at him on the wharf at Riverknoll, Cage could do nothing but challenge Noah to a duel. Witnesses at the time believed Noah, the son of plain Scotch-Irish Presbyterians who did not hold with notions of chivalry and dueling, would back down. But Noah had astonished the onlookers, including Charles, by accepting the challenge.

He was reputed to be a good shot.

A good shot. All during the night, lying awake in the dark I had thought of that. Supposing he killed Cage? I had argued, debated, told myself a hundred times that it was impossible, no one in the parish could outshoot Cage, but now in the cold, misty grayness of a quickly approaching dawn I was not so sure. It would take only a single bullet, one unerring bullet. . . . But no, I must not think of it. I would not *let* myself think of it. *Please, God*, I prayed, *please see him safely through, please, please. . . .*

I tried to focus my mind on something else, my own discomfort, my wet, cold feet, the numbness of my arms, the sky, the trees, on wisps of trailing mist still hanging over the tall grass in the meadow. Gradually an odd feeling crept through me. I could not place it at first and then suddenly it struck me—an eerie, almost breathless silence had settled over the wood. Unnatural. There were no sounds such as one would ordinarily associate with the out-of-doors when the diurnal animals were beginning to stir, no chirping, no bird twitterings, no snapping twigs, no rustling leaves; nothing. Just a curious and disturbing silence.

It went on, growing more intense, more ominous, more weird and unnatural. I forgot about Cage as a new fear gripped me. Undefinable fear. I could not explain it but my skin seemed to be literally crawling. It was as if I had been wrapped in an icy shroud, the terrible gravelike bindings of a mummy and placed in a tomb of silence, a great black void, empty of sound.

Suddenly a twig popped, exploding in the unutterable quiet like a bomb, sending an electric shock through my veins. My heart began to pound. Why? Why this fear of silence, this sudden fear of a snapping twig? What was there to be afraid of? Silences were as common in the woods as cracking twigs. A squirrel, a rabbit, some forest creature scurrying along had passed over a dry stick. Why must I quiver so? And yet I had the odd, creepy feeling that a foot, a human foot had stepped inadvertently on that twig, that even now as I lay cowering close to the damp earth someone who did not want to be seen was standing behind me, hiding, eyeing me with a cold, malignant stare.

I shivered, drawing my cloak tighter. If it is someone, I told myself after another long moment, they will eventually speak out, say something. I strained my ears—but there was nothing, nothing except the unearthly stillness. Above me the sky was growing paler and the fog, stirred by a wayward breeze, drifted in little patches. The sudden whirring of wings broke the silence and I saw a bush tremble as a startled bird flew off with a raucous cry. Then, slowly the Wood reverted to its normal pattern of sound, the small chirpings, the familiar clickings and creakings. Relief washed over me and I let out my breath in a long, shuddering sigh. Nothing was wrong, nothing. A predator, a fox perhaps, or a hawk circling high above had brought the forest creatures to a paralyzed stillness. That was all.

In a short while the muted thud of horses' hooves reached me, and presently I saw two horsemen enter the meadow. They were Noah Hayley and a young man (Hayley's son, perhaps?), both hatless but dressed in their stiff Sunday best, their red, coppery hair standing out like strokes of painted color in the pale gray light. Riding to the far side of the meadow they dismounted and tethered their horses to a green-sprigged beech. I could not see their faces, and their voices came to me only faintly.

A few minutes later Cage and Charles, who was to be Cage's second, arrived. Behind them rode Dr. Meggs. The sight of the old doctor in his sober black clothes, tall hat, the unsmiling, whiskered face beneath, and the black satchel he carried turned my heart cold. He brought a frightening aura into the quiet meadow, an aura of the sick room, of drawn shades and hushed weeping, an aura of dying and death. Once again fear sprouted, grew, mushroomed, all in the space of a moment or two.

Please God, I prayed, *not Cage, please God. . . .*

No one else came, no witnesses, no friends, no seconds to the seconds. It was to be a very private affair.

Cage, his long, lean figure elegant in dove gray breeches and a wine-colored coat, removed his hat and his blond head gleamed golden as the first rays of the rising sun cleared the tree-fringed horizon. He bowed to Noah Hayley, then to the young man. They stood mute, slightly turned away, ignoring him. Dr. Meggs placed the satchel upon the ground and opened it. The bag was not a medical one as I had supposed but held a pair of pistols.

Charles, the young man and Dr. Meggs came to the center of the field. I stretched my neck and cupped my ear, straining to hear.

"You will draw lots," I heard Dr. Meggs say, "to see who has choice of position and who will give the word to fire."

Dr. Meggs removed his high hat and I saw him place several pieces of paper in it. First, the young man reached into the hat, then Charles. The young man opened the slip of white in his hand and his freckled face lit up. "Papa!" he shouted, turning to Noah Hayley. "Papa, we have first choice on position!"

Dr. Meggs frowned. "Control yourself, Bart. A duel is serious business."

Apparently Dr. Meggs intended to observe strict ritual, a time-honored formality of which the young man (and myself) were ignorant. The young man squared his thin shoulders, rearranging his features in sober lines.

He and Charles drew lots again. The young man, once more unable to restrain himself, laughed, but under Dr.

Meggs's scowl quickly bit his lip and said nothing. Dr. Meggs spoke. "Mr. Hayley, when to fire will be your decision."

I felt sick. The duel had not yet begun and already Cage was at a disadvantage. Both position and the order to fire rested with Noah who, of course, would choose to have his back to the rising sun. But Cage did not seem the least perturbed. He lounged against a tree, hands in pockets, a small, half-amused smile playing about his lips. He was far too confident, too self-assured. It worried me. Though Cage, like Noah, had a reputation for being a good shot I found his air of nonchalance disturbing. "Never underestimate the enemy," Papa was fond of saying. I wanted to tell Cage that, I wanted to talk to him, to explain, to warn—be careful. *Please*, please.

But I could say nothing. I had to lay there, my heart beating like a hammer, frozen, wordless with apprehension.

The last of the mist had evaporated. Yellow light flooded the meadow and the scent of sweet grass filled the air, a lovely, nostalgic fragrance. A pair of birds flew overhead, fluttering, gliding black wing to black wing under the pearl blue sky. It was April, mating season, a time of new beginnings, not a time for spilling blood, not a time for dying. . . .

Noah and Cage had removed their coats and were coming forward to choose their weapons. I saw the gleam of a long barrel as Noah lifted a pistol from the opened bag. The sight of it, like Dr. Meggs's solemn garb, made me want to cry. Then Cage was taking his gun from the bag. He studied it, his lip curling in faint amusement.

And now the duelists were standing back to back, Cage still smiling. *Don't smile, Cage, for God's sake, don't smile!*

Dr. Meggs began to count—one—two—three and the men were walking away from each other. Ten paces. Pistols at ten paces. Where had I read that? In a book, a novel. The hero had defended his honor. At ten paces. But this was not a novel. It was real—all so terribly real.

They had turned. Cage and Noah Hayley were facing one another, their faces blurred by the mist in my eyes. I squeezed them shut. I could not look. I had fully intended to witness the whole thing, but I could not watch. I held my breath. *Dear God.* . . .

"Fire!"

I heard the word from a long, long way off. Two shots

rang out almost simultaneously in the still, April air. And an instant later I smelled the acrid odor of smoke. I kept my eyes closed and gritted my teeth.

Dear God! Dear God! *Dear God!*

Time stretched and stretched into an eternity of agonized uncertainty. The Wood still seemed to ricochet with the sound of those shots. And then through the roaring in my ears I heard Dr. Meggs say, "He's dead!" in a tone of shocked wonder.

Dead! Was there ever a word with such awful, despairing finality? Dead! In my mind I pictured myself dressed in black mourning, walking up the steps of Riverknoll, saw myself file through the drawingroom door with the other mourners, saw the coffin and Cage lying in it, his face so white, so still, like marble. . . .

"You killed him!" an angry voice exclaimed, cutting across the macabre picture. "You killed him!"

My eyes flew open. I saw Cage walking away, his bright hair shining like a helmet in the morning sun, Cage, still careless, still at ease. And very much alive! Alive! My head reeled, dizzy, light. I couldn't believe it. Alive! He was alive!

Dr. Meggs said, "Bart—I'm so sorry. I had hoped . . ."

"Don't touch me!" Bart swept the doctor's hand from his shoulder. "You killed him! All of you bastards—you killed him!"

"Now lad, don't take on so," the doctor's face colored. "I warned your father. I warned him. But he would not listen. It is sad, unfortunate—but it was a fair duel. It might have been Mr. Norwood."

"No!" the angry voice broke tearfully. "No—he—Mr. Norwood pulled the trigger before Papa could say, 'Fire!' "

"Why—my dear young man, that's completely untrue!" Dr. Meggs retorted, shocked. "I saw it all."

"*You!*" Bart's voice had become shrill. "*You* are one of *them!* You all band together, all you mightier-than-thou river planters—in your fine houses—darkies to fetch and carry from the day you were born. None of you ever worked a blessed day in your life. None of you! And you want me to believe that you can be fair? My grandmother's foot! You saw what you wanted to see here. Aristocrats— bah!" He spat.

Charles said, "Listen, Bart—this is no good. Let me . . ."

"Shut up, you lily-livered popinjay!" He was crying now, sobbing broken-heartedly. Noah Hayley lay very still, his body sprawled on the meadow grass. I was torn between pity and guilt-ridden happiness.

"Lad . . ."

"Go away, leave me alone!" he wept as Dr. Meggs tried once more to comfort him. "We don't need any of your help. I wouldn't touch your charity with a ten-foot pole."

Dr. Meggs motioned with his head to Charles and Cage. They mounted their horses and started to ride away, leaving Dr. Meggs with Bart who raised his fist and shouted after the riders. "You haven't heard the last of this! I'll get you back if it's the last thing I do!" His strident voice echoed across the field.

Charles said something to Cage, and Cage nodded in the affirmative. I knew that both of them would make some provision for the widow. It was part of the code. A gentleman always treated his opponent's survivors with a generous compassion; Corinne Hayley and her children would be taken care of. I must not fret about them or what had happened here. It had been a fair fight. Dr. Meggs had said so. It could have been Cage lying there now, dead, a bullet through his heart.

He was passing close now, so close I could see his booted legs clearly from my hiding place. And in those few moments as he rode by I forgot all about the sobbing son, forgot about the man who would never rise from the grassy floor of the meadow, forgot about compassion and the scene that in later years would come back to haunt me. Cage was alive, and in my youthful ignorance, nothing else seemed to matter.

Chapter 2

BY evening the news of Noah's death had spread all up
and down the river. Gossip, whispered asides and
shocked exclamations, authoritative declarations of mistaken fact, denunciations and praise, all in garbled bits and
pieces traveled quickly over the grapevine from plantation
to farm, from house to hovel, from stable to wharf. Everyone seemed to have an opinion they had to express.

". . . that Cage Norwood!"

"Imagine!"

"Corinne Hayley's the one should have been shot."

"Good thing his Papa and Mama are away."

"A hero!"

"Scandalous!"

At Barnabas Neale's birthday ball that night there was
talk of nothing else.

"They're saying you were the second, Charles," Barnabas, a stocky man with long, gingery whiskers, said to my
brother by way of greeting. "Is that true?"

We had come late, clattering up the circular drive to
stop before the brilliantly lit house already thronged with
guests. It was Papa who had detained us, Papa whose
political aspirations had kept him locked all day in the
study writing a speech for the coming legislative session.

"I can't imagine who would be telling you I had anything to do with the duel," Charles answered Barnabas's
question, his voice coolly evasive. He removed his cape and
handed it to Sam, the black butler.

"Rumor," Barnabas said and smiled.

Papa had not asked Charles the same question, afraid, I
suppose, he might force Charles into a lie, since a gentleman never disclosed his participation in a duel. But I think
Papa knew anyway and secretly approved, though publicly

he professed to uphold all laws—good or bad, as he said, even the ban against dueling.

"Is that Benton?" Papa inquired, anxious to change the subject. "Well, I do live and breathe," and he hurried after a stout man going into the library.

Barnabas's wife, Ellen Louise, fluttered through the dining room door. "Why—Adelaide! How nice. I'm so glad you could come."

"Thank you, Mrs. Neale."

This was my second ball. The first, last Christmas at Riverknoll, hardly counted for it had been a family affair, but tonight's was for grown-ups only.

"Would you care to freshen up?" Mrs. Neale was asking. She had narrow eyes in a thin, white face. Her voice came in gaspy, little whispers and she always looked as if she were on the verge of fainting.

"Why—yes, thank you," I answered reluctantly, standing on tiptoe, peering over her shoulder and through the open door of the dining room to see if Cage had arrived.

"The dancing has not begun yet," Ellen Louise Neale said, mistaking the anxious searching look on my face. "The darkies are just tuning up." I could hear the scrape of fiddles. "If you'd like, I'll go up with you."

"No, thank you, Mrs. Neale." A young lady always "freshened up" whether she needed to or not. "I know the way."

The upstairs bedroom mirror revealed to me a thin, excited girl with enormous brown eyes, flushed cheeks, a pointed chin and a rather large, unfashionable mouth. It was not a face that would launch a thousand ships nor one that men would swoon over. But it was all I had. Perhaps a charming smile, I thought, trying several on for size, might help?

Twisting my shoulders for a side view, I adjusted the wadded handkerchiefs stuffed under my décolletage. There, I thought, that's better. Then I bit my lips to make them look red. My gown was not the most flattering color, a rather bilious, flowered green, but Charles had brought the material back from Richmond as a gift and I could not have very well refused when he suggested I have it made into a ball gown, especially as he had been the one to persuade Papa to let me attend the Neales' celebration in the first place.

Standing there, gazing at my image, I recalled the Christmas ball—a disaster—small children racing about among the dancers, parents scolding and shouting, and Cage absorbed with the Benton twins. Charles, my own brother, had danced with me, and Mr. Norwood out of courtesy and Papa too. Humiliating, and we had been home by ten o'clock.

But tonight, I thought, bending to have another look, tonight would be different. It had to be. Cage would notice me. I had grown some since last Christmas, surely filled out somewhat? And my hair was fixed in a new, different way. Turning my head, I noticed a curl had fallen loose and I searched the dressing table for a pin to stab it back in place. I found one in a box, flounced in starched organdie. Everything in the bedroom (which belonged to Mary Neale, Barnabas's daughter) was flounced with white ruffles, mirror, bed, curtains, a chest of drawers, even the portrait of Mary herself on the dresser. Mary Neale, three years older than myself, had gone to an academy in Charleston for her "finishing" and there, rumor said, had met a Yankee who was now courting her. We had never seen him, did not even know his name. But nothing about Mary Neale would surprise us. Spoiled from childhood on by her parents and her brother, Henry, her every whim satisfied, I doubt she would be denied a Yankee husband if she wanted one. The Neales were not only rich but highly respected and would survive Mary's defection should it come to that.

One last glance in the mirror, a hurried retrieval of fan, of gloves, and I was ready. But midway on the descent of the long, curved flight of stairs I had a sudden, unexpected attack of stage fright. My mouth turned dry and my heart began to thump heavily against my ribs in a perverse and disquieting manner. It was silly, of course. There was no need to feel shy or afraid. I knew everyone who would be there tonight, had known them as far back as I could remember. Not one stranger among them, I kept telling myself, no need to cringe even if they should stare at my late entrance. They were all my friends. Even Cage.

I went on then, but had to pause again when I reached the threshold of the dining room, swallowing hard, trying to steady my watery knees. The room looked so different. Chairs and table had been pushed back against the wall to make room for the dancers who were going at it now to the lively strains of a reel. I bit my lips once more, then putting on a gay, careless smile, entered the room.

The fiddles swayed, sang and lilted, the effervescent music bouncing from wall to wall. Young bloods whirled their partners, while oldsters, standing or sitting, tapped their toes. No one noticed me, no one turned to look. No one said: "There's Adelaide." I sidled along the outer edge of the dance floor and found a chair.

Cage was partnering Elsie Young who fancied herself the prettiest belle on the river. She had a cloud of blond hair, a white and pink complexion, cornflower blue eyes and a mean, selfish streak yards wide. Now she was smiling up at Cage, her pointed, rabbity teeth gleaming between parted lips, her eyelashes quivering as if she had been struck by the ague. What an obvious fool she's making of herself, I thought with scorn. Men did not like women who threw themselves at their heads—so Charles had told me—and even from where I sat I could see the avid look, the bold desire on Elsie's face. Poor Cage. Gentleman that he was, he could do nothing but be pleasant and return her smile, that bright, beautiful smile dimpling at the corners, a smile that I loved to distraction.

The dance had ended; the darkie musicians in the alcove were mopping their brows, taking a breather before beginning the next tune. I opened my fan and waved it languidly under my nose, just as the other ladies sitting along the wall were doing, my lips parted in what I hoped was a discreet, but invitational smile. I tried to catch Cage's eye as he passed, his arm linked in Elsie's but they strolled on, heading toward the punchbowl without giving me a glance.

"Why Adelaide!" Mrs. Pettigrew exclaimed, hitching her chair closer to mine. A thin, sour-faced woman, Mrs. Pettigrew and her husband, August, a retired tobacco broker, were distantly connected to the Neales, cousins twice removed, I believe. They had come on a visit ten years earlier and had stayed on at the house ever since. I had been dimly conscious of Mrs. Pettigrew's presence, sitting in the chair behind, and I had hoped she would ignore me. A vain hope. Mrs. Pettigrew could ignore nothing, no one. "Didn't recognize you in that get-up," she said; her critical gaze scanning my gown.

"Good evening, Mrs. Pettigrew," I replied, giving her a perfunctory grimace, my eyes immediately shifting to the two at the punchbowl.

"Your papa letting you attend balls now?"

"Yes, Mrs. Pettigrew."

Cage certainly could not care for Elsie, I thought, not the least little bit. He had danced with her and it was only proper for him to invite her for a glass of punch. In a minute or two he would make some excuse and slip outside with the other men for a pull of real bourbon.

"Well—I do declare, the girls growing up so fast these days," Mrs. Pettigrew sniffed. "When I was a girl . . ."

She went on, but I wasn't listening. I kept smiling, willing with all my heart for Cage to turn his head and notice me, wishing his eyes would light up, his brows lift in a surprised, delighted look of recognition.

". . . and there's that Cage Norwood," Mrs. Pettigrew huffed indignantly, "fighting a duel over a woman! What's the world coming to? In my time . . ."

The music had commenced again and the men were choosing their partners. I held my breath, watching Cage like a lynx, my fingers crossed beneath the fan. He bowed to Elsie and she took his arm. Was he going to dance with her again? Yes. Oh, Lord, why, why, why? And they were playing a waltz. Elsie was batting her eyes and smiling that simpering smile. He was going to waltz with her. His arm slid around her waist. Of course she had probably asked him. "Oh, Cage—my favorite—the waltz—won't you please . . . ?" And it would have been rude to refuse, very discourteous, rude. He was holding her close, she was looking up at him. The pain in my heart grew. It hurt, it hurt so I could feel the tears pressing my eyes. But I went on smiling, fluttering my fan, showing the world that I did not care.

"And when his parents come back from Saratoga," Mrs. Pettigrew went on relentlessly, "I can tell you there'll be some hullabaloo. I understand William Norwood has given Cage an ultimatum. . . ."

If only someone would ask me to dance, I yearned desperately, someone, anyone, even Papa. But Papa was in the library together with Mr. Benton and Barnabas Neale, and I did not see Charles. It seemed that all the girls, even the married ones, had partners, Mary Neale, Sue, Margaret and Allegra Benton, Kitty Snowden with Horton Sands, Anna May with her husband, Thomas, and Henry Neale dancing with his wife, Rowena, his face red with exertion. Girls and ladies in bright ruffled yellow, in flounced pink lace, in apple green brocade, in blue silk and mauve taffeta, all whirling to a lilting tune in the arms of young men dressed in white, pleated shirts and dark evening coats. Cage stood out in the rainbow crowd like a young prince, graceful, elegant—one-two-three, dip and swing, one-two-three, dip and swing. And I had to sit there with the old maids, the matrons and gossips like Mrs. Pettigrew. A wallflower. The ignominy of it, the shame. I began to wish fervently, feverishly that I had not come at all. It would have been much better to have remained at home, lying in bed, staring at the ceiling, dreaming of the ball rather than being here, sitting so conspicuously, *unasked*, fluttering my fan, trying to cool my blazing cheeks.

" . . . of course it's lucky for William that Cage is not the eldest," Mrs. Pettigrew's voice sawed on. "Thank God, I say . . ."

If only I could leave, discreetly without being noticed. If only I could vanish into thin air or sink into the floor. The music stopped and then a moment later started again. Another waltz! I could not bear to look, the smile had grown thin, had disappeared. My stiff lips refused to put it back no matter how I tried. I stared down at my fan, my mother's, a gift from Papa. It had a real ivory handle, the silk painted delicately with roses, pink and yellow roses, buds and blooms peeping out from green leaves. I wished I were one of them, a rose painted on a fan, or a leaf, anything but Adelaide Carleton, fourteen, thin, plain, a wallflower.

"Miss Adelaide . . . ?"

I started, my eyes misted with tears lifting to meet the smiling ones of Cage.

"Miss Adelaide . . . ?"

Miss Adelaide. He had called me *Miss* Adelaide. He had never done that before.

"Miss Adelaide, may I have the honor of this waltz?"

The words seemed to reach me from a distant star. Were my ears deceiving me? Was it my imagination?

"That is, if you are not spoken for." He stretched out his hand. I stared at it stupidly.

"Miss Adelaide . . . ?"

Too overcome for speech I placed my hand in his and nodded mutely. He drew me from the chair and circled my waist and we began to glide away from the watching matrons. I thought I heard Mrs. Pettigrew gasp, but my heart was thumping so wildly I wasn't sure. *He* was holding me, my body moved with his to the music; my eyes were lowered, my head dizzy with excitement. I could smell tobacco, shaving lotion and soap mingled with whiskey, the heady, intoxicating odor of a young, virile man.

"Are you having a good time?" he asked into my hair.

"Oh—! Yes, yes! A marvelous, wonderful time!" And suddenly it was true. Never had the Neales' dining room looked lovelier, banked with blossoms and pine boughs and flowering dogwood. Strange I hadn't noticed those flowers before, but now they seemed to leap out at me, great bouquets of yellow jonquils and red tulips and early blooming jasmine, armfuls of lilac in pitchers and buckets and sweet, dainty violets in little white vases on the damask-covered table.

"They play well for amateurs," Cage remarked.

"Oh—yes, yes!" I agreed, my cheeks flaming, daring to look up at him at last. "Don't they?"

" 'My love is like a red, red rose,' " he sang under his breath, his eyes gazing over my head, " 'that's newly sprung in June.' Robert Burns set to a Strauss waltz," he explained.

"Yes." Cage knew all about such things. He had been to London, to Paris. He was educated, sophisticated. Strauss and Burns. I hoped they would never stop playing that waltz.

" 'My love is like a red, red rose . . .' " he sang.

"I adore love songs," I ventured.

"Do you?" His lips twisted in an indulgent smile, but his eyes were still fixed elsewhere.

"They are my favorites," I assured him.

"Mine, too," he murmured absently.

Someone brushed past us and he hitched me a little closer. For a few moments I could feel the hardness of his lean body, the muscles of his arm and it set my head to reeling dangerously again. "Crowded, isn't it?" he said, and then we were dancing decorously once more.

"Yes." The music was going to end, it had to, but I prayed in my heart that it wouldn't, not yet. I was dancing with Cage Norwood. If only I could be clever, witty, think of something humorous and make him laugh, so that he would find me amusing enough to ask me for the next dance. I wracked my brain trying to dredge up an anecdote, a tidbit of gossip, a droll phrase, but my mind was a hopeless blank.

"I see that the Gordons are here," he commented.

"Yes." He must think me terribly dull. Could I say nothing but yes and oh? For one tantalizing moment I thought of confiding in him, confessing that I had seen him duel that morning, and how impressed I had been with his bravery, his skill. Would he be pleased, flattered—or dismayed? Dismayed, most likely. Worse, he would think me a child, a prankish little girl who had indulged in a forbidden escapade. Gone would be the *Miss* Adelaide. He would be calling me "little princess" again.

Cage hummed under his breath, " 'Oh, my love is like the melody . . .' "

Love, he was singing about love. I shot a quick glance at him through my lashes. He was smiling, but not at me and his eyes had an excited gleam. I wondered who the smile was for and at the next dip I turned my head and saw Elizabeth Gordon, old Mr. Gordon's new wife from Richmond. She had auburn hair and a complexion like a magnolia petal. She was dancing with her creaky fusty husband, but she was smiling back at Cage.

Again pain stabbed at my heart. If only I could be tall, willowy and beautiful, and older, oh, yes, much older. And daring, like Elizabeth Gordon who did not care what people might think when she smiled at a handsome bachelor. Who could blame her? Her husband was at least twice her age and she was young and Cage was so charming. Women were always smiling at him.

"Thank you, Miss Adelaide."

Had the music stopped, the dance ended? So soon?

"You are welcome," I murmured dumbly. I hadn't noticed. Such a short waltz. Surely they could have played a few more bars, a minute or two longer?

"My pleasure," he said, leading me across the floor in the direction of the chairs. In a moment I would be there and he would be gone. I would sit next to Mrs. Pettigrew, and she would complain and gossip, telling me what a scalawag Cage was, wanting to know how my father and brother could befriend such a man, how they could permit me, an unmarried female, to dance with such a scoundrel. Cage was not going to ask me to dance again, he would have said something by now. My mind thrashed desperately, trying to think of something, anything to hold time back, to keep Cage at my side.

We had arrived; Mrs. Pettigrew throwing Cage poisonous looks, my empty chair waiting.

I turned to Cage. "I would like to dance a reel with you—when they—when they play one," I blurted out in a voice that trembled. I could feel the heat in my neck rising to my face.

Cage smiled. "Very well, Miss Adelaide. The dance after next?"

"Yes," I said, my cheeks burning.

But I never got to dance it with him. Papa came stalking into the dining room in a fury. "We are going home!" he announced, taking me by the hand. "I've had all I can stand from Benton." Papa and Mr. Benton were forever quarreling, mostly over issues like free labor versus slave, Mr. Benton maintaining that free labor was far more efficient and Papa saying it was a damn Yankee notion.

"Papa—no . . . !"

"Come along," he growled, ushering me by the elbow from the room.

"Papa . . ." there were tears in my voice.

"Get your wrap," he ordered, "and be quick! If I never see Benton again it will be too soon. The affront, the nerve, the stupidity . . . !"

"Papa, I can't go. I promised Cage . . ."

"Are you going to get your wrap or do you want to go home bare-shouldered?"

"But Papa—can't Charles take me?"

"Charles is playing cards. He will be here all night. Well . . . ?" His eyes were like thunder. I knew that look only too well. Useless to argue.

"All right, Papa."

I cried into a corner of my shawl all the way home to Green Springs.

Green Springs had belonged to Papa's family for almost as long as Riverknoll had belonged to the Norwoods. Like Sir Richard, Papa's great-great-grandfather had emigrated from England though he had no noble or even Cavalier pretensions. "Good stock," Papa would say, his underlip stuck out the way it did when he felt challenged. "Plain country gentry—and you won't find better than that anywhere." The "good stock" had constructed well for the main part of the house, dating from that first Virginia Carleton, still stood, its sturdy timber underpinnings mute testimony to practical foresight and a hardy respect for the vagaries of time and weather. Unfortunately the Carletons of later generations in adding two wings had done so in a rather haphazard manner for they matched neither the original dwelling nor each other. As a result Green Springs lacked the white columned elegance of Riverknoll or the Neales' beautiful white mansion, Beech Arbor. Still the treelined drive, the profuse flowering shrubbery and wide expanse of emerald lawn served to camouflage and frame the house rather attractively. And if the manor house fell short of grandeur the plantation itself was considered one of the most productive parcels in the parish, largely due, Papa claimed, to his innovative use of marl and guana fertilizer from Peru. The tobacco fields, the orchards, the kitchen garden, laid out in precise and geometrical design, all worked and kept in order by some one hundred slaves, gave bountifully. And though, as I later discovered, we were not really wealthy, we did afford a way of life that allowed for an openhanded hospitality, the groaning board, the invitation "to stay awhile" (which might mean months or even years), the frequent parties and balls, the blooded horses and the annual hunts. Looking back I can see where it was this sort of gracious, easy living that kept us comfortably provincial and ill-prepared for the tragic times to come.

It was two days after the Neale ball that we learned from Sissy, our black cook, that Noah Hayley's house had burned to the ground during the night. "They's all daid," she said as we sat at breakfast. "Mrs. Noah and all the chillun."

"Oh, no!" I exclaimed horrified.

"Are you sure?" Papa asked.

"Sho', I'se sho'."

Charles blanched but said nothing.

I looked down at my plate, a sick knot forming in my stomach. I wondered what Charles was thinking. Was he recalling the meadow flooded with sunlight, Noah alive one moment, a crumpled corpse the next? Was he hearing the shrill, childlike voice of Bart Hayley, "I'll get you back . . . !"?

"How did it happen?" Papa asked.

"Overturn' lamp, someone say," Sissy replied. "Poor chillun." Sissy was not one to waste sympathy on anyone beyond Green Springs. A tall, exceedingly thin darkie with prominent teeth and cheek bones she had been the only mother I had ever known and while she was devoted to Charles and me, and sometimes even tender, she rarely exhibited warmth to outsiders. That she did so now made the Hayley tragedy all the more awful.

"Poor chillun," she repeated. "I feels for the chillun."

I had forgotten the other children, of course. I had felt pity for Noah's son that morning but then Cage had ridden past, gallant, handsome, romantic and I could think of nothing but my own happiness because he had survived.

"How many were there?" Papa asked.

"Seems lak dey was tree—one girl, two boys." The oldest, Bart, the one who had acted as Noah's second, was seventeen, she said. She did not know the ages of the younger ones.

"That's the tragic side of dueling," Papa said. For all his quick temper Papa had a sympathetic heart. "Family men should never take to the pistol. If you young bucks want to shoot one another well and good, but not a man with a wife and children."

Charles grasped his fork in a white knuckled hand. "But, Papa, it was Cage who was insulted."

"Sad—very sad," Papa shook his head.

"And he never dreamed that Noah would accept the challenge and Cage's honor was at stake."

Papa sighed heavily. "I suppose you are right. Still—ah, that boy Cage . . ." Papa differed from most of the older gentry in the parish in that he liked Cage and, I suspect, secretly admired him. It was Cage's very recklessness, his wild living, I believe, which appealed to him. Papa's own youth had been spent under the shadow of a stern father who had died when Papa was only eighteen, leaving the management and responsibility of Green Springs on Papa's shoulders. He had never had time to kick up his heels, to duel and dance, hunt, gamble, drink and while away his time as Cage did. And though he expressed disapproval whenever Charles tried to follow this course, in Cage—someone else's son—he could well afford to relive a young and free manhood that had been denied him.

"It's not that I haven't a heart," Charles said. "I do feel sorry for—for the family."

"Yes," Papa said. "It's sad for the children."

"Noah was always a belligerent, truculent mule," Charles said. "And the fire wasn't Cage's doing."

" 'Course not," Papa agreed, commencing to eat again, knife and fork working in his thick-fisted hand. "No one says it is."

I ventured: "Perhaps the fire was God's judgment for Mrs. Hayley's sin."

They both looked at me in astonishment, Papa's fork held stiffly midway to his mouth. I felt myself grow hot with embarrassment. I was not supposed to know about sin, even in an abstract way, and to mention my knowledge of Mrs. Hayley's was indiscreet as well as horribly shocking.

"Well . . . !" Papa exhaled. "Well . . . ! Out of the mouths of babes."

"Haven't I told you?" Charles said to Papa, speaking from the authority of his seven-year seniority. "Haven't I said she ought to be sent away to school? Where is she to learn? Certainly not from . . . ," he lowered his voice, "not from Sissy. She's exposed to common gossip, has no proper chaperone as other girls do, she has no . . ."

"All right, all right," Papa, waving his fork. "I shall think about it. School—do you hear, Adelaide?"

"Seriously?" Charles wanted to know.

"Seriously."

Neither of them had given a thought to asking my opinion and school was the last place I wanted to go. If Charles had suggested it a year earlier I would have been delighted, but now in love with Cage, going away would be a torture, a cruel form of exile. Misery, like being sent to prison. Did Papa really mean it? Oh, why couldn't I have kept my mouth shut!

There was nothing to be heard for the next few minutes but the muted scrape and clink of cutlery, and then Papa said: "The price of tobacco has fallen again. I'm thinking of putting in cotton."

"Cotton?" Charles asked in surprise. "Why, Papa, we've never grown cotton here. Besides, what guarantee do you have that cotton prices will hold?"

They began to argue.

Relieved that I was no longer the object of their interest, I relaxed, watching Papa out of the corner of my eye. Perhaps by next fall he would have forgotten about school, perhaps it would vanish completely from his mind. The men went on talking. Soon my thoughts began to wander, settling as they so often did on Cage. I wondered how he had taken the news of the fire. Had it upset him, had it made him regret the duel? I was sure he had suffered twinges, for Cage had a kind heart. But what an awful thing to happen to the Hayley children, how terrible!

The next morning found me riding the leafy, wooded path toward the Hayley farm. I had thought about the fire many times during a long and restless night and in the early gray of dawn had finally decided to take Beau and have a look. Why I should want to see a burnt-out house remains a mystery, but the place drew me. Morbid curiosity, perhaps? Guilt because I had been happy over Cage's survival? I don't know. I simply felt this odd, almost obsessive need to go and so had started off after breakfast without telling anyone, covering the distance that separated us from the farm in less than an hour.

When I first caught sight of the Hayley chimney rising solidly above the tree tops I thought with a hopeful lift to my heart that Sissy had been mistaken. But a few minutes later emerging from the wood I had a full view of the house—or what remained of it, the chimney and one leaning wall. The rest was a blackened ruin. The fire had scorched the fruit trees in the front yard, some of which were covered with blossoms, a strange sight, a paradox. Life and death.

"Burned them all," Sissy had told me when I questioned her again later. The bodies had been charred so badly none of them could be recognized.

I rode up slowly, feeling sick, trying not to think of the children—or Mrs. Hayley—or Bart. Perhaps Noah had died the best death of all. Cleanly with a bullet through his breast.

I shivered as I brought Beau to a halt a few paces from the ember-strewn rubble. I sat there, staring at the gutted house, the smoke-stained skeleton of a bedstead, the ashes of an incinerated table, a chamber pot, a child's ribbed cradle, and the longer I stared the worse I felt. Such an air of desolation hung over the place, such an air of tragedy.

Why had I come? What earthly good had it done?

I wanted to turn Beau about and canter away, yet some kind of grim fascination held me. I sat in the saddle while Beau grew restless under me. It was the stillness which disturbed him and perhaps mesmerized me, the awful stillness of a house destroyed, deserted, an empty shell inhabited by ghosts. Except for the little snorts that Beau gave now and again and the shuffling of his hooves, an eerie quiet lay over the farm, a quiet without bird song, without the chorus of crickets, without the sound of barnyard animals. Even the wind was silent, holding its breath, waiting.

And suddenly I had the same, strange sensation I had experienced in the wood before the duel had begun, the feeling that someone was watching me. A cold chill clambered up my spine and I shivered. Wetting my lips I let my gaze slide from left to right, then back again. No one. No one at all. Only the ruins and the flowering fruit trees. After another long, painful moment I turned my head quickly. The wood behind me—the green budding trees and nothing else; nothing moved, nothing stirred.

And yet the feeling persisted. I scrutinized the trees, my hands clutching the reins tightly, my body tense, poised for flight. Was someone there, behind that oak? A shadow? I had passed through those oaks on the way and seen no one. My fear grew, turning my hands to ice. The ghosts of the dead haunting this spot, the departed souls of the Hayleys watching me with cruel enmity?

Suddenly mindless panic overwhelmed me, a panic I could not control. Wheeling Beau about, I dug my heels into his sides and fled.

Chapter 3

SINCE Cage would not inherit Riverknoll, Cage's mother, hoping, I suppose, to settle him down, had given him the Beacons, a small holding which had been left to her by a bachelor uncle. Situated near Charles City and comprising some five hundred acres of rolling bottom land the Beacons produced tobacco, a few vegetables and a varying number of blooded Morgans.

"Peasant's tillage," I heard Cage tell Charles with a wry twist to his lips. "I'll turn into a yeoman farmer yet."

Of course I could not blame Cage if he resented his older brother, Thomas, receiving the prize loaf while he, so much cleverer, so much abler, was getting a mere crumb. But I will say this for Cage, he did try, he did make an effort. He sent away for agricultural catalogs, for books on horse breeding, on marling and fertilizers, on fruit propogation. He installed a new barn and renovated the old house. He had the slaves try a new type of plow and even asked an animal doctor to come down and advise him on the best feed for his cows. For six months he did everything he could think of to make his venture a success, only to encounter bad luck at every turn. Worms ate his vegetables, his blue-ribbon stud took ill and died, and the overseer he had hired cheated him blind. It did not take long for the Beacons to slide into bankruptcy. Cage's father refused to loan him any more money and there had been a terrible quarrel (according to Charles) during which Cage's father had again enumerated his son's shortcomings, warning him to pull himself up and "quickly."

All this had happened before the duel.

And now the gossips speculated as to how Cage's father, when he returned from Saratoga, would react to this latest escapade. Since the duel had been fought over a common woman, most agreed that William Norwood would go into a towering rage for he was a stubborn, uncompromising old man who never made allowances for his younger son. The plain fact was that he did not really like Cage, never had. As far back as I could remember, William Norwood had shown a barely disguised resentment toward his son, a resentment easily provoked to anger. I don't know why, for I am sure Cage tried to please his father. He once told us, in half jest, that he hated quarreling with him and if he only could make the old man smile, if his father would pat him on the head in praise just once, Cage would gladly give up any or all of his vices. "It is a safe promise to make," he added wryly. "Papa rarely smiles—and at me, never.". Perhaps there was something in Cage's face, in his manner, his voice which evoked unpleasant memories in William Norwood's breast. Perhaps it was Cage's good looks, his easy charm which irked the old man. It was hard to tell. One never knew what Mr. Norwood was thinking. I doubt even his wife did.

. Papa must have been wondering about William Norwood and Cage, too, for at supper one night he said to Charles, "I surely expected the Norwoods back by now."

"Yes," said Charles. "Strange that some busybody hasn't written them."

"Mails are slow," Papa said.

"Yes. But news . . . ," with a quick look at me, ". . . of *that* sort always travels fast."

"Indeed," Papa said.

"Speaking of mail," Charles went on. "Horton Sands got a letter from his cousin in California. . . ."

"Who? Which cousin?" Papa asked. "I didn't think the Sands had kin in California."

"Lester Cooke, the Roanoke cousins."

"Never met them," Papa said, pouring gravy in a thick pool over his potatoes.

"Lester Cooke went to California a year ago—to the gold strike. Up to a place called Rainbow Gulch."

"Oh?" Papa said, looking up, raising his brows.

"Writes he's panning a thousand dollars a day."

"A thousand dollars!" Papa said impressed. "That's mighty good money for a day's work. Mighty good."

"Horton says he's thinking of going himself."

"Hmmm," Papa said. "Not likely. Isn't he engaged to that Snowden girl? What's her name?"

"Kitty," said Charles, "they call her Kitty."

The Norwoods returned unexpectedly from Saratoga the following Wednesday, fetched, as I later discovered, by a letter from Mrs. Pettigrew, repeating in full, lurid detail the neighborhood gossip concerning the duel.

I happened to be visiting Cage's sister, Theresa, at Riverknoll when they arrived. I had taken up with Theresa, shamelessly pushing a friendship I sensed she cared little for, out of a selfish desire to be closer to Cage. I sometimes wondered if my silly prattle, the oblique, offhand manner in which I brought up his name, fooled her, wondered if she found me as transparent as glass. If she did she gave no sign. Blond, with cold blue eyes, pretty when she chose to smile, but otherwise rather stern of expression for a girl of sixteen years, she was not someone I would have chosen as a friend—other things being equal. But other things were not equal. I was desperately in love with Cage—and she was his sister. Any morsel, any crumbs, any words she spoke of him fed my hunger and though these tidbits never quite satisfied my appetite, they did keep me from starving.

So I was there on that fateful Wednesday afternoon with Theresa, helping her untangle a skein of wool, when we heard the trap drive up to the front porch. A moment later William Norwood's voice came booming in through the French windows. "Is Cage at home, Moses?" Moses was the Norwoods' black butler.

Theresa spring to her feet, dropping the wool, and ran out to the hall. I sat there, my hands full of yarn, thinking with a sinking heart—they're back. Politeness required me to greet the Norwoods pleasantly, then to make my excuses and go home. But I did not want to go home, I did not want to leave. I was in a fever to find out what would happen to Cage, and from the tone of William Norwood's voice the portents were far from good.

A murmur of voices beyond the door brought me to my feet. Reluctantly, I showed myself. "Why—there's Adelaide," Mrs. Norwood said.

I smiled. "Good evening, Mrs. Norwood, Mr. Norwood —did you enjoy the baths?" Saratoga was famous for its hot springs; everybody who was anybody went at least once a year.

"Yes, indeed," Cynthia Norwood answered. She, like her daughter, had those pale, cold blue eyes. "I only wish it was not quite so far."

Mr. Norwood frowned. "Hello, Adelaide, how are you?"

"Fine, thank you." There was an awkward pause. "I was just about to leave."

Mrs. Norwood gave me the benefit of one of her limp smiles, a slight, tired lift to the corners of her thin mouth. "Please don't feel you have to go on our account."

I had been banking on that. Tidewater hospitality demanded that a guest be urged to stay, no matter how much the hostess might at a given moment prefer privacy. "But I don't want to be in the way—you've just returned. . . ." I protested rather weakly.

Mr. Norwood had stomped into the library. He, I was certain, did not feel bound by the amenities. "That's quite all right, Adelaide," Mrs. Norwood said. "I want to get into something more comfortable. So you and Theresa continue with your visiting."

Mrs. Norwood hadn't asked me to supper, but that was too much to expect. "We were unskeining wool," I said.

"Oh—well please, don't interrupt."

Theresa said nothing. I knew she was waiting for me to protest, to insist that I *must* leave, that Papa was looking for me to return soon. But I could not find it in me to oblige her.

"Well—I'll stay just for a little while," I replied, putting all the reluctance I could muster into my voice. "Theresa, you go on up with your mother. I'll finish the wool and slip on out when I'm done."

I went into the parlor, but did not shut the door. I would have given my left hand to be able to hear Theresa and her mother discussing Cage or better still to hear what William Norwood would say to his son when he got home. But I did not know how I could manage that. Meanwhile I fixed a skein of blue wool on a chair back and slowly began to unwind it into a ball. Theresa was knitting a shawl, blue and white. She had a half dozen skeins in her basket and I did them all, one after another. An hour went by. I had finished the wool and Theresa had not come down. Moses had gone in and out of the library once or twice, carrying a fresh bottle of wine to his master, but otherwise I neither saw nor heard anyone. I ought to go home, I thought, it isn't decent to keep sitting here when it is so obvious that the Norwoods don't want guests now.

I took a book from a glass-fronted cabinet. Ten minutes more, I promised myself, only ten minutes. Shadows had lengthened across the lawn, the clock on the mantel said a quarter to five. Suddenly my ears caught the sound of a horse coming down the long tree-arched drive. I held my breath as it drew closer. It stopped. I got up and peered through the window. Cage was dismounting. He threw his reins to a small black boy, and then I could not see him but I heard his heavy-booted step on the verandah.

"Is that you, Cage?" William Norwood's voice boomed in the silent hall.

"Papa!" Cage exclaimed. "Back so soon?"

I shrank into the shadows behind the half-open door.

"You sound mighty surprised," William Norwood said. "It's a wonder. You should have expected I'd be here pretty quick after your latest shameful exhibition."

"Papa—if you would let me explain . . ."

"Explain! What do you take me for? An idiot?" he demanded. "Well, come into the library. I don't want the servants to hear."

"I wish you would let me explain, instead of listening to people telling lies. . . ."

"Lies! I suppose the next thing you'll be denying it. Well . . ." The door shut.

I could not contain myself. I crept out into the hall and stood with my ear to the door, one eye cocked to the staircase. It was dark in the hall and if anyone should come I could slip into the shadows.

". . . ever since I can remember you've done nothing but cast shadows on the Norwood name," I heard William say.

"Papa—that's not true. Would you have me accept an insult?"

"Insult, bah! If Hayley insulted you, you probably deserved it. Oh—spare me your righteous protests. I know you well enough. You went to bed with his wife and he didn't like it—isn't that so? Well, isn't that so? Answer me, you damned fool!"

Cage murmured something I could not catch.

"He should have shot you outright—instead of offering to duel with you. You are a cad—a rotten cad. I don't care if they are yeomen—or whatever—a married woman is a married woman. Aren't there enough trollops in Charles City or Richmond to tempt you? Or have you gone through them all?"

There was a short silence and the clink of glass against glass.

"You make me sick," William Norwood continued in a voice dripping with disgust and scorn. "The sight of your face sickens me, d'you hear?"

"I hear, Papa," Cage said in a cold, still voice. "I've always made you sick, haven't I?"

"There was never anything in you to praise."

"You, Papa," Cage's voice trembled, "what is there to praise in you? An estate handed to you on a silver platter, not earned . . ."

"Cage—I warn you . . . !"

"Warn me about what? That you'll cut me off without a cent? Ha! I get mighty little now, an allowance that's a pittance."

"Don't sneer at it, Cage! It's enough to keep you in broadcloth and fine linen, enough to pay your gambling debts, to buy you good horseflesh. . . ."

"Enough—but barely. And that doled out with reluctance, with a scowl, with a grudge."

"You've had your chance. Your mother gave you the Beacons and because of your slovenly, lazy habits it has gone into bankruptcy."

"The Beacons was already halfway there when I took over—and you know it."

"I know nothing of the sort. All it required was a little hard work—application. Your brother Thomas would have known how."

"Yes, Thomas," Cage said bitterly. "Thomas the exemplary."

"Not an exemplar perhaps but certainly not an idler and a leech."

Again there was a small silence, then Cage said, "You

call me names Papa, but what are you? A reactionary old man . . ."

"Watch your tongue!"

". . . a stiff-necked, unfeeling, narrow, ignorant, petty . . ."

"Quiet!" William roared. "I shan't have you speaking to me like that, d'you hear?"

"You've never had the sense to come in out of the rain. Riverknoll is a success, not because of your efforts, but despite your lack of them. If I'm a leech, you are a bigger one, you. . . ."

"Get out!" the roar came again. "Get out! And I mean *out!* I want you away from Riverknoll within the hour, d'you understand? Away from the parish, away from Virginia. As far as I'm concerned this finishes it off. You're not my son anymore, so don't expect another penny from me. None, nothing. I don't want to see your face again. And if you ever set foot here, I'll have you horse whipped. D'you understand? Out!"

I did not wait to hear more, but slinking across the parquet floor, I quietly let myself out of the door, my ears burning, my eyes blinded with tears of anger.

I knew enough about William Norwood to realize that he would never retract his words, that if he had banished Cage, the banishment would hold. The old jackass! The heartless wretch! How could any father throw a son out into the cold, disown him, send him off without money or a place to go? Only a man with ice water running in his veins could do that, a narrow, ignorant man, just as Cage had said. And Cynthia Norwood, Cage's mother, living in awe of her husband, would do nothing to help her son either.

It was dark now and by the light streaming from the house I found Beau where I had left him. I stood for a moment, my hand on the bridle, watching the windows. The blinds had not yet been drawn in the dining room and I could see Moses setting the table for dinner. I wondered if William Norwood would allow Cage to dine with them before he left. "Out!" he had bellowed. "Out!" Not likely. Cage would never eat a meal there again, never sit at the table, in the chair that was his, never pick up a Norwood glass or a Norwood fork. The house was banned to him— the house, the plantation, the river, Virginia.

I would never see him again.

There was a raw ache in my throat as I put my foot into the stirrup and swung myself into the saddle. Then without looking back, I galloped down the drive, sobbing all the way as I went.

I found Charles sitting alone in the parlor when I came in breathless, my hair falling loose from its pins. "Good Lord!" he said, looking up from a game of patience. "Adelaide, what's happened? You look as if you've just seen a ghost."

"Mr. Norwood is sending Cage away!" I blurted out, "Oh—Charles—!"

"What?"

"Yes, it's true, it's true! Mr. Norwood got back from Saratoga and he was very angry, he yelled and he shouted, and he said that Cage made him sick and he hollered, 'Out!' and he told Cage he must never set foot in Virginia again."

I leaned against the library table, panting, pain stitching my side. "You—you can't—" I pleaded, my eyes swimming with tears, "—Charles, you can't let him go. He has no money, he has . . ."

I began to cry.

Charles got to his feet quickly. "Why, the old tyrant! When did this happen?"

"Now—just a while ago," I sobbed.

"Don't cry, Addie. It's all right. I'll go and see what I can do."

Papa was not at home that night, thank God. He was dining with Mr. Benton. I don't think I could have faced Papa, then. He would want to know how I had found out about Cage, what I had been doing at Riverknoll during a family quarrel. Had I eavesdropped? Questions which would have been a torment to answer. I sat down in a chair and waited for Charles to come back. I had no idea what would happen, what he would say. He would offer Cage shelter, of course. Charles was a friend of Cage's, he could do no less. But how would Papa feel? William Norwood was an old crony, a neighbor. To take Cage into our home would be an affront to William, and Papa had too much respect for the old man to hurt him in such a way.

I waited as the clock on the mantel ticked away, watching the slow, inexorable sweep of the minute hand. Time moved slowly, unbearably slowly. Joseph came in and asked, "Wuzzn't nobody comin' to supper?"

"Mr. Charles is out and I'm not hungry," I said despondently. "Later, perhaps." I could smell roast mutton and it made me ill.

At long last I heard horses on the drive, and I ran out. Two riders, Charles and Cage.

"Oh—I'm so glad—!" I began as they dismounted.

Charles's face was grim. "Go upstairs, Adelaide."

"But I can't. Oh—Cage—!" To be sent upstairs like a child when I wanted so much to hear, to talk*. . .

"You'd best do as your brother says," Cage said with a tired smile.

"But supper—"

"We'll call you when we are ready for supper," Charles said.

I went upstairs. Charles watched me go, standing in the hall, looking up to make sure I did as he asked. He must have guessed that I had eavesdropped at the Norwood house. The Norwoods would have never discussed their intimate family affairs in my presence, taking me into their confidence, so how else could I know about Cage? And now Charles was making sure that I was safely out of earshot before he spoke to Cage.

It infuriated me. I went in and shut the door, then stood with my ear to the panel, straining every muscle to hear. But all that came to me was the sound of footsteps and the closing of a door.

I started to pace the floor, biting my nails. What were they doing, saying? I was in a sweat lest Cage leave without my knowing, without my having the chance to bid him goodbye. I couldn't allow that. I couldn't. I stood for a few moments in the center of the room, my fists clenched tightly. It wasn't fair! It wasn't right! If I had been born a man I would be sitting in the library now with Charles and Cage, listening, putting in a word now and then, taking part in their discussion instead of being shut out, banished to my bedroom like a meddlesome child.

But I wasn't a man—I was Adelaide, a girl in love with Cage who was being sent far, far away.

I had to see him.

I went to my dressing table and quickly, with trembling fingers, began to tidy my hair, piling it high, jabbing pins into it every which way. It didn't matter what I looked like. The important thing was to hurry, for at any moment Cage might leave. He might or might not have supper with us, and I might or might not be called to join them, but it was a gamble I chose not to take.

Slipping out of the door and down the stairs, past the tall clock, my eye glued to the parlor door, I reached the hall and the next moment I was out in the damp, chilly darkness.

I crept around to the side of the verandah to the parlor window and finding a chink in the curtains peeked in. The windows were closed; they were sitting by the fireplace. I could not hear a word. If only I could read lips, I thought. They both looked serious, Charles with a fine line drawn between his brows, Cage, for once, without a smile on his handsome face.

I waited a long time there in the dark, peering into my own house like a sneak thief, no more the wiser than I had been upstairs in my room. They talked on and on. My legs went numb and the one eye pressed to the window began to ache. Still I stood there trying to decipher the expressions on the men's faces, Charles's frown, Cage's earnest eyes.

Presently an odd, though familiar, feeling crept over me. Again it was much like the one I had experienced in the wood and at the burned site of the Hayley house; the feeling that someone was watching me. I turned from the window.

A half moon threw a thin, watery light across the drive, dappling the leaves on the bay tree planted on the edge of the lawn. It was an old tree, the trunk wide and gnarled, and as I stared at the bay it seemed that a large shadow under the branches gradually took on the configuration of a man in a low, slouch hat and a long cape, a mysterious, ominous-looking person. A cold little shiver ran down my spine. Who was he? Why should that silent, faceless creature be watching me? I shrank back against the house, prepared to scream if he should make a move, frightened enough to call out, revealing my presence to the two men inside if need be. But the shadowy figure stood very still. Very still. My mouth went dry and my lips moved, but no sound came. I could hear the beat of my heart in the silence—and nothing else.

Then the wind sighed in the branches and the leaves made a rustling sound. I screwed up my eyes, trying to see if the slouch-hatted man moved. I took a step closer, then another.

There was no one there! No one. Just an empty black shadow. See! I told myself triumphantly, letting out my breath, it is only a trick of light, the way the moon rays strike the tree trunk.

I went back to the window.

Cage and Charles were on their feet, shaking hands. They were saying goodbye. Charles clapped Cage on the back and shook his hand again. Cage picked up his hat and I ducked into the shadows, flattening myself against the wall. A minute later Cage came out of the front door alone.

I swallowed, my throat suddenly gone thick, overcome by a terrible shyness. He was stuffing something into the saddle bags at the side of his horse. In another moment he would be swinging up into the saddle itself. Then, putting spurs to his mount, he would go galloping down the drive and the night would swallow him up.

Panic plucked me from the porch and I ran down the stairs, skirts flying. "Cage—! Cage—wait!"

He turned. I saw his face in the dim moonlight, his brows raised in surprise.

"Wait—! I—I wanted to say goodbye."

"Little princess," he said, with a wan smile. "How did you know I was leaving?"

"I know, I knew. Oh, Cage—I can't—it will be so terrible. . . ." I struggled for words. My tongue felt awkward, unwieldy. "Couldn't you stay?"

"No, princess, I can't."

"But where will you go?"

"I don't rightly know—yet. But you needn't worry your pretty little head about me, princess." The thin smile seemed to tremble on his lips.

"But Cage—what did Charles say?"

"He thought New Orleans would be a good place. I have friends there and I like the city." He paused. "As a matter of fact, the more I consider New Orleans the more it appeals to me. What do you say, princess, what's your opinion of New Orleans?"

"New Orleans—" I whispered. He might as well have said Timbuktu. "I've never been."

"Then—if I go you must come and visit me." He gave me a mock bow.

"Oh—Cage—I—it's so far. What will you do there?"

"What I would do anywhere, I suppose. Earn my living for one, though I don't seem to be good at anything but dueling and cards. Perhaps I shall gamble for my bread."

"A professional gambler? Oh, Cage."

"Shocking isn't it? A professional gambler. That ought to make Papa really angry." For a moment the smile had vanished, giving place to a bitter twist of the lips. "But then what does it matter?" He put his hands on the reins.

"Cage—wait," I pleaded. Time had run out. He was going, there was so much to be said, so much pressing hard in my chest, on my tongue, all the unspoken torment of love, and in half a minute, less, he would have vanished. "Cage—," so much and all I could whisper was, "Cage— oh, Cage, please kiss me goodbye."

"Why, princess—!" he said in surprise.

His arms went about me gently and he bent his face, his lips brushing my cheek. At his touch an electric thrill shot through me and I flung my arms about his neck and for a fleeting immeasurable instant his mouth pressed mine. And then he was detaching my arms, holding me by the wrists. "Be good, princess," he said. "Come to see me in New Orleans. All right?"

I stood in the drive and watched him go, stood there until the last echo of the horse's hooves faded, stood there with tears coursing down my cheeks, not caring if Charles saw, not caring about anything or anyone, except that Cage had gone and left me feeling like the last lonely person on the face of the earth.

Chapter 4

IT was not until I had stumbled back into the house and dragged myself up the stairs that I realized I had not even asked Cage to write to me. How could I have possibly forgotten? Oh, what a ninny, what a fool! Letters were the one means by which I could still keep in touch with him. And I had not given writing a thought.

But then it struck me that Cage would probably be corresponding with Charles and I could get Cage's address from him. I knew it was not proper for a young lady to initiate a correspondence with a man, but by this time proprieties hardly mattered. The one person whose opinion I valued was gone. Cage would not think ill of me. I had asked him for a kiss, as forward and brash a request as any, and it hadn't shocked him at all.

At the memory of his kiss a sudden, sad sweetness overwhelmed me and I sank down on the bed, my fingers touching my lips where only a short while ago Cage's mouth had pressed. There, I whispered, *there!* It seemed that if I closed my eyes I could still feel his arm about my waist, smell the male tobacco-shaving-soap odor, feel that delicious thrill run through my body. A man who kissed a girl like that surely must feel something, shouldn't he? And at the Neales' ball he had asked me to dance. *Me*, Adelaide. We had waltzed to Strauss and he had sung, "My love is like a red, red rose . . ." I closed my eyes again and hummed the tune. What a lovely evening that had been. If Papa had not gotten into the argument with Mr. Benton—all sorts of wonderful things might have happened.

Cage, Cage, I whispered and with all the romantic, foolish abandon only a girl of fourteen can feel, I threw a kiss to the night outside my window.

42

Within a week Charles had a letter from Cage. He read part of it to Papa and me at the dinner table. ". . . friends have put me up in the French quarter. Not the best of lodgings, but adequate enough. Tomorrow I will be introduced to a private club where cards are played. Stakes are rather high, but I think I can manage, thanks to your loan."

Papa said, "You loaned him money?"

"Not much," said Charles. "Well, Papa, what would you have me do? If ever a man needed a friend, he did."

"I'm not criticizing you, Charles boy. But I don't think I approve of Cage gambling for his bread and butter. A gentleman plays cards, certainly, as a matter of—I should say—sport, but to make it a profession . . ."

"He had no choice, Papa."

I tried to imagine Cage, suave and debonair at the gaming table, his long, slim fingers dealing cards. I'll write to him, I thought. I'll ask Charles for his address and write to Cage tonight.

Papa said, "Well, what else does Cage say?"

"Hmmm." Charles eyes skimmed the page. "Nothing much. Oh—he does send his love to you and Adelaide."

His love. My heart skipped a beat. Cage sent his love. But then he had included Papa, too; perhaps it was nothing more than a polite gesture. One did that in a letter, love to Mama, to Aunt Betsy, to a favorite pet. It was a formality, expected. On the other hand . . .

"Adelaide—?" Charles was looking at me in an odd way. "Adelaide, I wish you could see yourself."

"Why, why? What's wrong with the way I look?" I asked, puzzled.

"You are the perfect picture of a moonstruck maiden, if I ever saw one. All gooey-eyed and silly."

"Who? Me?" My face flamed. "You're wrong, Charles, you are positively wrong."

"Am I?" He stared at me for a long moment. "I wonder. Could it be that you are harboring a passion for our Cage?"

"Of course not!" I denied hotly. "Of course not! Whatever gave you such a dumb idea?"

"Now that I think of it, you did cry a bucket of tears when he left."

"I always cry when people leave, and you know it. You are just trying . . ."

". . . and the way you positively change color every time Cage's name is mentioned," Charles continued.

"It's not true! It's not true!" I shouted.

"What's more," Charles went on resolutely, "I also recall how you used to hang on his every word. . . ."

"Please—Papa—" I turned to him, pleading. "Make Charles stop. Make him!"

Charles wagged his finger. "All those blushes and little smiles—"

"Charles!" Papa rebuked. "Leave off teasing your sister. Can't you see she's still a child? And even if she were old enough I should hope to God she would have better sense than to want somebody like Cage."

"I thought you liked him," Charles said.

"I do, I do. Lots of spirit, that lad. I like him, but not as a son-in-law, not as a husband for Adelaide. He will marry some day, I'm sure, and let's hope he will marry a girl who can keep a strong rein on him, he'll need that. Some girl who won't let him break her heart."

I did not want to hear about Cage marrying "some girl." It was like a knife twisting in my heart. He was not going to marry "some girl." He was going to wait and marry me.

"I think Cage Norwood will make a perfectly good husband," I said stoutly.

Both Papa and Charles looked at me, and to my dismay color flooded my face.

"Well," said Papa, "well, well. Could there be some truth in Charles's teasing? Hmmm?" He gave me a sharp look. "You haven't been throwing yourself at the lad, have you? Well . . . ? Answer me, Adelaide, have you?"

"No—certainly not!" I denied hotly.

"See that you don't! I won't have a daughter of mine making a fool of herself. Let people clack their tongues about the others—silly geese tossing their empty heads and blinking their eyes. But not you, Adelaide."

"Yes, Papa."

"There are plenty of fine young men who will come courting you when the time is ripe, my dear."

"Yes, Papa." I did not want "fine young men," I wanted Cage.

"There's the Sands boy. What's his name? Horton. Horton Sands."

"Papa, Horton is Kitty Snowden's beau."

"He is? Then I must have him confused with the Young lad. Now, there's a fine, upstanding . . ."

Papa warming to his subject went on, enumerating the various young men of the neighborhood, their families, their qualities, their eligibility. I soon stopped listening. I heard his voice and I said, yes, Papa and no, Papa in the right places, but all I could think of was the letter I planned to write Cage. It was plain, though, that I never could ask Charles for Cage's address. Somehow, in some way I would have to get my hands on Charles's letter without his catching on.

That afternoon while Charles was out, I sneaked into his room, opened the desk drawer and found the letter. The return address was written in Cage's thick, flamboyant hand, "Cage Norwood, 16 Bourbon Street, New Orleans, Louisiana." I would remember that. I didn't have to copy it; the number, the street pinned itself firmly to my memory.

Instead of closing the drawer I stood there, gazing down at the envelope while a little voice within me seemed to say, *why don't you read it? You've come this far, why not go all the way?* There were parts that Charles had not read aloud, one whole page his eyes had skimmed over. What had Cage said in that page? I couldn't, I can't, I told myself even as my hand reached for it.

My fingers trembled as I withdrew the paper. Holding my breath, I listened for a step on the stair, then began to read quickly, furtively. The first part of the letter was about his journey, some of which Charles had already read, and then I came to the page which he had omitted.

". . . the women here are fantastically beautiful," Cage wrote. "You wouldn't believe the beauties. From the lovely aristocratic lasses of the neighboring plantations, the Creoles with their Spanish and French blood, dark hair, snapping eyes, high bosoms [I had the decency to blush here], to the quadroons on Market Street, soft, peachy skins, lovely! Lovely! I tell you I am slightly overwhelmed by it all."

I refolded the letter and tucked it back into the envelope. Then I slowly closed the drawer. I wished now I hadn't read the letter, wished I hadn't seen those warm, praising words describing the women of New Orleans. But what could I expect? Cage was a manly man; a red-blooded male could not possibly remain indifferent to the charms of the opposite sex. And those Creoles, the quadroons, he admired as he admired all beautiful things. They meant no more to him than a lovely scene, a painting, a sunset. No matter how many there were his heart would remain intact —the heart he would some day give to me.

Writing to Cage took most of the night. I cannot remember how many letters I began, tore up, and began again, but at last I succeeded in penning something which sounded neither too forward nor too impersonal, the sort of letter that, hopefully, carried a hidden message between the lines. Mailing it was not easy—I had to sneak it out and over to Harrison's Landing, but I managed. And then I began to wait for an answer. Two weeks, I reckoned, one week for the letter to reach New Orleans and another week for it to return, that is, if Cage answered right away. The two weeks went by and then another two for good measure. Cage wrote to Charles again, but made no mention of me. He did not even send his love. I had read his entire letter (once more on the sly) and it was all about the card games Cage had played, about the people he had met. Jay Cooke, one of the Roanoke Cookes, was also in New Orleans. There was not a single reference to me.

Had he received my letter? The mails were not to be trusted. I was certain, the more I thought about it, that my letter had gone astray. So I wrote another, much like the last. And again I waited.

A whole month went by.

Had Cage forgotten me? Already? I thought of all those lovely women with their snapping black eyes, peachlike skins and high bosoms. And me, here, so many miles away. Out of sight, out of mind.

Another two weeks passed. And then an idea came to me. I dismissed it at once, but it kept coming back and back until I could think of nothing else.

I would go to New Orleans.

I would go there all by myself and I would make him see

that I was no longer a child. He had sensed it the night of the Neales' ball and when he kissed me, too. If he had stayed he would have known. And now—I refused to give him up to some grasping female in New Orleans who would make him unhappy and miserable. He was mine—I wanted him—and once I got to New Orleans and we talked he would realize that I was the only girl for him, just as he was the only man for me.

It seemed so simple until I began to give serious thought to the journey itself and the insurmountable obstacles that lay in my path. It was one thing to sneak off to Baker's Wood for a few hours and quite another to make a long, secret trip to a distant, unknown city. Furthermore, for a young, unmarried girl to travel without a male protector or at least a chaperone was unheard of. People would stare, nudge one another knowingly, ask embarrassing questions. Perhaps I could endure that part, the raised brows and the snickers, but how was I to get away from Green Springs? How could I manage to leave without anyone knowing, without being seen?

I stewed over the problem for several days until the answer came in the form of a letter from Aunt Tildy. God bless Aunt Tildy! My mother's eldest sister, Mathilda Hampton, widowed for the last ten years, lived some miles down river at Brandon. Childless herself, she had taken a fond, maternal interest in me ever since my birth, a fondness which I reciprocated. Now she was writing to ask if I would like to accompany her to White Sulphur Springs. She would be gone two months and would enjoy having me with her. "I haven't written to your Papa for permission first," she said, "because the last time I did so on such a matter he forgot all about it. So I leave that part of the arrangements up to you. Write as soon as you can and let me know."

I showed Papa the letter. "May I go?" I asked, a plan already formed in my mind. "May I?"

"I see no harm in it," he said grudgingly. Papa found Aunt Tildy somewhat overbearing. He liked his women to be soft and pliable, and Tildy was nothing like that, but she did have a high place in society, a fine house and carriage, plenty of money and no one to leave it to but me, her goddaughter.

It was arranged that I take the paddle boat, traveling with Mr. and Mrs. Snowden who would leave me at Brandon and proceed on their way to Norfolk where they intended to visit with relatives. To Aunt Tildy I wrote that I was sorry but I could not leave Green Springs because cousins on Papa's side of the family were staying at the house. How I would explain that lie and the others that were now necessary, I shuddered to think. Perhaps, I wished in a sudden, wild surge of hope, Cage will ask me to marry him right away, and if I came back to Green Springs and Riverknoll as Mrs. Lewis Cage Norwood. . . .

The idea thrilled me to the core. I thought of all the elopements, of couples who had run off to Richmond to be married and how quickly scandal had died down in the face of the bride and groom's happiness. Perhaps—

But first I must get there.

Since Papa never wrote letters I had no fear he would suddenly take pen in hand and address Aunt Tildy. The rest seemed easy. I left with the Snowdens on a warm June morning with the golden sunlight dimpling the broad, blue river. Papa and Charles kissed me and Papa told me to be good. The Snowdens were kind people, solicitous, and I had one or two twinges of guilt as we sat in the lounge of the boat playing three-handed whist, looking the very image of a sedate young girl going to visit an aunt.

It was a brief, uneventful voyage.

I had already told the Snowdens that Aunt Tildy would not be able to meet me, explaining in a voice as bland as cream that she had important business with her lawyer the same afternoon the boat docked and had asked if my escort would bring me to the house. I sensed the Snowdens were somewhat taken aback by this false news, that they felt Aunt Tildy should have made allowances, but good manners prevented them from commenting in my presence. Aunt Tildy, of course, taking her servants with her (she always traveled in style) had already departed, and I had a bad moment or two after we reached the house when I could not find the extra key usually left under a flower pot on the window ledge. The Snowdens were eyeing me suspiciously as I fumbled about and insisted on going inside with me. Thank goodness they were pressed for time and did not stay but a few minutes. It was with a great sigh of relief that I saw their hired hack disappear down the street.

The next morning I was on the wharf inquiring for passage to New Orleans. I had money. Papa had given me a generous sum before I left so buying my ticket was no problem. The ticket master's nasty stare and the shocked murmurs of several female passengers were just as I had expected, but within the hour the boat had sailed, and looking down at the river gliding past, I could think of nothing except the look of astonishment on Cage's face, the raised, fair brows, the stuttered words of greeting. From there I let my mind wander—I saw the surprise turn to pleasure and then delight. He would take my hands, kiss each one in turn, and then draw me into his arms. "Adelaide, my darling," he would whisper, "I didn't dare hope—your father—but now that you are here. . . ." And his lips would meet mine.

It was raining when we docked at the Canal Street wharf in New Orleans, a warm, misting rain. Beyond the wooden pier the ground had been churned into greasy, puddled grooves by the constant flow of carriages, wagons and carts until it resembled an enormous hog wallow. Some of the carriages, I noticed, were mired to their hubs, others rocked dangerously as they tried to make their way forward.

I had brought only a carpet bag with me (my trunk I had left at Tildy's) and I clutched it tightly as I was handed down the gangplank by the purser, trying to pretend for all the world that someone was going to meet me. The wharf was thronged with people, sailors, merchants, country folk, travelers, river gamblers, all shouting, talking, gesticulating, a cacophony of strange sounds and voices that bewildered and confused me. I tried to push my way through the crowd past the rumbling wagons to a line of carriages I had seen earlier from the ship's deck. But the crush was impossible and finally I simply had to let the host of debarking passengers carry me along.

"Can I help?" a husky male voice inquired.

I turned my head. A man with a dark beard was leering down at me. His gap-toothed smile and his wet, gleaming eyes drove terror into my heart.

"Thank you—no. I—I have a carriage waiting."

"Oh?" he said dubiously, taking my elbow. "Then let me assist you."

At his touch all the whispered horror stories I had heard of strange men abducting young women came back to me in a terrifying rush, tales of villains who whisked innocent girls off to God-knew-what unmentionable fate.

"Come along . . . ," he urged, his breath hot on my cheek.

Panic seized me and I jabbed my elbow into his ribs, and with fear giving me strength I rammed my way through the milling crowd, heedless of glaring eyes and muttered curses.

Breathless, mud-spattered, with bonnet rakishly askew, I finally managed to reach a waiting carriage. "May I hire you to take me to Bourbon Street?" I asked between gasps. The driver was an elderly darkie with graying whiskers. He looked respectable, dependable, safe.

"Yas'm. Let's help you in, m'am."

Sixteen Bourbon was a lodging house. One entered it through a wooden door and came into a courtyard. The landlady had a little office at the foot of a staircase. She was a stout, moustached female, formidably jowled with thick black brows that met over a large nose. When I asked for Mr. Norwood her eyes swept over me from the muddied hem of my gown to the top of my bonnet. The hard, puzzled look she gave me did not help to shore up the shaky poise which had already received such a damaging blow on the wharf.

"I am Mr. Norwood's sister," I added hastily as she continued to stare.

"Sister? He said nothing about—"

"It's a surprise," I put in, giving her a nervous smile. "I've come all the way from Virginia to see him."

"Hmmm," she murmured, eyeing me again. "If you say so. His room's at the top of the stairs."

I hesitated at the door, my fist lifted to knock, my heart thumping so loudly I thought I would faint. I swallowed, licked my dry lips. Now that I had arrived, what would I say? I did not know. I was suddenly so terrified, I believe if it had not been for the moustached landlady still staring, still watching me from down below, I would have turned and fled.

I knocked.

"Come in," the well-remembered voice invited.

Trembling I opened the door.

He was there, standing near a small, manteled fireplace, and when he saw me his jaw dropped. "Adelaide—!"

Unable to speak, I clutched my bag, my lips parted in a faint, uncertain smile.

"Well—of all—!" He looked past my shoulder as if expecting someone else to appear.

"I—I came alone," I said, answering the question in his eyes.

"Alone?" he asked incredulously.

I nodded mutely.

"You mean—alone—to my lodgings here—"

"No," I said. "I came alone all the way from Green Springs." My knees suddenly went weak and I must have swayed slightly for he said quickly:

"Adelaide—here—please have a chair. You are wet from the rain, too, I should have noticed. Give me your shawl—your bonnet. A glass of sherry?"

Seated in a high-backed chair with a small glass of sherry to restore me I felt a great deal easier. Cage shoved a footstool across the floor and placed himself at my feet.

"Now tell me," he said, "this is incredible—you made the journey alone—you came with no one?"

"I came with no one."

"But your father—and your brother—surely they would not allow you to do such a thing. Your papa especially—"

"He—Charles and Papa—didn't know."

"But how—?"

"I told them I was going with Aunt Tildy to White Sulphur."

"Oh," he said, his mystification still apparent. "And you came all this distance—alone, because you wanted to have a look at New Orleans?" He took my hand and I felt myself go all hot and cold. "My dear Adelaide . . ."

"I wanted to see *you*, Cage," I said earnestly, looking into his face. "I don't care a fig for New Orleans. I wanted to see *you*."

"Why, Adelaide! I'm flattered, truly flattered. It always does the heart good to know friends have missed me. But, my dear little princess, such a jaunt!"

There was reproach and kindness in his voice, but he

still did not understand. "I would have walked all the way, Cage." My throat felt dry and hoarse, despite the sherry. "Even if it were twice as far, I would have walked every step of the way."

"Adelaide—"

"I lied to Papa and it hurt, but I would do it again if I had to. It's been so—so miserable since you left, and I couldn't stand it any longer."

"My dear princess—"

Oh, God! Why couldn't he see? "Cage—I love you!" I cried, choking on the pain, unable to bear his not knowing. "I love you so much, I thought I would die if I did not see you again."

He dropped my hand and getting up from the footstool stood, looked down at me.

"Adelaide," was all he said. But his eyes told me everything and I did not know which was worse, the momentary gleam of amusement in them or the look of compassion which followed. It was dreadful, terrible—like being stretched on the rack. Yet I *would* go on, obstinately, desperately. . . .

"I love you," I repeated, my eyes swimming with tears. "I love you—and—oh, Cage, don't you—*can't* you love me at least a little back?"

"Of course I'm fond of you, it goes without saying. . . ."

"I'm not speaking of fondness, Cage. Love, I'm talking about love."

"My dear—I would give anything not to hurt you."

"Then you mean no?"

"How can I put it without. . . ."

"It would be better, much better," the lump in my throat was enormous now, "better if you said straight out. Please."

"I am afraid it is no, my dear."

He did not love me.

I had made a fool of myself just as Papa had warned, an utter, clumsy, shameful fool. He did not love me. I should have heeded Papa's advice, listened to him, not thrown myself at Cage, not opened myself to pity.

"You are still so young, so very young, Adelaide," Cage said, breaking an awkward silence. "A child."

But he was wrong. I wasn't a child, not anymore. I may have been one when I came into the room, this shabby room with the rain streaking down the dirty windows, but I did not feel like one now. It had taken only a handful of humiliating minutes, five, ten perhaps, for my childhood to fall away. I had grown infinitely older and wiser, it seemed. And I knew then, as surely as I knew the feel of the glass in my hand and the floor under my feet, that I would never, never bare my heart so openly to a man again.

Chapter 5

I did not weep. Thank God, I did not weep, though hot tears pressed painfully against my eyes.

Cage sat down again at my feet and took my hand, his eyes reflecting paternal solicitude. He began to talk of puppy love, of growing up, and how someday I would have many beaux, boys my own age, young men who would adore me. He spoke of sweethearts and courtings, words and more words that went on and on and meant nothing to me. I loved him, I still loved him, I would always love him, but the humiliation and pain turned me deaf.

He considered me a child. The waltz, the kiss, the "Miss Adelaide" had been formalities—small, polite kindnesses, the sort of gestures an adult would make to please a youngster. I was a child and a plain one at that (face it, Adelaide, face it!), lanky and graceless. How could I compare to the peach-skinned quadroons, the sloe-eyed Creole ladies, the Tidewater belles with their pink and white porcelain skins?

"I must write to your papa at once," Cage's voice reached me dimly. "Your father—"

Papa!

I came back to full consciousness with a jolt. "No! No, you can't write Papa!" I exclaimed. "I shall die if you do! You can't!"

"But—Adelaide, be reasonable. How are we to get you home?"

I had never thought of the return trip. All my effort, my will, my energy had been concentrated on reaching New Orleans. And, too, in the back of my mind, there had been that glimmering hope that Cage would propose immediately, that when I came back to Virginia (with Cage forgiven by his father in my fantasy) it would be as Mrs. Lewis Cage Norwood.

What an idiot I had been!

"I can't let you go alone," Cage was saying. "And I am unable to take you. I'm *persona non grata* at home as you well know. We will have to arrange with your family. . . ."

"No! No!" I exclaimed. "Charles and Papa must not, must never be told. I came alone and I can very well return alone."

"I cannot allow you to do that."

"But—you must. . . !"

"Adelaide, please." He thought for a few moments. "There might be an alternative. Let me see. I could, I suppose, get someone else to take you."

"No!"

"Please—let me think. Hmmm. Yes, yes—I think I have it. Horton Sands's cousin, Jay Cooke, is here in New Orleans. He owes me a favor and I believe I can persuade him to act as your escort."

"Who? Jay Cooke? I don't know this—this Jay Cooke. I don't know him! I don't want to go with a stranger, I want to go by myself," I argued, heatedly, flushed, miserable. To be fobbed off, to have someone grudgingly escort me as a favor seemed like a further humiliation to add to the one I had already suffered.

"Adelaide—be sensible. Try," Cage pleaded.

I sat without answering, my mouth set in a resolute line.

"Very well, then, I have no choice but to ask your father or Charles to come fetch you."

"No!" the cry was wrung from me.

"Jay Cooke, then."

There was another long moment of silence. "Either your father—or Mr. Cooke. Which will it be?"

I could see that it was useless to argue, that if I continued to remain adamant Cage might very well throw up his hands and decide to send for Papa after all.

"Well—" I took a deep breath. "All right," I capitulated grudgingly.

"Good. He's a fine person, you'll like him, Adelaide. I'll talk to him right away. He lives just round the corner. Will you be comfortable waiting? Something to eat perhaps? I can have my landlady . . ."

"I'm not hungry." It was all solved for him; the runaway

waif made comfortable, offered food and then packed off under guard.

"I shan't be but a few minutes."

He left, closing the door softly behind him. My first thought was that I could cry now, no one would see me, I could let the tears I had successfully held in check flow. But I felt strangely empty, unable to shed a single tear or wring out a single sob. I leaned my head back on the chair cushion and sighed heavily. Cage was sending me home. What would I say to Papa, to Charles? To the others? For no matter how well my secret was kept the real reason for my absence was bound to leak out.

I would not go home, I suddenly decided. I could never live the scandal down. I would go to Aunt Tildy's. I would have this Cooke person take me to Brandon and there I would wait until Aunt Tildy returned from White Sulphur. I would make up some excuse, some lie to hide the time lapse between my leaving home and her arrival. I did not want her, or anyone, to know.

I suppose I should have been too devastated to care about scandal, too heartbroken to be concerned about what people might say. But I had been weaned on a fear of gossip. It was an aversion that ran in my blood, infused into me through the years by Papa, by Charles, by Sissy. Whatever happened, one must be careful to avoid a situation that would make people talk. It should not have mattered, now especially, since the future seemed so utterly bleak and futile, but it did. Even at fourteen lifetime habits are hard to break, and in the midst of my misery I was still able to shudder at the thought of Mrs. Pettigrew's clacking tongue.

Well, I promised myself, I shan't be grist for her mill. I shall slip into Aunt Tildy's house while she is still away and settle myself there as if nothing had happened.

Sighing heavily once more I looked around, observing the furnishings of the room more clearly than I had earlier. It was a shabby room, not the sort I would ever associate with a fastidious man like Cage; peeling wallpaper, a stained, sooty ceiling and grimy windows on which the rain spattered. A bed, partially hidden by a faded curtain, stood in an alcove, a bed on which Cage slept. . . .

I felt myself blushing and turned my head away. A

washstand, a wardrobe. Very plain. And a table and four straight chairs. Did he receive visitors here? I wondered. Certainly no decent lady, not even an escorted one, would come to such a place, a bachelor's lodgings. Well, I had flouted convention—God knows I had. I squirmed again at the memory of my declaration, the look of pity in Cage's eyes.

I must have dozed off for I recall suddenly jerking my head upright, my eyes flying open, the momentary, bewildered panic of awakening in a strange room before I recognized my surroundings. Cage had not returned. For some reason his continued absence frightened me, although I told myself there was nothing to be afraid of, nothing to fear. It was simply taking him longer than he had thought. And yet my uneasiness grew and my heart continued to hammer inexplicably against my ribs.

I sat for a few minutes, hands folded, trying to bring some measure of calm to the thumping thing in my breast, when suddenly I felt a little chill draft move along the back of my neck. No sound, just that small flowing chill like a puff of cold breath. And I knew with some sort of harrowing, animal instinct that the door behind me was slowly being inched open. It was a stealthy movement, sly, frightening, the sort of unnerving, imperceptible stir that makes one break out in goosebumps. I wanted to turn my head, to cry out, but I was too frozen to do either. The chill crept up my arms, up my spine, squeezing at my heart, my throat, raising the hairs on the back of my neck. I seemed to be caught, suspended in a horror-struck moment of time, the room falling away to the charred ruins of a house, a stark chimney, a leaning wall. And the moment went on and on, until a terrible blackness threatened to engulf me entirely. A strangled sound rose in my frozen chest and with a superhuman effort I moved sideways, grasping the arm of the chair, moved only a split second before I heard a gun discharge and felt a hot breath pass my cheek as a bullet splintered into the opposite wall.

I screamed.

The door slammed shut. Running footsteps, a few moments of silence and then the landlady shouting, "What is it? Qu'est-ce que c'est?"

I staggered up from the chair, but I was trembling so hard I had to sit down again. I perched on the edge, my body taut, my head turned, facing the closed door.

"Qui est là?" I heard the landlady demanding in a loud, stentorian tone.

Minutes seemed to pass. Then several masculine voices spoke outside and soon there were steps upon the stairs. When Cage came through the door I had a few moments of giddiness as the room and his face swam frighteningly before my eyes.

"Adelaide—!" he exclaimed, "you're white as a ghost. What's happened?"

"Someone—someone . . . ," I began, wetting my lips, unable to continue because the giddiness had returned.

"Here—lie back," he pressed me into the chair and put my feet up on the hassock. "Jay—get the brandy—in the cupboard."

I had a blurred impression of a tall, broad-shouldered man opening the cupboard. "Cage—I—"

"Don't try to talk now. Here—" The glass was at my lips. The liquid burned like fire and I coughed, sputtered and coughed again, tears misting my eyes.

"Better?" Cage asked. He gave me his handkerchief and I dabbed at my eyes.

"Someone," I began again, "someone tried to *shoot* me." Both men gaped at me.

"The bullet," I said, closing my eyes for a moment, swallowing hard, ". . . the bullet went past. . . ." I waved my hand vaguely.

Jay Cooke walked over to the mantel. "Well, I'll be a . . . she's right! Here's the hole . . . !" He bent over and picked something from the floor. "The bullet's still warm."

Cage had gone very white. "My God, Adelaide! How did it happen? Can you tell me?"

I nodded. "Yes." Haltingly I told him how I had fallen asleep, how I had awakened and shortly after heard or felt the door opening. "The shot came only a minute or two later—although it might have been longer."

"My God!" Cage repeated. "My God! You might have been hurt, killed."

Jay Cooke frowned at the bullet in his hand. "I can't understand it. Obviously this young lady must have been mistaken for you, Cage. That chair would hide anyone sitting in it from the door. Or it might have been some maniac on the loose."

"I don't know," Cage said. "I've no idea."

There was a small silence. "You haven't introduced us," the broad-shouldered man said.

"I am sorry," Cage apologized. "Mr. Jay Cooke, this is Miss Carleton."

Jay Cooke gave me a slight bow. I was still too nervous to notice much about him except that he had dark hair and dark eyes.

"Cage is hardly known in New Orleans," Mr. Cooke said. "He has many acquaintances, like myself, but is not known enough to make enemies. Later on perhaps."

Cage laughed. "Now—Jay—I'm not a bad fellow."

"I didn't say you were—and perhaps Miss Carleton does not find this incident so amusing."

"No," I said. "I don't."

"I am sorry," said Cage. "It was rude of me to joke about such a matter. But I cannot imagine—wait!" He snapped his fingers, his eyes lighting up. "Wait! I think I have an explanation. This room—*this* room, according to my landlady, was formerly rented to a smuggler, some notorious pirate, she said, who had cheated his partner—or was it a go-between? No, I think she said partner. At any rate the smuggler found it necessary to keep moving from one place to another because his partner had threatened to kill him. It was probably the partner—who mistaking Adelaide for the smuggler, shot the gun, then ran."

I shuddered.

Cage said, "I should not have left you alone. I feel responsible, terrible. I did not mean to be flip a moment ago—will you forgive me?"

"Yes," I said, looking into his eyes directly for the first time since I had made my ill-fated declaration of love. "Yes."

"Good. I am going to inform the police about this—shooting at defenseless girls—my God!—but first I should make arrangements for you to spend the night where you will be comfortable and *safe*—above all *safe*. When I think . . ."

"It's all right, Cage," I assured him, suppressing another shudder. "I'm all right." I did not want to talk about it.

I was put up in the home of an Episcopalian minister,

the Reverend Brookewaite and his wife, Amanda, trans-
planted North Carolinians. They were kind. I don't know
what Cage had told them, but they asked me no questions
nor did their manner in any way suggest they were curious.
I was grateful for that.

The following afternoon I said goodbye to Cage from
the same wharf from which I had disembarked the day
before. Oh, how eager I had been, excited, fearful, yet with
such high hopes! A different girl, a child. Had only a day
passed? It seemed so long ago. Jay Cooke had gone to
check last minute arrangements and Cage and I were alone.

"I've lodged a complaint with the police," he said. "But
it's doubtful they'll find the culprit. He's probably long
gone by now."

"Yes," I said.

There was an awkward pause, then Cage said: "You will
forget this—this episode, forget me. In a month's time, two
at the most, I wager I will be gone completely from your
mind."

"Yes," I said in a tight voice. *I would never forget,
never.* "You are right, of course. It was stupid of me.
Forgive me."

"Princess—I did not mean to hurt you."

"It's quite all right. You haven't hurt me. And Cage—
please don't call me princess. Adelaide—or Miss Adelaide."

He smiled, but before he could comment, Mr. Cooke
arrived.

"Everything seems to be in order," he said.

"Goodbye, Cage." We shook hands. And I walked up
the gangplank, my head high, my face carved in stone,
trying to act as if my world had not fallen apart.

I stayed in my cabin all the first day and part of the
second and then hunger drove me to the dining salon. Jay
Cooke had inquired, of course, by way of the steward,
whether I was ill, if he could do something to help. Otherwise he had not tried to communicate with me. When I
came into the salon, he was already there. He rose and
pulled out a chair. "Good evening, Miss Carleton," he said.
"I am glad to see that you are feeling better."

"Much, thank you." I had told him, through the steward, that I was suffering from a migraine.

"Those headaches are incapacitating," he murmured, his
eyes running over the menu.

I thought I caught a faint note of sarcasm in his voice and gave him a sharp look. But his features were sober, serious.

"Are you any relation to the Lester Cooke who went to California?" I asked politely.

"He's my brother. Quite rich now, from what I've heard."

"Gold?"

"So he says."

He went back to studying the menu.

"I recommend the ham," he said after a few moments. "It's the best they can offer. Salted, preserved, it's much safer than the rotten meat I was served yesterday. Do you like ham?" He looked up at me, one brow raised quizzically.

"Yes. It will do."

"Mmmm. There's isn't much choice," he said, his eyes regarding the menu again.

He was older than Cage, by how much I could not tell. He was dark, swarthy like a gypsy, with broad shoulders and muscles that seemed to bulge disconcertingly against the seams of his coat.

"Will you take wine, Miss Carleton?"

"Some elderberry, please."

"Elderberry?" His mouth turned up in a small smile. "I'm afraid one does not generally drink elderberry with an eight-course meal. Burgundy, perhaps?"

It was then that I had my first inkling that Jay Cooke and I were not going to get along.

"*You* may not drink elderberry wine with an eight-course meal," I said in a precise, even voice. "But I do."

There was a slight pause. "Very well, elderberry it shall be."

By the time our food came I was ready to faint with hunger and it took an enormous amount of self-control not to attack my heaped plate like a starveling. The waiter served me elderberry—to Jay Cooke, a red wine. We ate in silence, however, for I was too busy concentrating on my food, on the necessity to eat slowly with ladylike grace to take much notice of my table companion. But when I had finished the last bite, he spoke:

"Would you like another serving?" His gaze rested for a

fraction of a moment on my polished plate. "I can get the waiter. . . ."

"No, no, thank you," I said, wanting more, still hungry, but determined not to let him know.

"There's dessert," he pointed out. "I believe some fairly good chocolate mousse." And when I hesitated, he added, "I'm having some. You must try it."

"Well—I'm quite full, but if you recommend it, I believe I shall."

He signaled for the waiter. I wondered how much Cage had told him, if he knew why I had come to New Orleans. But—no—Cage was a gentleman, I reminded myself, he would disclose nothing that might give me cause for embarrassment.

The mousse came. It was delicious.

"I've often wondered," Jay Cooke remarked, leaning back in his chair, "why it is thought proper for gentlemen to relish their food more than ladies."

"Ladies have delicate appetites," I said, rather primly.

"Pshaw! I don't believe that for a minute."

I turned a deep crimson. Had he seen through me, guessed how hungry I was and how much I had wanted another serving? He was watching me now, his black eyes twinkling.

"Believe what you will," I said.

He removed a cigar case from his inner pocket and extracted a cigar. "May I?" one dark brow raised. The match flared, lighting up his dark face. There was something feline, something latently dangerous and disturbing in those features. I was liking him less and less.

"I always think," Jay Cooke observed, "how much easier, how much simpler it would be for you ladies to say, 'I'm hungry,' or even, 'I'm starved,' and to go right on and attack your food with gusto."

"That would be vulgar," I said.

"No honest appetite—whatever it may be—is vulgar."

The flush on my cheeks deepened, but I said nothing. It embarrassed me, this talk of appetite. And though I was not quite sure what he meant, I knew that the appetite he referred to had little to do with food.

"Do you find that shocking?" he asked.

"Yes—yes, I do." Why must he pursue it? Couldn't he see that I was uncomfortable? For all his fine clothes and educated drawl he was apparently not a gentleman. Decidedly not. A man of breeding, certainly one that I had only just met, would engage in polite small talk—the weather, the ship, the food we were eating, anything but a discussion of "appetites."

"I find that sad," he remarked ruefully, tapping the ash from his cigar. "Sad. I somehow felt that beneath your prim exterior a person of great warmth and honesty existed, a girl of feeling, a . . ."

"Mr. Cooke—I don't think . . ."

"Please—let me finish. A passionate girl who would make some man very happy. What I cannot understand, Miss Carleton, if you will forgive me . . ."

"Mr. Cooke—I must say you presume . . . !" I exclaimed, very red in the face, angry, bewildered. Passionate, what did he mean by passionate? "I prefer not to hear . . ."

"What I cannot understand," he went on blandly, ignoring my heated protest, "is why all that youthful ardor should be wasted on a man like Cage Norwood."

"*How* dare you . . . ?" I spluttered, outraged now, rising to my feet. "Why you—you—don't you *dare* say one word against Cage Norwood. Why, you—you aren't fit to shine his boots!" flinging the banality at him like a gauntlet.

He laughed.

Speechless with rage, I wheeled and stalked across the salon, colliding with a waiter near the door. From behind me I could still hear that deep male laughter. Murmuring an apology to the startled waiter, I brushed past him, and with tears in my eyes fled to my cabin. There I threw myself on the narrow berth and for the first time since my debacle with Cage wept bitter, despairing tears.

After that my whole being shrank from encountering Jay Cooke again. He was a cad, a barbarian, a monster. Why should I subject myself to his odious company? I would remain in my cabin, starve if need be, rather than endure his vulgar conversation. But when I began to think of his secret, mocking smile as he contemplated my empty chair in the salon, my ire rose. Why should I give him the satisfaction of besting me? Why should I capitulate, let him know by my absence how he had hurt me? I would not have him laughing behind my back, thinking that I was a shrinking violet, a coward. No, better to beard the lion in his den, better to have him believe that I didn't give a hoot for his opinions. So I forced myself to appear punctiliously in the salon for meals, though it cost me dear to sit at the same table with him three times a day. I ate with him, but I did not speak.

He tried to coax me from my silence.

"Cage did not divulge anything to me but your name and destination, if that's what's worrying you," he said at one point. And at another, "I simply put two and two together. But I assure you, your secret is safe with me."

I said nothing. I pretended I had not heard, that he was not there. I refused to be trapped into another insulting debate, one that he was sure to win.

When the ship left coastal waters and started up the James River, I finally condescended to speak. "I would like to debark at Brandon," I said. "My aunt—Mrs. Hampton —lives there—and I've been thinking I ought to pay her a call."

One brow went up. "Not going home?"

"Not yet," I said.

"Don't want the neighbors to talk, eh? Afraid of a little tiddle-taddle, are you?"

"If it is all the same to you," I said acidly, ignoring his gibe, "I should like to terminate my journey at Brandon. But you needn't leave the boat." He had been planning to go on to Richmond after depositing me at Green Springs. "I can find my way."

"I would not dream of letting you go unescorted."

"Thank you for your concern, Mr. Cooke," I said stiffly, "but I prefer going alone."

"You are determined?"

"Yes."

His eyes went over me in a rather bold manner, and though I tried to summon a feeling of wrathful indignation, it would not come. No man had ever looked at me in quite that way, and those dark, luminous eyes in their upward, probing sweep of my figure gave me a strange little thrill, one which, after a momentary struggle, I succeeded in suppressing.

"Such iron pride—but so young, so untried . . ."

"You need not bother with the pretty words," I said.

"I had not meant them to be 'pretty,' simply a true assessment."

"Oh, stop it!" I exclaimed, exasperated.

He laughed, and I think if I had been a year or two younger I would have hit him.

When we reached Brandon, he saw me down the gangplank, and into a hired buggy. "Goodbye," he said, extending his hand, and when I made no move to reach for it, added, "Can't we part as friends—at the least, for all my trouble?" He smiled ingratiatingly.

"Goodbye," I said coolly. "And thank you for—for your trouble."

His hand was still extended and I could do nothing but give him mine. He held it for a few moments, then let it go. "Take care," he said.

Once the carriage started off, I sank back in relief, hoping I would never see him again. *Never.*

It was mid-afternoon when I reached Aunt Tildy's door. The house with its shades drawn slumbered in the hot June air, the roses in the garden already drooping with heat. I found the key under the flower pot and opened the door. The minute I stepped into the cool entry hall and saw that the furniture in the parlor was no longer sheeted I knew something was wrong, terribly wrong.

"Adelaide . . . ?"

My head jerked up. Aunt Tildy was standing at the top of the stairs, a look of astonishment on her face.

Chapter 6

I had to tell her. There was nothing else I could do. I had to tell her everything from the beginning, confess my love for Cage and how I had deceived Papa (and her) and gone to New Orleans. I had to tell her what Cage said and how I had been brought back to Brandon, hoping to find an empty house. It was a long confession, one that I made haltingly in an agony of shame.

Aunt Tildy listened without comment until I finished.

"I do declare!" she said, letting out her breath. "I do declare!"

I waited for the scolding, the punitive words, the lengthy reprimand, my head lowered, not daring to look her in the eye.

"If your Papa only knew . . ."

"Oh, please!" I flashed at her, my voice breaking again. "Please—don't tell him."

"I expect he'd skin you alive."

"Yes . . ." A tear rolled down my cheek. I did not see how, in all conscience, she could keep my horrible transgression from Papa, but I hoped, I hoped.

"I won't ask you if you are sorry. I can see that you are."

"Yes," I said in a small whisper. I was sorry that I had opened myself to rejection, to humiliation, sorry I had made a fool of myself. But I could not be sorry for loving Cage; that would never change.

"If only I could push time back," I said wretchedly. "If only I had never gone."

"Too late for that now. Consider yourself fortunate that worse did not happen."

"Cage was really very kind."

"I should think so. But a girl traveling alone . . ."

"Oh!" I said, suddenly remembering. "I nearly forgot. I was shot at, Aunt Tildy."

"Shot at? Where? Why?"

I explained what had happened.

"How dreadful! You might have been killed, child. How terrible!"

"Yes." I thought it best not to tell her about the bearded man who had accosted me on the wharf.

"It all goes to show what can happen when you forget you are a lady and act in an unbecoming, if not dangerous, manner. Do you get my meaning?"

God's punishment. "Yes, Aunt Tildy."

She contemplated me for half a minute, chewing her lip. "It seems to me, child, that you are truly contrite."

"Oh, yes!"

"So I see no point in discussing this with your father or with Charles—it would only upset them."

"Oh—Aunt Tildy . . . !"

"But," she continued sternly, "I hope you have learned your lesson. A girl, even if she loves a man, never throws herself at him, never even *tells* him. When she marries, perhaps—but even so it is done discreetly, using good taste. It is all very well for a man to declare himself, to make all sorts of wild avowals, get on his knees, swear undying love, but for a well-brought-up woman to do more than smile or flutter her eyes is distinctly unfeminine."

"It seems so unfair," I said.

"Well—who says it isn't?" she asked rather sharply.

When I finally returned home to Green Springs, Papa and Charles wanted to know if I had a good time at White Sulphur, and I recited my rehearsed little piece about the hot springs and how they still smelled like rotten eggs. I told them all about the latest in the women's fashions I had seen there and about a fictitious masked ball which Aunt Tildy and I had attended. Fortunately Papa and Charles did not question me beyond their initial polite inquiry. They were too taken up by the recent published writings of some man called Henry Ruffner, who, I gathered, was the president of Washington College.

"What does *he* know?" Papa grumbled. We were sitting in the library after supper with the windows wide open, hoping to catch a cooling night breeze. "Mr. Ruffner—holed up there in his ivory tower, saying the free Northern states are prosperous, while we here are decaying and going to hell in a basket."

"Well, Papa," Charles said, "he doesn't exactly claim we are going to hell. . . ."

"Might as well—give me that." He snatched the pamphlet Charles held in his hand. "Here—here it is," he said, turning a page. "Right here in black and white. '. . . the South—cultivation spread over vast fields that are wearing out—stagnation—positive decay . . . instead of the stir and bustle . . .'—in the North, he means—'a dull and dreamy stillness . . .'—that's us here in the South—'broken, if broken at all, by the wordy brawl of politics.' Now what do you call that?" Papa demanded, red in the face. "What do you call that? And from a Southerner, too."

"He does point out a few truths," Charles said reasonably. "We don't have any manufacture here in Virginia to speak of, commerce and navigation, what there is, is mostly run by Yankee interests."

"Pshaw!" Papa exclaimed scornfully. "Let the Yankees soil their hands with commerce, they aren't suited for anything else. We are gentlemen here in Virginia—gentlemen, and proud of it."

"I am not decrying the gentlemanly way of life, Papa, but you can't eat on that, you can't run a plantation on that."

"Ah—there you go! Next thing you'll be talking like Mr. Benton, saying we ought to free the slaves."

"No, Papa, I wouldn't go that far," Charles smiled.

Their conversation continued. Something was mentioned again about the plummeting price of tobacco. If it went any further, Papa said, we would all have to tighten our belts. The conversation got more and more boring, and I soon found myself adrift in a daydream, a fantasy which I had devised since I had come home to Green Springs. It centered around Cage, of course, and in it I saw myself receiving a letter in which he asked my forgiveness. "I acted rather brusquely," he would write, "but out of consideration for you, my darling Adelaide. You are so young —I do love you—and it is hard for me to wait, but when you are sixteen . . ." My head—the head and brain that had grown up so quickly in New Orleans—told me that such a dream was utter nonsense. Nevertheless I went on dreaming it. Somehow it helped to ease the pain.

My fantasy letter never came, of course. But Cage did write to Charles. "He's going to California," Charles announced at dinner one day. "To the gold fields. He and Jay Cooke."

To California! My heart sank. If I had once believed New Orleans to be as remote as Timbuktu, California, by contrast, seemed like an infinitesimal pinpoint in the universe, a far distant planet.

"Cage has asked me to come along," Charles said.

"You?" Papa exclaimed in surprise. "I should think you have better things to do."

"He writes that men are making fortunes overnight along the Feather and American Rivers. There's still plenty of gold. A new strike every day."

"Hmmm," Papa said, picking his teeth with his thumb nail.

"There's not much capital involved in such a venture," Charles said. "One can get outfitted, if one is sensible, fairly reasonably. And there's the fare—he recommends going by ship, then crossing the Isthmus and taking ship again on the Pacific side."

"He's thought it all out, has he?"

"Yes, he's made his decision. He's leaving shortly, as a matter of fact, but he is waiting to hear from me first. Then if I don't choose to accompany him, he and Jay Cooke will leave together."

Papa continued to worry his tooth with his nail.

"Horton Sands is going," Charles said.

"Is he?"

"Yes. It seems like such a sure thing, Papa. And if I made a few thousand dollars, why—we wouldn't have to think about selling that acreage up near the old well."

It was the first I had heard about selling acreage. Papa was so proud of Green Springs, nothing short of financial embarrassment would cause him even to contemplate parting with a small parcel of it.

"Do you want to go?" Papa asked quietly after a long silence.

"Yes—I rather think I do. That is if you find you can get along without me for a few months, sir."

He wanted to go. I knew Charles well enough to see how

eager he was to join Cage and how hard he was trying to hide that eagerness.

"It might be a fool's chase," Papa pointed out.

Charles smiled. "But then again it might not. Like playing cards, Papa, only I believe the odds here are much better—in my favor, that is."

"Hmmm," said Papa. "Well, I shall think on it."

Papa did not take long to come to a decision. I am sure falling tobacco prices had greatly favored his response for we were hard up for ready money that summer; even I, nursing my unhappiness, could sense that. And perhaps Papa too, had caught a little of the gambling fever associated with the California Gold Rush. He gave Charles six months. "A year at the outside."

Charles was delighted but no more than I. Charles would be my link to Cage, a very personal link. He would be with Cage every day, talk to him, live with him, join in his ventures, and through Charles I would be close to doing the same thing.

"You *must* write," I impressed upon Charles for at least the fifth time. "I want to hear everything that happens, what you see, what you do."

"I shall indeed, little princess," he said, smiling happily at me. "I shall even start a journal—just for you."

"Promise?"

"Cross my heart and hope to die," he said, in a mood to promise anything.

I don't know if Charles ever commenced his journal, but he kept his word about writing to me. I received my first letter from him a few weeks later, sent from a place called Chagres in Panama.

"You wouldn't believe the throngs making this mad dash westward," he wrote. "Men from all walks of life, a few with their wives—all bursting to get to the gold fields as soon as possible. We, of course, are no different in our enthusiasm. But here we are, stuck in this godforsaken sink hole, awaiting a steamer to carry us up the coast. It rains constantly, pours like water sluicing out of a bottomless bucket, a humid, tropical rain. Everything stays wet, clothes, supplies, ourselves, with nary a dry spot to be found. There is no housing so we must perforce bed down as best we can on blankets under the nearest trees. Food is scarce and fire impossible. We are subsisting on the raw meat of turtles and what fruit we can forage. Many have already succumbed to fever. But our little party, I am happy to say, is surviving fairly well. Our spirits remain undaunted. We while away the time by talking of what we will do with our gold when we find it. This morning Cage said that he hopes to become a millionaire and buy us all out along the river. I think he is still smarting under old man Norwood's edict."

Of course he was, poor darling. And I could not blame him for feeling bitter, for wanting to show his hidebound father that he could be a success. He was so superior to his brother, Thomas, to whom he bore little likeness. Thomas favored his mother; the cold blue eyes, the arched nose and thin lips, a very correct and frigid gentleman, frozen into the old school at twenty-four. He married Kitty Snowden toward the end of July that year in an elaborate, guest-thronged wedding at Riverknoll.

Kitty Snowden had broken her "understanding" with Horton Sands when he had gone blithely off to California, and no one could blame her for choosing Thomas (who Aunt Tildy called a "bird in the hand"), even if the interval between Horton's leaving and her marriage was indecently short. Despite the talk, everyone who mattered had come to the festivities, friends, neighbors and relatives, some from as far away as Durham. Only Cage was absent. No one remarked upon it, no one seemed to notice. He had already been forgotten by kith and kin, by former associates, by all, it seemed, except me.

I remember standing in the packed hall lit by hundreds of white candles, waiting for the bride to descend the stairs on the arm of her father, thinking of the letter nestled safely in my reticule. Charles had written again, this time from San Francisco where they had arrived safely after a long and boring voyage. "Cage livened it up somewhat," Charles wrote, "by winning fifty dollars from a Boston lawyer. He believes it a sign, a good omen, if you will, of times to come. I hope so."

They had put up at the Union Hotel, he said, and were

lucky to get rooms at seven dollars a day with board.
"Hordes of people have descended upon this place already
teeming with thousands," the letter went on. "The harbor is
crowded with ships' masts—eight hundred, Horton
counted—many of these vessels deserted by captain and
crew alike. Everything is dear. Eggs go for twelve dollars
a dozen, flour at twenty-five dollars a sack. Cage laughs at
it all. . . ."

I could almost hear that laughter, see the golden head
thrown back, the fine lines of his throat.

Suddenly Mary Neale, clutching my arm, brought me
back to the present. "Here she comes!" she whispered.

The bride, her face glowing beneath her veil, was descending the stairs. She was being married from Riverknoll
instead of her own home because the Norwood mansion
could accommodate a larger crowd. She looked so happy,
so proud. I watched, my throat catching, my eyes suddenly
swimming with tears. Oh, if that were only me, wearing my
mother's wedding gown and veil and coming down the
stairs of Green Springs with Papa, with Cage waiting at the
bottom to claim me as his bride.

"I always cry at weddings, don't you?" Mary Neale said,
dabbing her eyes with a handkerchief.

"Yes," I said, reaching for mine, "Yes, I do."

I was at Miss Fenway's Academy for Gentlewomen in
Richmond when I received my next letter from Charles.
Papa, as I had guessed, had quite forgotten about his
promise to send me off to school, but I had not. I wanted
to go. There were too many memories at home associated
with Cage; memories that had become as painful as throbbing wounds. Everywhere I looked, everywhere I went, I
saw his face, heard his voice and laughter. Papa said the
house would be lonely without me, and I believe he regretted Charles ever having suggested the Academy in the first
place, but he did not try to change my mind. "I'll be home
for Christmas," I reminded him, adding, "After all, Richmond isn't the end of the world," as if I hadn't once
thought so.

Charles's letter, forwarded by Papa, came as a shock.
Horton Sands had been killed. Charles, Cage, Jay Cooke

and Horton had gone up the Sierra mountains to a camp known as Devil's Gulch. There they had each staked out a claim, banding together to build a large sluice box sometimes known as Long Tom, a popular contrivance used to separate the gold from the gravel and debris. The pickings were lean, the work hard. "Added to that," Charles wrote, "the surroundings here would confound the devil in Hell —hence the name, though I am told conditions are pretty much the same in all the mining camps. Such a collection of cutthroats and ruffians I have never seen, discards, untrustworthy characters from all around the globe, Italian, French, English, South Sea Islanders, Spaniards, Chinese, East Indians, a veritable Tower of Babel. Some of them do nothing but get roaring drunk. Tempers run high. The wonder is that all of us haven't been killed instead of just poor Sands."

Horton had been stabbed to death one night while sleeping in his tent. All four of the men had pitched their tents in a cluster, no more than six feet apart, yet no one had heard or seen the intruder. "Cage believes Horton was mistaken for him," Charles wrote. "But I very much doubt it. Why should Cage be singled out? And yet he fails to be convinced. I don't think I have ever seen him quite so disturbed. He spoke of some shooting incident which occurred in his rooms in New Orleans and wondered if it had any connection. But wouldn't elaborate. I think it's a case of nerves.

"I have written to Mr. Sands, but since shipping the body home is close to impossible, we shall have to bury him here."

I felt dreadfully sorry for Horton's family, and I went to their home with Papa to pay my condolences. But all during that hour as we sat sipping tea in the darkened drawing room, making hushed conversation, I thought and worried about Cage. It was not like him to be troubled by matters of personal safety. He was always so cool in the face of danger, so seemingly indifferent. I remembered how calm he had been at Baker's Wood before the duel. Why should he be disturbed now? Did he have some enemy, someone who had sworn to kill him? Perhaps the man he had played cards with on the ship or another he had met at

Devil's Gulch bore him some grudge. I worried for him—
and for Charles, too. As for Jay Cooke, I never gave him a
thought.

I had come home for the Christmas holidays when the
next letter arrived. The three men had returned to San
Francisco.

"Those that say fortunes are to be made in the mountains exaggerate," Charles wrote. "The work is unceasing,
backbreaking, tedious. There were many days during
which we profited nothing, some when we could only pan
four dollars for ten to twelve hours of toil, and some days
when we considered ourselves lucky indeed to make ex-
penses. So we have come back to the City where the real
wealth lies, where for small capital one can go into business and prosper beyond anything the gold fields have to
offer."

After describing the various ventures open to them, he
said, "Cage feels that since he has a flair for cards he will
put his talents to work. Gambling is the sustenance of life
here. There are dozens of gambling saloons and parlors, a
good many of them clustered about Portsmouth Square in
the center of the city and though gambling has been out-
lawed on Sundays, it goes on nevertheless at a brisk pace,
seven days a week, morning, noon and throughout the
night with no stop. Faro, poker, dice, monte, every form of
gaming you can think of. These places are dens of iniquity
and I won't go into detail, little sister, lest I burn your ears.
There are no women of decent breeding, what females one
sees are best left unnamed."

I knew what he meant, of course, though I was not
supposed to. "Bad women," as they were obliquely referred
to in polite society, and then only in whispers. Prostitutes.
Gentlemen avoided them, I was told, but I knew otherwise.
Hadn't Papa said, "A man has his appetites"?

Thinking of appetites I suddenly recalled Jay Cooke and
the conversation I had had with him on the boat coming
home from New Orleans. What was it he had said? "No
honest appetite is vulgar." I shuddered. A disgusting man. I
had no doubt at all that he patronized these women. Did
Cage? But I did not want to think about that.

There was the usual spate of parties and dances given at Christmas along the river. I attended most of them with Papa as my escort, speaking to people, shaking hands, eating, even dancing, all done, however, as though I were moving through a dream. Without Cage these festive gatherings were meaningless. Gone was the nail-gnawing fear, the tremulous heartbeat, the breathless anticipation which had made the never-to-be-forgotten birthday ball at the Neales' so exciting. I did not even care whether or not I was asked to dance, and because I did not care I seemed to be dancing more than I ever had before, partnered by Thomas Gordon, Alex Young and Rooney Benton. And if I had been asked the next morning what they looked like, how they danced, what they had said, I would have been at a loss for words. Papa seemed pleased, though. He said that I was beginning to bloom, that I would surely be a "belle" someday.

It meant little to me. If I could be a belle I wanted Cage there to see, to smile at me, to know. The other young men seemed pallid, innocuous and dull when I compared them to Cage. They did not interest me. I did not care. The only bright spot during those weeks was the anticipation of another letter.

It was the middle of January and I was back in school before I heard again from Charles.

As always I skimmed over the preliminaries, the description of scenes in San Francisco, the foggy weather, the curse of high prices, my eye searching for the one name that held meaning for me.

"Cage," Charles wrote, "has literally lost his shirt. He has taken up with that gambling crowd at the Bella Union —and they've stripped him. They are card sharks, cheats, con men. Cage cannot understand that the rules do not hold here. That honor and honesty are unknown words at the Union. Well, he was a sorry mess, I can tell you. Fortunately he has two good friends. Both Jay and I still have cash and the three of us have decided to go into a real-estate venture. Land here can do nothing but go up in value. The City is growing by leaps and bounds. We feel we cannot fail."

Nor did they. Subsequent letters informed me of complicated transactions of lots bought and sold on Market Street and Yerba Buena Island from a man by the name of E. P. Jones. Charles began to send money home to Papa. It embarrassed Papa, not that the money wasn't put to good use, buying seed, renovating the more dilapidated slave cabins, procuring new plow horses, but he would have much preferred that the money had come from the gold fields. Dealing in real estate smacked of trade, and gentry —certainly the sort of Old World gentry Papa believed in—never soiled their hands with trade. Still, the money was not refused.

Cage bought a bank. "He's changed the name to Norwood and Company," Charles wrote with a note of exasperation. "I told him, and Jay Cooke has agreed, that banks are proliferating here like mushrooms. Cook and Company (no relation to our Jay), Wells Fargo, Adams and Company, Naglee, to name only a few. It is a dubious venture, but Cage persists."

Nevertheless, Cage prospered with his bank and during the following summer news came that he was building himself a house. "I think it is a monstrosity," Charles said. "One of those popular structures embellished with Gothic spires and gewgaws. We call it 'Cage's Folly.' What on earth he wants with such a huge house, I have no idea."

But I did. He was thinking of getting married. A bachelor did not build a huge house unless he had matrimony in mind.

"He's joined the Vigilantes," Charles wrote in another letter. "A band of men who are little more than scoundrels and whose aim—*they* say—is to bring law and order to San Francisco. Cage is the only gentleman among them, if you want my opinion. But he claims he's going into politics, and these men are powerfully situated, men who will help him get ahead."

The house, then, I thought with an upsurge of hope, is for entertaining his political friends. Of course. That was it! He must have a proper place, a grand residence with which to impress the important men who would sponsor him in his political career. Not marriage—politics. He would marry, but not in San Francisco. There were no women of breeding there, and Cage would never marry beneath him. He would marry a Virginian, and maybe, just maybe, it would be me. Yes, I still nourished that dream, still hoped that William Norwood would relent and invite his son to return, that Cage would finally fall in love with me.

I was back at Green Springs permanently now, trying to interest myself in local gossip, in picnics and barbecues. Then came a rather disturbing letter from Charles. "Cage," he said, "has hired himself a private detective. He got this notion that someone is following him. I don't know why. It's so peculiar. The detective is a lean, dark fellow with a drooping moustache and a lisp. Jay Cooke says he reminds him of a juggler he once saw in a circus. We try to laugh at it, but Cage is most serious. So far the detective has not been able to find a single suspicious soul. We—Jay and I—believe that it is all in Cage's mind. He does get jumpy every so often—something he never did at home. Can't understand it. Maybe it's being rich that makes him so nervous."

We had a great deal of rain in August, warm, slanting rain that usually fell in the early mornings and lasted until noon. Afterwards when the sun shone, moist heat would rise from the river in steamy vapors, spreading inland preventing the fields from properly drying out. More than a quarter of the tobacco rotted in the ground. Papa talked of planting rice as they had in the Carolinas, but nothing came of it. Aunt Tildy arrived for a visit. A brief one. She and Papa did not get along too well. She wanted to know if I had any steady beaux and why not and how did I expect to get married if I moped about in the library reading books. "Girls get stoop shouldered and squinty eyed reading," she remonstrated with Papa. "Adelaide will never catch a husband that way."

Privately she alluded to my New Orleans escapade only once. "I hope you've completely wiped Cage Norwood from your mind," she said.

"Yes, Auntie," I lied. "Yes, I have."

And then the fatal blow fell, the terrible blow that I had not wanted to think about, the thing I always told myself would never, never happen.

The news arrived in September. I remember the day, warm with Indian summer, a golden glow shining over the river, the trees turning yellow, the roses in their last, riotous bloom. The letter was waiting for me on a salver in the hall when I came in from a visit at Riverknoll. I recognized Charles's thick scrawl and picked up the envelope eagerly, removing the glove from my right hand with my teeth.

I tore the envelope open and smoothed out the pages, my eye skimming hurriedly over the sentences. At the bottom of the first page the words leapt out at me.

". . . Cage was married yesterday."

Chapter 7

HER name was Lillith.

Charles did not say who she was, whether she was young or old, pretty or plain. He made no mention of family, background, birthplace or antecedents. He did not even give me a last name. Just Lillith. Lillith, now Mrs. Lewis Cage Norwood.

I could have died. I wanted to.

I remember carrying the letter in my hand up the wide staircase past the tall clock, down the gallery and into my room. I remember shutting the door carefully and locking it. Then I sat down on the bed. Had I been mistaken? Had I seen something in Charles's letter that was not there?

My eyes hastily scanned the trembling pages once more. "*. . . Cage was married yesterday.*"

The words had not gone away. They were still there. I gazed dumbly around the room. The void under my heart was frightening, a terrible empty space. Married. The end of everything, the end of hope, of dreams, of future happiness. He had been the kingbolt, the cornerstone, the fulcrum of my life. He was the beginning and the end of each day, the stuff of nighttime dreams and daytime fantasies. It was only for him that I smiled, for him that I preened, for him that I had wanted to be popular and beautiful. And I had lost him, lost him to a faceless woman by the name of Lillith.

I got up and went to the open window. The day had turned chill and drab, clouds covered the sun and the roses in the garden seemed pale and colorless, a mockery. Beyond the arched trees, the river ran cold, a dreary gray. The light had gone out of everything, sky, water, earth and time was slowly closing in on me like an iron trap. What was there to look forward to now? What, except to go on with this unbearable hurt under my heart?

My eyes fell upon the roof of the verandah below the window. I stared at it for a long time. No, I thought dully, it is not far enough. I would only break a bone or two, sprain an ankle and then I would have to explain. The thought of explaining, of talking, of seeing Papa, Sissy, people, anyone, was like a rope of hemp about my neck. Somewhere deep inside in the midst of my abysmal despair a small nugget of intelligence told me that this was bound to happen; inevitably a man like Cage, handsome, of good family and wealthy to boot, would be snared by some clever woman, but I was in no mood to reason rationally. The pain was blinding, and my only agonized wish was to find a way to end it. Why go on living, suffering?

I went to my dressing table and began to paw among the bottles and jars; an unguent for mosquito bites, cream for roughened hands, rose water, a box of headache powders given to me by Dr. Meggs ages ago. I sat down and began to eat them all, the powders, the unguent, the cream. I found some water color paints in a drawer and ate them, too. The taste was horrible but I forced them down. Ought I to write a note? I wondered, waiting for the ungodly mess in my stomach to take effect. Should I pen my last words to Papa saying that I had died for love like a Walter Scott heroine? Papa would write to Charles and Charles would tell Cage and Cage would be heartsick. He would be sorry, regret that he had ever married that Lillith woman. In my mind I could picture his face, handsome, sad. Yes, I would write that note; he might even weep.

But before I could find pen and paper, the rose water, paints, powders and unguents suddenly began to churn in sickening nausea, rising in a great bubble, bringing the bitter taste of green bile to my mouth. I ran to the wash basin and began to retch, my body convulsed by paroxysm after paroxysm. My breath came in gulping, heaving gasps as I clung to the commode with cold, clammy hands. I heard a pounding on the door and Sissy's voice, then Papa's. I tried to stagger across the room to open it, but a new spasm caught me. I was going to die, for sure, this was the end. Over—all over. And suddenly I was not too certain that I wanted to die, after all.

I heard a cracking sound and Papa's voice, "Adelaide—!", and then a long time later I felt Sissy's cool hand on my forehead.

They put me to bed. I was too sick to care if they found Charles's letter or not. I even doubted whether Papa would put two and two together, connecting my sudden illness with Cage's marriage. Dr. Meggs was called, and he wanted to know what I had eaten to make me so sick. "Oysters," I said. "I bought them from an old fisherman who stopped down at the wharf."

He "tsked" and "tsked" and felt my pulse. "I've always said oysters in September were bad for the digestion."

Aunt Tildy came a week later. I was up and about by then, looking pale and wan. "You've grown terribly thin," she said, adding with a stern look, "I want to have a private talk with you."

The anticipated and dreaded talk. "Aunt Tildy—some other time," I said, trying to put it off.

"There is no other time."

"Now, miss," she said, after we had gone up to my room and shut the door, "what is this about oysters?"

"I was foolish to eat them, Auntie. . . ."

"I should think so. And . . . ?"

She waited for me to go on, but I could find nothing else to say.

"Your father tells me Cage Norwood has just been married. Did you know?"

"Yes," I said in a small voice, meeting her shrewd, intelligent eyes for the barest of moments.

"And those 'oysters,' did they have anything to do with it?"

"No," I lied, forcing my eyes back to hers. "No."

She studied me, her lips pursed. "I'm not going to press you, Adelaide, but I want you to listen to me. You will look back on this some day and laugh. . . ."

Had Cage said that too? You'll laugh? No—he said that I would forget. As if I wanted to, as if I could.

". . . oh, yes, I realize that you think you will never laugh again. Well, my dear child, you are mistaken. Your infatuation will pass. And don't tell me it's not infatuation but pure, passionate love. Ha! There is no such thing, my dear. And the sooner you learn that, the happier you will be. I know, believe me, I speak from experience."

There was a wry twist to her lips. "I suppose you are wondering why I should say that?"

I looked at her and saw a dour old lady with frizzed,

iron gray hair and dark eyes that could be soft or hard, stern or compassionate, an Olympian of wisdom, but far removed, I felt, from the "experience" of young mortals like myself.

"I was a year older than you," she went on, "when I fell—what is the term—'madly in love?'—yes, I suppose that's what it's called. I fell madly in love with a young man—and he swore he loved me. I won't tell you his name, so don't try to guess. Well, this young man courted me off and on for six months. Whenever he came to Brandon he'd take me to parties, teas and the like. I kept waiting for him to ask Papa for my hand, but he didn't. I thought it was shyness which held him back and so said nothing. Then one fine day I heard that he was to be married—that he had been engaged all along to some sweet young thing. . . ." She looked away, staring for a long time out the window, her jaw a hard line. She's still angry, I thought, after all these years, she's still angry and she wants *me* to laugh. "Well," she continued briskly, "I got over it. And then I met Mr. Hampton. I was not 'madly in love,' but he made me happy, far happier than the young man ever could."

I wondered if she had said that just to make me feel better or if she really meant it. But it did not matter. A hundred stories of jilted young girls and blighted romances could not keep me from believing in love or erase Cage from my adolescent heart.

"Dear Charles," I wrote the day after Aunt Tildy had safely gone, "I was quite surprised to learn that our mutual friend, Mr. Norwood, had married. Naturally I am curious —you know how females are when they hear of weddings. You say the bride's name is Lillith, but you tell me nothing else. You must write more, describe her and the wedding itself, of course. Being Cage's close friend I'm sure you were his best man." I then launched into a spritely account of a fictitious picnic to make it look as if my inquiry into Cage's marriage was merely of casual interest.

Charles replied that Lillith was a widow with a two-year-old daughter whom Cage had legally adopted. He said nothing else, and this curious silence about the bride from my brother who had been so eloquent on a number of lesser subjects, gave me the strong feeling that he disapproved of the marriage. But why, I could only guess. Perhaps Lillith was older than Cage; as a widow she might very well be. That gave me comfort somehow, and I liked to picture her well up in years, the beginning of wrinkles at the corners of her eyes and an ugly mole on her chin. But knowing Cage as I did, I soon realized that he never would have chosen anything but an attractive woman to be his wife. What did she look like then? Tall? Short? Dark or fair? My unsatisfied curiosity grew and finally I wrote to Charles again, boldly throwing pretense and caution aside, asking for more details. He ignored my questions, however, and Lillith's face continued to remain a blank in my mind.

A year passed. Mary Neale had married her Yankee suitor and gone to live in New York State. People buzzed about it, called her traitor, said, wasn't it a shame, but she went merrily off without a backward glance, and the gossips soon had other things to talk about. Kitty Snowden, Mrs. Thomas Norwood these past two years, had two children in quick succession and was expecting a third. "You'd think she'd have waited, it's positively indecent. . . ." Henry Neale was courting Rowena Sands. If Rowena refused him, Mrs. Pettigrew said, she would be considered an old maid. "Twenty, you know," clacked the tongues, "and not getting any younger." Of Cage Norwood no one spoke at all.

Nor did Charles mention him, though he continued to write long letters to me. He and Jay Cooke were still in business together, still dealing in real estate, still prospering. Papa grumbled that Charles ought to come home, and but for the money we received I think he would have ordered him to. Production along the river had fallen off that year; disease, an infestation of nematodes and an untimely hailstorm reduced some harvests by half. Many of the planters were cutting down on their slave population by selling them to traders from the deep south where the demand was still high, or leasing their darkies to the new factories in Richmond. Papa would do neither. He felt these practices were inhumane, and for once he and Mr. Benton were in agreement. Perhaps if Papa had been hard pressed he might have gone along with the current trend, but because of Charles's generosity we did not feel the pinch at Green Springs as they did elsewhere.

Meanwhile, life went on for me in a kind of a numb void.

Voices and faces, the news and gossip seemed to reach me over long, empty distances. I nibbled at my food, grew thinner, my complexion sallowed. No beaux came to call. I went to fewer and fewer parties and finally ceased going to any at all. Thankfully, Papa, engrossed in politics, did not notice. He was always fuming about something; factionalism was rampant in Virginia then. The Tidewater, guarding its old aristocratic ways, pitted against the Piedmont, the Shenandoah against the Transalleghany. Papa opposed the building of a railroad that had been touted by Norfolk as benefiting commerce along the river, Papa claiming they ought to concentrate on improving the James and Kanawha Canal instead.

Then in the summer of '55 an epidemic struck. We had always been subject to yellow fever and malaria in the Tidewater, but this was the worst attack in memory. Some likened it to the black death of the Middle Ages. It started in Norfolk, brought over, it was said, by a steamer from the West Indies. A stricken crewman on board managed to infect several civilians before he succumbed and from then on the disease spread rapidly. By the end of August people were dying like flies, seventy, eighty or even one hundred passing away daily. We heard that entire families had been wiped out, mother, father, grandparents, children, servants, and because the supply of coffins soon ran out, mass burials became necessary.

The plague soon moved upriver, and Papa was the first among us to fall ill. Dr. Meggs, who had gone to Norfolk to offer his assistance (with doctors from all over the states —forty physicians from New York, Philadelphia, Baltimore and Washington alone), was hastily summoned back. I wrote immediately to Charles begging him to come home. Green Springs had been put under quarantine and no visitors were allowed, both negroes and whites strictly confined to their plantation and house. Nevertheless, Aunt Tildy, hearing of Papa's illness, came bustling up from Brandon. Dr. Meggs scolded and said she ought not to have taken the risk, but I was glad to have her.

I was frightened. Papa had never been sick a day in his life that I could remember, and it unnerved me to see him lying in bed, weak from retching, his eyes glazed over with fever. Then after the fourth day his temperature returned to normal and I breathed a sigh of relief. But Dr. Meggs warned Papa not to get out of bed. "You've gone through the first stage," he said. "If you are lucky that will be all—but if you are not . . ."

Papa was not lucky. The following morning after we believed he was on the mend, he had a severe nose bleed and his fever returned. From then on he went downhill rapidly, his skin turning the ghastly yellow so characteristic of the disease. We took turns sitting by his bedside, nursing and waiting on him, Aunt Tildy, Sissy and I, tiptoeing in and out of his shade-drawn room with basins of cool water to wash his fevered body. He suffered dreadfully, tossing and turning, winding the bed clothes about him, often unaware of our presence, mumbling and sometimes shouting deliriously. There was nausea and vomiting and terrible headaches that set him to groaning pitifully. We could do nothing but sponge his brow, keep his linen changed, soothe, sit, watch and wait. The smell in his room was horrible. Dr. Meggs said we were not to open the window for the fresh air would be harmful. Aunt Tildy disagreed. "What does the old fool know?" she would murmur under her breath, and after he left she would fling the windows wide. The odor persisted however, the sour-sweet odor of sickness, of sweat and vomit and fear.

I grew more and more apprehensive as I sat by his side, peering into his face, hoping for a sign of change. If Papa went what would I do? I had heard the old platitude spoken often enough of people who watched loved ones die—"all my life I took him (or her) for granted"—and it had never meant anything to me until now. I had taken Papa for granted. He was a part of my life, a part of me like my hand or my foot or my eyes, things one accepts as a matter of course until possible loss looms like a dark, threatening cloud. I could not imagine the days ahead without Papa, Green Springs without the sound of his voice, his heavy tread on the stair. I did not *want* to imagine it. "You must not die!" I would whisper urgently while the oil lamp flickered and flared and the tall clock chimed the black, waiting hours. "You must not!" For the first time I forgot completely about Cage and thought only of Papa, my earliest memory of him, a tall, looming shape above a pair of black varnished boots, and the smile on his face as he bent to me. "Give me your hand, princess." I wept silently and I prayed as I never had before—for God to spare him.

But He did not. Papa breathed his last just before dawn on the tenth day of his illness. He died thinking that it was my dead mother's hand he held instead of mine. "Judith," he said, his face brightening in a strange and frightening way, "Judith . . . ?" And then he was gone.

I was still sitting by his bed when Aunt Tildy, white and drawn, came into the room to ask how he was.

"He's dead," I said and wondered why my voice should sound so odd, so far away. "He's dead."

There was a sick feeling in the pit of my stomach, and as I got slowly to my feet the room suddenly vanished into darkness.

I don't remember much after that. I knew I was ill, that I might die, that Aunt Tildy was with me, and sometimes I recognized Sissy's frightened black face. I had terrible visions, nightmares of burning houses and screams of children. Sometimes I was in a burning house myself, the flames licking all around me, higher and higher; I could feel the heat, smell the smoke, the acrid burning of carpets and curtains, and I would open my mouth to scream, but no sound would come.

The dreams continued for ages, it seemed, and suddenly they went away. From a muted distance I heard Aunt Tildy say, "You are going to be all right."

I opened my eyes. Moonlight was streaming in through the fluttering curtains. I could smell the mock orange planted near the verandah and the wet, dew-soaked grass.

"Have I been sick a long time?" I asked.

"Four days," Aunt Tildy said, looking old, very old.

It seemed like four years. "Papa . . . ," I said, weakly, suddenly remembering.

"He's been buried, Adelaide. We had to—the heat. He's in the family plot next to your mother."

It was too soon for Charles to come home, but I asked anyway. "Charles . . ."

"Not yet," she said.

Unlike Papa, I did not go into the second phase of the illness. I began to recover. But my convalescence was a long, slow process, disheartening and trying. The fever had left me feeling boneless, weak and trembling. Every movement was an effort—combing my hair, tying a shoelace, pulling a gown over my head. To cross a room or climb the stair was like wading through hip-deep water on leaden limbs. Often I had little desire but to sit for hours at the bedroom window, looking out at the river and thinking of nothing. Aunt Tildy and Sissy fussed; I ate like a bird, they said, and they set all sorts of tempting dishes before me. Gradually, by slow degrees, I began to mend, much to their relief.

We at Green Springs were not the only ones who had been struck by fever. Among our neighbors not one family had escaped the illness, the shadow of death. Ellen Louise Neale, Barnabas Neale's wife, with her breathy speech, was gone. Grandpa Joseph Sands, both of Kitty Snowden's parents, the Woods's two younger children, five-year-old Tricia Benton, as well as numerous darkies, had died. In nearby Richmond, which had lived through the same epidemic, we heard that cholera was now sweeping the city, and for a time we feared it would spread, engulfing us all in a new horror. But fortunately it did not, though over two hundred people died in that city.

When Charles came home a month later he found black crepe fluttering from the doors of the mansions up and down the river.

"I should have left San Francisco a year ago," he said, blaming himself for not being at Green Springs when Papa took ill.

"But there was nothing you could do," Aunt Tildy protested. "It all happened so fast."

Charles had changed. He looked older. He had grown chin whiskers and a large, curling moustache which he kept tugging and twitching. It seemed to me that his shoulders had broadened; he looked manlier, more assertive, perhaps because he was now master of Green Springs.

"Are you rich?" I asked shyly.

"Not as rich as I should be to do some good here." He gave me a small smile. "The plantation is in worse shape than I had imagined. It will take a lot of money, Adelaide." He began to talk of building up the soil, of trying corn, perhaps cattle too.

After a long while I screwed up my courage. "And how is Cage getting along?" Very casual, as if he were some distant acquaintance.

"Well enough, I suppose," Charles answered after a slight pause. "We haven't been seeing much of each other this past year."

"You haven't quarreled, have you?"

"No," he said noncommittally, "no, nothing like that."

I wanted to ask if Cage had had any children, if he and his wife seemed happy, in love, but the coolness in Charles's voice discouraged further inquiry.

As the weeks went on I noticed that Charles received mail from Jay Cooke, but not a single letter from Cage. Perhaps they *had* quarreled, perhaps the rift between them had occurred over some business matter, a dispute which left them both too angry and rancorous to reestablish their friendship.

It was surprising how easily Charles stepped into Papa's shoes. For a young man who had done nothing more arduous at home than race his black stallion, ride to hounds or play cards, he showed a remarkable capacity for work. He did his own overseeing, rising at five-thirty in the morning and working through most of the day, supervising, planting, cultivating, fertilizing, and at harvest time curing the tobacco, then selling it himself in Richmond. In his spare time, little as it was, he began to court Anna May Gordon, Hale Gordon's daughter by his first wife. They were married a year later in a quiet, but lovely wedding at Merinowe. All my contemporaries were married by then, the Benton girls, the Snowdens, the Sandses, even Theresa Norwood who was Mrs. Ernest Young now. People said, "You will be next, Adelaide."

I had no desire to be next. I was nineteen and well on my way to spinsterhood but it did not bother me in the least. The one man I wanted to marry, had ever wanted to marry, already had a wife. Her name was Lillith.

"I've invited Gordon Woods for supper, Adelaide," Anna May, my sister-in-law, said one afternoon. "Such a nice young man, home from the University."

This was the first of the "nice young men" we had to supper at Green Springs. Anna May tried, at first subtly, then brashly, to snare a husband for poor Adelaide, her husband's old maid sister. To this day I do not know if her efforts were prompted by a desire to have me out of the house, or by a genuine concern to see me married with my own husband and home. It was hard to tell with Anna May. A pretty, blond-haired girl, she wore a perpetual sweet-as-sugar smile. Nothing seemed to disturb her, nothing made her angry, displeased or unhappy. Never did she raise her soft-spoken voice, give an unkind look, or utter an unkind word. I often wondered as I watched her at mealtime or in the parlor in the evening as she sat knitting or embroidering (some needlework was always in her hand), what went on inside her head, what she was thinking and feeling. It piqued my curiosity. But I never found out.

So the would-be beaux came and went. They came mostly, I suspect, because Charles had generously set aside a tidy sum as a marriage portion for me. They certainly were not drawn by my looks or my charm, and though I was polite enough I encouraged none of them. A single evening usually sufficed; a dull supper in the company of Charles, Anna May and myself, and afterwards an hour or so of suppressed yawns and awkward silences in the stuffy parlor. Only the truly hardy returned for a second time and not one ventured a third.

Anna May, though expecting her first child, kept trying. It was an effort made at great sacrifice, since women in the "family way" were expected to remain sequestered from the public eye. Nevertheless she braved those hopeful suppers, wrapped in an immense shawl even on the warmest of evenings. Charles said nothing, but I could tell he wanted me married, too. He would sit in Papa's chair by the fire with his pipe, and when I would catch him staring at me, he would look down at his book or newspaper and sigh heavily.

I think it was those heavy sighs that finally decided me. I knew that he was thinking of Papa then, and how Papa's dearest wish was to see me married. I could have ignored Charles, of course, and remained a worry and burden to him—and Anna May—the unmarried auntie to his children, but it would have made life uncomfortable for us all. Their anxiety became so contagious I was forced at last to do some weighty soul-searching. It took me some time but

I finally—and reluctantly—arrived at the painful conclusion that pining for a man I could never have was selfish, if not useless. Cage was gone, married, immutably removed from my life. I might remember him, carry him deep in my heart, but day-to-day living among others had to go on. I had to face reality and the sooner, the better.

It was then I began to take notice of the unattached menfolk and so became aware of Barnabas Neale. I had always thought he was a frequent visitor to Green Springs for no other purpose than to discuss plantation business with Charles until I realized it was me he most often addressed, my opinions he usually sought. His face and figure, hitherto a nebulous shadow on the periphery of my preoccupied mind, suddenly took form, and I looked at him now more keenly. What I saw was not displeasing.

Barnabas Neale. I had known him all my life. A friend of the family, a kindly country squire, younger but on a par with Papa, a settled man with a wife and children, I never dreamed I would ever contemplate him as a possible suitor. But—I asked myself—why not? Not handsome, but dignified, he was of medium height, about forty-five or forty-six, with sparse hair ringing a bald spot, thick chin-whiskers and gentle, brown eyes. He was fond of me, I could tell, and the thing I liked about him was his air of ease. I never felt constrained in his company, never felt that I had to force myself to make small talk. Even the silences which occasionally fell between us seemed comfortable. For me that meant a good deal. I wasn't very good at flirtation, never having quite mastered the art of fluttering my eyelashes or waving a silly fan. Nor could I indulge in empty flattery. Thank goodness Barnabas was a man who could not be taken in by such artifices.

He had been widowed for almost three years now, his children were grown and married. His son, Henry, and his wife, Rowena, and their young son, Ted, lived at home in one wing of Beech Arbor, and the daughter, Mary, of course, resided in New York with her Yankee husband.

He was lonely, he told me one evening as we sat on the verandah steps listening to the cicadas in the weeds beyond the clipped lawn.

"I know I am old enough to be your father," he said, "but I want to marry you. I love you, Adelaide. And I promise I will do everything to make you happy."

Very short and to the point, not the impassioned proposal a young girl might expect as her first, but then, I thought, I had left all that sort of thing behind—all my dreams of passion had died the day I received the letter telling me Cage had married.

"I won't talk to Charles," Barnabas went on, "unless I have your consent first." Charles, of course, as my older brother, had taken Papa's place. Form required that his permission be granted. "I hope you will say yes."

He had said nothing about my loving him. No questions asked. If he had, I would have told him the truth, perhaps he guessed, perhaps that is why he did not ask. But I was fond of him. And I was sure that would be enough.

"Thank you, Barnabas, I shall be honored," I said. "Please do speak to Charles," and offered my cheek for him to kiss.

Chapter 8

BARNABAS was a gentleman. Mild mannered, soft
spoken, in many ways like Anna May, but with more
depth and without her sugary sweetness, he was the essence
of courtliness. I cannot recall ever hearing him raise his
voice. I suppose being human he must have felt anger at
some time or other, but if he did he never gave the least
sign. He was such a contrast to Papa and Charles, who, if
irked, would forget themselves and erupt with an oath even
in my presence. Barnabas always spoke courteously, whether
to me, his gentleman friends or to the lowest field hand.
Even in our more intimate moments he never deviated from
his gracious, considerate manners. And if our marriage
lacked passion, I did not notice it. I was brought up to
believe (by innuendo mostly) that a wife submitted to a
man's needs out of duty and that her reward for these
physical interludes of, thankfully, short duration were
crowned by motherhood.

The only flaw I could find in my new husband was his
obsessive tidiness. He was meticulously neat in his person,
in his work, in everything he did, his eye constantly on the
alert for a slightly crooked picture frame, a book out of
line on the shelf, a carelessly placed fork on the dinner
table. If his boots had not been shined to a mirror gloss he
would deliver a reprimand, spoken in a quiet voice, but a
reprimand nevertheless. Other than this extraordinary need
for precision, other than my caution about not leaving a
shawl on a chair or my stockings on the wardrobe floor, I
found being married to Barnabas pleasant. My status as a
wife, more importantly as the wife of a well-off planter of
good family, insured me a place in society above the
barbed prattle of tongues. I no longer had to shrink at the
meaningful glances, the little asides, the whispered, "She's
plain, you know." In the past I had told myself that these

SHADOWS OF THE HEART 93

little snubs did not matter, but now I realized they had hurt more than I cared to admit. No more. Because I was Mrs. Barnabas Neale the stigma of "spinster" had been erased. I was no longer that unattractive, uninteresting Miss Adelaide, a young woman one spoke to condescendingly, if at all. The same ladies who had politely ignored me now fairly gushed, embracing me if we happened to meet as if I had just come home from a long journey. Even Mrs. Pettigrew smiled and called me "my dear Adelaide."

I was not bitter. It amused me. I invited them to my small dinner parties and little teas and smiled demurely, wondering what they would say if they knew what I was thinking. Except for Kitty Norwood they were all shallow-minded, empty-headed fools with scarcely enough brains among them to puddle a demitasse. It was strange, too, how I had never noticed their lack of intelligence until I became Mrs. Neale. It was as if I had come into a new and different world, vaguely familiar in its background, but peopled with men and women I was meeting for the first time. My mind had been too full of other matters, I suppose—Cage primarily—for me to give much thought to the neighbors and friends I had known, at least outwardly, for a lifetime.

"Can you imagine?" exclaimed Cynthia Norwood, raising her pale brows one afternoon as I handed her a cup of tea. "The Benton girls are allowed to read whatever they choose. I had it on good authority from Theresa. They have even read that dreadful woman—what *is* her name?—Stull?—Stowe—yes, that's it, Harriet Beecher Stowe! It's her book, they've read, that awful *Uncle Tom's Cabin*."

There was a collective gasp of shocked sensibilities, and I wondered what they would have said had they known that I, too, had read Stowe's novel years ago when some girl had smuggled it into the Academy.

"I daresay they share their father's abolitionist views," Mrs. Sands said. "He is a disgrace—Hugh Benton is a disgrace, and if it were not for that sweet wife of his, I would cut him dead."

The sweet wife, Alice Benton, reputedly a direct descendant of Thomas Jefferson, came from an old, old family, and she numbered among her friends and kin several prominent people who were frequent guests at her home. To be invited to one of Alice Benton's parties was considered a mark of high favor, whatever her husband's politics, and there were those who toadied to her shamelessly. Alice knew it but seemed to enjoy their flattery.

"My girls never read at all," Mrs. Woods said, drawing her lips together. "Books have a tendency to addle a young female's brain. Let the boys read, I say."

"It's easier to raise boys," Mrs. Sands said. "Although . . . ," she paused, raising a handkerchief to her eyes. "They do go off when they're grown and mine . . ." She sniffed and everyone lowered their eyes, remembering Horton's death at the Devil's Gulch mining camp in California.

"Now, now, poor dear, don't take on," Mrs. Pettigrew soothed. "You still have the other two."

"Yes," Mrs. Sands agreed tearfully, dabbing at her eyes again. "Thank God for Frank and George. But if Horton had not been persuaded to go by . . ." She stopped short, blushing crimson, throwing Mrs. Norwood a guilty look.

There was a long moment of silence during which Cage's name seemed to hang in the air, then Mrs. Pettigrew said, "I do believe I'll have another one of those lovely cakes, Adelaide," and the assembled ladies began to talk again.

I hoped for a child. As time passed and none came my hope turned to active longing, a yearning that was difficult to conceal. I wanted a baby not only because it was expected that I bear my husband one, but because I truly wished for a child of my own. Despite my contentment with Barnabas and my busy schedule as mistress of Beech Arbor, there were still moments when I experienced a queer feeling of emptiness, a sudden void under the heart, like a blow struck when I least expected it. I believed that a child could fill that void and I looked with envy upon other women who had babies. When Mary Neale came to visit and brought her year-old son (but not her Yankee husband), I thought that even though she had defected to the alien North, she, too, had been blessed. I told her how fortunate she was and she laughed. "You will have dozens, Adelaide. Just wait and see. Once they start coming there will be no end. Just look at Charles's wife."

I liked Mary Neale. I got along splendidly with both of Barnabas's children, although at first I thought they might resent me. "Why should we resent you?" Henry Neale asked when I ventured to tell him one evening as we were dining. "You have made Papa very happy. And you take such good care of him. You're a fine wife, not like some I could mention who marry older men." He was referring to Elizabeth Gordon, the lovely young thing Cage had once flirted with. "There's never been a breath of scandal attached to your name."

Yes, I thought, no scandal. Aunt Tildy and I had kept my trip to New Orleans secret. And, of course, I had my plain looks as defense against gossip. Who would associate a sallow-skinned girl, thin and unobtrusive, meek and shy, with scandal? Not Adelaide Carleton Neale.

In the autumn of that same year, 1859, a disturbing event took place.

Though we women were not supposed to be interested in politics and seldom, if ever, discussed affairs of state, leaving that to the men, the news of the raid on Harper's Ferry on October 16 shocked us so, we could talk of nothing else for weeks. It seemed that a man by the name of John Brown, an insane fanatic (Theresa Norwood said that his grandmother and mother had both died in an asylum) with a long beard and mad eyes, had gathered a band of cutthroats together, crossed the Potomac at night and, seizing the federal armory at the Ferry, had killed the mayor. In addition they had taken several leading citizens into custody, including Colonel Lewis W. Washington, great-grandnephew of George Washington. Our own Governor Wise had ordered out the militia and then appealed to the federal government for aid. Brown's avowed aim, it was said, had been to incite a slave uprising all over the South, and although the culprit had been captured, subsequently found guilty of treason and murder and sentenced to hang, his outrageous deed had left an ominous pall over the river plantations. For some time now there had been increasing tension between North and South, and Harper's Ferry had done nothing to ease it.

"The Yankees want to destroy us!" Mrs. Pettigrew, very red in the face, exclaimed one afternoon. "They paid that awful creature, Brown, to attack the armory. Yes, indeedy, it is a well-known fact. Prominent people in New York paid John Brown. Well—I can tell you, they'll see our mettle soon enough. Why, Mr. Pettigrew says he'll stand up to the Yankees barehanded if need be. He's willing to show them!"

Mr. Pettigrew was a thin, little man, sparse of hair with a timid smile, and the vision of him standing up with clenched fists against a horde of devil-tailed Yankees would have been amusing had not this same sentiment been voiced heatedly by others.

"We'll fight to the last man." "Trifle with us, will they?" "Give them a drumming they won't forget!" "Kill the bloody, arrogant thieves!"

There were cooler heads, of course (Barnabas's among them), who felt that confrontation could be avoided. John Letcher, newly elected governor of Virginia, assuming office on the first of January, 1860, did not share the secessionist views of his predecessor, Henry Wise. He wanted Virginia to stay in the Union if this could be done honorably. The word "honor" carried a lot of weight, for the truth was that there were not that many slaves in Virginia (three-quarters of all white Virginians owned no slaves at all, according to Mr. Benton), but there was a great deal at stake in terms of tradition, a way of life, a feeling that Virginians were astute enough to govern themselves without the unwanted interference of Washington. It wasn't that Virginia stood against the Union, *per se*, either. As late as April our state convention voted against secession. (The three leading Richmond papers, however, leaned toward breaking away, one of them calling Lincoln, "a hideous chimpanzee from Illinois.")

But after Fort Sumter the debate died suddenly, irrevocably.

On the very day that the Virginia convention sent three prominent citizens to a conference with President Lincoln in a desperate last-minute attempt to avert hostilities, the Fort was bombarded and fell to the seceding South Carolinians. When President Lincoln issued a call for 75,000 volunteers to put down the rebellion, Virginia, who was unwilling to furnish federal troops to coerce South Carolina, a sister state, voted to secede.

Barnabas and I happened to be in Richmond during that historic April week, and I shall never forget the white hot fever generated by the crowds milling through the streets. On April 19 a Confederate flag was hoisted atop the Capitol flagpole, and that night from our windows at the Ballard Hotel we watched a mile-long torchlight procession wind its way down Marshall and Broad Streets. Bands blared, drums rolled and voices rose from hundreds of throats in stirring chorus as line after line of marching men filed past, the cadence of their tramping feet echoing above the music. Women wept, children screamed, while overhead rockets burst and Roman candles flared, throwing the excited faces of the throngs into garish relief. We laughed, cheered and exchanged shouted quips with the crowd below. Predictions were that the Yankees would be beaten in less than a month. Two at the most, an ebullient young man told us. "In sixty days the Confederate flag will be waving over the White House in Washington."

Robert E. Lee was asked to take command of Virginia's military and naval forces and he accepted. Regiments were formed, arms and uniforms gathered, supplies assembled, and before we could catch our breaths we were knee-deep in what we thought would be a victorious, short-lived war.

All our young men went off to fight: Kitty's brother Tom, Frank and George Sands, the oldest Davis boy, Clem Young and Gordon Woods (my would-be suitor) and Henry, Barnabas's only son. Henry along with Charles enlisted in the Cavalry under Jeb Stuart. I remember how handsome both men looked when they came home for a brief leave dressed in their gray uniforms, gold-braided, sashed and sabered, wearing sweeping felt hats on their heads. Rowena, Henry's wife, put on a brave face when they left, but my sister-in-law, Anna May, expecting another child, broke down and cried bitterly as she watched Charles mount his prize black stallion and ride away. It was the first time I had seen placid Anna May overwhelmed by an emotion and it shook me. I tried to hide my own apprehension by comforting her. "You'll see," I said, "it won't be for long. He will be back before the baby is born."

Charles did come back, but not until years later, and not to Green Springs. He was taken prisoner at a place called Rich Mountain where William Norwood, Cage's father, lost his life.

That was early in the war, early as I look back now, for even after we got news of Charles's capture and William

Norwood's death we were still caught up in a kind of delirious, patriotic euphoria, believing victory and the end of fighting was only a matter of weeks. When we heard that Jeb Stuart's cavalrymen were on their way to join Joseph E. Johnston's army on the peninsula, we were immensely cheered. The horse-mounted troops had passed through the streets of Richmond lined with jubilant throngs singing and playing "Dixie," while pretty girls tossed flowers and kisses at their gallant fighting men. Yes, soon the war would finish, soon, very soon, we told one another in those soft green April days of 1862.

As the months went by, more and more of our neighbors enlisted, though the Conscription Act had exempted men above thirty-five as well as the owners of twenty or more slaves. William Norwood had been one of the first older men to go, and perhaps because of his untimely death, the others, feeling a little guilty, soon joined up; Tom Pettigrew (little Tom), Alex Sands, Jim Woods, Dr. Meggs, even Hugh Benton, our one and only abolitionist—and, of course, my own Barnabas. Since his daughter had married a Yankee, he felt as great a need to show his Southern sympathies as Mr. Benton, and he went off to join the gray-clads, leaving me at Beech Arbor, a house suddenly silent and empty.

The women at home coped as best they could. Most of the slaves had run away, and all but the sorriest of horses had been commandeered by the Army, so that there was no one to plant the tobacco fields that spring, and they lay fallow. But we were able to raise enough foodstuffs to keep us comfortably fed, more so than the unfortunate city dwellers. By now the Yankees had effectively bottled up the Southern ports, and a good many of the blockade runners heralded early on as daring and heroic soon proved to be profiteers, and instead of sorely needed food, medicines, machinery, guns and ammunition they brought in shiploads of luxuries, liquors, cigars, perfumes and silks, which they auctioned off at exorbitant prices. The ordinary necessities of life became dear or completely out of reach. At Riverknoll, Green Springs and Beech Arbor we deplored these selfish, money-hungry scoundrels as traitors and went on growing potatoes, squash, beans, corn and black-eyed peas, trying to keep at least one milk cow from the army agents, who did pay us for what farm animals they took, but in Confederate dollars and very few of them.

Spindles were brought down from the attic and the older women taught the younger ones the lost art of weaving. We wore our homespun proudly. Misfortune had drawn us together; shallow gossip and petty quarrels vanished overnight. Again I was surprised (pleasantly this time) to discover how I had misjudged my friends. Not weak-kneed, fluttering and shrinking as I had expected, but rallying to the cause with strength and stiff-lipped courage. Even Anna May, once she had dried her tears, bore Charles's incarceration with admirable fortitude. Aunt Tildy closed her house in Brandon and came to stay with me, and wonders of war—and its exigencies—she and Mrs. Pettigrew, whom she never could abide, became staunch friends. Mrs. Pettigrew herself emerged as a tower of strength. Indefatigable, she mended, wove and knitted, nursed the sick among us, cheered our flagging spirits and took over the cooking at Beech Arbor until we could replace the darkie cook who had fled. It was she who delivered Anna May's baby. I never thought the day would come when I would embrace her with such warmth and affection as I did when, after the long, arduous night, she brought my nephew into the world.

Deprived of our menfolk, too busy and too financially embarrassed to entertain as we had in prewar days, we still managed to remember each other's birthdays and anniversaries with small parties and quiet little dinners. We socialized at our weekly sewing circle where we rolled bandages, knitted socks and exchanged letters from our fighting men, serving tea, sweetened with sorghum now, but in the same silver pots. We still said, "Come stay awhile," meaning it, still tried to keep up with the old ways, clinging to the routine and geniality we had always known. But in the backs of our minds lurked the frightening awareness of our vulnerability to attack along the river James, the highroad to Richmond, capital of the Confederacy.

Then one morning in early June a grayclad Confederate officer came to Beech Arbor warning us that the Union General, McClellan, was planning an assault on Richmond by way of the river. "Best to make for the city," he advised. "Richmond is well fortified and hundreds of families have already taken refuge there. I strongly urge you to do the same."

We held a hurried council of war. The Norwood women, the Bentons, the Sands and the Snowdens, all our neighbors decided to leave at once, locking their houses, hoping by some miracle to find them unharmed when they returned. Theresa invited Anna May and her four children to join her at her in-laws, the Youngs, since their large house in Richmond could accommodate them easily. Rowena, my step-daughter, would go to her cousins, the Fanchons, at Big Lick. But Aunt Tildy refused to budge.

"I hear that McClellan, the Union general, is a gentleman," she said nodding her grizzled head assertively. "An honorable man, from reports, one who makes allowances. If we don't scurry off like rats from a sinking ship we have a better chance of saving our possessions."

"A Yankee—a gentleman?" they chorused scandalized.

"You must have lost your mind," Mrs. Pettigrew declared.

"I have not," Aunt Tildy denied firmly. "I was forced to leave Brandon, but I'll be a goose's cousin if I let the Yankees chase me one step further. *That's* retreat, Mrs. Pettigrew, that's *retreat*." She turned to me, her face flushed with indignation. "Well—Adelaide—what do you say? Do we stay—or run?"

"Of course we'll stay."

Why, in God's name, I gave in to such a rash, foolhardy course remains a mystery to this day. I think if I had tried to argue I might have persuaded Aunt Tildy, but I suppose the word "retreat" made me feel guilty and so I agreed to remain at Beech Arbor. Whatever my reasoning, the decision was one we both came to bitterly regret.

It could not have been more than two days after our neighbors had departed when Hattie, the darkie cook, came racing up the drive to tell us between gasps that she had seen a ship flying the Yankee flag approaching from down river. Aunt and I hurried upstairs to the bedroom window where we could have an overview, and there we watched with sinking hearts as the first of the ominous-looking gunboats appeared, followed closely by another and another, a long line of ships sailing past on their way to Richmond. It was a frightening sight; vessel after vessel, their guns bristling, their decks crowded with ranks of bluecoats, gliding silently by like monstrous ships in a dream.

"I never really believed they would get this far," Aunt Tildy murmured. And the unspoken thought lay between us. *Trapped!* We were cut off from Richmond. Yankees below and above, Yankees all up and down the river, there was no escape now, however much we might want to flee.

The next morning before dawn we heard the booming of guns, the sporadic thunderlike rumble of cannon. The silences between bursts of fire were short, portentous, becoming shorter as the hours wore on, and soon there were no silences at all.

Now the incessant booming, the distant cracking, rat-a-tat of artillery continued without a pause, filling the air, bouncing from wall to wall, rattling the window glass in every room of the house. Dishes clinked and shivered in the china cabinet, floors shook, chandeliers swayed. For three days the unseen battle raged, its thunderous clamor deafening our ears. We could not shake the sound, hide, stop our hearing; the noise was always there, savage, savage, frightening. Sleep came fitfully, sleep full of maleficent nightmares. The negroes who had not left locked themselves in their cabins, as terrified as we were. Later we learned that the fighting had taken place at Harrison's Landing and Malvern Hill only a few miles upriver, but for us at Beech Arbor it might as well have been fought on the front lawn.

Still we pretended. We went about our daily routine, seeing that the cheese crocks were properly covered and the hams in the smokehouse turned. We gathered new rose petals for sweet-smelling sachets to put between the linen sheets, we sewed, we crocheted, we polished silver. Two women, hemmed in by the enemy, alone in a large, empty house that shook and trembled with every heavy burst of fire. Catching a fleeting glimpse of my white, strained face and frightened eyes in a mirror, I wondered if it would not have been infinitely easier, more sensible, really, to give vent to our feelings, to weep, to talk, to say what was uppermost in our minds. *I am so afraid.* But convention held us like a vise, and we continued to speak of trivialities while fear lay locked in our hearts.

Then suddenly, ominously, the guns were still. And

somehow that silence seemed more terrible than the booming sound of battle, a silence like an enormous question mark. We sat in the parlor all that day, I remember, working on a quilt, not speaking, our needles moving in and out of the cloth while every nerve strained for the slightest break in that awful stillness. Toward evening rain began to fall. We had an early supper and went directly to bed. The rain continued, a steady drumming on the roof, pattering at the windows through the night, and in the morning we woke to find that the Yankees had docked at our landing.

Aunt Tildy came into my room. "They are here," she said, her face white as milled flour.

Barefooted I ran to the window and stood there, too frightened to do anything but stare at the bluecoats swarming over the wharf.

"We must do something," she said. "I am an old woman, but you . . ."

Rape! I could see it in her eyes. A word that never passed the lips of gentlewomen, never directly.

"We could hide," I said, my mouth dry as dust. They had reached the lawn, a sea of bluecoats. The wagons were rumbling down the long drive—wagons and caissons, and men on horseback who had taken the river path.

"Where? The slave cabins are the first place they will look." She tapped at her teeth. "I have it! You will be preg—with child."

"Aunt Tildy . . . !"

"With child. Quick, get into your clothes. Hurry! They will be at the front door in a minute. Get into your clothes and put a pillow under your skirt."

"But I can't show myself!"

"You will—it's the only way. They will never molest a woman who is expecting. And make yourself ugly, for God's sake! Twist your hair tight in a knob. Wear that mended homespun. Hurry!"

We stood in the hall and heard the jingle of bridle bits and the rattle of sabers in scabbards. The knock on the door came a moment later and my heart jumped like a living thing. Aunt Tildy opened it. "Yes?" she inquired, calmly, as if she were greeting a passerby. "What can we do for you?"

I saw the blue trousers, the blue coat and brass buttons and behind that a host of blurred faces under peaked caps. My heart leaped another notch.

"Colonel Brighton, m'am." The officer removed his hat revealing graying hair and a furrowed brow. The maturity of his looks was somewhat reassuring and I let out my breath. Not a devil, but a middle-aged man, tired, respectful, a mature man who might act like a gentleman. There was hope. "We have many wounded," he said, "and we must requisition your house as a hospital for the United States Army."

"But . . . ," Aunt Tildy said, giving him an embarrassed smile, "my niece here is—uh—in the family way."

The Yankee said: "We shan't harm you, m'am," and then the blurred faces began to shoulder past him, blueclad men of all sizes and shapes, the gaunt, hollow-eyed walking wounded, the bloody, limping ones helped by a comrade's shoulder, and the gory, white-faced, inert bodies carried in on litters. They poured over the threshold, ignoring us as if we were part of the fixtures, fanning out through the downstairs rooms and up the staircase, more and yet more, thousands it seemed, dirty, smelling, the look of death stamped on their features. We could hear the tramp of boots over our heads, the squeak and rumble of protesting furniture. "Only the real sick for the beds!" a voice shouted.

From where Aunt Tildy and I stood I could see our sofas and chairs and the red velvet carpets in the drawing room being covered with the sick and the dying, placed cheek by jowl like so many logs. From them rose a discordant chorus of groans mingled with pathetic calls for water. Someone was sobbing. The stench of putrefying flesh and unwashed bodies was overwhelming.

And yet they came.

I felt ill; I wanted to faint. I could think of nothing but one of our own, Barnabas or Charles, perhaps both, suffering somewhere, wounded, helpless, in pain, their throats parched with thirst.

"What shall we do?" I whispered to Aunt Tildy.

"I'll tell you what we shan't do," she hissed. "We shan't give them any help."

Two able-bodied bluecoats were coming down the stairs, their arms laden with an assortment of stolen articles, gilt-backed mirrors, silver cups, jewelry. A soldier meeting them on the stairs, said, "The colonel gave orders there was to be no looting," and the two thieves laughed. "We won't tell him. These are *pressed*, you fool, pressed."

Aunt Tildy glared at them as they, still laughing, went past. But they took no notice of her.

"We can't keep on standing here," I said. "What shall we do?"

"Does the plantation office have a key?"

"Yes," I said. "If they haven't requisitioned that, too."

The plantation office where we kept our books and records was at the back of the house overlooking the kitchen garden. We hurried to it and to our relief found the room empty. When I closed the door and turned the key in the lock, Aunt Tildy said:

"Now that I think of it, that locked door won't mean a thing if they really want to come in."

"Let's hope they're too busy to bother with us."

"Busy stealing," she said sourly.

The loud, brassy cackling and squawking of hens and the honking of geese drew us to the window. A half-dozen soldiers were rounding up the poultry. From the region of the barn we could hear shots. "They've got the pigs, no doubt," Aunt Tildy said, her mouth a hard line. In the short time that had elapsed since the first of the Yankees came up the drive, every sign of vegetation in the back garden had been trampled, churned into muddy ruts under the wheels of wagons and horses. Craning my neck, I could see that one of the tobacco fields had blossomed with tents.

"They will have to let us go," Aunt Tildy said grimly. "I shall speak to that colonel after they've settled down somewhat. I'll speak to him and order him to give us two horses so we can get to Richmond."

Night came and we arranged ourselves as comfortably as we could, Aunt Tildy on the small horsehair sofa, I in Barnabas's large chair. From time to time we heard the sound of axes ringing on wood outside. "The trees in the orchard," Aunt Tildy said. "I expect they're wanting firewood." After a while the axes fell silent and an uneasy stillness descended over the house.

I awoke some hours later, my throat and mouth parched with thirst. I remembered the bucket of water kept in the passage by the kitchen door, well water, drinking water, sweet and cool. The more I thought of it, the drier my mouth became.

Finally, unable to bear my thirst, I lit a candle and softly, very gently, let myself out the door. I could hear the muffled groans and snores of our uninvited guests as I traversed the hall and reached the passage. Raising my candle for better light I felt my heart jolt as I spotted a dark body lying directly in my path. A Union soldier. Was he dead? No—for he was groaning softly, and the bandages at the side of his head were stained with fresh blood.

"Water . . . !" he pleaded. I went quickly to the bucket and filled a cup with the dipper. Coming back, I knelt and lifted his head and placed the cup to his lips. Not until he began to drink did it occur to me that I was aiding and abetting an enemy. If Aunt Tildy knew she would be furious. But then I thought of Charles, wounded, a prisoner. Perhaps some compassionate Yankee lady was even at this moment putting a cup of lifegiving water to his lips.

"Thank you, m'am," the soldier said. "I—I tried to find it on my own."

"Was there no one to help you?"

"Too many of us," he said with a grimace that passed for a smile. His face was the color of green cheese.

"Your wound," I said. I lowered his head to the floor and turned my back, tore an upper, still-clean flounce from my petticoat. Then by the light of the flickering candle I removed the old clotted bandage from his head, cleansed the wound as best I could and wrapped the flounce up and over his brow, tying it securely. "That ought to do it," I said.

"You—you are an angel of mercy," he whispered in a voice edged with pain. "I—I shall be forever grateful—shall remember you in my prayers."

"There—there is something you might do now that would help us," I said hurriedly in a low voice. "My aunt and I want two horses; we would like to get away."

"Ah—m'am," he sighed, "if only I could. I—I am merely a private. I could not even get myself a cup of water."

"Yes—of course—I should have realized that." I stared at him, the wounded Yankee soldier with the ashen face and bloodied head, gazed at him, suddenly overcome with a strange, eerie feeling of *déjà vu*, a feeling that somewhere, at some time I had seen or met him before.

"You—you sound like a Southerner," I said. "You are from Virginia?"

"No, m'am—Indiana."

He was lying. I knew it at once. I had never been to Indiana, never known anyone who had lived there, and yet I could sense he was lying. Why? Perhaps because as a Southerner he was ashamed of fighting with the Yankees?

"What is your name, soldier?" I asked.

"Bernard West—m'am."

It was a name that rang no bells. And yet, and yet . . .

I peered at his features in the feeble light of the candle. Now that I had a closer, more objective look, there was something about him that I found unsettling. What? He had cold eyes. That was it. His eyes, even in pain, held an inflexible hardness that disturbed me.

"You cannot stay here on the floor," I said.

"It's all right, m'am. After a bit I can manage to crawl back into the parlor. It's better that way—thank you."

I helped myself to a dipper full of water, then left him. It was not until I got back to the little office that I realized I had forgotten to wear the pillow which had been my disguise. But I doubted if Bernard West knew of my "condition" and even if he had I hoped he would say nothing.

The next morning when Aunt Tildy approached the colonel requesting horses, he informed her it was out of the question, that we could not leave. "Your niece can have her baby here," I heard him tell Aunt Tildy. "We have doctors, not enough, but medical assistance is available."

Aunt Tildy took the colonel's refusal as an insult. He was a dastard, a bully, a jailer of women, the lowest form of creature. Did he think he could keep her, Mathilda Hampton, a prisoner? "We are leaving," she announced to me between gritting teeth. "The sooner the better."

That night while the men slept we stole out of the house, and keeping to the shadows crept down the long, tree-lined avenue. We dared not steal a horse, although we had considered it, but they were tethered too close to the men. It was dark and we clung to each other as we stumbled forward, afraid that we might be discovered at any moment. But the anticipated, dreaded alarm never sounded and by cutting through the trees we managed to evade the sentries posted along the upper drive. When we finally reached the river, we paused a moment to steady our trembling legs. Then taking a deep breath, we set our faces northward, to Richmond.

Chapter 9

IT was a nightmare journey—that much stands out—a fearful, foot-weary, heart-pounding trek. When I recall the terror, the exhaustion which dodged every step, the hunger we suffered, I wonder that we ever survived. We hid in the woods—I don't know how many times—skirting the path, sidestepping pitched tents and straggling bands of enemy soldiers returning from the battle of Malvern Hill, scurrying to cover whenever we heard the jingle of harness or the tramp of boots. Aunt Tildy, though a woman of iron spirit and great courage, was well up in years now, and it distressed me to see how she struggled to keep going on painfully swollen feet. But she would not go back, she would not give in. If it had not been for the kindness of an occasional refugee like ourselves we would have starved. A half-loaf of bread, a handful of carrots, a cup of milk—food given generously by people who had nothing themselves. Toward the last we met up with a yeoman farmer fleeing with his family in a wagon, and we rode the remaining few miles crammed among mattresses, sacks of wheat, rotting apples and the farmer's five children, the youngest, mere babes, who wailed without pause.

Richmond had never looked so good. When we appeared on the doorstep of the Hamptons (kin to Aunt Tildy's dead husband) there was a moment when I felt their shock would overcome good manners. But manners won out.

"Of course you are welcome," Mrs. Iona Hampton gushed. "Dear Lord, if we can't do for our own, then what?"

The fact was they were hard pressed themselves. Prices for mere necessities had soared sky high; flour, bacon, sugar, lard, coffee (when one could get it) had tripled in the last year and a half. And we had nothing to offer but the clothes on our backs. Still they embraced us, providing us with a roof and beds, sharing whatever food they were able to obtain.

Aunt Tildy said, "I would have done the same."

When we had recovered from our flight and could take stock of our surroundings I was amazed to learn how the more affluent Richmonders went about enjoying themselves in spite of the war. Elaborate parties and dances were thrown nightly. Theatre entertainments, musicales, picnics and dinners graced the social calendars of the privileged few, sending them on a frenetic round of gala events as if there were no battles being fought, no wounded and dying arriving daily by railroad car, no hardship suffered by the rest of the population. We heard stories of blockaded luxuries obtained for the use of the President's lady, Mrs. Jefferson Davis; gourmet food, fine wines, silken gowns and Parisian bonnets.

Aunt Tildy said the rumors were vastly exaggerated. However that may have been, we ourselves lived modestly, and despite the talk, never wavered in our belief for the cause. We came together again with our former neighbors, the Sands, the Bentons, the Norwoods, and with them joined the other women of Richmond in daily visits to the hospitals where we wrapped bandages, bathed fevered brows, fed the infirm or wrote letters home for those unable to do so. Those visits were far from pleasant. Although the doctors felt that gentlewomen such as ourselves should be shielded from the sight (if not the care) of the more seriously wounded, we could not help but be aware of their terrible suffering, the groans and shouts of agony, the mutilated, living corpses brought in on stretchers, soldiers who had once been whole and happy men, like our own, going blithely off to war. But however difficult it was, we continued our hospital duty, the shrinking and the brave, all of us traveling by foot and by carriage to that horrible sinkhole, trying to help in the best way we could.

One afternoon Theresa casually remarked, "We've heard from Cage."

The name dropped like a stone into the sudden hush that fell among us as we sat over a table piled high with strips of white linen.

"He's coming to Richmond to join up," she said.

"Bless him!" I exclaimed, surprised that it was me speaking, surprised at my steady voice, at the lack of secret excitement his name would have once evoked. "Did he say when?"

"The letter was written from New Orleans, so I expect it will be any day now."

"It will be good to see him," I said. Like an old friend, I thought, pleased with myself, an old friend. Aunt Tildy had been right; all the passion, the torment, the death-defying love I had felt for Cage had disappeared with the passage of years. My encounter with him in New Orleans had become so dim in my memory it seemed that it had happened to a different girl, someone else, not Mrs. Barnabas Neale. How good it was to be free of that feverish, consuming adoration, how good it would be to face Cage, have him take my hand in greeting without falling completely to pieces. Thank God Barnabas had come into my life, canceling the unhappy past, making the present orderly, comfortable.

"Will Cage be bringing his wife?" I asked with polite interest.

"He did not say," she replied. "The letter was very short."

A week later a little black boy came to the house with a note addressed to Aunt Tildy from Cynthia Norwood. "Cage and a friend have returned from San Francisco," it said. "And you and your niece are invited to supper."

On the ride over Aunt Tildy gave me a shrewd look. "I hope you are still not pining for that man," she said.

"Of course not," I laughed. "You forget I am a married woman."

Sam of Riverknoll had been installed as butler at the Youngs and it was he who opened the door to us with a wide grin. "He's hyah," he said, wagging his head toward the open door of the drawing room. "The young massa is hyah."

I turned to look.

And realized at once that I had made a terrible mistake. I should never have come. I should have made some excuse, any excuse and stayed behind. I should have known, I should have guessed.

He was standing with his back to us and at the sight of his tall figure and the sun-streaked, golden head, my carefully prepared feelings, my assurance and poise fled, and a thousand and one bittersweet memories rose in a swift, overwhelming tide. I tried to quell it, I tried, I tried. But it was useless. It was as if time had stopped and I was fourteen again and Cage had never gone away.

But I mustn't, I mustn't . . .

And then we were walking across the hall and Cage turned and exclaimed:

"Why—! If it isn't Miss Adelaide—and Aunt Tildy!"

The thunder in my ears all but obliterated the sound of his greeting. I hated myself. Again I tried to bring my tumultuous heart back to some semblance of calm. But I failed—miserably. My knees were shaking and my throat was dry.

"Cage Norwood," I murmured as he bowed over my hand. "It has been such a long time." Was *that* my voice, so cool, so soft-spoken, so deceptive of the painfully loud clamor under my ribs?

"And Jay Cooke is here also," Cage went on. "You remember him?"

Jay Cooke! My God! Another devastating shock. Jay Cooke, of all people! *Here.* It was one thing to have him mentioned in Charles's letters, a bodiless name, but for him to appear suddenly, out of the blue in the Youngs' drawing room . . . Why? How could this be happening to me? Jay Cooke—Cage. Two devastating shocks in the space of as many minutes. To find myself disintegrating in Cage's presence was difficult enough without having to face Jay Cooke, the man who had escorted me home from my humiliation in New Orleans, not so dim a memory now but painfully fresh in my mind.

"Oh—how stupid of me, of course you haven't met," Cage was saying, suddenly remembering the circumstances under which we had.

Jay Cooke was standing near the fireplace watching us, a faint, mocking smile curving his lips. I wanted to turn and run, but instead I forced myself to smile.

"It's Mrs. Barnabas Neale now, isn't it?" Cage asked as he presented me to Jay Cooke.

"Yes," I said. "Mrs. Neale. Delighted, I'm sure, Mr. Cooke. My brother mentioned you more than once in his letters from San Francisco." I marveled anew at my being able to talk at all, let alone utter banal pleasantries.

"I hope Charles spoke kindly," Jay Cooke replied, looking at me with that direct penetrating gaze of his as if he could see into the very back of my mind. "I am sorry to hear that he is a prisoner of the Yankees."

"Yes—yes . . . it was a blow." I had to sit down. The stays of my corset were biting into my flesh, cutting off my breath. It was warm in the room, airless. "We were quite distressed at the news. . . ." Where was my fan? I must have dropped it somewhere in the hall when I first saw Cage. And it was so hot, so very hot. "My aunt," I said, looking about for her, my eyes desperately seeking her face among the assembled guests. "Have you met my aunt?"

Oh, why did he have to come? Why did Cage have to come? Why couldn't they both have remained in San Francisco?

"How do you do?" I heard Aunt Tildy say, and then Cynthia Norwood was asking, "Aren't you well, Adelaide? You look so flushed." Cage's mother, terrified of catching the fever, always noticed heightened color in others.

"A little warm," I managed, dreadfully embarrassed, my cheeks turning a deeper shade of red.

"I'll have Sam bring you some punch."

It came in a tall, fragile glass. "Please put it down," I said, indicating the table next to the chair where I had been seated. My hands were shaking so I did not trust myself to hold it. I leaned back against the cushions, my gaze traveling the room. I saw all the familiar faces, the Bentons, the Sands, the Woods, the Norwoods; no strange woman. Cage had not brought his wife. If he had I'm sure he would have mentioned her, introduced her. I wondered if she was unhappy about having to stay behind. Did she miss Cage, had she wanted to come? Again I tried to picture her, tall or short, slim or stout, light or dark-haired, but her appearance remained as vague as it had always been.

I lifted the glass and sipped at it. From the corner of my eye I saw Jay Cooke disengage himself from Aunt Tildy and start across the room toward me. I had a moment of terrible panic but then Allegra Benton arrived, accompanied by her brother and several of his fellow officers, all of whom had come home recently on leave, and Jay Cooke got diverted by the flurry of introductions and subsequent talk. Thank God! The last thing I wanted was for him to draw me into a conversation. I had nothing to say to him. I sipped again at the punch, wishing with all my heart that I could be somewhere else.

At supper Cage sat next to Allegra Benton. The youngest of the Benton girls, she had been a child when Cage had gone away. Now she was seventeen with creamy bare shoulders, a slender throat, pink mouth and dark lashed, cornflower blue eyes. She was fluttering those lashes now, smiling at Cage, who seemed attentive, paying her pretty compliments, no doubt, as only he could do. Jay Cooke sat between Aunt Tildy and Theresa. Every once in a while he would dart a glance across the table and I would quickly avert my eyes. I hardly tasted my food, a plain meal, indifferently cooked, but it might as well have been brandy-basted ham and candied yams for all that I noticed. I could think of little but how to get Aunt Tildy home as soon as was decently possible without arousing her suspicions.

However, Aunt Tildy was not quite ready to leave. After supper Mrs. Norwood took her upstairs to show her the rag rug she had just completed while the rest of us gathered again in the drawing room. The talk, as always, was of war and its attendant horrors.

"They tell me," said one of the officers who had come with Allegra, "that the entire city of Fredricksburg has been sacked by the Yankees. Sheer, wanton vandalism is what they say. Those bluecoated dogs running through the streets, tearing priceless heirlooms from homes, throwing precious chests and carved chairs, books, pictures, fine china into the road like rubbish. The place is a shambles, and . . ."

"Oh—Von," Allegra interrupted, putting her hands over her ears. "I don't want to hear about it! I don't want to hear any more ugly stories. It makes me ill—ill!" She shivered. "Might not we have a little music instead? Theresa, would your mother mind?" This was said in deference to the house's mourning for William. "We could sing a few patriotic songs," she added hopefully. "And we'll all feel much better instead of getting all gloomy with this depressing talk."

"I'm sure it's all right," Theresa said. "Perhaps Adelaide could favor us with a piano selection and a song."

I blushed. "I—I don't think I am in voice tonight," I said, clearing my throat pointedly. "Perhaps—you, Allegra . . ."

"Come now, Adelaide," Cage said, turning the full light of his smile on me. "You play so well. I'll sing—and you won't have to do anything but run your fingers over the keys. All right?"

I did not want to play but there was no way I could refuse. "Nothing morbid," Cage bent and whispered in my ear. "None of those awful war songs."

Nothing morbid. I wondered if he felt badly about his father's death. Did he regret that the old man had died without ever having forgiven him? Would he have returned if William Norwood were still alive?

"We're waiting," Allegra reminded impatiently.

"Yes," I said, catching myself, searching my brain for an appropriate song.

"Well . . . ?"

I started with "Listen to the Mockingbird," innocuous enough and Cage caught it on the third bar. He had a clear, melodic tenor, an excellent voice, and when we had finished there was a burst of applause.

"Sing 'Call Me Pet Names,' " Allegra implored, her eyes bright. "Do you know it, Adelaide? Cage? Oh—then do it!"

Again Cage's voice filled the drawing room and he gave the blatantly sentimental words such meaning goose bumps broke out on my arms.

> "Call me sweet names, darling.
> Call me thine own.
> Speak to me always in love's old tone."

He placed his hand casually on my shoulder and his fingers seemed to burn the exposed skin, shooting quicksilver through my veins. Quicksilver, ice and fire. I had missed him. It was the truth, I couldn't pretend, no matter how I tried. I had missed him. I had longed for him. Time, years, a century—nothing. Even in those moments when I thought I had forgotten, he had been there. I knew that now. Oh Cage, Cage . . . !

"Speak to me always . . ."

The room had grown very hot again. My cheeks were flaming. It was unbearable to sit there playing the piano with Cage beside me, knowing that I could never have him, that he was married to someone else, that I was married to Barnabas. Playing that song as if it had no meaning at all.

Finally it was over. I got up from the chair.

"You're not going to stop, are you?" Allegra asked in dismay.

"Yes," I said sharply, thankful that Aunt Tildy was not in the room to see my heated face. "Perhaps someone else can take my place."

They were all looking at me in a funny way, all those surprised faces turned to me. "Pardon," I murmured and hurried from the room.

My cheeks were still hot and I went across the hall to the small sitting room and stood by the open French windows, breathing in the cool night air. I had been there only a minute or two when a voice behind me said:

"Mrs. Neale, does this happen to be your fan?"

I wheeled about.

"I am so sorry, I did not mean to startle you," Jay Cooke said. His tone was sober, apologetic, yet I caught a suspicious flicker of amusement in the depths of his dark eyes.

"You did not startle me," I said, taking the fan, then adding a grudging, "Thank you," and when he made no move to leave, I said, "Thank you very much," in a tone I hoped indicated dismissal.

"My pleasure," he said.

I turned and looked out the window again, staring into the black darkness, hoping that he would take the hint and leave.

"My presence embarrasses you," he said after a long moment of silence.

"Quite frankly, it does," I said stonily, my eyes fixed on a distant star which appeared only in my imagination for I could not see beyond the verandah.

"I am sorry to hear that." Another long pause. "You needn't be afraid, I shan't breathe a word of your—your journey to New Orleans."

"I should hope not," I said loftily, opening my fan and fluttering it under my chin. "And if you were a gentleman you would not mention it now."

"Perhaps I am not a gentleman." There was a slight mocking edge to his voice.

I turned. He was dressed very correctly, very fashionably in black broadcloth and white stock, the conservative evening clothes of a proper supper guest. But somehow—it was hard to define—somehow he seemed too *big* for his clothes, as if his heavy muscled shoulders would burst through the cloth. He looked earthy, like a peasant in masquerade.

"Perhaps not," I said.

"Even so, I would hate to think we could not be friends, Mrs. Neale."

"I have nothing against you."

"I suppose I shall have to count that for something." He was smiling at me, that taunting smile which had irritated me so years ago and which to my consternation I found still did. "You have changed since I last saw you."

"Ten years would change anyone," I said.

"Except me?" he said as if reading my mind.

I did not reply.

His eyes flicked over my bare shoulders. I had worn an evening dress for the occasion, yards of blue silk over a vast crinoline, low cut with capped sleeves. It was an old dress; we all wore our crinolines, that archaic monstrosity of the '60s throughout the war, not knowing if we were still in fashion or far behind the current mode. But at the moment I did not concern myself with fashion; I resented Jay Cooke's appraisal.

"But I *have* changed," he went on. "I've grown older and wiser. And you—you have become a woman, I can see that." Again his bold eyes caressed my skin. I bit my lip to keep myself from blushing. How dare he!

". . . a matron, as the saying goes. Quite settled, rather staid . . ."

"Mr. Cooke! *Please.* Your opinion is of little matter to me." Anger was boiling up despite my attempt at control. "As a matter of fact I find this conversation rather tedious."

"Do you? Let me finish, quickly then. Nevertheless, matron that you appear to be, I see underneath that composed exterior the girl still, the same passionate girl who defied convention to come. . . ."

"Mr. Cooke . . . ! It seems that you have said all these things before, so if you will . . ."

He gave me another swift, eye-stripping appraisal and my temper burst. "You—you are the most—the most ill-bred . . ." I searched for a word, ". . . ill-bred scoundrel! And now you *must* excuse me." I swept past him and was almost to the door when he said:

"His wife is dead."

It was as though I had been shot between the shoulder blades. I stopped in midstep, my back to him.

"She died two years ago."

I stood there, rigid, drawing in my breath, suddenly forgetting everything, my embarrassment, my anger, my chagrin. Free! All I could think of at first, the only thing that came into my head was that Cage was no longer married, that he was a widower, *he was free*. But even as the thought ran through my head like wildfire, I was conscious of Jay Cooke behind me. He knew. He had seen through me as Aunt Tildy had not; he knew I was still in love with Cage. I turned. He was smiling. I would have killed him, and gladly, if I had been able to.

"She died under rather mysterious circumstances," he went on in that bland, drawling voice of his. "Do you want to hear about it?"

"No," I said, the word coming out between my teeth. "No. Not from you. If Cage wants to tell me, he may, but I do not want to hear it from you."

"Very well," he said, and shrugged. "I would not have told you anyway—it is not my place, as you so aptly imply. But I merely wondered if you were still interested."

"I'm not!" And with that I sped from the room, slamming the door behind me.

Of course I was interested. And I hoped against hope that Aunt Tildy would learn the details from Cage's mother. But Aunt Tildy did very little to satisfy my curiosity. "Cage is a widower now," she told me on the way home. "A widower and from what Cynthia says, he's not only lost his wife, but most of his money. She says that the only thing he has left is that big house he built. And the little girl. It was *hers*, you know. The child is in San Francisco with a housekeeper or nurse, something like that." She yawned.

I longed to ask her about Cage's wife, who she was, how she had died. But I was afraid that an excess of interest on my part might result in a barrage of questions, questions which I could not answer without giving away my feelings toward Cage.

"I don't like to cast doubt on Cage's patriotic motives," Aunt Tildy continued, "but I wonder if he didn't come home because he was penniless and had nowhere else to go."

"Oh—Aunt Tildy! Surely you don't believe that army pay would entice him? It's hardly worth a pauper's effort."

"Hmmm. Perhaps you are right."

I did not see Cage again until he and Jay Cooke came to say goodbye a week later. I had learned through Mrs. Pettigrew (who went right on in Richmond, as she had done at home, garnering and imparting bits of gossipy news) that Cage had been a frequent visitor at the Bentons, seeing Allegra during his brief stay and the knowledge had lain like a knife in my heart. Cage, always attracted to a pretty face, had sought out Allegra, unmarried, young and beautiful. Could I blame him? He was going off to a bloody war and possible death and he wanted to make each day, each hour, count. Why shouldn't he spend his time with a lovely, coquettish girl instead of a married woman—one who had made a fool of herself in an incident which had been painfully embarrassing both to him and myself?

At least he has not forgotten me altogether, I thought, as he and Jay Cooke came into the small, cramped parlor. He has remembered me enough to come and see me before he leaves. That was the crumb I had to console myself with. But it was better than nothing, much better when he took my hand and smiled.

"We're off to the wars," Cage said gaily.

The men were not in uniform yet and they joked about it. "Homespun, Jay," Cage said. "Homespun is all they issue these days. We've missed out on the gaudy plumage."

I wanted to tell him that no uniform could improve his appearance, a handsome figure in gray broadcloth, wide black cravat and ruffled white shirt. I yearned to tell him so many things, yearned to beg him to take care of himself, to be cautious, not foolhardy, to be brave yet prudent, to come back alive. I wanted to say that I still loved him, that for me nothing had changed. But all I could do was utter the usual empty, worn phrase, "Let us pray that the war will be over soon."

"I doubt it," Cage said with a wry smile. "McClellan is marching on Richmond again."

"And Grant, I hear, is moving up the Tennessee River," Jay Cooke added with a flippant edge to his voice.

I ignored him. "You did not have to come back, Cage," I said earnestly.

"I don't see how I could have done anything else," he replied.

Aunt Tildy clapped her hands. "Brave words, Cage, brave words."

"Not so brave," Cage said. "I came back because—well, it is hard to explain. But Virginia stays with you—in your blood. I couldn't sit out there and see her invaded by the Yankees." He stopped short, seemingly embarrassed by this sentiment and my heart went out to him.

Jay Cooke put his hand over his breast and in a jeering voice recited:

> "Breathes there a man with soul so dead,
>   Who never to himself hath said,
>   This is my own, my native land?"

I turned to him, my cheeks burning. "Certainly, *you* had no cause to return." Oh, how I hated him! Insufferable devil. Why did he have to make a mockery of these precious minutes of farewell between Cage and myself?

"I came for the fun and excitement, Mrs. Neale," he said politely. "I would not have missed this quarrel for the world."

"It's a wonder you did not join the Union army then," I said tartly.

"They wouldn't have me."

Cage laughed. "Jay Cooke would rather be caught dead than be called a patriot, eh Jay?"

He shrugged. "Oh—I'm not so sure."

I searched hurriedly in my mind for something to say, something nasty and biting, but Aunt Tildy forestalled my reply by asking, "Would you boys like some brandy? I believe the Hamptons still have some. It's quite all right, Cage," when he started to protest, "they won't miss a drop or two."

We drank to the rebel cause, to their health and their safe return while my eyes clung to Cage's face, memorizing every feature, every nuance of his smile. I no longer cared if Aunt Tildy noticed. Cage was leaving me and it was worse than the farewell at Green Springs for this time he might die as thousands of other soldiers had died on the battlefield, sabered, shot, blown to bits, and the thought was unbearable, unthinkable.

"Time, Jay," he said with a smile, setting his glass down.

Stay! I wanted to implore, to weep, *don't go!*

We were in the hall. He stooped and kissed Aunt Tildy, then his lips were on my forehead, too, cool lips, a friend's, and it was all I could do not to throw my arms about his neck and hold him, just for one moment longer.

"We can't leave you out," Aunt Tildy said to Jay Cooke and offered her cheek.

"I would be affronted," he said gallantly, kissing her. "And Mrs. Neale," Jay Cooke said.

I stiffened, but he seemed not to notice. He grasped my shoulders with hard, almost hurting hands and then to my consternation kissed me full on the mouth. It could not have lasted more than a second or two but it was a kiss that did strange, frightening things to me, and when he released me I was too breathless with outrage to do anything but stare at him.

"Goodbye, Mrs. Neale," he said as coolly as you please.

And I hated him more than ever, for it was Cage's mouth on mine that I had wanted, Cage's last, tender goodbye.

Chapter 10

WHEREAS in the past I had been worried over Barnabas's safety (how "safe" Charles was in a Yankee prison I could only hope) I now lived in an agony of suspense over Cage. It was shameful to be more concerned about a man other than my husband, almost like committing adultery in my mind, but I could not help it. Nor did guilt or stern self-chastisement do anything to alter my feelings. I lived constantly with a small pain gnawing at my stomach as I avidly followed the progress of the war. Both men were in the Army of Northern Virginia, Barnabas fighting under General Longstreet, Cage under Thomas J. Jackson (later to be known as "Stonewall"). Manassas Junction, Chantilly, Sharpsburg. Every battle would send me along with the other women down to the telegraph office for news. I would wait with the crowds outside in the street for the printed lists of the wounded and dead, sitting erect in the buggy, stony-faced and silent beside Aunt Tildy and Mrs. Hampton, my cold hands concealed in the folds of my shawl, twisting and turning the ring on my finger until a bleeding blister had formed.

God!—those hours of torment, of waiting, waiting. I used to think how much better it would be if I were in the front lines with the men, beside them, facing enemy fire than here in this awful limbo of apprehension. When at last the lists were posted, my eyes would hastily scan the page looking for Cage's name, then satisfied (one more reprieve!), I would furtively search for Barnabas Neale's. My guilt was compounded by the frequent thought that I had made a mistake, that I had married in haste. Why hadn't I waited? I should have refused Barnabas and remained single. I did not let myself consider that waiting for Cage might have been a futile gesture. I did not want to recall that he had just recently spent his time with Allegra

Benton before he went away, that he now wrote to her and not to me. Cage had become part of my fantasy again and I could not let go.

Meanwhile, high society in Richmond set a hectic pace, their parties, balls and dinners thronged with guests, it was said, who drank champagne which sold for three hundred fifty dollars a dozen. Shakespearean plays were put on at the New Richmond Theatre; and the Mosaic Club, uniting Richmond's literary and musical talents, gave readings and concerts in the more elegant and private homes of the city. "What good does it do to be sad?" Allegra Benton asked, tossing her head. She had a dozen beaux dancing attendance, young, handsome officers who were only too delighted to escort her to parties and suppers. One would almost think that the hospitals were not overcrowded with the wounded, that rumors of barefoot soldiers unable to procure boots were untrue, that the less fortunate in the poorer sections were not going hungry.

Nor did my chagrin arise from envy, for we were invited and actually attended several of these functions, but I never enjoyed them and always came away feeling that I had somehow betrayed our loved ones who had to shoulder the dreary, dangerous work of war.

Snow fell in Richmond in the middle of March, and when it thawed, the roads leading to the city became quagmires, making it difficult, if not impossible, for farmers to bring their produce to market. Foodstuffs, already costly and in short supply, rose even steeper in price. Citizens tightened their belts and a group of women of the poorer class, faced with starvation and driven by desperation called on Governor Letcher, explaining their plight. But all he could, or would, give them was sympathy.

Turned away from peaceful petition the delegation suddenly became a mob. The women joined by boys and men loafing on Capitol Square managed to arm themselves with hatchets, knives, and a few pistols and headed toward Main Street. Shouting "Bread!", they began to smash store windows and take food, but soon they were seizing clothes, shoes, dry goods and luxuries, anything they could get their hands on. Aunt Tildy who had been shopping for yarn got caught on the edge of the crush and admitted when she came home, white and breathless, that she had been more frightened of the mindless, hungry mob than she had been of the Yankees.

Mayor Mayo, Governor Letcher and President Davis, she told us, had appealed to the rioters without effect until the troops were brought in. At that point President Davis took out his gold watch and said he would give the mob five minutes to disperse, then he would order his men to fire. Threatened, the unruly crowd broke up and quickly melted away.

The year wound itself out. Barnabas came home on a short leave, looking old, ragged and gray. There were deep lines in his forehead and at the sides of his mouth, and he walked with a limp. Rheumatism, he said. I begged him to ask for a medical discharge, but he would not hear of it. "As long as my son is fighting, I will too." he told me. We had received no word from Henry in a long time.

Barnabas's great wish was to conceive a child before he returned to duty. I bore with him out of compassion, out of pity, out of guilt, for I found I no longer wanted his child. The baby I had once yearned to have meant nothing to me now. I was too full of Cage. When Barnabas left he kissed me and I knew he was waiting for the words, "I love you," but I could not say them, even a kind lie was impossible now. "God keep you" was the best I could do.

Richmond's hospitals became more crowded than ever, the flow of wounded and maimed mounting with each engagement. They arrived by every available means of transport, wagons, ambulances, private carriages, hired hack and railroad car; men in tattered uniforms, without shoes or boots, armless, legless, bloodied and hungry. Sometimes they lay at the train station for hours in the sun or rain because there were not enough stretchers or able-bodied men to move them. People took the wounded into their private homes (we had two); hotels, boarding houses, stables, every available accommodation pressed into service was swamped by this deluge of the ill and the maimed. There were never enough doctors, and though they worked around the clock many of our wounded died for lack of attention.

I went every day now to the hospital on Chimborazo Heights. I had never gotten used to it even in the early days when conditions were far better and I had to force myself to go. The foul smells, the lice, the festering sores, the groans and the screams of those undergoing amputations without chloroform nearly drove me mad. And yet, I could not keep away. What if—I would say, as I mopped the sweat from yet another white face—what if this were Cage?

It seemed that we had been at war all our lives. When I thought of Green Springs, Riverknoll or Beech Arbor, it was like thinking of places that I had known centuries ago when I was very young. It did no good to remind myself that I was only twenty-six, not eighty-six, for it seemed that I had lived such a long, long time. I felt aged, tired with a weariness that hung on me like the shabby clothes I wore, a fatigue that no amount of sleep could dispel.

In June I received a letter from Barnabas. The troops were going into Pennsylvania, he wrote jubilantly, chasing the bluecoats into their own territory. "We'll show the Yankees," he said, "we'll teach them a lesson they're not likely to forget." It was the last letter I ever received from him.

He died there in Pennsylvania, at a place called Gettysburg.

His death filled me with superstitious horror. I felt that somehow by loving Cage I had willed my husband's demise. Common sense told me that was ridiculous, but I could not help thinking God was punishing me for wishing I had never married him. I cried copious tears at the memorial service we held at our church. (The actual burial had taken place at Gettysburg since there had been too many dead, thousands we heard, to bring any one of them home.) Barnabas had been a good man, a kind man and deserved better than me. He should have married someone else, someone who could have made his last days happy, someone who could have said, "I love you," and given him a child.

After Gettysburg the fortunes of war went slowly but inexorably downhill for the South. Dressed in black mourning I still put in my hours at the hospital, staying longer now as if to assuage my guilt. Cage's older brother, Thomas, was killed on the Rapidan River, the Woodses lost their two youngest from acute dysentery at a hospital in Georgia. The death lists grew longer and longer. Everyone had lost someone—a husband, a brother, a sweetheart, a son. I began to hate the war with a passion. Silently as the days dragged by I cursed it, calling upon God to damn both sides for allowing the slaughter to continue. There were moments of anguish when watching one more half-starved young lad die at the hospital in pain and distress I feared for my sanity. No one, not even Allegra Benton, had received a letter from Cage in months.

To me the end of the war came almost anticlimactically. Anyone with an ounce of wisdom could have foreseen it. Handicapped by lack of industry and adequate transport, by lack of food, clothing, manpower and medicines, everything in short which an army needed in order to win victories, the South struggled on through the bitter campaigns of '64 and '65. Only her morale, her blind, uncompromising faith in the nebulous thing called the "Cause," her valor, her extraordinary courage against overwhelming odds kept her afloat.

On the second of April we received news that Petersburg had fallen and Lee had advised the evacuation of Richmond. This time Aunt Tildy needed no persuasion to leave. We both agreed that it would be better to try to return to Beech Arbor than to remain in a city deserted by the Confederacy and left to the mercies of its more desperate citizens. Aunt Tildy herself had seen what an unruly mob could do and was not about to test their mettle again. Rowena was still at Big Lick and the Bentons, the Norwoods, and the Sands had already left, but Anna May elected to stay with the Youngs. Her two younger children had taken ill with the measles and she was afraid to move them.

We invited our hosts, the Hamptons, to come with us but they declined, saying their house was the only home they had and they felt that their presence would protect it. Aunt Tildy tried to argue, telling them she had once thought the same, but they would not listen. Wishing us well they gave us their buggy, a dilapidated contraption worn by years of hard usage, the upholstery ripped and torn, the stuffing out in places, the wheels rickety, jarring at every turn. The horse that went with it was hardly in better shape, a tired emaciated nag with stark ribs showing through a mangy hide.

How we managed to hold that rig together in the crush

of flight with people, refugees, bewildered men and frightened women, lost children and drunken looters dashing madly up and down the streets, I'll never know. The traffic was wild, impossible. We were jostled by vehicles of every description, carts, buggies, landaux, carriages, lumbering wagons, all heading in the same direction toward the bridges which spanned the James. After a breathless, tooth-jolting chase we reached the bank, crossing the river on the tail of the Confederate rear guard minutes before the bridge itself blew sky high with a mighty roar. I thought the horse would give up the ghost then, but Aunt Tildy, rising from the seat, laid the whip on the galled back with such force the sorry beast had no alternative but to stagger on.

The long, jiggling ride back to Beech Arbor was accomplished in silence and dismay. The once beautiful, graceful, white mansions facing the river were now in a state of ugly ruin, shutters hanging, windows broken, doors agape. The flowers, the shrubs, the rolling lawns were all gone, lying bare in the April sun, churned to a puddled, muddy morass. In one three mile stretch we saw not a single tree standing. They had all fallen to the Yankee axe. Though we knew Virginia winters could sometimes get very cold and that the wood had probably been used for warmth as well as for cookstoves, we could not help but think that a good part of the destruction had been wanton, and the closer we got to home, the more certain we became.

Our worst fears were borne out when we looked upon Green Springs. It had been fired. We sat in the buggy on the river path, numb with exhaustion, gazing at the blackened chimneys, the gutted second-story bedroom where I had once dressed for the Neales' ball. My room, Papa's, Charles's—the carved wainscoting, the high white ceilings, the carpets, the pictures, the clawed dressers—all gone. Tears stung my eyes as I stared at the broken windows, at the soot-blotched walls, at the verandah where I had sat so many balmy evenings. And the clock, I wondered, the tall clock on the landing that used to tick so comfortingly away, unhurried, solid, had it been burned too? I could not bear to go inside and look.

We had anticipated disaster but the reality before us seemed incredible, a house that had withstood almost two centuries of living now a blackened shell.

"I suppose we can expect the same at Beech Arbor," Aunt Tildy said, her voice shaking.

But Beech Arbor was still standing, miraculously intact, evacuated, empty. It was the inside which had been left a shambles. The furniture had all but disappeared, the mahogany chairs, some more than a century old, the sideboards and breakfronts, the dining room table, even the rosewood piano had apparently fallen under the axe just as the trees had. The carpets were in ruins, the draperies torn and muddied. Worse than the destroyed furniture and the stained, boot-scratched floors was the utter loneliness of the house, the empty echo of our voices the way the house whispered and creaked through that first long, sleepless night. Carpets, curtains and tables could be replaced, but the dead could not. Their ghosts, Barnabas, Thomas, William, seemed to trod the bare floors, speaking in low whispers behind closed doors, watching us from the top of the shadowed stairs with accusing eyes. We had survived and they had not.

We heard of Lee's surrender some two weeks later when Anna May came to Beech Arbor with her children, the smaller ones recovered from the measles but still pale and sickly. The Youngs had brought her. She said Richmond had been a hell (yes, she used that word), a cauldron of fire and looting and drunken revelry. And it was the Union forces who, having entered the city on the third of April, finally managed to quell the rioters and put out the fires.

We tried to pick up the pieces while we waited for the men who were still alive to come home.

Henry was the first to arrive. Mustered out at Appomattox and allowed to keep his horse by promising not to take up arms again, he had ridden to Big Lick where he had fetched Rowena and their son, Ted. Shaggy-haired, black-bearded, gaunt and wearing tattered clothes, he gave the appearance of a scarecrow, but a grateful one, nevertheless, glad to be alive. Now that Barnabas was dead he was master of Beech Arbor. And Riverknoll, the Norwood's large estate, would go to Thomas's fatherless little boy, Cage's nephew. Perhaps Cage, if he were still alive (and he must be, he must!), as the heir's nearest male kin would be appointed guardian to run the plantation. And what would

Charles do? How changed everything was, how different from what it had once been.

I did not know what would become of me. I realized that Barnabas must have made some provision for my welfare (he had made out a will, leaving it with a Mr. Jones in Richmond), a small annuity perhaps, but the future seemed so vague and shadowy, a future I did not want to think about.

Some of our negroes had come straggling back, confused and just as frightened as ourselves, not knowing where to go or what to do. Henry could not pay them a wage, but he told them if they wished to work he would provide the land, the seed, the tools and a share in the harvest. Other planters followed the same course, though most of them, like Henry, were hard put to find the money even for seed.

Henry had been home several weeks when Charles arrived, looking like death, emaciated with hollowed eyes and a greenish pallor to his skin. He was not staying, he informed us. He had come back only to get Anna May and the children and as soon as he could borrow the train fare, they would all leave. A man in Boston had offered him a job as assistant to a manager of a clothing emporium and he had accepted with alacrity. A clothing emporium! I thought Aunt Tildy would die of shock.

"Your father must be rolling in his grave," she told him. "To think of it! A Carleton, a shopkeeper!"

But Charles did not care. Green Springs, as well as the other plantations along the James River, was in ruins, and he wanted nothing now but a chance to earn bread for himself and his family. In my heart I could not blame him.

After Charles left the others came limping back, those few men among our neighbors who had survived, a ragtag collection of skin and bones, the halt and the lame, the disillusioned and the bitter. I saw them, watched them, greeted them, all the while my eyes going past their faces to the river path, looking for the one face I longed to see. Each day that passed without a sign of Cage was a torment, but I would not let hope die. He *would* come home, he was alive, he *would* come—it was a litany, a prayer, a charm repeated three, four, six times a day. I would go over to Riverknoll on the slightest pretext, bringing them a jar of sorghum, a basket of produce, asking advice on jelly making, the refurbishing of an old gown, whatever, just in the hope of hearing something about Cage. Cynthia Norwood and Theresa knew why I came but said nothing. The pretense at all costs had to be kept up, the truth concealed. I sensed they thought me brazen, forward, unladylike, that I, with my husband hardly cold in his grave (though he had been dead for two years, a widow properly mourned for three), should show interest in another man. But I no longer cared what they thought or what they might whisper behind my back.

When Cage finally did return it was not the Norwoods, however, who gave me the news, but Jay Cooke.

He came up the avenue one afternoon, past the stumped trees, riding a Morgan, a sleek black stallion, the first well-fed piece of horseflesh I had seen in years. He was not dressed in a tattered uniform as the others had been, but wore an impeccably tailored dark coat with matching trousers, a starched white linen shirt topped by a high collar and on his head an assertive, wide-brimmed, felt hat. His face was clean shaven and though thinner than when I had last seen him, he was by no means gaunt or bony. Like the horse he looked well-nourished, healthy, disgustingly so. Still, the sight of him stirred a hope in my breast.

"Mrs. Neale!" he exclaimed, coming up the steps, his hand extended. "As I live and breathe!"

"Good evening," I replied, not able to hide the tremor in my voice. If Jay Cooke was here that meant Cage . . .

"Ah!—I can tell by your warm greeting how overjoyed you are to see me," he said with a mocking smile on his lips. "Yes—to answer the question in your eyes—yes, Mrs. Neale, he's come home. And—in one piece."

I closed my eyes in silent prayer.

"Well, aren't you going to ask me to come in after bringing you such good news?"

"Of course!" I exclaimed, liking him for the first time. At the moment I would have felt kindly toward my worst enemy, kindly, warm, wanting to embrace the whole world. Cage was alive—he had come home! My heart leapt, my blood tingled.

"What can I offer you?" I asked happily, ushering him into the bare drawing room. "I am afraid we have no brandy, but there is wine."

"Elderberry?" he raised a brow in mock memory.

But I forgave him. "It will be a moment, excuse me, the servants—everyone has gone to Charles City for the day."

"It is quite all right. No hurry."

I got the wine from the kitchen cabinet and poured a glass, my hand shaking. Oh God, I thought, wanting to jump, to skip, to dance. *Cage is home, he is alive!*

"Thank you," Jay Cooke said when I handed him the glass. "Your husband died, I was told."

"Yes—at Gettysburg."

"My condolences," he said lightly, and drank, his dark eyes watching me over the rim of the glass.

"And how long must you go on wearing black?" he continued after a short, awkward silence, his disconcerting gaze never leaving my face.

"Another year," I said, suddenly deflated, uncomfortable. Jay Cooke could do that to me.

"A pity. It does not become you," he said.

"I can't help that."

"Yes, you can." He put his glass down and leaned forward. "You can marry again."

"Mr. Cooke—I don't see . . ."

"Why not? It isn't that you were so wildly in love with Mr. Neale, were you?"

I said nothing.

"And you don't want to be a widow for the rest of your life, do you?"

Again, I remained silent.

"And it isn't because you lack a suitor, because you don't. You have one, an ardent petitioner. . . ."

"Mr. Cooke—I don't see . . ."

". . . me. I want to marry you."

Stunned I could only stare at him. Had the wine gone to his head? Or was he baiting me?

"I suppose I should not have been so precipitate, but I've given the matter a great deal of thought—"

"*Please!*" I broke in. "Please don't joke. I do not find a proposal humorous."

"I am not joking," he said. His eyes were sober, very dark, frightening now. Was he mad, unhinged by the war? They said many had lost their senses under heavy bombardment.

"But—but you hardly know me," I stumbled.

"I know you very well, much better than you know yourself. Ever since that day when I walked into Cage's lodgings in New Orleans and saw those wide brown eyes, I thought, now there is a girl I would like to have once she's grown into a woman."

"But—but that's ridiculous!"

"Is it?"

He rose and came over to the sofa where I sat, standing over me, looking down. "All during that hellish, foolish, damned war I thought of you. Ah! I can see you still do not believe me."

He took my hands and pulled me to my feet.

"Mr. Cooke—please—I don't . . ."

"Why? What have you got against me?"

"Nothing—but . . ." I stopped short. Why should I have to explain my feelings to this man, a stranger who meant nothing to me?

"But there is Cage, is that it?" he goaded.

"Please—let go of my hands."

"It *is* Cage. My dear Mrs. Neale—Adelaide—he is not worthy of you. For all his admirable qualities the truth is he can't love you."

"Why not?" I asked sharply, my heart constricting, forgetting for the moment that Jay Cooke's hands were gripping mine with a painful urgency.

"Because he can never love anyone but himself. The dear boy is likeable, but I'm afraid, selfish and egotistical. . . ."

"You're wrong! You're wrong! He's none of those things!" I blazed up at him.

He stared at me for a long moment. Then his eyes suddenly leapt to flame, and before I could tear my hands from his he pulled me into his arms and his mouth came down on mine. My breath caught in my throat as I tried to struggle free. But he held me fast, crushing me against his lean, hard, muscular body, his lips pressing, demanding, hungry, and for an instant I felt myself drawn into a strange, new, dizzy excitement, felt my knees go weak, my heart pounding, felt lost, thrilled, afraid. . . .

And then I was pushing him away. "How dare you! How dare you," choking with fury, my hands pressed to my scarlet cheeks. "Leave at once! you—you . . . !"

He smiled.

"Get out!" I shouted. He kept on smiling, a devil's smile. "I never want to see you again. Never! Don't you—you dare . . . !"

"All right, all right, I get the drift," he said coolly, picking up his hat. When he reached the door he turned. "But please consider my offer, won't you, Mrs. Neale?"

"Never!" I hurled at the closing door.

It was on the following day that we received a call from Mr. Jones of Richmond, the lawyer with whom Barnabas had left his will. A fussy little soul with bushy side whiskers, Mr. Jones was dressed in a black, rather shabby frock coat much mended but neatly pressed. He apologized for taking so long to reach us.

"The situation has been disruptive, to say the least," he muttered, clearing his throat, shuffling through a sheaf of papers he had brought in a carpetbag.

The will was short and began with no unexpected clauses. Henry was given the plantation, "all buildings thereon including the manor house, the furnishings." Mary, Barnabas's daughter, received the family jewelry, all of which had been pilfered by the Yankees. Cash money was divided between Henry and myself, Confederate money, now worthless.

" 'Also'," Mr. Jones cleared his throat and read on, " '. . . also to my dear wife, Adelaide, I bequeath shares in the Cramwell Iron Works of New Jersey . . .' "

"New Jersey!" I exclaimed.

"Well, yes," Mr. Jones said apologetically. "Mr. Neale told me that he had bought stock years ago on the advice of his new son-in-law as a favor. The young man was just starting out as a stock broker. . . ."

"But he never said anything to me. Oh, well, I suppose he was too ashamed of investing his money, whatever the sum, in a Yankee enterprise."

"To be sure, to be sure." Mr. Jones, embarrassed, his cheeks pink, cleared his throat again. "But—Mrs. Neale, I believe from one standpoint it was a most fortuitous investment. You see, during the war, iron works made guns, all kinds of military material—well, to put it concisely, the stock your late husband acquired is now worth over ten times what he paid for it—and still going up."

The amount, quoted in cold, hard Yankee dollars,

stunned me. It was extraordinary, more so because it was unexpected. I would be comfortably well off for the rest of my life—and from our poverty-stricken standards, a rich woman.

Rich!

When I had recovered from the shock my first reaction was one of delirious excitement. I began at once to make plans to celebrate my good fortune. A barbecue, I thought —I would give a lavish outdoor picnic and barbecue on the lawn, a party to which I would invite my neighbors, their relatives and friends, acquaintances, everyone up and down the river (even Jay Cooke was included, for in my new magnanimity I forgave his rudeness).

I had our old servant Moses, who had come back with a few of the other darkies, scour the countryside for hams, chickens, ducks, geese, anything he could find in the way of foodstuffs, telling him that price should be of no concern. It would be like the old days, a feast to share with the people I loved, people who had been through so much and like me never thought they would feast again.

They all came, Cage too. He had called on us the day after Mr. Jones's visit, offering his condolences for Barnabas, glad that my bereavement should not be weighted down with poverty, too. When I first saw him I had the impulse to ask, "Why didn't you write, why didn't you send me one word, one . . . ?" But his smile, his warm handclasp banished the thought from my mind. He was there, with me, his fair skin bronzed by the sun, his blue eyes cool and bright, his face honed to a new masculine handsomeness. I wanted to fling my arms about his neck and tell him that I had prayed for him every night, that he had been in my thoughts, that it was his name I always looked for first on the casualty lists, but I said nothing, only sat and listened, my eyes fastened to his face as he explained to Aunt Tildy and the other members of the family his last days of the war.

He came again the next evening and the following afternoon invited me to ride with him to the Beacons to see if the new owner would sell him some mules.

"We're reduced to buying mules now," he said wryly, wrinkling his nose, "instead of blooded horses."

I had gone with him, wishing I did not have to wear black, wishing that I could look more attractive, wondering, too, if Cage was courting me. Was he? Was he smiling in a special way at me now, a smile different than his others had been?

He kissed my hand when we parted, his lips lingering for a moment longer than I thought propriety condoned. And my heart began to beat with a new hope.

He called on me every day for a week after that, bringing small, inconsequential gifts, walking arm in arm with me along the river path, attentive, his eyes smiling, his intentions becoming more and more clear.

But it was at the barbecue that he asked me to marry him. He had drawn me away from a group of people on the verandah. "Adelaide, I do believe you were going to lend me a book—on marling, was it?" he said, linking his arm with mine.

He led me into the library. I could feel the warmth of his hand through the cloth of my sleeve. My knees were trembling. He shut the door. "There's something I want to say," he said, looking at me, his eyes alight. "And it has nothing to do with books." I sat down on the sofa, because of my knees, and tried to look appropriately puzzled. He came and sat beside me. My heart was beating so fast I thought I would suffocate. He took my hand, turned it palm up and kissed it. A little electric thrill ran up my arm and I could feel my cheeks go hot.

"I've always admired you, Adelaide. When you came to me in New Orleans—no, please don't look embarrassed, we can speak of that now—you were still a child and my heart went out to you—and I thought what a fool I am to send her back—but you see, you were so young. . . ."

Somewhere deep inside, even as I gazed rapturously into his eyes, a voice cried, but there was Lillith! What of Lillith? But his words, the words I had so yearned to hear for so long drowned out that horrid voice.

". . . and now, coming back from the war, after being so close to death, I've learned to appreciate the good, the truly noble things of life—the friends, the people, who are dear to me, who have always been—Adelaide, you would do me such an honor—if you only would—by becoming my wife."

I swallowed. I knew that I ought to cast my eyes down in maidenly fashion, I ought to make some sort of protestation for form's sake, but I could only gaze at him, my heart in my face and say nothing.

"Perhaps—perhaps I should have asked Henry first, he being the head of the family? Or perhaps I should give you more time to think?"

"No," I said quickly, too quickly perhaps. But I was afraid that none of this was true, that in a moment I would wake and find that it had all been a dream. "I—it isn't necessary to ask Henry. I am flattered by your proposal. . . ." The words were stiff, not at all like the ones clamoring in my breast.

"But—were you going to say 'but'? Please don't. I fancied that you hadn't changed your mind since New Orleans, that you still loved me."

Oh, but I do, I do! I wanted to cry, *I do with all my heart!* but I couldn't. That sort of impetuosity had died when I was fourteen. I was afraid to be eager, afraid.

"It hasn't changed, Cage."

"Then it is yes," he said, leaning over, kissing me lightly on the lips. "Yes?"

"Yes," I smiled. "Of course, it's yes."

Not until hours later did I recall that he had not said he loved me.

We had gone from the parlor to the verandah and Cage had taken Henry aside. In less than ten minutes from the time I accepted Cage's proposal, the announcement had been made to the assembled guests, and they began to crowd around me, congratulating me, wishing me happiness. Aunt Tildy and Rowena both kissed me with tears in their eyes.

Now, the last of the barbecue guests had long since departed and I, worn out by excitement and feverish joy, had retired early. I lay in the dark on the large feather bed that I had once shared with Barnabas, my mind going over and over the scene in the parlor, Cage kissing the palm of my hand, Cage asking me to marry him. "I fancied that—you still loved me," he had said. He admired me, he was fond of me, perhaps he had meant to say more. Perhaps my primness had discouraged him. He did love me, I was sure he loved me.

But as the night wore on and sleep still eluded me, a

cold, little suspicion began to creep into my head, a small, malicious thought which Jay had put there earlier. He had come up to me during a lull in the party when I was standing alone near the coffee urn. "I'm afraid I cannot offer congratulations like the others," he said, a sardonic twist to his lips. "It's not sour grapes, you understand, the rejected suitor, but a genuine concern for your well-being."

"Oh?"

"Yes, I am not at all sure you are doing the right thing by marrying Cage."

"*I* have never been more sure," I replied haughtily, resenting him for trying to spoil my happiness.

"Are you? I believe you are making a big mistake."

"What a horrible, audacious thing to say! I never asked for your opinion, Mr. Cooke. If you cannot wish me happiness then the least you can do, as a gentleman, is to keep silent."

"How can I keep silent when I see you throwing yourself away?"

"I—I refuse to listen to you." I started to walk past him, but he took my arm, lightly with just enough pressure in his fingers to detain me. "Ask yourself one thing, one thing only, Adelaide Carleton Neale—am I sure Cage Norwood is not marrying me for my money?"

"Of course not! How dare you even suggest such a thing!"

But now his words came back to me. I tried to push them away, but they simply refused to go. *Was* Cage marrying me for my money? Of course, he wasn't. It was ridiculous to entertain such a notion even for a moment. But *was* he? And if he was not why hadn't he said he loved me, the cold little thought asked. Why hadn't he declared himself, kissed me passionately as Jay Cooke had done? Because he was a gentleman, a man of refinement, of breeding. Then why had Jay Cooke been the first to call on me at Beech Arbor? Cage had not come to see me until the day after the news of my inheritance had spread up and down the river. Why hadn't he written to me, why . . . ?

I thrust my hands over my ears, trying to still that nasty, cold voice of reason. I didn't care. I didn't care if he was attracted to me because of my money, if he didn't really love me. I wanted him. I wanted Cage, had wanted him for so many years, had ached for him and now I would be his wife. His wife! I knew I could make him love me, if he did not now he would love me later, eventually. I knew so down to the very marrow of my bones.

I had said yes, I will marry you. I was going to be Mrs. Lewis Cage Norwood and nothing short of death would change my mind.

We were wed quietly in Richmond a month later. Only our immediate families attended the small ceremony, the Norwoods and the Neales. Jay Cooke was the single outsider. But I was too happy to be embarrassed by his presence, too elated to care. As for him, if he still had any feeling about Cage's quick courtship, our hurried marriage, he said nothing, gave no sign. He wished us both well; his lips as he brushed my cheek were cool and impersonal.

Cage did not want to stay at Riverknoll, though Kitty, Thomas's widow, had begged him to buy the plantation. She could not run it herself and it would be years before her young son was old enough to take over. She had received several offers, mostly from Yankees, one a New Yorker who was buying up all the land he could persuade the impoverished planters to sell. River property was going cheap, two dollars an acre where once it had sold for one hundred and fifty dollars. Thinking that Cage was embarrassed for funds, I offered to buy Riverknoll from him, but he refused.

"It's not that I am too proud to take your money, Adelaide, sweet, but I am simply not cut out for farming." His mouth curled into a smile. "Ironic, isn't it? When I once would have given the world to own Riverknoll. But Adelaide, if it were offered to me on a silver platter I wouldn't take it. You have only to look around you, the burned-out houses, fields abandoned to weeds, stumps and undergrowth, fences destroyed, cattle gone. Let's face it—the South is dead as the dodo. And what is left of the corpse will be buried by the carpetbaggers. No, Adelaide, my future, ours, lies out West in California. There are fortunes to be made there, wealth, prestige, power, if you will. California. That is where we shall live." He took my hand. "You don't mind leaving, do you?"

"No—I have nothing here. Papa dead, Charles gone, nothing. Will we go to San Francisco?"

"Yes. I have a house there. I'm sure you know that.

Charles told me he had written you. Cage's Folly, it's called, not a folly at all, but a beautiful house. A beautiful house. And I do have an adopted daughter, Octavia. I suppose you know that, too."

"Yes," I said, waiting, expecting him to tell me about Lillith. But he said nothing, and I had not the courage to ask.

Part II

FOLLY

Chapter 11

WE had gone by way of the Isthmus, that steaming strip of jungle-choked land which divides the Atlantic from the Pacific, the journey made easier since Charles and Cage had first crossed it because of the new railway. Taking ship on the other side from Panama we sailed up the California coast, breaking our voyage at San Pedro. From there we proceeded northward, a tiresome, rather rough passage that took two more weary weeks before we reached the harbor mouth of San Francisco.

I remember leaning against the ship's rail, straining my eyes, all aflutter, thinking how promising to be starting a new life by entering it through a place called the Golden Gate. Cage teased me—he said I looked like a small child who had been given a lollipop. But I could tell from the way his eyes smiled that he was just as excited as I.

There were a series of exasperating delays as we made our way through the anchored shipping vessels flying flags from all over the world, so that we did not tie up at the dock until late afternoon. Standing on the deck I looked down at the city that was to be my new home, a treeless, overgrown metropolis fanning out from a shore-front conglomeration of wood and adobe buildings, the polyglot houses climbing inland over sandy, chaparral-covered hills. It appeared new and raw, unfinished, not what I had expected.

We debarked amidst confusion. I had never seen so many foreign faces nor heard the babble of so many foreign tongues. Charles had once written me that the Gold Rush had brought men from all over the world, French and Malays, Germans, Chinese, Mexicans, Peruvians, dusky South Sea Islanders, as well as Yankees and Southerners, but his descriptive powers had fallen far short of the actual picture. Now I saw them with my own eyes, these aliens, these strange men who had emigrated from distant lands, lured by the glitter of promised wealth, the swarthy Spaniards in serapes, the Chinese in baggy trousers with black queues and slanting eyes, Malays wearing their ugly little knives called *kris* at their waists, miners straight from their mountain diggings, sunburned, unshaven, their red shirts blobs of brilliant color in the crowd. Clinging to Cage's arm I looked at them all with a kind of fearful awe. There were few women—one or two respectably attired, like myself, on the arm of an escort, the others in pairs or singly, common-looking, hard, their cheeks painted, their eyes bold. Whores, I was later to learn, who had come down to meet the ship and the woman-hungry sailors.

Cage, keeping me protectively in tow, expertly elbowed his way through the heterogeneous throng, the bellicose hawkers selling their wares, the drunken derelicts begging for a coin, the dandified townsmen who had come to collect cargo or mail. "It's a sight, isn't it?" Cage smiled, speaking loudly above the noise.

"Yes." His smile encouraged me, reminded me that I was happy, I was in love, that I need not fear the squalor and stench and the noisy crowd of the wharf, that it was but a passing scene.

Cage hired a hack and when our luggage had been safely strapped to the roof we started out. A furious wind was blowing down through a gap in the hills, clouding the air with whirling dust so that I could see nothing but the blurred shapes of people hurrying past dim store fronts. But Cage apparently had better vision for he kept remarking on the changes since his absence, the new buildings which had gone up and the old landmarks which had vanished.

"A new bank!" he would exclaim, or a new clothing store, a bakery where there had formerly been a cafe.

It was dusk when we clattered through a pair of iron gates and down a short tree-lined drive and reached the house itself. "Here we are!" Cage exclaimed proudly, handing me down from the hack, his eyes shining up at the Folly. "What do you think?"

Think—! I stared at the house, speechless, appalled.

"Well—? Tell me."

"Why—it's—it's lovely," I said, trying to hide my dismay, totally unprepared for what I saw. Charles, of course, had said it was a monstrosity, but Charles was inclined to be highly critical of architecture which did not reflect the Greek revival style of the Tidewater mansions, so I had not paid much heed to his word. But now that I was here, I saw what he meant. The house had been named the Folly for good reason. It was ugly, no other word could describe it—a misalliance of Italianate, Tudor and Gothic with spires and mushroomlike towers and cast iron grillwork worked in fanciful gingerbread.

"I knew you would like it!" Cage, happy as a schoolboy, linked my arm in his, still looking up at the house, his eyes rapt with admiration.

"Yes—of course I like it." The dying sun had caught the windows in one last crimson blaze and they appeared for all the world like savage, bloodshot eyes. I shivered.

"Cold? How thoughtless of me, darling," Cage said. "You're chilled through. Come, let us go inside where it's warm. Ah, how I've missed it!"

The door opened as we ascended the steps to a deep-shadowed porch. A woman stood on the threshold, a mulatto, with graying tightly curled hair pulled uncompromisingly back from a high forehead.

"Welcome, Mr. Cage," she said. Her accent was not of a Southern darkie but what it was I could not guess.

"Martha," Cage said, "I want you to meet my new wife. Adelaide, sweetheart, this is Martha, our estimable housekeeper."

She had light brown eyes, cold and hooded. "How do you do, Mrs. Norwood." She did not welcome me as she had Cage, did not curtsy (as our house darkies at home would have done), or even offer her best wishes for our new marriage. She did not even smile. There was only that chill, "how-do-you-do" and those hard eyes looking me through and through.

"Well," Cage said, still pleased with himself. "Come along then." Martha stepped aside and for a moment I thought Cage would lift and carry me across the threshold, but instead he bowed and with a sweep of his arm ushered me through the door.

I found myself in a large entry way dominated by a curving staircase. At the foot of it, rising from the newel post stood a bronze statue of a half-nude woman supporting a beaded lamp in one upheld hand.

A girl suddenly appeared at the head of the stairs.

"Papa . . . !" she exclaimed, and in a flurry of skirts and long black hair, flew down. "Papa . . . !" she cried again, flinging herself into Cage's arms.

"Octavia—pet!" He kissed her, then laughing held her away by the wrists. "How you have grown—goodness how you have grown!"

"It's been four years, Papa. A lifetime. I never thought —oh, Papa!" She embraced him again. "I never thought to see you again."

"Didn't you, now?" He smiled at her, his eyes crinkling at the corners and a little pang of jealousy, no more than a twinge, passed through my breast. "You ought to know it would take more than a war to down your old Papa."

"And you weren't shot, or hurt, not once?" she questioned excitedly. "Oh—Papa you must tell me all about it. I was so proud of you—and why aren't you wearing your uniform? I told all the girls you were a . . ."

"Wait—wait!" He put his fingers to her lips. "We shall have lots of time for that. Right now I want you to meet your new mother."

Her back stiffened. There was a long silence, then she turned slowly, staring at me as I stepped from the shadows. She had the most beautiful eyes I had ever seen on anyone, man or woman. They were wide set, a deep violet, black fringed. "You may call me Aunt Adelaide," I said with a smile. "We need not be formal."

She did not return my smile, nor did she speak. She simply stood there, staring at me. She was fifteen perhaps, not more than sixteen, and she did not like me. It came as no surprise. I had anticipated some resentment, hostility, for very few children, unless they were grown like Barnabas's, take immediately to a new stepmother. But I was confident that once we got to know one another, respect if not fondness would develop between Octavia and myself.

"I've looked forward to meeting you," I said warmly.

"Yes," she murmured, then turned back to Cage. "Can't I speak to you alone, Papa?" she asked petulantly.

"Not now, my dear. That would be discourteous. Later, perhaps."

She tossed me a quick, hostile look. "If she . . ."

"Aunt Adelaide," he corrected.

"If Aunt Adelaide would like to rest now, mightn't we have our talk?"

"I don't mind in the least," I put in with an affected lightness, wanting to start off on a happy, pleasant note, wanting things to run smoothly. "I'll go up and have a wash and lie down for a bit. You two go ahead."

"You're sure you don't mind?" Cage asked.

"Not at all." A little wizened man had already carried our bags upstairs. "If someone will show me the way?"

"Of course. Martha will be glad to." She had been standing unobtrusively by and she came forward now.

"I shan't be long," Cage promised.

Octavia with a triumphant smile linked her arm in Cage's, and they went into a large room and shut the door.

"This way," Martha said.

She led me past the bronze lady-lamp and up the winding, red-carpeted stairs. We went along a narrow corridor, its walls crowded with oversized gilt-framed pictures and mirrors. Stopping before a door, Martha flung it open, standing aside to let me pass.

I came into a little anteroom, a sort of sitting room furnished with a velvet sofa, chairs and a writing desk. Beyond it was the bedroom itself, and when I entered it I was immediately struck by the sight of two whole walls paneled from floor to ceiling in mirrors. They made the room look vast, a huge room, opulent with red velvet draperies, red-flocked wallpaper and a thick red carpet on the floor. Over my head hung a rock crystal chandelier, suspended from a sky blue ceiling on which fat cupids holding garlands of flowers had been painted. The cupids seemed to be a motif, for they were everywhere, sporting along the wooden friezes, carved on the mantel and the headboard of the satin-covered bed, fashioned on the backs of teak chairs and even in the legs of the small satinwood tables. Cupids and fruit and flowers. Not in my wildest fancies could I have pictured such a room, nor Cage, who had such impeccable taste, in it. And yet he had spoken so glowingly of the house, loved it he said.

The woman was watching me with her cold, brown eyes.

"It's—it's a bit large," I said self-consciously, not knowing what else to say, for she seemed to be waiting for some comment.

"Mr. Cage finds it quite comfortable."

"Yes—yes," I said, my eyes moving to the bed, wondering if this was the room he had shared with his first wife. "Very nice—and so tidy."

Tidy! Was there ever an inadequate word to describe such an extravaganza as I now found myself in?

"We try to keep it that way," she said.

"Is there—is there a large staff?" I hated myself for stumbling, for being so tongue-tied and ill at ease. Why should I feel intimidated by a darkie servant? But I did.

"There's myself, the cook, Doreen, a maid, Lucinda, and Gandy the houseman." She did not invite me to meet them.

"Such a large place to manage," I murmured.

"Twenty rooms. But then we've only had Octavia to do for."

"Yes." There seemed to be a chilly reproof in her voice, intimating that the work, unhappily, would be doubled now that I had come. "If you feel it necessary to hire more..."

"Mr. Cage does not care to have more than four servants."

"Oh." She did not like me, nor did I like her. I wished she would go, not stand there looking at me with those inflexible, stony eyes. I could have dismissed her, but strangely enough, I, who had had servants all my life, could not find the words to do so.

I went to the dressing table and unpinned my hat before the small glass. I could see that she was still watching me, her somber figure reflected as four in those huge, impossible wall mirrors.

"I hope that you will find everything you need," she said, breaking a long silence. "If you do not, you have only to ring." She indicated a tasselled bell pull.

"Thank you," I said. Then after hesitating, I added, "If it isn't too much trouble, I should like some hot water."

"Certainly. I will have Lucinda bring it up. There is a bathroom," she indicated with her chin a closed, ornately carved door, "but the plumbing does not often work."

"I see." I played with the feather on my hat. My eyes went to the bed again.

"This was Mrs. Norwood's boudoir," she said as if reading my thoughts.

"It's lovely." I murmured the lie, feeling ashamed and resentful. Why should I have to lie? Why should I be conversing at length with this woman at all?

"Mrs. Norwood—the first Mrs. Norwood, that is, Miss Lillith, thought so." For a fleeting moment her eyes seemed to soften. "It was a fit setting for her, everything here bought at great expense, the wallpaper, the draperies and the mirrors, especially the mirrors. You see," she said, her eyes going over me, "she was very beautiful."

"So I have heard." Another lie. I had not heard anything. Cage had said nothing about his dead wife, had not even mentioned her name.

There was another awkward silence. I wondered why she continued to remain. Was there something she wanted to say, to tell me? But I could not bring myself to ask.

I went across the room to the low table where my dressing case had been deposited and began to undo the straps. Apparently the maid's duties did not include unpacking for the mistress. But I did not mind; I had waited on myself for such a long time, the lack of service bothered me little. It was Martha's scrutiny which disturbed me.

"My mistress—Miss Lillith, died very young," she said after a long pause.

"So I understand."

"She died in this room—but then I suppose you know all about it."

"Yes," I said, knowing nothing and suddenly not wanting to.

She gave me a curious sidelong look. She knows I'm lying, I thought, she knows. I turned from her and took out my brushes, my comb and my slippers.

"Sometimes," she said and her voice startled me, because she was right at my back and I had not heard her move across the room. ". . . sometimes Gandy says he sees her ghost in here."

"He does?" I said with an attempt at amused indulgence, an attempt which fell flat. She was still behind me. "The little man who brought up my bags?"

"Yes, that's him. But, I think he's very foolish. I don't hold with ghosts, do you?"

"No," I said. A cold sick knot began to form in my stomach.

"Gandy says that he sees her at the dressing table but not in the mirror, of course. He sees her combing her hair of an evening just before the lamps are lit. She had long black hair, you know, and he says he can hear the crackle as the comb goes through. 'Gandy,' I says to him, 'Gandy, you have an imagination.' But he swears Miss Lillith is here." She was speaking now in a low, husky whisper and the cold sickness swelled up through my breast, lodging an icy lump in my throat.

"He claims he smells her scent—she had it 'specially made up for her, you know, jasmine. It was a jasmine perfume. How she loved it, and sometimes I wonder . . . ," her voice trailed off.

There was a long eerie silence and into it there seemed to seep the faint, faint odor of jasmine, a ghostly scent, sweet and cloying. Had it been there all along, unnoticed until this moment? Or . . .

I gripped the edge of my case so tightly my knuckles turned white. "Martha," I said, turning, "Martha—if you don't mind, I think I should like that hot water. I'm very tired, please . . ."

She stepped back, her face bland, masklike. "Yes, Mrs. Norwood. Yes. I'll have Lucinda bring it up right away."

When she finally closed the door behind her I sank down on the bed. My knees were shaking and my heart was pounding. Dreadful woman! How dared she speak to me like that! What gall! Uppity, Aunt Tildy would have said, and dismissed her at once, sending her out to the fields. I had bungled badly, mismanaged the entire interview. I should have been imperious, authoritative, in command, not apologetic and stuttering over my words. Apologetic, my God!

But I felt that if given the chance to do it over again, I could not have behaved differently. It was not only Martha who intimidated me, but the overwhelming room itself, the lush hangings, the thick carpet, the gilt carvings, the mirrors, and that insidious, lingering odor of jasmine. This was Lillith's room and I had come as an intruder, the classical, the despised, the unwelcome second wife.

I rose from the bed and took my dressing gown from the case, a creation of watered silk which Aunt Tildy had given me as a wedding present. Lord knows where she got the money to buy the material for she, like everyone else at home, was poor as a churchmouse. I had begged her to come with us, but she would not think of it. "Leave Virginia?" Her eyebrows had gone up in shock. "And for that heathen country? Why—I'd be like a fish out of water."

Her house in Brandon having been destroyed in the latter part of the war, she had stayed on with Henry and his family, rather than return to her husband's relatives, the Hamptons, in Richmond. I thought of her, her iron will, her independent air. *She* would have coped and scolded me roundly for not doing the same.

I got into my dressing gown and sat on the bed, waiting for Lucinda to bring the hot water. I thought again of Aunt Tildy, of Henry and Rowena, and Ted, grown into a handsome lad since his stay at Big Lick. What were they all doing now? I wondered. At this hour it would be night at Beech Arbor and they would be long asleep. The house would be quiet except for little, nocturnal creakings and the soft wind sighing in the chimneys. A river barge would be passing, sailing up the James, its mournful horn tooting in the dark. Then stillness again, a curtain fluttering in a draft, a sleeper muttering, the clocks ticking. The smell of polished wood, the simple elegance of a hand-turned bench, the wide-planked floors. I missed Beech Arbor, I missed them all, missed them with a dreadful, longing ache. I . . .

But how silly that was, how foolish! Here I was married to the man of my dreams, in his house as his wife and I could do nothing but sink into maudlin homesickness like a child. How ridiculous! I rose from the bed.

Where was that hot water? I couldn't imagine what was taking the maid so long. I felt dirty and grimy and wanted a bath badly. I went to the door and cracked it open. A gas light flickered in a wall sconce and along the dimly lit corridor shadows swarmed thickly. A heavy oppressive silence pervaded the house, and though I strained my ears for the sound of a voice or a step I heard nothing. I closed the door softly and turned back to the bed, feeling suddenly very tired. Where was Cage? Surely he did not have to spend the entire evening talking to Octavia. Surely he must realize that I was alone?

But of course he did, I told myself, trying to revive my

spirits. But it was hard, very hard. I felt cold and alone and strange. Presently, as I sat there I had the odd impression that I was being watched, that old, unsettling feeling I had not experienced in years. And as always there was no rationale to it, none whatsoever. There was no one in the room, no one but me. Nerves and exhaustion, I told myself. Still the feeling persisted, the cold hand laid on my heart, the raised hairs on the back of my neck. All those heavy red curtains. My eye traveled the room; anyone could hide behind one. Perhaps a servant spying on me? A servant curious to observe the new Mrs. Norwood? Suppose there—*that* one!—was it moving, ever so slightly, a ripple of velvet . . . ?

I got up, my hands balled into fists, nails piercing the palms of my hand. I walked over to the nearest wall hanging and fumbling for the draw string, pulled it. The curtains swished as they swept apart—and to my horror I found myself looking into the eyes of a woman, wide-set eyes of the deepest violet blue.

The scream rose in my throat, rent the air, before I could think and I heard Cage's voice behind me exclaim, "My God!"

Chapter 12

IT was a portrait, life-size, painted with extraordinary realism.

I shrank back from it, trembling, turning to face Cage.

"What the devil are you doing here?" Cage asked in a low, tight voice, his face white as chalk.

I felt cold, sick. He was angry and I had never seen him really angry before. Even when his father had banished him he had worn a mocking, wry smile, had made a bitter remark or two, not spoken like this, his eyes blazing in a terrible, white face.

"I said—*what* are you doing here?" he repeated, his fists balled at his sides, his blue eyes piercing through me.

I wet my quivering lips and tried to speak.

"Well—?" he demanded.

"She—Martha—our bags were brought up to this room," I stumbled like an idiot, pointing to our luggage which had been set against the wall.

He saw the bags and the tight set of his shoulders relaxed.

"I wasn't expecting the picture, you see," I went on. "I—oh, Cage! Please, I'm sorry I screamed." I could not bear for him to be angry with me.

"I wrote to Martha, telling her explicitly . . ." He went to the bell pull and yanked at it.

"Draw the curtain," he ordered, waving at the portrait.

I did as he asked, but not before I noticed the picture's likeness to Octavia. It was Lillith, of course, Lillith wearing a black gown with a single red rose tucked in the low cut neck, a red rose nestled between milk white breasts.

"It was a mistake," Cage said, the hard edge to his voice gone. "I'm sorry I lost my temper. But even if I were a boor I would have had better taste than to put you in my first wife's bedroom."

151

"It's all right," I said. "I'm sure Martha did not understand."

He took my arm. His own was trembling. Why? I wondered, why?

"We won't wait," he said, "I'll have Gandy bring the bags."

We went out and he led me back along the corridor and opened another door. The room was not quite as large as the one we had left; it did not have the sky blue ceiling, nor the cupids, nor—thank God!—the tall mirrors, but it did have plush, plum-colored drapes and the woodwork fairly crawled with carved cabbage roses.

"Much better, isn't it?" Cage said, smiling at me, kissing my cheek.

"Much," I agreed.

It was not until later, not until we were sitting in the large dining room on satinwood chairs at the immense oblong table, just the two of us (Octavia had pleaded a headache) with candles in the center, that I wondered if Martha had deliberately chosen to ignore Cage's written instructions by putting me in Lillith's room. Cage had wired the news of our marriage and had followed the telegram with a letter to Martha asking that the "plum room" be made ready. Martha claimed that she had never received the letter.

Cage accepted her statement without question. More than that he did not chastise her for her blunder, a mistake a well-trained housekeeper would never have made. I did not tell him what she had said in that room, how she had frightened me, the words themselves now seemed petty, foolish, and Cage would have laughed at them, as I should have done then.

"More wine?" Cage asked, reaching for the cut glass decanter.

"No, thank you." Martha had served our dinner silently, unobtrusively, though I had been painfully aware of her presence. Every now and then I would catch her watching me, her hard, tan-colored eyes slightly narrowed, and I could very well guess that she was wondering why Cage had married me, a pale, plain, spiritless twenty-seven-year-old widow.

"You've hardly touched your food," Cage said, refilling

his glass again, for what must have been the eighth or ninth time.

"I'm not very hungry."

I was thinking about Octavia, my new stepdaughter. Did she really have a headache or was it an excuse to absent herself from the table? Was I that odious to her? Perhaps not. Perhaps she did feel unwell. I must have an open mind in regard to Octavia, I had to. For I could see how fond Cage was of her, just as if the girl had been his. I did not allow myself to think that perhaps this fondness might be due to Octavia's resemblance to her mother. Instead I convinced myself that Cage liked Octavia because he loved children and his stepdaughter had come to him when she was still very small.

"You haven't had a chance to see the rest of the house, Adelaide," Cage said. "I'll give you a guided tour after dinner."

"I would like that."

Octavia's trust, if not fondness, I must win. There was nothing much I could do except come to some kind of terms with her. But the housekeeper . . .

"There's a ballroom," Cage said, the decanter in his hand once more. "A *real* ballroom. We don't have to push back the chairs in the dining room for a dance as we did at Riverknoll."

"How lovely!"

The housekeeper was a servant and servants, though they no longer could be sold, could easily be sent packing.

"Are you sure you wouldn't like some of this wine? It's imported from France. No?" He drank, savoring the taste on his tongue.

"Riverknoll," Cage went on, giving a short laugh. "To think I once wanted *that*—wanted it so badly, you cannot imagine, Adelaide. Wanted it—and now I have this—so much superior."

"Much superior," I said barely listening, engrossed in my own thoughts.

It would not be easy, I reminded myself, telling Martha she must go. "Your services are no longer required," I pictured myself saying. But then when I thought of those strange eyes, hard and cold, my heart quailed. Perhaps Cage could do it for me.

"Cage . . . ," I said, hesitating, wondering how to put it, ". . . Cage, how long has Martha been with you?"

"Martha? Why she came when—when I got married—the first time—maybe twelve, thirteen years ago."

A long time. "Do you—do you feel she's indispensable?"

"Yes, I do." No equivocation in those three words. Still I went on. "This is a big house—and running it with a small staff takes some doing."

"Indeed, and my dear Adelaide, you needn't worry about it at all. Martha is quite capable, very efficient. She will take care of everything."

She came into the room then and began to remove the plates. I wondered if she had been listening at the door for she threw me a cold, malevolent look. I tried to meet her eyes with a look of my own, but her malicious stare made me drop my gaze.

"Brandy," Cage was saying. "Let's have that good imported brandy, Martha. There's some left, I presume? Good. Brandy and coffee in the drawing room."

It was late—I was bone weary and would have been happy to retire early for Cage and I had not had much chance to be truly alone since our marriage. At Beech Arbor there had been the constant ebb and flow of relatives and friends who, feeling cheated of the usual nuptial festivities, had decided to call on us, some guests staying for days. Even our wedding night had been given over to callers. I had spent the best part of it waiting in trepidation upstairs for Cage while he, down below, feeling duty-bound had entertained several of his old comrades-at-arms who had come to pay their respects to the new bride and groom. By the time Cage had come up to bed I had worked myself into a fine state of nerves, the sort of panic one might expect from a virgin bride, not a widowed woman. But Cage was too full of spirits to notice and our marriage was consummated wordlessly, quickly; my fears as it turned out were for nothing. Sleeping with Cage would not be too much different than sleeping with Barnabas. The thing I had missed, however, that I especially wanted from Cage, were the little endearments, the intimate husband-wife talk that would bring him closer to me.

But we had not had the opportunity. There had been clothes to unpack, wardrobes to be cleaned out, and papers to sign. From the outset I had insisted on giving all my investments over to Cage as a proper and loving wife should. He had protested, saying I ought to keep at least a few bonds as my "marriage portion," but I told him that I had no head for business, that I trusted him to do with the money as he thought right. "Think about it, at least," he had urged. "No," I had replied, "my mind is made up." He had taken me in his arms then, kissed me, told me I was the most generous woman he had ever known. It had been a glowing moment, one that I wanted to stretch and stretch, but before it was over a knock on the bedroom door announced a fresh batch of visitors.

Nor did we have occasion to be alone on the long journey across a continent and a sea, crowded as we were on trains and ships by the many emigrants coming West to seek their fortunes, not in gold now, but in the rich silver deposits of Nevada. All through those tedious, uncomfortable hours of travel I had promised myself that once we got to Cage's home, *our* home, we could be together, we could close the door on the outsiders, the distractions, the world and have our privacy. Perhaps then Cage would say the words I wanted so much to hear, perhaps then he would speak of love.

And here we were, the Folly at last—and still not alone. The garish house, the unpleasant housekeeper, the hostile stepdaughter could all be forgotten if only Cage and I could be by ourselves. But—not yet, not yet. In the drawing room Martha continued to hover on the edge of my vision, pouring brandy, arranging the coffee cups, stepping back into the shadows, standing there, an intrusive though withdrawn figure, ostensibly waiting for further instructions.

"This," Cage said, pointing to a large, heavy clawed table covered by a crimson, gold-fringed shawl, "belonged to a Spanish grandee. It was supposed to have come over with Pizarro."

"Lovely," I murmured.

Dare I ask Martha to leave the room? I was mistress at the Folly now; it was my place to tell her that she would not be required to stay.

"And this," Cage went on, linking his arm in mine as we paused before a life-sized marble statue of a muscular Greek discus thrower, "is a copy of well-known antiquity."

It was dreadful being afraid of a servant, a fear that I

had never imagined possible. I could not go on this way. I had to make a stand, the sooner the better. I must.

I turned, "Martha . . . ?"

But she had gone. The strange part of it was that though she had left the room I still felt her presence; it lingered, unpleasantly, like an aftertaste that remained on the tongue.

"Let's have some brandy," Cage said.

It had a nutty flavor, very good, very potent. I had a sip, no more. Cage downed his, rather fast for brandy, and poured himself another.

"Coffee?" I asked, lifting the pot.

"No—I'll stick with the brandy. Coffee keeps me awake."

"Cage," I said, lowering my voice, trying once again, "would you feel upset if I made several—ah—adjustments in the staff?"

"What . . . ?" he said. "Change the servants?"

"I thought . . ."

"You've only just arrived, Adelaide. They may seem like a scruffy lot at first glance, but I assure you they're efficient and loyal, that's the important thing—loyal."

"But . . ."

"I wish you wouldn't keep harping on it, Adelaide," he said rather testily.

I kept silent. It would not do to quarrel, not on our first night at home, not with Martha listening at the keyhole.

"Have more brandy," he said, splashing some into my glass. "Go on, drink up. It will take your mind off your worries."

I had another sip to please him, wondering what worries *his* mind dwelled on. He went on drinking the brandy, a slight frown between his eyes.

"Cage," I said, breaking a long silence. "Are you glad to be home?"

"Glad? Of course." His lips twitched. "But I did not think—did not dream the place would be so full of memories."

Memories! The word was like a door slammed in my face. Of course he would have them, memories of the life he had lived away from the Tidewater, mementos, remembrances of the years spent here, memories of which I had no part. I had already realized in a vague sort of way, that Cage had a past removed from mine, but not until he had spoken just now had it hit me so forcibly. There was a whole, long chapter in Cage's life to which I was not privy, ten years which had belonged to him and another woman, ten years which had completely excluded me.

I looked around at the baroquely furnished room crowded with glass-beaded lamps, carved walnut tables and velvet chairs, the walls hung with gilt-framed mirrors and pictures of scantily draped women gamboling in deep green forests—and I thought of Lillith. A "fit" setting. This was all Lillith's, Lillith's and Cage's. This house, this Folly had belonged to them. They had lived here together, sat in this very room side by side, drank from these same brandy glasses, looked at the same pictures. And while the bed upstairs in the blue-ceilinged room would not be mine, Lillith's ghost, her spirit would hover over me wherever I laid my head, just as surely as Martha's presence hovered in the shadows.

"Yes, memories." Cage's voice had begun to slur. The decanter clinked against the glass. "Not all happy ones, my dear, not by a longshot, in case you are wondering. But on the other hand . . ." He looked around at the walls, the ceiling, ". . . we had some high old times, too." He smiled to himself as he tipped the decanter and sloshed the liquor into his glass. "Well, Adelaide, aren't you going to ask me? Don't you want to know all about it?"

He was drunk. I had never seen Cage drunk before. Of course I knew he drank; there were very few men who did not, but I had always assumed that he carried his liquor like a gentleman. Papa had said that one of the acid tests for a man of good breeding was his ability to drink and not show it. Tonight Cage was showing it.

"Cage," I began, "you're tired, perhaps . . ."

"You haven't answered my question, Adelaide. Don't you want to know about what went on, don't you want to know about those ten years with Lillith?"

"Cage, please . . ."

"Well—my dear, I would not tell you anyway. You are too much of a lady." His hand shook as he drained his glass. "No—you are too fine a person, too kindhearted to be told." His blue eyes suddenly flooded with tears.

"Oh—Cage!" Moved, I got up and went over to him, sitting down at his side, taking his hands in mine. "What is it, darling? I can't bear to see you unhappy."

He looked at me, biting his lip, struggling for control.

"I—I'm all right. Just a momentary weakness. Please—Adelaide," he withdrew his hand from mine, "please, don't—don't—don't make it worse than it is. I hate scenes. If there is anything I cannot endure it's a mawkish scene."

I felt my face go stiff.

"Ah, there—I've done it and I am a cad. I'm sorry, my dear," Cage apologized. "I don't mean to hurt your feelings. I—it's coming home—that's all—a little sentimentality, nothing more. I'll be all right. Why don't you go on up to bed—I'll join you presently."

"Are you sure you want to be alone? Are you . . . ?"

"Yes—please. Just a few minutes."

But it was almost dawn before I heard his uncertain step on the stair.

We had guests for luncheon the next day. John Shelby, a former business associate of Cage's, and his wife, Clara. Cage had warned me beforehand that Mrs. Shelby was a brash, outspoken woman and a gossip to boot. "Half of what she says is sheer fabrication," he had said. "If it were not for John I doubt I'd have her under this roof."

"If you dislike her so," I had replied, "wouldn't it be simpler to invite John for a 'bachelor' evening of cards instead?"

"I couldn't do that. John would see through it and feel slighted. He dotes on the woman, though God knows why. He's a very shrewd business man—and right now he's thinking of setting up his own company. Mine stocks. Silver mine stocks. There are millions to be made yet in the Comstock."

The Shelbys arrived promptly at one. They were not at all what I had expected. I had pictured John Shelby as tall, thin, with flashing gold teeth, attired in loud checks, and his wife as short and stout, gaudily dressed with yards of pearls twined about a sagging throat. Nothing could have been further from the truth. Mr. Shelby, a dignified man of medium height and graying hair wore a conservative black broadcloth suit, and Clara Shelby, considerably younger than her husband, a vivacious, pretty woman looked as if she had just stepped out of an illustration in a Parisian fashion magazine. A crushed green velvet porkpie hat with a single plume sat jauntily on a mass of brown curls and her dress, following the lines of her narrow waist and full hips featured an apron front, looped up over a brightly colored petticoat. She made me feel quite provincial for I still wore the modified crinoline.

"My dear," she said in an aside to me as we were sipping our prelunch sherry, "I hadn't realized that you arrived only just yesterday. If I had known, we could have postponed this visit."

"It's quite all right," I said. "I don't in the least mind."

"You shall want to go shopping, I'm sure." Her eyes flicked over me. "I know a seamstress who is an absolute genius. You ought to wear colors," she went on when I said nothing, "bright colors would suit you better than dove gray. It does nothing for the complexion."

I suppose I should have resented her criticism, but it was delivered in such a pleasant voice I did not mind. Later I was to find that Clara Shelby could unloose the sharpest barbs in that sweet voice of hers, and her victims hardly felt the pain until long afterwards. However, in all fairness, she was never deliberately unkind to me, and I felt from the first that she liked me, and if she found fault it was because she meant to be helpful.

"Will you be entertaining soon?" she asked.

"I don't know. Perhaps. You are the first of Cage's friends I've met so far."

"Oh? Then I feel flattered. He has scores and scores of friends. Some of them are quite dull, some . . ."

"Mrs. Shelby?" It was Cage, calling from across the room. "Would you come here to settle a dispute between your husband and myself?"

Octavia joined us in the drawing room a few minutes later. I had not seen her since our initial encounter in the entry hall for she had avoided both supper and breakfast. Her manners in the meanwhile had scarcely improved. She wore a sullen look on her pretty face, the mouth turned down, the eyes resentful. She barely said good-day to me; to Mrs. Shelby she gave a grimace that passed for a smile. Efforts to draw her into conversation met with incomprehensible murmurings or stony silence. Her palpable resentment made me uneasy and I was grateful for the company of the Shelbys at lunch, grateful for Clara's ceaseless chatter even though it concerned people and places unknown to me. Octavia sat through it all, eating little, and as soon as we left the gentlemen to their cigars she excused herself,

saying she felt indisposed, a statement somewhat at odds
with her look of rosy health. I wondered why she had bothered to make an appearance at luncheon unless she had
done so only at the urging of Cage.

"Shall we go out into the garden?" Clara suggested.

The garden at the back of the house was a pleasant
surprise, a thoughtfully laid out bower with a high, stone
wall and neat, brick-enclosed beds of blooming roses. It
had an arbor shaded by two silvery acacia trees and a
flagged walk, the borders planted with a profusion of autumn flowers, lavender and pink gentians and bright yellow
chrysanthemums. We went and sat in the arbor.

"Adelaide—I may call you Adelaide?" Clara's light
brows lifted. "Then you must call me Clara, Adelaide; I
will confess you are not at all what I expected."

"Am I not?" I asked smiling.

"No—after Lillith . . . ." She paused, her face suddenly
flushing. "But of course you know about Lillith."

"Yes. Yes, Cage told me—everything." I hated myself
for not confessing the truth. If I had done so perhaps Clara
would have enlightened me, for suddenly I wanted to
know, I wanted very much to know. But to admit ignorance on the subject of my husband's first wife was to
acknowledge that our marriage was not the intimate, personal relationship a marriage was supposed to be.

"Quite frankly," Clara said, "I think Cage Norwood has
made a far wiser choice this time."

"Why, thank you, Clara," I said, feeling flattered.

"Yes, indeed," said Clara, rearranging her skirts, "and
you mustn't mind Octavia. She's still a child."

"I try not to," I said. "I can't blame her really for
resenting a stepmother. But I feel sure when she gets to
know me she'll soften up."

"Perhaps."

"She seems very fond of Mr. Norwood."

"She adores him," Clara said, "as much as she can adore
anyone. She's a very cold little person, at least that's my
impression."

"No—I think you are wrong. She flung herself at Mr.
Norwood—literally—when we arrived yesterday. But then
I suppose she would, her own father having died when she
was quite small."

Clara lifted her brows. "Who told you that? Though I

don't think Octavia remembers her own father, perhaps not even who he was—the subject is very hush-hush, she's adopted and passed off as Cage Norwood's child—but her real father died when she was ten."

"Ten . . . ? How could that be? I understand when my husband married the first Mrs. Norwood her child was only two. Surely," I lowered my voice, "surely, her father and mother were not divorced?"

"Divorced?" She laughed. "They were never married, my dear. Lillith and the man, Octavia's father, were never married. The girl is a love child—to put it politely. Illegitimate, if we are to be frank."

Illegitimate! The word seemed to ring out shamelessly, a word that until now I had only heard spoken in a hushed tone. Octavia, Cage's foster daughter, was illegitimate. I wished Clara had never told me.

Chapter 13

I had been too shocked to notice Martha until she spoke. She was standing very close, no more than a foot away from us.

"Mrs. Shelby," she said in a cold, dead voice, her eyes alive with anger. "Mrs. Shelby."

She must have come along the flagged path to the arbor without making a sound. How much of our conversation she had heard I could not guess.

"Really!" Clara Shelby exclaimed. "You do creep up on one."

"Mr. Shelby wishes to see you," Martha said.

"Tell him I'll be along shortly," Clara answered.

"He says he wishes you to come at once."

"I can't imagine—oh, very well then." She rose, smoothing her skirt. "I'll be back, Adelaide—unless you want to come in with me?"

"No—I'll wait out here."

Martha stepped aside to let her pass. I thought she would follow Mrs. Shelby but she did not. She waited until Clara had disappeared through the side door of the house, then turned to me.

"You must not mind what that woman says," she said. "She has a loose tongue."

So Martha *had* heard. What disturbed me, however, was not her eavesdropping (inadvertently or not) as much as her open criticism of Clara Shelby.

"Martha . . ."

"What she says is a lie," she went on, ignoring the warning note in my voice.

"Please—I think . . ."

"A downright, scurvy lie!" The cold fury, the belligerency in her voice struck an uneasy note in my heart. "Octavia is Mr. Norwood's child. She was born nine months after he and her mother were married. She's legitimate. Legitimate!"

The woman was speaking irate nonsense. "I don't choose to discuss this with you." How could Octavia be Cage's daughter when Charles had written me at the outset that Cage had married a woman with a two-year-old child? And Cage had not been in California but eighteen months when he took Lillith to wife. Furthermore, why should Martha be so upset? This was none of her affair.

"It's slander," Martha muttered. "Slander. And I'll see to it—I'll see to it . . ." Her eyes narrowed and in the dappled shade of the arbor they glinted with a sinister light. They gave me a queer turn, those eyes. They did not seem human.

Suppressing a shudder, I got to my feet. "Martha—I don't want to discuss Miss Octavia," I repeated. "Please, let me pass." For one horrible moment I thought she would bar my way, but then she moved and I left her, going up the walk, feeling those terrible eyes trained on my back.

When I entered the house through the French windows of a little side parlor, I did not go directly to the drawing room, but stood there, my hands pressed to my cheeks, trying to collect my thoughts. Could Martha have been speaking the truth? Octavia—Cage's child? But he himself had said that she was a foster daughter, legally adopted by him. Was he trying to protect himself? Had he committed an indiscretion, then later rueing it, married the mother? But where had he met Lillith? In New Orleans? Supposing he had known her there, supposing he had been having an affair with her when I came, throwing myself at him . . .

My heart was beating so fast I had to sit down. I had to collect myself; I couldn't go to pieces simply because a servant had made a statement contradicting Clara Shelby's. Should I believe Martha—or Clara? Cage had labeled Mrs. Shelby a gossip, saying that half of what she repeated was "sheer fabrication." Still, why should she tell me that Octavia was illegitimate, that her real father had died when she was ten? Her allegation was just as shocking as Martha's. Well-bred women did not have children out of wedlock, at least none that I had ever known. In the novels I had read they either died conveniently or had their babies in secret and then gave them away and after that remained forever a spinster, "repenting." Even if Lillith had been forced, assaulted, taken against her will, she would never have kept the baby. And Cage, a gentleman, would have never married a woman with a "love" child.

Unless he loved her very much.

I twisted the ring on my finger. Why should it matter? She, Lillith, her marriage to Cage, everything that concerned her belonged in the past. She was dead and buried, the years she and Cage lived together irretrievably lost. This was another decade, another year, another season. It was Cage and Adelaide now—and what went before had nothing to do with us. All that time had been swept aside. I must remember the Folly was mine, that *I* lived here now, in the present, today; yesterday had vanished.

Except for the memories.

I could not get the picture of Cage out of my mind, the picture of him as he sat, brandy glass between his hands, a look of brooding nostalgia on his face, saying, "I didn't dream the place would be so full of memories." What had he been thinking of? Was Octavia his? He was the last person I could ask, and yet I felt I had to know. I wanted to know everything about him. A door had been opened into the past, one door revealing other doors, and I longed to know what lay behind each of them. Never mind my resolve that bygones were bygones. That was my mind talking, not my heart. To be shut out was too painful. I loved Cage and I wanted to share every aspect of his life. But who could I ask? Certainly not Clara Shelby.

Then I thought of Charles. He had been displeased with my marriage. Just before Cage and I had left Beech Arbor I received a short note from Charles saying that he believed I had used poor judgment in my choice of a second husband but wished me well all the same. I had been hurt by his tone and had not written to him since. But now I decided I would write a long, chatty letter just as I had done in the old days when he had gone off to the Gold Rush, and in this one casually, tactfully ask about Octavia. Of course he might not tell me—he had ignored my questions then—but now that I was Mrs. Cage Norwood perhaps he would react differently.

The sound of a footstep and the rustle of a gown broke into my thoughts and turning I saw Clara Shelby peering in through the glass door.

"Oh—so there you are!" she exclaimed, coming into the room. "I looked in the garden—and you were gone."

"Yes, well—it got a little cool."

"But why are you sitting here?"

"I—I was feeling a little faint," I said, not knowing what else to say.

"Faint? My dear, you aren't . . . ?" her eyes swept over me in a quick, assessing glance, "expecting?"

"No—no, I wish I were," I answered, my face turning scarlet.

"Adelaide—you actually *wish* for a baby—*now*, so soon, when you are just starting out here in San Francisco? If one happens there is not much you can do, but to *wish* . . ."

"With all my heart. I would give anything to have a child. Wouldn't you?"

"What . . . ? And lose my figure? I know you must think me awfully selfish but I have no great overweening desire for motherhood. It's the truth. The thickening waist, the forced seclusion. No, no, not for me."

I did think her selfish and her statement shocking, but said nothing.

"Well, enough said on *that* subject. But you do look peaked, my dear. It's no wonder, I expect, after your journey. And we've overstayed our leave. We'll be going as soon as I can tear Mr. Shelby away. You know how it is when men get to talking business—I don't bother about it—I find it awfully dull, don't you?"

"Yes—I leave it to Cage."

She came closer and lowered her voice. "I got a ragging from Mr. Shelby. He says I'm not to talk to you about Mr. Norwood's wife or child—not a word." She paused, her eyes rolling toward the door. "It's that Martha—she's a spy—take care—she has eyes and ears that travel everywhere, I swear."

A spy? For whom? Perhaps Clara meant a snoop.

". . . there's lots I could tell you, but I daren't. Mr. Shelby has warned me. Personally I think he's afraid of . . ." Suddenly she straightened up and put her fingers to her arm in mine and whispered, "I'll lay you odds she's got her ear to the door now." Raising her voice, she said loudly, "Shall we join the men?"

We went out into the hall. No one was there but at the

far end I heard the soft click of a closing door, and the sound sent a shiver up my spine.

Shortly after breakfast the next morning Cage left for the City. "Business," he said, kissing my cheek absently. "I shall try to be back in time for dinner."

I hated being left alone. I wanted to go with him, but he was meeting a group of men and could not take me. Wives did not go to business meetings. I might have spent the time visiting the shops, but Cage had not suggested it. "You and Octavia can get acquainted," he said, lifting his hat and gloves from the hall table.

Octavia had appeared silently at breakfast and then gone up to her room again. I wondered how I was to become acquainted with her as she rarely made an appearance. Perhaps I ought to make the first move, I thought. Perhaps part of the trouble was shyness. Being painfully shy myself as a girl, I could understand shyness in others. I would wait for a bit, and then if Octavia did not show herself again, I would seek her out.

After Cage had gone the house seemed very quiet. The servants were supposedly busy with their separate tasks, but I neither saw nor heard them. Martha had introduced me to the others, Doreen, the cook, a short, fat darkie with a squint, Gandy, the wizened little man who saw ghosts and Lucinda, a pretty young girl with café-au-lait skin. They all appeared to be efficient; none of them were friendly.

I stood for a moment or two longer in the hall, then went into the library. It was much smaller than the drawing room, more sensibly furnished. There were large leather-covered chairs, a sofa, a square desk and book shelves covering two entire walls. I chose a book at random, *Tom Jones* by Fielding. I flipped it open. The pages were uncut. It was a dull book, if I remembered correctly, but I sat down with it in my lap and stared at the printed words.

Book I. Containing as . . .

The house seemed to settle around me in a deeper, heavier silence. I had seen the whole of it the afternoon before, Cage taking me from room to room, showing it off proudly, the many bedrooms, the huge ballroom covering the top floor, the little alcoves, the anterooms, the towers and the turrets. His pride in the Folly was a puzzle to me. It was one facet of his personality—this love for gewgaws and graceless furniture—I had never suspected, for I had always assumed him to have the best of taste. And yet I could understand how in a way the Folly's expensive, garish furnishings could act as a symbol of affluence, of security. Cage while living at Riverknoll had very little he could call his own, and then he had been literally thrown out to fend for himself. The Folly had been his revenge against his father, against the fact of his disinheritance and the threat of poverty.

The Folly was my home, too. I must try to like it for Cage's sake if for no other reason. Yet—I wished it were not quite as large, or opulent, or smothering, not quite as strange. But, I told myself, familiarity would come with time. I would get used to it, might even grow to like it. I went back to the book in my lap.

Book I. Containing as much of the Birth of the Foundling.

There was a clock on the mantel I had not noticed before. It was oval-shaped, standing on clawed legs with two china cupids embracing above the white, dial face. A noisy clock, now that I had become aware of it, the sound of its ticking filling the room. Tick-tock-tick-tock!

My eyes returned to the printed page, but the sound obtruded, and gradually as I listened I became more and more uneasy, a little afraid. Funny, I thought, how the ticking kept growing louder and louder, how ominously, how portentously it echoed in my ears, rebounding from wall to wall, swelling into a thundering duet with my loudly beating heart. And now I sat frozen, frightened as the ticking swelled even louder, as if it were the voice of some malignant, raging enemy, someone who meant me harm, someone terrible, louder and louder, TICKTOCK-TICKTOCK, shouting, drumming, pressing upon my brain relentlessly. TICKTOCK . . .

I sprang up; the book fell to the floor. God knows where my fancy was taking me. It was only a clock. An ugly clock at that. I picked the book up and with shaking hands replaced it on the shelf. My nerves had been playing tricks on me. The strange house, the newness, the fatigue from the long, tiresome journey had conspired to make me sensitive to everything, even the homey sound of a ticking clock. And yet no matter how I reasoned, I found that I could not remain in the library. Not now, not alone.

I went out and ascended the stairs. Octavia's room was down at the end of a long corridor. I paused before her door, biting my lip, then lifted my hand and rapped on it.

"Who is it?" came a voice.

"Adelaide."

There was a long pause. "Come in."

She was sitting on a chair near the window in her petticoat. I could see at once that it had been a mistake to think of her as a child. She was well developed, slender waisted, full breasted. She looked at me with hostile, violet eyes.

"Hello," I said, smiling with a great deal of effort. "I thought we might have a little talk."

"About what?"

Despite her mature figure she was still childish, an impertinent child, but I chose to ignore her rudeness.

"Oh—I don't know. I feel it's high time we got to know one another."

"I don't see why," she said.

I bit back a sharp retort and went on calmly, "I suppose you could say that since we are going to live under the same roof, it might be more pleasant if we did so as friends."

"Must we?"

I fought with my temper. Above all I must not show anger. "No—but don't you think if we both love Cage that it would please him?"

She gave me a long, long look. "Does my father love you—really? Does he?"

"Of course he does," and my eyes dropped before her intense gaze.

"You are so different from Mama," she said.

A flush stained my cheeks. "I am hoping that you won't hold that against me." Lillith's portrait flashed through my mind, the white skin, the black hair and the violet eyes. "Yes, I am different. But I cannot help that."

"I had believed my father would never. . . ." she paused.

"Never marry again? But he did. He's a young man still. Come now, Octavia, you didn't expect that he would remain a widower for the rest of his life, did you?"

"I don't see why not!" she retorted.

"Your mother's memory will always remain . . ."

"Why did he marry *you?*" she blurted out. "Why? You're not even pretty. Was it for money?"

A red mist seemed to swirl before my eyes, blinding me, and my first angry impulse was to lash out, to strike the insolent, pretty face. She had thoughtlessly wounded me where it hurt the most and I clung tightly to self-control, warning myself that it would be a mistake to let her know how I bled. I had remained standing during the interview since she had not asked me to sit down, but now I groped for a chair and lowered myself into it. "That was an awful thing to say," I told her when I could find my voice. "Rude and cruel."

She kept silent, her eyes hard and defiant.

"I won't ask you to apologize, because you are just mannerless enough to refuse. It is difficult for me to realize that you are—are Cage's daughter."

Still she said nothing.

"Whatever you say—or think, *I* am Mrs. Norwood now. You will simply have to accept that."

She shrugged. "It's none of my affair—really." Her voice broke and she turned her head but not before I saw a suspicious tear glitter in her eye.

My rancor softened. "You are unhappy," I said, drawing in my breath. Of course, what did I expect? How mulish of me to think that a few words, a smile would pave the way to friendship. "You are unhappy and angry." She kept her head turned, staring out the window, and for a while I did not speak. Then I went on, "I would have felt the same, perhaps, if my father had remarried. You see, my mother died, too—only I never knew her, she died shortly after I was born."

I saw the line of her jaw quiver, but she said nothing.

"I love your father very much," I continued, "and I am going to do my best to make him happy. I shan't press myself on you." I rose. "I only hope that with time . . ."

"I don't want to talk about it," she said.

I left her sitting in the same position, looking out over the drive, her back a silent reproof.

Cage did not return for dinner. Instead a note delivered by messenger in the late afternoon informed me that he would be unable to come home until the next day. An important man by the name of Ralston was supposed to join their business meeting, he wrote, and since he was afraid the conference would last until the small hours he thought it best to put up at a hotel. "I am sure you understand," he said. "I'll make it up to you, my dear."

It was a blow—and it did disappoint me. Our second night at home and the first spoiled because . . .

But I pushed the thought from my mind. I must not find fault with him. Cage was anxious, eager to get ahead, to make a success of himself. How different than the devil-may-care, ambitionless Cage of the river that I once knew. I ought to be proud, not critical. And we had the rest of our lives together, all those days, weeks, months, years, stretching into infinity. Cage and I. We were married. I still found it hard to believe. Whatever else intruded, the unpleasantness, the hostility, the coldness, the anger, I had that reality to warm myself with. Cage was mine. We were husband and wife.

After I read the note a second time, I went to the kitchen to tell Martha that Cage would not be having dinner at home. When I opened the swinging door, I was surprised to see that the staff had visitors. They were all sitting around the table eating and drinking, our four darkie servants, Martha, Lucinda, Doreen and Gandy, with three colored women and a very black negro man. The minute I came in a hush descended on the room. They all looked at me with blank faces and then at Martha.

"I—I'm sorry," I stammered, too flustered to wonder why I, as mistress of the house, should apologize. "I—I did not mean to interrupt."

They kept gazing at Martha expectantly, as if they trusted her to rescue them from what must have been an embarrassing moment for them as well. She got to her feet. "What is it you wish, Mrs. Norwood?" she asked, very polite, not servile, but with just the proper amount of respect. Yet there was that hard look on her face, a look that came dangerously close to scorn.

I told her about Cage.

"Very well—you will be dining alone, then."

"Alone? I thought . . ."

"Octavia is going out." No reason given, where, why, just that flat statement.

"I see." I waited, thinking she might still offer some

explanation concerning Octavia. But she said nothing. Nor did she give an introduction or an accounting of her guests who were wining and dining at the master's expense. I waited another moment or two and finally feeling foolish left the room. As soon as I shut the door behind me, I heard the hum of voices commence and I fought the urge to bend my ear to the keyhole before I finally walked away.

The rest of the day passed very slowly. I wrote my letter to Charles, giving it to Gandy to post. Supper alone in the dark, wainscotted dining room was a ghastly affair. Lucinda waited on me this time, silently, without a word while Martha stood near the service door and watched. Her shadow loomed large on the wall, and the only sound she made was when she whispered to Lucinda, instructing her to remove one dish and set another before me. I ate little and what I did eat seemed to lodge in my throat. I could have had a tray in my room and avoided the ordeal altogether, but it would have been a cowardly act, one more little retreat, and God knew I had retreated too much already.

Lucinda's hands shook a good deal as she served me, and at first I put it down to nervousness. Perhaps she had been hired only recently or perhaps serving at meals was not her usual job. I had the strange impulse to reassure her, to tell her not to be afraid, that I was new also, new, clumsy and a little afraid. But I could not utter a word. Martha's presence seemed to fill the room, just as the ticking clock had done in the library.

Toward the end of the meal Lucinda dropped a dessert dish, pudding I think it was. She let out a small scream, and her face turned an ashy gray as the dish fell to the floor with a tinkle of broken glass. It wasn't me she was frightened of, however, it was Martha. She looked at her out of distended eyes, her mouth quivered. "Miss Martha . . . ! I don't know what happened—it jus' slipped," she quavered.

"Get a cloth and mop it up," Martha said in a cold, hard voice. "And hurry!"

"Yes, m'am, yes, m'am," and she scurried off.

No apologies were made to me.

"Will you be taking coffee in the drawing room, Mrs. Norwood?" Martha asked.

"Yes—yes, please." I did not want coffee, I did not want to go into the drawing room. But something told me that I must keep up with the routine, I must not show fear as Lucinda had done.

The coffee was hot, bitter. I drank it slowly.

"Brandy, Mrs. Norwood?"

"No, thank you—and—and Martha," I swallowed. "You need not wait." How coolly, how casually the held-in words had come out after all. "I don't think there will be anything else. Thank you for the dinner—it was excellent."

Her eyes narrowed for a moment, then she left the room. I did not relax, but sat with my head held at the right angle, calmly sipping coffee though the cup when I finally put it down rattled in the saucer.

I retired early, bolting the door of my room securely. But what was there to be afraid of? Surely I could not believe for a moment that Octavia or Martha would attack me? Still, the drawn bolt gave me a feeling of safety. Undressing quickly, I got into bed, turning my back on Cage's empty pillow.

I must have fallen asleep immediately for I remembered nothing until I woke with a start at the sound of a chime striking somewhere in the corridor. I had no idea of the time. I counted nine tones but, of course, it could have been much later. I turned my pillow over, punching it up and settled myself comfortably, shutting my eyes, only to have them pop open again. I tried once more, a different position, the covers tucked firmly about my chin, but again my eyes flew open. I then went through the usual ritual of the insomniac, telling myself that it was ridiculous, I was tired, ergo I must sleep, it was night and in the morning I would be worn to a frazzle if I did not get my proper rest. I tossed and turned and twisted. I counted sheep, did the multiplication tables, took deep, soulful breaths. All in vain. I lay on my back and stared at the shadows. A wedge of moonlight had worked itself in between a gap in the curtains, spilling over the bureau and the carpet in barred light.

Suddenly I heard a soft click, the tiniest, microscopic sound but it ran through me like a shock. I levered myself up on my elbows, my elbows, my eyes, round as saucers, staring.

Click. There it was again!

My head swung about. And peering through the gloom I saw that the door knob was slowly turning! Everything inside me seemed to freeze. Someone was on the other side of the door, someone was trying to get in, silently, stealthily. Oh God! There was another click as the knob turned back and the hair on my head seemed to stand straight up. I wanted to shout, to scream, "Who? Who is it?" but my throat was clogged with fear. The knob twisted once more, and the door seemed to bulge (I swear!) as if a hand were pressing against it. Thank God for the bolt. Thank God I had had the intuition, the silly fear to draw that bolt.

I heard a small, scratching sound now, a slight pawing, so tiny a sound it was hardly more than a rustle. My lungs felt tight as I strained my ears, listening, listening.

Gandy sees her combing her hair—she had long, black hair, you know—Lillith . . .

No, I thought, no. I won't think about it. Mice, that is what I hear, mice. But how could mice turn a knob? I won't think about it, I won't think about it, I repeated silently.

After a long while I caught the faint sound of footsteps walking away. Still I sat as I was, straight as a ramrod, clutching the bed clothes to my chin, rigid, listening. Finally the clock chimed again, twelve times, the witching hour. Who had been at my door? Martha? Octavia? Or one of the servants? Sleep, of course, was now impossible.

I got out of bed and lit a small, shaded candle, then blew it out almost at once. I had the odd, inexplicable feeling that it was safer for me to remain in the dark.

I tiptoed to the window and parted the curtains. The bedroom was above the garden and I looked down at it now washed by bright moonlight, the sharp black shadows etched along the walk and under the arbor. As I gazed out into the night a thin plume of smoke rose from beyond the garden wall, and then a soft glow appeared as if a fire had been lit there. Fear returned, a different kind of fear this time, a fear of fire. Cage had told me that fire was one of San Francisco's great hazards, explaining how conflagrations had swept through the city during the '50s, reducing entire blocks to smoking rubble. Even now, after ordinances had been passed prohibiting the erection of wooden buildings, Cage maintained, fires were still common, still cause for alarm.

I opened the window and leaned out, watching the glow, but the fire, or whatever it was, seemed contained. Perhaps someone was burning rubbish, and although the hour seemed late for such a domestic chore, I could think of no other explanation.

It was a balmy night and very still. As I watched the rosy light beyond the garden wall I caught the faint sound of singing, a curious chanting to the tap of a drum. For a few moments I thought I had imagined it, but no—it was there, a rising, falling chorus of voices. It was hardly more than a murmur, like the ebb and flow of the sea on a far, distant shore. Song, prayer, hymn? I could not tell but it went on for some time. Then it stopped and a female voice began to speak. Though I strained to hear, her words were muted, indistinguishable at times from the little sporadic breezes whispering under the eaves.

I shivered. Goosepimples sprouted along my bare arms, but I did not close the window. There was something hypnotic about that voice, something compelling, frightening yet fascinating.

When she had finished the chanting began again, louder now, and as I listened it grew even louder, a hypnotizing, rhythmic, repetitious swelling of voices. Soon it began to take on an abandonment, a wildness, a pagan frenzy while the drums echoed through the dark night like a gigantic, throbbing heart. The savage cadence took hold of me, entered every pore of my body, sang and pulsed in my blood, beat in my heart and my brain. Then suddenly, as if a giant hand had swooped down in the moon-drenched night, the voices and the drum ceased and the red glow went out. There was nothing now but the silence, and gradually into that quiet vacuum crept the homely chirp of crickets and the humming of nocturnal insects.

In the morning I rose early, just as the sun was peeping over a gray horizon. Dressing quickly, I stole down the stairs into the garden. I wanted to see if those nighttime voices, the fiery glow, had been a dream or a fantasy of mine. In the harsh light of early morning it seemed so unreal, so improbable. The garden glistened with dew, the gentians, the late roses drooping damply as the first rays of the sun caught spun webs of droplets in delicate rainbow hues. I went past the arbor to the brick wall on the far side, the same wall which lay in direct view from my window. I was hoping to find a gate which led to the vacant, tree-bordered stretch beyond, the place where I had seen the fiery glow. Otherwise I would have to reach it by way of the road, in full public view, and a passerby, to say nothing of the servants, might think my actions a little strange.

To my surprise, I actually found a gate, a small wooden one, hidden by a clump of oleanders. The hinges squeaked as I went through. It was dark under the trees and the ground beneath my feet wet and slippery with fallen leaves. I had taken only a few steps when I came out into a small clearing shaped in a circle where the weeds had been trampled into the sandy soil as if by many feet. In the center of the clearing stood a flat rock and in front of it lay a heap of gray ashes. I went up to the heap. It had a queer odor, a stench like burnt chicken feathers, and indeed I noticed a few blackened feathers beside the pile. With the toe of my slipper I brushed some of the ashes aside. A tiny red ember winked up at me like a malevolent eye, and I shuddered.

It had been real, no dream, the chanting and the fire and the voice that had gone on in its hypnotic monotony. What was it? I stared at the heap of ashes, unable to pull my eyes away, and though the sun was shining brightly now, I seemed to be in a dark place, a place cold and frightening and full of evil.

Chapter 14

CAGE came home that forenoon in such a happy, exuberant mood I hated to spoil it with a gloomy, depressing account of beating drums and charred feathers.

"Adelaide—I'm going to be a rich man!" he cried, tossing his hat in the air. "A rich man!" He laughed, sweeping me up in his arms, kissing me.

"Oh, Cage, I'm so glad!" I loved to see him this way, his eyes sparkling, his face bright. Later, I promised myself, I would tell him all about it later, but for now I wanted to bask in the warmth of his happiness.

"Ralston—the tycoon, remember my mentioning him?" he asked. "Well, Ralston is setting up a new company, a silver mining company, and I am one of the few who's going to be allowed to buy in. Just think! Those silver kings are making millions, Adelaide, millions! They've branched out into real estate, banking, hotels, theaters, they're building mansions for themselves on Telegraph Hill, throwing their money around like rajahs. Money! Money is power, Adelaide, power! And my dear, thanks to your generosity . . . ," and here he bestowed a resounding kiss on my cheek, ". . . I'll soon be able to join them."

"Oh—Cage—how wonderful!"

His excitement was contagious. I did not know much about business affairs, but I remembered how chance investment by Barnabas had eventually brought me wealth, and I was sure it would do the same for Cage. Not that I cared a great deal for money, in itself, or for the life of a rajah, but I knew how important it was to Cage. He was an aristocrat, born to move in the best circles and although Tidewater society looked down their noses at business as crass and Yankee, the fact remained that in San Francisco the best circles were haloed with money. I knew that. Cage

176

had explained it all to me on our journey. "There's no such thing as genteel poverty there," he had told me. "You are poor, getting along, well off or wealthy. What you were before—rogue or prince—does not matter. The 'best' families got their start in the Gold Rush of '48. Sure I know San Francisco has many illustrious names from Virginia, the Hunters, Charles Fairfax, the Randolphs, Botts, but my dear, when they arrived they put their shoulders to the wheel, either in the mines or in banking or as lawyers. They made their financial success, climbed up to the top, just like anyone else. They're 'best' because they have grace, certainly, breeding, of course, but most of all because they have money. There's no claptrap in the new West, none of this leaving estates to the oldest son and letting the others go to the devil. Every man, if he's got any gumption, and just a little luck, has a good chance of becoming a millionaire."

Cage took my hand, led me into the dining room. "This calls for a drink!" He went to the sideboard and brought out the brandy. He looked at the bottle and shook his head. "No—not brandy, champagne. Martha . . . ! Martha!" he called.

She was there in the wink of an eye. "Do we have champagne? I've just made a business deal, a lucky one, and we want to celebrate."

"Yes—I believe we might have a bottle or two, Mr. Cage."

The champagne, not having been chilled, was warm; it tickled my nose.

"There's very little risk, Adelaide," Cage said. "In case you are worried about the money."

"I'm not worried," I said and smiled.

He returned my smile and it went to my head more than the champagne. "I'm glad I had it," I said.

"Here's to us," he said, lifting his glass, grinning at me over the rim.

"To us," I echoed. We drank.

"The good book says, 'Blessed are the poor'. That's a lot of hogwash, Adelaide. Pure hypocrisy invented by poverty-stricken parsons. There's nothing blessed about being poor, nothing blessed about hunger, about want, about ragged clothes."

I wondered if he had ever gone hungry or had ragged

clothes. Had he been that destitute when he lost his
money? But he would have sold the Folly surely. Still, as I
understood it, the house was mortgaged. Perhaps he had
suffered during the war, although he spoke little of his
Army experiences, and I had never pressed him. I had the
feeling that what had happened during those years was
painful, best forgotten.

"I'll buy you diamonds," he said, splashing more champagne into our glasses. "Diamonds and emeralds; do you
like emeralds?"

"I've never had any."

He laughed. "Tomorrow I want you to go into town and
order up a dozen gowns. Ball gowns, too. We are going to
entertain, Adelaide. We are going to have dinner parties
and galas such as this town has never seen."

"But Cage . . ." So soon, I thought. I wasn't prepared. I
would much rather have met his friends at small lunch-
eons, little intimate affairs such as we had given for the
Shelbys, guests two or four at a time. I was no good at
large gatherings among strangers. Barnabas and I had led
such a quiet life.

"We can afford it, I assure you," Cage went on, mistaking my hesitation. "Big parties are good investments, Adelaide. You have to put on a front for these people. Success
breeds success. And if I want to go into politics—which
has considerable appeal for me, I don't mind saying—then
I have to entertain. Well—what do you say, Adelaide? You
won't have to do much. Martha is very good at organizing
these socials."

"Of course," I said, wishing he hadn't brought in Martha's name. "It will be delightful. When would you like to
have your first dinner party?"

"A week from next Saturday night."

"Oh—Cage . . ."

"That should give you plenty of time. I'll write out a list
of guests and you can send the invitations. Martha will do
the rest."

He was very merry at lunch. "I've hired a carriage with
an option to buy. Well—my dear—we need transportation
and this is a modest one—later we shall get something
bigger. It is at your disposal whenever you like. For myself
I have purchased a hunter, a lovely brown thoroughbred.
She'll come tomorrow. She's a real beauty. Three years old,

lovely legs. Do you think you might want a riding horse, too?"

"For the City—I—I don't think so."

"We have plenty of room to keep them." The stables were situated in the back, well beyond the garden. Gandy, Lucinda and Doreen had rooms there. "Well—think about it. I want you to promise me you'll think about a lot of things, Adelaide. We don't want to get the reputation for penny pinching, do we?"

"No—of course not, Cage." He was like a small boy in a pie shop. An endearing, lovable, handsome boy. I had not been reared to admire ostentatious display, but if display is what he wanted, then I would spend, buy and dress outrageously, like a peacock even, in order to make him happy.

It was not until after lunch as we were sitting in the parlor at the side of the house (the room which had a partial view of the garden) that I suddenly remembered my night's eerie experience. Again I hesitated to tell Cage but after a few minutes of self debate decided he ought to know. With a frown between his eyes he listened to my story of voices, the beating drum and fire and of the feathers I had found in the morning. When I had finished he said:

"Adelaide—are you *sure?* Are you certain you did not imagine these things? Sometimes . . ."

"No, Cage, no. Come, I'll show you."

He was surprised at the gate in the wall. He had not known, he said, that it was there. "The workmen probably put it in," he said, "when they were building the house—for easier access."

I did not know why it would have been easier to come through the garden—surely nonexistent when the house was built?—than simply to come from the street, but I said nothing.

"The adjacent property belongs to me also," Cage explained as we went through the trees. "I bought it because I did not care to have close neighbors."

When we emerged into the clearing I stopped suddenly, so suddenly Cage bumped into me. The flat rock was gone! There were no ashes.

Cage brushed past me and walked into the center, looked around. "Adelaide . . . really, my dear, you must have dreamed the whole thing. I thought such a story was—what?—a little preposterous?"

I stared at the empty place, my hands twitching the sides of my skirt.

"Adelaide?"

"No," I said dully. "No—it was here—the ashes—the rock."

"But you can see for yourself there is not a sign of either—and a rock is not all that easy to remove."

"They were here," I repeated, chilled through, more afraid than I had been before. I had *seen* the rock, had touched the smoking ashes with the tip of my shoe.

"Adelaide . . . ," he sighed heavily, patiently. "My dear —I am not saying you are fabricating. Perhaps there was a fire here, some vagrant—Lord knows the City is full of them, disappointed, flat-out miners and such. One of them may have built a fire in this lot last night and cooked himself a stolen chicken."

"Perhaps." But what of the chanting, the singing, and the voice that went on and on? What of the beating drum and the wild, rising throb of its rhythm?

"Come—let's go back to the house. You're looking very pale, Adelaide. I do believe you haven't gotten over the effects of the journey, yet. That's all it is. Nerves." He took my arm.

"Nerves," I echoed, wanting to believe him. Hadn't I always been a rather fanciful person? Uneasy recurring dreams, that feeling of being watched, my obsessive anticipation of disasters that never came about, all were the products of an imaginative mind. And yet—I could have staked my small clutch of jewels against any odds that what I had seen and heard the previous night—and this morning—were real.

The following day I set out for the City on a shopping tour in the carriage, with Gandy as my driver. A small, wrinkled man, light skinned like Martha, Gandy had a slight limp when he walked. But he knew all about horses and looked very pleased and important as he sat on the box, waiting to hand me in. I had asked Cage if it would not be a good idea to invite Clara Shelby along as she knew all the best shops and places to go. But he said no, he preferred that I did not pursue a friendship with her. "She has a loose tongue," he said. "Besides Gandy is well acquainted with the mercantile section. He can take you anywhere you wish to go."

Gray clouds overhung the dun-colored hills as we clattered downward toward the sprawling city. Beyond the ragged waterfront the slate-gray bay was dotted with tall-masted ships, sails furled, the naked spars rocking slightly with the tide. A wind was blowing in from the sea, lifting dust and debris in little whirlwinds, sending ripples of sand shifting across the road. On either side the vegetation, what there was of it, trailing vines and clumps of scraggly chaparral, was covered with a film of fine, yellow sand. We passed few houses at first, wooden structures mostly, some of them no more than shanties with tar-paper roofs, and then we came to an entire section of elegant homes rising behind prim, iron-picket fences and built in a crescent facing a park. After that we were on the flatlands, the streets we traversed now covered with board planking and the horse's hooves rang out with a thumping, hollow sound.

The traffic grew heavier—carts, barouches, carriages, landaux, wagons and horsemen vying with each other for the right of way, plowing up dust where the planking had worn through. We had to detour in places as the streets were being repaired or torn up to make way for what I later learned was called, "Nicholson Pavement," a type of paving stone that unfortunately proved impermanent. Shops and store fronts became more numerous; wares were displayed out on the open sidewalk and hawkers called to the passersby. A mixture of foreign faces and colorful dress could be seen among the pedestrians, the same blend of humanity I had noted when we disembarked from our ship, the slant-eyed yellow men rubbing elbows with Yankees and dark-skinned Latins, slouch-hatted miners and dandies (gamblers, Gandy said) elegantly got up in black broadcloth and frilled white shirts. Most of the population seemed to consist of men, young men in their twenties or early thirties.

Gandy stopped the carriage in front of an emporium sporting a red and white striped awning. As he was helping me alight I saw Clara Shelby coming through the door.

"Mrs. Shelby . . . ! Clara!"

Her face lit up. "Well, I do declare—Adelaide! How nice! Have you come to do some shopping? Oh, but you said you would have me along when you did," she reminded with a wry face.

"I—I didn't want to inconvenience you." I could not repeat what Cage had told me. He did not want me to become an intimate friend of Clara's, but I saw no harm in spending a few hours with her. I was lonesome. San Francisco seemed so strange, so different, so unpolished. It had none of the gentility, the air of deep-rooted tradition and gracious living one encountered in a city, say like Richmond, a city whose streets one could stroll down feeling a sense of timelessness, of security, a city in which I felt at home. San Francisco was alien to me, and seeing Clara Shelby's familiar face in a sea of unknown ones was a welcome sight. After all Cage had not *forbidden* my speaking to her.

"Inconvenience? Nonsense!" Clara exclaimed. "I'm hard put to know what to do with my time. Are you looking for gowns?"

"Yes—Gandy seemed to think that this store . . ."

"Pooh! They have nothing here that will suit you. Really. Let me take you to the City of Paris, a beautiful establishment. Shall we go in your carriage or mine?"

"Oh—let's go in mine." It occurred to me that Gandy would be sure to report my meeting with Clara Shelby to Martha and from there it would go to Cage. But then I thought: what of it? I can't very well be rude to Clara.

"Do you mind if we stop at O'Conner and Moffat's to pick up some material and a pattern?" Clara asked when we had started out.

"Not at all."

As we were crossing Market Street, Clara pointed out the tramways, cars drawn by small locomotives known as steam dummies. "They're not very safe," she commented. "They are forever running out of control. Why just the other day one smashed into a carriage, killing a man and his wife. I understand the city fathers have ordered each car to be proceeded by a man on horseback ringing a bell. Oh, well, nothing beats the carriage. Speaking of carriages, is this hired? Or have you bought it?"

She talked all the way to Moffat's and never stopped for breath even when we finally got to the City of Paris. The store was in the heart of the mercantile section, large, imposing with an interesting facade. I must say I was impressed, especially with the merchandise. I had never seen such a beautiful assortment of laces and silks, bonnets, gowns, wines, liqueurs and perfumes. Oh—the delicious, delicate scents! At home I had not worn cologne or perfume—Papa had thought only cheap women did. But these were from Paris, and Clara assured me that society women would rather be caught without their gowns than without their Esprit de Paris or Rose Attare.

"You haven't been introduced to society yet, have you?" she went on. "Well—I shall tell you it's the Southerners who prospered in the Gold Rush who set the tone."

"So Cage has told me."

"Snobs most of them—though some lost all their money in the war—backed the wrong horse, you see, and their wives are taking in boarders now. You'd think the others, the ones who did well, would give them a hand—not on your life. Oh, well, it doesn't worry me. My husband is a Georgian—he's rich and so they speak to us, but barely, if you know what I mean."

"No—I don't, not really."

"You'll soon find out. Of course, you're Virginia, old family, too—and I understand you brought your husband a fine dowry. Stocks in some Northern company, was it?"

I colored. Cage must have said something to her husband and he probably repeated it to Clara. I wished that Cage had been more discreet. Even so this was not a subject I felt Clara ought to mention, much less discuss. A lady never did. For all her fine clothes and elegant taste I was beginning to see where Cage might be right. She had a loose tongue. She had no business talking about private matters, such as Octavia's parenthood, I now remembered, and certainly no business questioning me about my so-called "dowry."

"It's all right, you needn't answer," she continued. "I can see I've stepped on your toes. Forgive me—I do get carried away."

The ill feeling, the awkward few minutes were swept away when we began to look at the gowns. I tried several on and bought two, a day dress of dark blue figured muslin and a ball gown of pink, inset with yards and yards of foamy lace. "You can wear pink," Clara said, nodding in approval. "But perhaps a little touch of brighter color—something near the neckline?"

"No—I think it would clash, don't you?"

"Not at all. Your complexion is so pale, you need something to give you a . . ." She bit her lip, searching for the right word.

"A livelier look?"

"Oh, well, you said it, not me."

Our purchases made and packed into boxes, we followed the store clerk as he took them out to Gandy waiting on the street. An open landau stood next to our carriage. In it sat a woman decked out like a bird of paradise, fairly glittering in a green satin gown trimmed with row after row of mauve flounces. Set rakishly over hair so red it could not possibly have been real was a flamboyant green and mauve plumed hat.

"Who is *that*?" I whispered to Clara.

"My dear, her name is Ellen Sharpe. She is one of our more notorious ladies of the evening."

It took me some moments before I could digest what Clara meant by "lady of the evening," then I turned crimson.

"You mustn't take on," Clara said, an amused look in her brown eyes. "The City's full of them. Ellen happens to be one of the more exclusive—what shall I say?— courtesans. A senator is keeping her. It's the poor girls in the houses. . . ."

"Houses . . . ?"

"Brothels, my dear. You *are* naive. There are the brothels or boarding houses of varying degrees, then the cribs, tiny barred rooms where the meanest of them, the Chinese girls. . . ."

"I don't want to hear about it," I said, shocked. Along the James River women, gentlewomen, that is, never spoke even obliquely of brothels. Though we knew they existed in Richmond, especially during the war, not one of my friends ever let the soiled word pass her lips.

"Oh—all right, then. But I wonder . . ." She bit her lip, giving me a sidelong glance. "Never mind."

We got into the carriage and Gandy clucked to the horses. "Would it be all right if we stop at my dressmaker's?" Clara asked.

"Of course. Just tell Gandy where to go."

She leaned out the window and shouted, "Take us down

Kearney toward Pacific. I'll tell you when to stop." She turned to me. "Mrs. Taggard asked me to come in for a fitting this week and I thought you wouldn't mind since her place is close by."

"Certainly—I don't mind at all."

It was a scruffy neighborhood. The narrow streets were lined with two story wooden houses leaning against one another in woeful disrepair; steps sagging, paint peeling, and windows cracked or broken. The planked walks, littered with refuse, had gaping holes, while here and there a scrawny tree struggled up from a nettle-choked yard.

"Come in," Clara invited after she had instructed Gandy to stop before one of the houses. "I want you to meet Mrs. Taggard. She's really a dear. Perhaps you might order a dress, too. Frankly, I like hers much better than the ready-made."

The seamstress was a young woman, a plump little soul with three small children. She ushered us into her parlor scattered with scraps of material, spools of thread and numerous little poufs sprouting pins and needles. Clara's dress was not quite ready for a fitting, but if she would wait, Mrs. Taggard said, until she finished a seam or two and a few tucks Clara might try it on.

"Adelaide," Clara said, "why don't you go on? I can get a carriage at the for-hire around the corner to take me back. I might be here for hours."

"You're sure you'll be all right?" I was tired and I did want to get home. Cage would be waiting for me. "Well— if you don't mind, then."

When I emerged from the house, Gandy was not sitting on the box. I looked to the left and right, biting my lips. He was nowhere in sight. I supposed that he had grown restless and had taken a short stroll. Stepping into the carriage, I sank down on the cushions, resisting the temptation to remove my shoes. My feet ached unbearably—I was more spent than I had thought.

I waited patiently, waited as the minutes ticked by. The deserted street was submerged in a gray, late afternoon light making the dismal houses on either side appear even more dreary and cheerless. Their windows were shuttered like hooded eyes, unfriendly and sinister. Not a soul was visible, not another vehicle or horse, not even a stray mongrel dog. The air was so still; the dusty street and the houses coming to a point in the distance like a street in a pencil sketch. Only the twitching ears of the patient horses harnessed to the carriage gave any sign of life.

Presently a fog began to creep over the rooftops, sifting down like dirty smoke, curling in wisps above the ground. I pulled my shawl tightly about my shoulders and peered through the window. Where was Gandy?

I thought of getting out and going back into the house, but changed my mind when I realized that if Gandy came and found me gone, he might stroll off again. So I waited, getting angry, then anxious, then angry all over again.

The sky darkened, the fog grew more dense, wrapping itself around the carriage like a chill shroud. Even through the isinglass window I could smell it, dank, rotting with an iodine odor from the sea. Then suddenly I heard the faint sound of footsteps and as I listened they drew closer, a heavy, slow tread. Not Gandy's, for Gandy limped. These were steady, even steps, echoing hollowly upon the plank walk and there was something sinister about them as if the owner of those heavy boots knew that I was sitting in the carriage, a woman alone and helpless. What had Mrs. Taggard said?—I hadn't listened to her chatter as she and Clara conversed. But now I vaguely recalled she had mentioned something about the Barbary Coast being only a few short blocks away and spreading so that she might be forced to move. The Barbary Coast, a sinkhole she had called it, full of outlaws, thieves, cutthroats and low women. The Barbary Coast and Mrs. Taggard's front door now lost in the opaque fog.

The footsteps came on, not hurried, taking their time, weighted with menace, like the steps of a confident, stalking huntsman sure of his prey. I was seized with terror, the kind of terror that came to me in nightmares, the terror of watching eyes, of entrapment. And the fog continued to swirl, to shift, thicker and thicker, obscuring even the horses' heads, isolating me completely in a world of blinding mist. My heart was now hammering against my ribs, my throat was dry. I can't sit here and wait, I thought. God! I had my hand on the door handle when a man's figure loomed suddenly out of the swirling fog. I flung open the door, a scream poised in my throat.

The man stopped and the scream died.

"My! What a surprise! If it isn't Mrs. Cage Norwood," came a familiar voice.

And I found myself looking into the mocking eyes of Jay Cooke.

Chapter 15

H E was impeccably turned out in charcoal gray, the cape of his greatcoat thrown back to reveal a crimson lining. Sweeping the tall hat from his head he gave me a deep bow. "Mrs. Norwood—a pleasure!"

I could only stare at him, my hands clutching my shawl.

"Did I startle you?" he asked anxiously.

"Yes—yes." My heart was still hammering. "I was expecting Gandy, my coachman . . ."

"And not me, of course."

"I had no idea—this fog—he'd gone off and when I heard footsteps, I naturally thought it was . . ."

"Naturally. I am sorry if I frightened you."

"Only—only for the moment."

"Thank goodness for that. I would not cherish the role of bogey man." He was watching me, his lips curved in a small, wry smile.

"It—it was just such—such a surprise—seeing you here. . . ." I took a deep breath, forcing myself to meet his eyes calmly. He said nothing, apparently waiting for me to go on.

"How are you, Mr. Cooke?" I finally managed, relieved now that it was Jay Cooke rather than the beetle-browed villain I had fully expected to emerge out of the fog.

"Never better," he said, his white teeth showing in a broad smile. "And you, Mrs. Norwood? Has this marriage agreed with you? Oh, but I forget my manners. I never did congratulate you, did I?"

"No," I said, my relief suddenly tempered with discomfort, as I reminded myself that Jay Cooke could be prickly even in the role of gallant.

"In fact, if I recall, I made several unkind remarks."

"Yes."

"So I did. But you must forgive me. Put it down to the

envy of a rejected suitor, disguised as a wish for your happiness, of course. One is apt to say thoughtless things in such situations, and I'm sorry."

It was a graceful apology, spoiled however, by the taunting look in his eyes. He did not mean it, obviously, and I rose to the bait.

"I am sure if you had set your mind to it," I said tartly, no longer uncomfortable but annoyed, "you could have thought of something more appropriate."

"Perhaps. But you see I was speaking from the heart. The heart has a voice of its own, Mrs. Norwood, and the mind cannot *always* control what it says. Can it? You, of all people, should know that, you, a creature of impulse."

"Indeed! And am I to have one of your philosophical lectures now? If so, please spare me." The man had an insufferably long memory. I once thought we had left Virginia never to see him again. I might have known better. "What brings you to San Francisco?"

"Why—the same thing that brought Cage—money, or at least a good honest living. Besides, I consider San Francisco my home. Why do you ask? Curious?"

"To be perfectly frank, I don't really know why I asked. What you do or where you go matters little to me."

"How sad—I was hoping—but never mind. More to the point. Are you aware that this is a most disreputable neighborhood? Dangerous, in fact. I am surprised that Cage has allowed you to come to this section of town."

"Cage doesn't know," I said, ruffled. "I brought a friend to her seamstress—and would have been long gone had not my coachman disappeared."

"Unreliable, that coachman of yours. He must have gone down the block to the Golden Nugget. Did you say his name was Gandy? Hmmm—if it's the Gandy I know, then he's changed. He was a teetotaler in the old days."

Dusk had come and it was rapidly growing darker, although the fog had begun to thin somewhat. I peered down the street. "Is the Golden Nugget far?"

"Two streets away, but you aren't thinking of looking for Gandy, are you?"

"No, but . . ."

At this point the seamstress's twelve-year-old boy emerged from the house followed by Clara Shelby.

"Oh—Adelaide!" she exclaimed, "you're still here.

Thank goodness. I had no idea it was getting so late and Tom was about to fetch me a carriage, but now I'll go home with you. Thank you, Tom. But—oh, my dear," seeing Jay, "I didn't realize you had company."

"This is Mr. Cooke," I said. "A friend of my husband's."

"Oh yes, Mr. Cooke—I believe we met—some years ago." Clara dimpled up at him. "You have business in this neighborhood?"

"No. I was just passing when I noticed Mrs. Norwood stranded. It seems her coachman has deserted."

"Really? Well, that's the way servants behave these days." Clara fluttered her eyelashes coquettishly. "Shiftless, no feeling of responsibility."

"Unfortunately true—not only of servants but of others as well. Allow me to drive you ladies home."

"It won't be necessary," I put in quickly. "I think Mrs. Shelby and I can manage."

"In the dark? In the fog? And in this neighborhood? Don't be ridiculous. No, I insist. I left my horse tethered up the street. It won't take but a moment to get him."

He disappeared into the mist and Clara climbed up beside me. "I must say!" she sighed ecstatically as she peered out the back window. "What a handsome devil, isn't he? I never knew him too well, my husband did. I don't think Mr. Cooke and Cage Norwood were close friends, though they did go off together to fight the war, didn't they? Never married as far as I knew. Is he married now?"

"I didn't ask." Clara Shelby was not only a gossip but a flirt as well. Why should she care if Jay Cooke was married or not?

"Did he say what brought him to this part of town?" she inquired.

"No, he did not and I didn't bother to ask him."

"Well . . ." She let out her breath. "There are several of those fancy sporting houses in this section, you know what I mean—not the best ones. But all the same gentlemen of quality sometimes frequent the lesser houses, gentlemen who'd rather not be seen going in and out of such an establishment in the more fashionable part of town."

"Clara . . . ," I had great difficulty in keeping my voice level. "Don't you think you are jumping to conclusions about Mr. Cooke?" Why must she make such indecent insinuations? Fancy women, fancy houses. She certainly knew a great deal on the subject, more than a well-bred lady should.

"Well—think about it, Adelaide. He tethered his horse up the street—and then started to walk—doesn't that tell you something?"

"It tells me nothing at all," I answered coldly.

We heard the clip-clop of horse's hooves, and a moment later Jay Cooke's tall figure, leading his mount, appeared out of the gloom.

It was dark night now. The buggy swayed as Jay Cooke climbed into the seat. We saw his shadow bending over the carriage lamps, and then they bloomed into soft, fuzzy light, casting a yellow shine over the mist-dampened roadway.

"Jay Cooke," Clara mused as the carriage lurched forward. "Yes—I recall now, he and your brother had a falling out with Mr. Norwood when your husband got married —the first time, I mean, but I expect you know all about that."

"Yes." The curious thing was that at the mention of Cage's first marriage my annoyance with Clara vanished. I knew I should have been just as nettled with her reference to Cage's private life as I was to Mr. Cooke's, but the fact remained that I was involved with Cage and not with Jay Cooke, and Cage's continued silence about his past baffled me. Sitting there beside Clara as we rode through the darkness, I was tempted, as I had been when I had first met her, to throw my carefully nurtured decorum aside and confess that I knew nothing, to say that neither my brother, Jay Cooke nor my husband had told me a word. I wondered if she would be shocked to find me discarding good Tidewater manners as I nestled up to her and whispered, "I want to hear all about it. I want to know all about Lillith, everything, down to the tiniest detail." But again convention triumphed and the moment vanished. And I realized (as I had done before) that I would never have the courage to admit my ignorance, never have the courage to ask.

We continued to bowl along at a fairly good clip when suddenly the carriage halted with a jarring squeal of wheels, throwing Clara and me forward on our seats.

"What is it?" Clara cried. "What's happened?"

I opened the door. Jay Cooke had jumped down from

the seat and was bending over a man lying prone on the street.

"Someone's hurt," I said. "Or drunk."

Mr. Cooke was kneeling now, cradling the man's head. "Can I help?" I called.

Then I saw that it was Gandy with a gashed, bleeding head wound. "Can I help?" I repeated, moving closer.

"Unconscious," Jay said, trying to staunch the flow of blood. "He must have been hit from behind. Do you have a handkerchief? Mine's all sopped through."

I gave him my handkerchief, suppressing a shudder. "How did it happen? Why? A thief after his money?"

"Or the carriage."

"The carriage?" I said shocked. "But why, when we found him *here?* I don't understand."

"I did not want to say anything earlier for fear I might have been mistaken and alarmed you ladies over nothing. But there was what I thought looked like dried blood on the driver's seat of the carriage."

"Oh . . . !" The fog shifted and moved, a cold mist laying an icy hand on my face.

"Someone must have bludgeoned him while he was waiting for you, then carried him away, perhaps intending to return for the carriage, but was frightened off."

"It seems so . . ."

"Only a theory, we'll find out more when Gandy comes to."

Jay Cooke lifted the little man in his arms as if he weighed no more than a child. His head lolled forward, his face a ghastly blue in the reflection of the carriage lights. "I'll have to put him on the floor," Jay Cooke said. "It might not make a pleasant ride for him or for you ladies."

"I don't mind."

Clara, pulling her skirts in fastidiously so they would not touch Gandy, vowed that she would change to a seamstress who lived in a more desirable neighborhood. "To think— that I've been going there all these years, with goodness knows what dastards skulking about." We did not speak again until I bid her goodbye at her doorstep. From Clara's house it was but a short ride up the hill and to the Folly. By that time I was trembling so with fatigue and nerves I took Jay Cooke's offered arm gratefully as he helped me from the carriage.

Cage was not at home. I was relieved in one sense—I hated to think of him pacing the floor, wondering where I had been—but disappointed in another, I wanted him; I missed him. I could have done with some comforting, for I had realized on the long, rumbling journey back across town that if I had gone out a little earlier from the seamstress's house to the carriage I too might have suffered a blow like Gandy, or, as Clara darkly hinted, worse.

And Martha's reaction did nothing to soothe me. When Jay brought the still unconscious Gandy into the house, she turned a livid color and her eyes held a look that seemed suspiciously close to fear. Martha, unflappable Martha afraid? It was the first time I had seen a crack in her armor, and despite my own apprehension, I could not help but wonder. Did Gandy mean so much to her? Was this cold, frigid woman in love with the ugly creature? Not necessarily in love, even fond of? And why was she afraid?

"Shall I go fetch a doctor?" Jay Cooke asked.

"No, no," Martha protested. "I can doctor him better than any of them quacks, Mr. Cooke. Just bring him back to my room."

I asked her, "Is there anything I can do?"

"No—thank you." And she hurried off after Jay Cooke.

I was sitting in the drawing room, my hat and gloves still on, when Jay came back. "You mustn't worry about it," he said. "Gandy's already coming round. It's not as bad as I first thought and Martha is a great one for nursing, for herbs and simples. But in the future I wish you would remember that there are some sections of this city which even the hardiest dare not trespass. Gandy should have known that—but, of course, as a servant he would follow your orders."

I wanted to ask what had brought *him* to such a disreputable neighborhood, but instead I murmured, "I didn't know."

There was a long silence. "Adelaide . . ."

I lifted my head. He was gazing at me, his dark eyes luminous, softened with a gentleness that disturbed me even more than the mocking, jeering light I often saw there.

"Yes, Mr. Cooke, what is it?"

There was a slight pause. "Nothing," he said, finally,

buttoning his greatcoat. "I'd best be going. I'll come and pay a formal call on Cage later."

I did not want him to leave. It was strange, a man I disliked so—and yet I dreaded being alone even for a short while. "Whatever you say," I murmured, not knowing how to ask him to linger. "Oh—and thank you, thank you for bringing me home."

"It was my pleasure."

I listened to his boots echo hollowly as he crossed the hall; the door opened, then shut with a decisive click.

Twenty-eight guests had been invited to our dinner party, twenty-eight, the seating capacity of the large oak table in the dining room. Cage had wanted to ask more, but then we would have had to serve a buffet-style supper, and Cage wanted this first social affair to be a formal sit-down meal.

I, of course, had thought twenty-eight was far too many. Cage pooh-poohed me. "When I become a millionaire," he said, "I shall build us a real palace, an estate in Menlo Park or Millbrae and then our dining table will hold fifty, maybe more." The prospect appalled me. How could I ever be hostess to fifty when the notion of twenty-eight threw me into a quiver? Even writing out the invitations had tied me in knots, all those names to address, fourteen couples with blank faces, men and women, who, excepting for the Shelbys and Jay Cooke and *"friend,"* were strangers to me. "Dear Mr. and Mrs. Fairfax," I wrote in my best hand, "we should be honored to have . . . ," and I wondered if the Fairfaxes were rich snobs as Clara had said or nice folk, well bred, mannerly and kind, who happened to have a lot of money. Entertaining except for large casual barbecues and picnics had never been easy for me, even at home among the friends and neighbors with whom I had grown up. As a guest I had done tolerably well, but playing hostess in a formal setting had always put me in a state of nerves. Now here, in this alien city, the prospect of having to stand in the receiving line, even with Cage next to me, having to smile, to meet all those probing eyes and shake all those cold, limp hands was an ordeal I anticipated with dread.

If the preparations had not been taken so completely from me, perhaps I could have occupied my mind with various tasks, choosing a menu, ordering the wines, arranging the flowers and place cards. But everything had been left to Martha. She knew the guests, she knew who should sit next to whom, the precedence, the protocol. She had supervised dozens of dinner parties before my arrival at the Folly and was well acquainted with the little feuds, the likes and dislikes of Cage's wide circle of friends. Now that Gandy had recovered (he said he never saw the man who hit him and had nothing in his pockets for which he might have been robbed), she could devote all her energy to the coming event. I was merely to be the gracious, charming hostess, so Cage remarked, a statement which made me wince inwardly.

After I had sent the last invitation off by messenger, there was still nearly a week left until the dinner. The hours dragged. I wrote letters; I wrote to all my friends in the Tidewater, in Richmond. I wrote to people I had barely known. I read until my eyes ached. I walked in the garden. I had no wish to take the carriage and ride into town, besides Cage had given both Gandy and me such a scolding for allowing Clara Shelby to lead me "astray," I thought it best not to go anywhere for the time being. At home, at Beech Arbor or Green Springs I would have had callers. But here, in San Francisco, except for Clara, I had neither friends nor acquaintances. There was no one even to exchange a few words with; the servants were busy. Cage was gone all day and most evenings, and Octavia had left to visit a friend in Rose Valley.

One morning I decided to tour the house to see which rooms should be aired in the event that some of our guests might want to stop the night. But here, too, I found that Martha or Lucinda or both were ahead of me. Dust sheets had been removed from the furniture in four of the bedrooms, the huge, carved fourposters freshly made up with starched ruffled spreads, the bureaus, wardrobes and tables gleaming with wax polish, the lamps cleaned and provided with new wicks. Still I went on with my tour, walking the long corridor, peeking into room after room rather absently for I had nothing better to do. When I came to Lillith's bedroom, I hesitated a moment, then suddenly, on impulse, slipped through the door and closed it softly behind me.

I stood motionless for a few moments in the curtain-drawn dimness, feeling like a sneak thief or a trespasser on

forbidden territory. I remembered Cage's anger. He had
not liked my being in Lillith's room. He had thought it bad
taste.

I stared at the bed, the smooth satin cover, the carved
headboard, the cupids, the forget-me-nots and roses. Lush,
extravagant, sumptuous. I went across the deep-piled
soundless carpet and stood over the bed, my imagination
pulling me down forbidden paths. Cage had made love to
Lillith here, held her, kissed her, even as he did me. Perhaps with more passion? Perhaps murmuring over and over
into that black hair, *I love you*, the words that I so longed
to hear myself? Had she loved him, too? Had she lain here
at night and waited for the sound of his step on the stair,
for the rattle of the knob turning in his hand? Had she
smiled when she saw him, catching her breath, "Oh . . .
Cage?"

I bent over and touched the cover, running my finger
along the smooth, slippery satin. She was dead and no one
had told me how she had died. Young, Martha had said,
she died very young; but nothing else. Had it been in
childbirth, the mother and baby both succumbing? I
wished suddenly, fervently that I could have a child, Cage's.
It would be mine and his, Cage's and Adelaide's, something we had, just the two of us, a memory which Lillith
could not share.

I looked up and suddenly froze. The room, empty until
now, had been invaded by several people, women dressed
in brown muslin, each pale and wide-eyed. It took a moment before I realized that the women were all me, my
image reflected in the many mirrored wall. How serious
these other selves seemed. They did not appear to look with
approval upon this invasion of a dead woman's privacy. It
was not the sort of thing Adelaide Carleton of Green
Springs would do.

I ignored the mirrors and went across the floor to the
window and thrust the curtain aside. It was raining, gray,
dismal rain, splattering against the glass, slanting down
past the sodden trees into the the muddy street beyond
the gravel drive. The hills on the far horizon were somber
under the leaden sky, their glaucous dreariness stabbing me
like a pain. I leaned my head against the cold glass, trying
not to give into a sudden homesickness, trying not to think
of Beech Arbor or Green Springs in the rain, the way the

magnolia leaves glistened and the wet shrubbery gave out a fresh odor of damp earth and growing things. I must not remember the fallen petals of lilac, the roses, the mock orange or the dogwood dripping with moisture, the sound of rain in the gutters, the pitty-pat on the verandah roof. I must not think of it, I couldn't. I was Cage's wife now. My home was the Folly. I was happy here.

Yes—*yes*, very happy.

Sighing, I let the curtain fall in place. I turned back to the room, my eyes going to the opposite wall where I knew Lillith's portrait to be. I stared at the wall for a long time, my heart beating in a queer, erratic way. I had only that one brief glimpse before Cage had ordered me to close the curtain. Should I . . . ? A desire to see Lillith's face again, to study her picture at leisure took hold of me. Why not? a small voice whispered. What harm would it do? Who would know? Martha was preoccupied in the kitchen and Lucinda, once she tidied our room, never came upstairs. A quick look then, just one.

Swiftly I crossed to the pull, tugged at it, and the red portieres swished apart with a silky sound.

My heart dropped. Somehow, in some foolish way, I had hoped my first brief impression of Lillith had been in error, hoped against hope that people exaggerated her beauty. They had not. She was, in truth, the most beautiful creature I had ever seen. The black-lashed violet eyes were set in a face of incomparable symmetry, the nose, the mouth, the slightly high cheekbones, the perfect jaw all harmonized to make up the unblemished whole. The gown she wore revealed creamy white shoulders, the red rose lying against a lovely bosom. No man looking at her could help but love her. And once having her and loving her, could never forget.

What a wild presumption on my part to imagine I could take her place. How could I, pale and dowdy with my browns and grays, my sallow complexion and colorless hair, me, a wren, compete with this brilliant peacock? Tears filled my eyes, and I turned from the picture, only to find that the room had come to glowing life with a half dozen portraits of Lillith. She smiled out at me from the mirrored wall, the polished dressing table, the bureau, her violet gaze jeering at me, freezing my heart. I could smell her scent, the jasmine perfume, sweet and cloying; it lay along my nostrils, a reprimand, a reminder. Her lips were curved so seductively over teeth small and lovely as pearls. In a moment she would speak, her voice low and thrilling. *I am Lillith,* she would say, *and who are you?* Yes, who am I? The room was full of her, the bed, the dressing table with its flounced skirt, the blue ceiling with its cupids and the bed—ah, yes, the bed. I was the intruder here, a *voyeur*, a peeping Tom. *Do you believe in ghosts?* Martha had asked. And I felt the cold creep along my arms. Yes, Lillith's ghost was here, a palpable, haunting spirit. And she did not like me. I could feel that she was jealous, that she resented me. Her eyes seemed to have turned scornful, the smile malignant. I had taken Cage from her, no—more than that—I had come into her sanctuary, her boudoir, a place that Cage had not wanted to share with *me*. And she did not like my intrusion, she . . .

Suddenly I heard a door slam down below and my heart jumped. The multi-reflections of Lillith faded into the background as I strained to listen. Had Cage returned? How embarrassing if he should catch me here. What could I say? I turned quickly and just as I was about to pull the curtain I saw a white envelope lying on the floor at the foot of the portrait. I picked it up.

It was the letter I had written weeks ago to Charles.

Chapter 16

IT had never been mailed. I turned it over in my hand. There were several smudge marks surrounding the wax seal. Had the letter been opened, read? Anger made my hands tremble. I forgot about the room, about Lillith, about the possibility that Cage might even now be looking for me, might be coming up the stairs. How dared Gandy be so careless with a letter of mine, an important one, too, one which I was anxiously hoping would be answered?

I hurried out of the room and paused at the top of the stairs, looking down the stairwell. Gandy, not Cage as I had thought, was walking across the hall, carrying a box on his shoulders.

"Wait!" I shouted, "Gandy, wait!"

Descending the stairs, I suddenly realized that perhaps Gandy had never mailed any of the letters I had written here, that perhaps he had been instructed by Martha not to do so. The thought made my knees shake with fury.

"Gandy," I said, holding out the envelope, "I gave you orders to have this mailed two weeks ago—and I have just found it upstairs. Now, why was it not mailed? Why?"

He goggled at me and his dusky complexion seemed to pale.

"I'm waiting," I said, glowering at him, "I'm waiting for an explanation."

"I dunno—I guess I must—I mustah dropped it."

"Dropped it upstairs in one of the bedrooms?"

"I dunno," he repeated.

"I'd better talk to Martha," I said, sweeping past him.

Martha disclaimed all responsibility. "He's sometimes careless," she said, her face an impassive mask. "I sent him upstairs to move some furniture about two weeks ago and the letter must have fallen out of his pocket. Where did you find it?"

199

"In one of the bedrooms," I said. She did not have to know it was Lillith's. "How can I be sure Gandy's not done the same to my other mail? I've written to quite a few people since I have been here."

"Your letters went out," she said quickly, too quickly.

Perhaps they had, but I sensed that she lied about the letter in my hand. She must have met Charles when he and Cage were still close friends, when Cage was courting Lillith perhaps, and she must have guessed or read that my letter contained questions about Octavia's birth and had (for some reason that was a mystery to me) resented it. And yet I could not confront her with an accusation. She would deny it, of course. Then what?

She was still looking at me, almost defiantly now, waiting for me to make a move. But I could not. My wrath and indignation melted under those cold, stony eyes. She intimidated me. I hated her for it, hated myself.

"Hereafter," I said, "I shall either post my own letters or have Mr. Norwood do it."

"As you think best, Mrs. Norwood."

I did not tell Cage about Charles's letter. Perhaps I might have done so had the contents been different. In a sense I had gone behind Cage's back by making an inquiry on a private matter which, had I the courage, should have been directed toward my husband rather than my brother. What I did do, however, was suggest again that we hire another servant, an errand boy.

"Gandy has too much to do around here," I pointed out, "keeping shutters, plumbing, doors in repair, the garden tidy, doing all the heavy work. I think it is unfair to expect him to run small errands too."

"Well—if you like, then," Cage said with seeming reluctance. "Ask Martha."

"Martha? Oh, I wouldn't trouble her." Ask Martha? Not likely; she would have one more flunky of her own, one more ally or spy. "I'd just as soon do the hiring on my own."

"Martha might not like that."

I stared at him. It was on the tip of my tongue to say, Martha is your servant, I am your wife. "I'm sure she won't mind in the least," I said and smiled.

"All right. Do it, if that's your wish. Just be sure he is

discreet. I don't like to employ servants who blab our business all over town."

"I'll make very sure," I said.

Clara Shelby sent over her seamstress's father, McCorkle, a grizzled old miner down on his luck and crippled by rheumatism. He chewed tobacco incessantly, was rude, dirty and stank. But he was from Georgia, a Cracker, most likely bigoted and I felt there was little chance he would be hobnobbing with Martha and the others. I wanted someone I could trust, someone who would make sure my mail came and went properly, and perhaps provide me with a shield against Martha's ever watchful eye. He seemed glad enough to get the job, eight dollars a week, plus a room over the stable and all he could eat.

What I had not counted on, however, was McCorkle's overweening self-interest. I did not discover this until much later when I noticed him toadying up to Martha and forced the truth from him. He confessed that at the outset Martha had made it plain that it was she who ruled the kitchen, if not the house, and that if he wished to eat well and have a bit of whiskey into the bargain, it would be prudent to be friendly. By then I saw no point in dismissing him for I realized only too well that Martha could persuade anyone I hired in the same way.

In the meanwhile time spun itself slowly out toward the inevitable dinner party. Two days before the event, in a flurry of doubt and nerves, I had rattled down to the City of Paris in the carriage to buy another gown, convinced that the one I had purchased earlier would not suit. When I brought it home and tried it on in front of the mirror, turning slowly round and round, the smile faded from my lips and I realized with a sinking heart what I had always known. Though the dress was indeed lovely, no color, cut or style was going to change me into the beauty I so longed to be. I was still the same Adelaide; no miracle had been wrought. Who was it who said you cannot make a silk purse from a sow's ear? Aunt Tildy? Or was it Shakespeare?

It did not matter. I was stuck with my face, the long jaw, the brown, no-color hair. The figure was passable— but not the face. If only I could borrow one for the night, borrow Lillith's perhaps, the porcelain white skin, the bowed lips, the misty, violet eyes. Would Cage look on me differently then? Would there be a certain bright gleam in his eyes as he took me into his arms, holding me close, kissing me passionately, whispering over and over again, *I love you, Adelaide, I love you—only you.*

I took the dress off and had Lucinda press it before she put it away.

The evening of the dinner party finally arrived. All that day I had kept to my room, staying out of harm's way, listening to the clatter and hum of the preparations going on below. Martha had hired extra servants, trained waiters, in addition to porters, and I could hear the clatter and thump of chairs as the men brought them down from the attic above. After dinner we were to have a short musicale, nothing elaborate or too highbrow, Cage had said, but just enough entertainment to settle our stomachs. He had invited the singer Anna Bishop to perform. "She's world renowned," he had informed me. "Trills like a bird."

He had Gandy help him dress, and I wondered why he did not get a real valet, but supposed it was because of his general antipathy to servants. It was strange to me, this antipathy, especially in a man who seemed so extravagant in other respects. I was secretly buoyed up to note, however, that he seemed a little nervous himself; his brandy glass was never far from his hand, and when I heard the rumble of an early arriving carriage in the drive, I had to swallow the impulse to ask for a dram of brandy myself.

I don't think any Christian led to an arena of famished, growling lions could have been more terrified than I as I descended the stairs to meet our first guests. They were the Mr. and Mrs. Fairfax about whom I had been curious. He had a high forehead and bored expression; she had predatory eyes. I could feel them assessing me, looking me up and down, see the fleeting expression of astonishment, banished by a cloying, "My dear—how wonderful to meet you!" when they each in turn took my hand.

After the Fairfaxes there was a pause when nothing happened and no one came. Cage and I stood in the hall, waiting. Cage rubbed his gloved hands along the sides of his trousers. "I wonder if I have time to pop into the library for another drink," he said. We could hear Mr. and Mrs. Fairfax speaking in the drawing room. My uneasiness grew. What if the rest of the invitations have not been delivered, I thought. Should I have entrusted them to Mc-Corkle? What if we had to spend the rest of the evening with the Fairfax couple, all that food and wine, and the long table set with twenty-eight chairs, and Mrs. Fairfax's eyes looking at me all the time?

I was working myself into a panic when I heard the clatter and grinding of wheels in the drive. Then they were upon us, one couple following another. Faces, voices, laughter, a great crowd filling the hall and the drawing room beyond. Cage was easy with his guests, now, his nervousness gone, shaking each male hand, bowing over the ladies', passing them to me with a brief introduction. So many people I had never seen before, so many names to remember, my mind whirled in confusion. The Shelbys when they arrived seemed like old and reliable friends. I embraced Clara with a warmth that even surprised her. It was so good to see a familiar smile, a face I knew, a pair of eyes that did not look at me as if I were a freak in a side show.

Jay Cooke came with a Mrs. Landfer, a pretty, young woman who dimpled charmingly when she smiled. "You look very fetching tonight," Jay Cooke said as he took my hand and kissed it. I thanked him for the compliment, suddenly realizing that Cage had made no comment on my dress, on the way I looked. Too nervous, I told myself, he had been too nervous to notice.

At dinner Cage sat at the head of the table, I at the foot. On my right was Jay Cooke. Had Martha seated him there to be perverse? On my left was a Mr. Thillon, or Trillon, I couldn't remember, but his eyes kept straying to the low cut neck of my gown, keeping my face in a permanent flush.

Jay Cooke leaned over and said, "Don't let the old goat make you feel uncomfortable. After all he's only human, a man, and besides he's very drunk."

"He's a cad!" I whispered back fiercely.

"Most of the men at this table, despite their high society pretensions, are, you know."

"No, I didn't know."

I looked around. They all seemed to be having a good time, all dressed in faultless evening clothes. No one was as drunk as Mr. Thillon, no one was shouting or gesticulating rudely. The women, too, seemed well behaved. On Cage's right sat a blonde woman, not so very young, but beautiful nevertheless. She was dressed in black, a startling contrast to her light, yellow hair.

Jay Cooke bent his head. "I see you are looking at Mrs. Walters. The hair is dyed, my dear."

I thought that a crass thing to say, even if it were true. Now that I noticed, though, perhaps it was dyed. Cage was paying her an inordinate amount of attention, ignoring his other guests, his chin resting in his hand, whispering in her ear, while she smiled and fluttered her lashes.

I tried to look away, tried to ignore them, tried to speak to Jay Cooke, to fuss with the food on my plate, but my eyes kept coming back to them.

Mr. Thillon tapped my arm. "My dear," he said and hiccuped loudly. "My dear, are you curious about that woman?"

Jay Cooke said, "I'll have you hold your tongue, Thillon. This is a lady you are speaking to."

"Lady . . . ?" He looked at me, staring at my bosom again. I colored. "Forgive me, Lady Norwood," and he hiccuped once more.

A woman's musical laugh caught my attention. She was very pretty too.

"Who is that?" I asked Jay Cooke. I had been introduced to her, but her name and face, like the others, had run meaninglessly through my head.

"Anna Bishop, the singer."

"Oh—yes," I said, remembering, "and the man with her is Mr. Bishop."

"No," he said, "Sir Henry Bishop, Anna's husband, is still in England. The man she is with is Robert Nicolas Boscha, the French harpist."

"I see. He's to accompany her when she sings."

"I'm afraid you don't see. Mr. Boscha and Anna Bishop are living together as man and wife. They eloped a few years ago, Anna without bothering to divorce her spouse."

An adulteress and openly flaunting her paramour!

I looked down at my plate, my face crimson. I felt humiliated, shamed. Never, never would I have entertained such a woman at Beech Arbor. It would have been unheard of, unthinkable. Adulteresses were not received in the Tidewater; doors were closed to the Anna Bishops.

And here she was under my roof, by my invitation, chatting with my dinner guests. Had Cage known? "She trills like a bird," he said. Surely not Cage, a Norwood, the product of so much good breeding. Mrs. Bishop was a singer, an entertainer—he couldn't have known.

"My dear," Jay was saying, "don't look so put out. Half the women here—and a good many of the men—are no better than Anna Bishop."

"I don't believe it," I said resolutely.

"Mrs. Norwood," Jay Cooke said, his voice heavy with patience, "I'm surprised your husband hasn't given you a better understanding of society here in San Francisco."

"He has told me that quite a few old and respected families from Virginia are represented in the City."

"True—but that's only a small portion and many of them, I must admit, have kicked over the traces. This place is at the other end of a continent, a new city, and an exciting one in many ways. The past makes no claims. I'm not specifically condoning immoral behavior, but one must be broadminded and accepting. You can't be an ostrich with your head in the sand."

"I'm not an ostrich," I blazed, resenting his patronizing tone. "I am a mature, fully grown, intelligent . . ."

"You're a child, Mrs. Norwood, forgive me, a protected, naive child."

"I *beg* your pardon, Mr. Cooke, but . . ."

Suddenly Mr. Thillon hiccuped loudly in my ear. "Sh—she'sh his mistressh—that's who sh—she'sh. Mrs. Walters ish that—what'sh his name?—Cage—Cage Norwood'sh mistressh."

I glanced quickly at Jay Cooke. But, engaged in conversation with the woman on his right, he had not heard.

"I'm telling you," Mr. Thillon went on, leaning toward me, winking. "She—she'sh his mistressh. Don't believe me, d'you? Ask anyone, Mrs. Walters and Cage Norwood." And he sank back in his chair, his head nodding affirmatively.

Was he speaking the truth? Mrs. Walters, Cage's mistress? I couldn't look at her, I couldn't. Oh, God, God!

Anna Bishop—and now Mrs. Walters—Cage's mistress!

I don't know how I got through the rest of the meal. I suppose I said the right words in the right places for the most part, though sounds and voices seemed to be coming to me through a nightmarish, dreamlike trance. But every now and again I would jolt to awareness like a sleeper rudely awakened, conscious of someone looking at me in an odd, sly way. I remember one woman especially, a matron with carefully piled and curled, iron gray hair, whose stare I caught several times. "Aha!" her eyes seemed to say, "so this is the plain little heiress who bought herself a handsome husband."

I wanted to take her by the shoulders and shake that look from her eyes. I wanted to tell her that she was wrong, that I loved Cage, that he loved me, that money had nothing to do with our marriage. I wanted to shout it, to scream, to weep. But instead I sat like a wooden figure, a pain under my heart, a fixed smile on my lips. Every pretty face was a threat, an enemy. Had this one, the young thing with the chestnut hair, or that one, the supple-waisted girl with flaxen curls been Cage's mistresses also? Why were there so many beautiful women among his friends? And why was Cage so attentive to Mrs. Walters? Was there a *Mr.* Walters? Or was she living in sin, too?

Afterwards I remember sitting on a chair in the drawing room, one of those delicately carved chairs brought in earlier by the men. Behind me were rows and rows of the same kind of chairs filled with black-coated men and colorfully gowned women, all staring at my back. A man was seated at the piano and presently a woman dressed in green shot silk came out from behind the portiere. She was pretty, too. She began to sing. Anna Bishop, of course. She sang several songs in a sweet, melodious voice. "Lorena"? "Home Sweet Home"? The drinking song from *La Traviata*? I cannot recall. People applauded and she sang again. And all this time that terrible pain under my heart. "You look dreadful," Clara Shelby whispered in my ear. "Are you ill?"

I had the impulse to say yes, yes, I feel sick, I have this terrible headache and I must go upstairs or I shall faint. Perhaps I could manage to faint? I thought of the bed in my room, the cool white pillow, the comforter that could be drawn up over my head, shutting out the light, the noise, the babble of voices, the curious stares.

"No," I said. My disappearance would serve only to fuel further talk. People would say that I was ill-bred as well as plain. Or perhaps they would whisper, gathering in small corners, nodding their heads, smiling as they told one another how narrow-minded, how old-fashioned, how straitlaced I was. Everyone's husband had a mistress, and what if he did invite her to a dinner party?

"No," I repeated. "I'm all right."

"You look so white," Clara said.

"It's this color, the color of my gown. Blue never did suit me well."

Later on as we stood about while the waiter passed among us with trays of champagne and cakes, I glanced across the room and saw Cage in earnest conversation with Mrs. Walters. She was smiling up at him, her eyes blinking coyly. I drained my glass and took another. His mistress. A leaden weight seemed to be dragging me down. In another moment I would be shouting for help. I felt I had to talk to someone. I couldn't go on carrying this load, this awful compression squeezing my heart. There was always the hope that Thillon in his drunkenness had been mistaken; perhaps he had confused Cage with someone else. I had to ask. I couldn't wait. The evening would drag on forever. It was long past midnight now, and the drawing room and library still remained crowded with guests.

The champagne I had drunk wiped out my inhibition, my reticence. I went up to Clara Shelby. She would know if anyone did. "Clara," I said, "may I talk to you in private?"

We went into the library and I shut the door behind us. "Clara . . . ," I hesitated, biting my lip, "Clara—what do you know about Mrs. Walters?"

"Mrs. Walters? Why, she's supposed to be a very astute business woman," Clara replied. "She has money, made a great deal of it in real estate."

"What—what is her association with Cage?"

"My dear," she said, a look of compassion coming into her eyes. "Someone has been talking. And I thought *I* was a gossip. Really—it would be best . . ."

"She is his mistress, is she not?"

"No—no, of course not."

"She *was* his mistress, then?"

Clara said nothing, but her silence confirmed the truth. My eyes filled with hot, stinging tears and I turned my face away. I wanted so desperately to weep, but knew that I could not, must not make a spectacle of myself. Mrs. Walters had been Cage's mistress. That was the bald, unalterable fact and there was no way I could hide from it. None. His mistress. She had shared his bed, like Lillith, and Lillith had been his wife and I was jealous of her. But Lillith was dead. Her portrait might hang upon the wall, but it was only a picture, a memory. She was in her grave, gone forever. She could not sit at the table and smile up at Cage, could not flutter her eyelashes, move her shoulders coquettishly, laugh and talk and tease. She was dead, but Mrs. Walters was very much alive.

"My dear," Clara said in a soft voice, touching my arm. "You mustn't take on so. I'm sure Cage didn't realize that Fanny had been married to Mr. Walters, that she was who she was, else he never would have invited them."

So, there *was* a Mr. Walters, or was Clara trying to make it easy for me? Kind, sympathetic Clara, and I had thought her a shrew and a gossip.

"He was never wildly in love with her, she told me so herself," Clara went on.

"You knew her?" I said, hurt all over again. Somehow Clara knowing this Fanny seemed like a betrayal of friendship. How could any decent woman consort with a—a mistress?

"Slightly. She came into Cage's life at a time when he needed someone—after—after Lillith died. It didn't last very long."

Had they slept in the bed upstairs in Lillith's room, or in the one Cage and I now shared?

"You mustn't let it worry you," Clara repeated. "A man has—has needs, a real man, that is. You couldn't expect someone like Cage to live without—without female companionship."

"No," I said, my throat tight. I had always heard that Cage had women, affairs of the heart, but it had been rumor, vague talk, the kind that only succeeded in casting a romantic aura about an already dashing young man's head. And, too, I was never sure that these rumors had much truth in them, not even the one about Mrs. Corinne Hayley, the woman who had caused the duel. But now I saw it differently.

"There were others, were there not?" My voice broke in spite of myself.

Again her silence was like a confession.

"Who . . . ? How many?" It was an effort to speak, the lump in my throat had grown so enormously.

"Why do you torment yourself, Adelaide? What difference does it make? There is no one now. And he married *you*, it's *you* he loves."

But he had never said so, I wanted to cry, he's never said he loved me.

The last guest had gone, the Hunters had been ensconced in the green room, the Putnams in the gold. I was in my wrapper, sitting before the mirror, wearily unpinning my hair.

"I can't seem to undo my blasted cravat," Cage said, appearing at the door of the dressing room. "Give me a hand, darling, won't you?"

I got up and began to undo his cravat. My hands were trembling, but he did not seem to notice.

"Wonderful party," he said, weaving a little.

"Yes," I said, not looking at him.

"You were magnificent, darling."

I lifted my eyes, color flooding my face.

"Cage—I . . ."

"I couldn't have done without you. No really, Adelaide." He was smiling down at me.

"Cage . . ."

His arms went around me and he drew me to his chest, and for one split second my body stiffened. Then he was kissing me, his lips pressing mine, holding me close, kissing me again and again. A warm giddy joyfulness spread through my veins, my head spun, my heart raced. I kissed him back, feverishly, passionately, forgiving him everything, forgetting those other women. They did not matter. I loved him. Clara was right—he had married *me*.

Chapter 17

OCTAVIA came home from Rose Valley the following Saturday, looking miserable, her eyes bloodshot and puffy, her face white and strained. But when I asked if she were ill, if I could help, she flounced past me and up the stairs. A half minute later I heard the door of her room slam shut.

"What do you suppose happened?" I asked Martha. "I'm positive she's been crying."

We were both standing at the bottom of the stairs, gazing up. Martha had her hands on her hips, her mouth drawn in a tight line. "It's them snobs," she muttered between her teeth. "Them snobs. Someone's been talking 'bout her mother. I'd kill 'em if I could, kill 'em."

I was beginning to discover a few things about Martha, one was that she had a soft spot in her flinty heart for Octavia, the other that the depth of her anger could be gauged by her slipshod grammar and the way she clipped her consonants. Ordinarily, she was careful of her language, speaking precisely in a Yankee accent. She was angry now.

"Maybe I ought to go up?" I suggested.

"No," she said emphatically. "She don't want anyone when she's this way. No one 'cept me."

"Why? What could those people have said?"

"It ain't for me to tell you."

I wanted to shake her, and yet all I could bring myself to do was to give the limp argument, "But she's my step-daughter and it is my business. . . ."

"Ask Mr. Cage then," she replied shortly and began to ascend the stairs.

Cage was not all that easy to ask. First, there was my own reticence, secondly there was his. Except for that first night when he seemed overwhelmed by what he described as "memories," he never spoke of Lillith or the past. Thirdly, he was infrequently at home. Business, he told me, kept him in town. Sometimes it was two or three in the morning before I heard him coming up the stairs, sometimes he would send a note explaining that an important business meeting was detaining him overnight. I tried to understand, I reminded myself over and over that Cage was ambitious, he was a young man with a future. He wanted to go into politics, to be state senator, perhaps even governor of California, and I, as his wife, should be sympathetic and proud of his efforts.

And yet, pinned to the back of my mind was the picture of lovely Fanny Walters, our dinner guest and Cage's past mistress, as well as the nameless, faceless others. There was no denying—ever—that Cage Norwood was attractive to women, that they gathered about him as bees to a honeypot. The long, sleepless nights I spent wondering, worrying, telling myself *not* to wonder or worry. He had married me, hadn't he? But strange how reason, rationality, deserts one in the wee black hours before morning, how the imagination can run rampant, how little nasty rumors can play on reality and become so graphic. Suppose, I would say, suppose he is even now embracing some pretty young thing, a girl with white skin and large eyes, misty eyes or violet ones like Lillith's, kissing her, telling her, promising her outlandish things.

And then I would hear the bedroom door open, I would smell the whiskey, listen to his tiptoeing steps and let out my breath. He was home, I was safe. I had nothing to fear. He had come back, back to me. And when a few minutes later, he would slip into bed I would turn to him and he would take me in his arms, and I would forget, my mind wiped clean of all those miserable hours of waiting, of anticipating the worst, of morbid fancy. "Cage," I would say, and feeling his heart beating against mine, I would think what a fool I was, what a fool to worry.

Those nights soothed me, but sometimes in daylight, through the lonely hours my doubts, my anxieties would return. Octavia and I came no closer. At mealtimes I could feel her watching me covertly with half-shut eyes. There was no approaching her, no softening, no way I could break through that shield of animosity. I soon found that Martha was her champion, Martha her confidante, Martha her foster mother. The two of them shut me out so effectively, I felt more than ever like an unwelcome guest at the Folly, not its mistress.

Nor did the house itself grow on me as I had hoped it would. It remained, like Octavia, at arm's length. I tried to interest myself in the garden, planning new flower beds, new bushes, new trees. I even went so far as to have McCorkle spade up little designated plots. But it all came to nothing. I don't know why. The house was one I could never like. It was not so much its tastelessness, the rank, rococo decor and oversized furniture, but a feeling of hostility which seemed to emanate from the plush hangings and soft velvet sofas, a feeling that I did not belong, that I was not wanted. And those mirrors—everywhere—in the drawing room, dining room and side parlors, mirrors in the entry way, along the corridors, in the bedrooms, gilt framed, carved with cornucopias of fruit and entwined with giant acanthus leaves, polished glass reflecting, doubling, tripling all that it saw. Sometimes at dusk just before the wall sconces were lit, when ascending the stairs or suddenly opening the door of a room, I had the eerie, fleeting illusion (like Gandy) that Lillith's ghostly image had been there only a moment before, a phantom trapped for a split, blurred moment in the reflecting glass. Then a light would flare—a lamp wick bloom, and she would vanish.

I got so that I hesitated before going into an unlighted room, dreaded the shadowed staircase and long, dark hall. It was no use telling myself that my nerves were playing tricks on me, that my fancy was burgeoning into the absurd. No use telling Cage about it; he would only pat my hand and offer me brandy, his remedy for everything. As the days drew in I asked McCorkle to light the lamps, wall brackets and chandeliers well before twilight. He seemed surprised at my request but said nothing, only grunted an affirmative. I knew he would discuss it with Martha, guessed that she might smile at the news, perhaps laugh. But I did not care. If only I could resolve all my anxieties as practically, as simply as the curtains could close out the fog, how much easier my life at the Folly would be.

As the weeks wore on I decided the best remedy to combat my unrealistic fear was to fill my time with interests, social doings, charities and teas that would take me

away from the house. Clara Shelby, happy to have me
express a wish to meet her women friends, introduced me
to the Ladies' Needle Club, a sewing circle that made gar-
ments for the poor of San Francisco. The Club met twice a
month at the various homes of its members, "society" ladies, a mixture of young and old, some pretty, some plain,
all with money and prestigious names. Sitting in their company through a long afternoon I sometimes felt as if I were
back on the James River before the war, when there was
nothing to occupy our minds but petty scandal and the
latest in fashions. Several of the women urged me to volunteer my services at the Godspeed Mission Orphanage and I
fully intended to do so. But somehow I never got around to
it.

I knew they talked about me. Once arriving late at Mrs.
Fairfax's home, I had found the front door ajar and slipped
in without knocking. Hurriedly divesting myself of my
cloak and draping it over a chair, I crossed the hall to the
morning room. I had my hand on the door knob when I
heard my name.

". . . and to think that such a lady as Adelaide Carleton should follow in that creature's footsteps." It was Mrs.
Fairfax who was speaking.

I stood there very quietly, holding my breath, waiting to
hear the next words.

"Indeed," Clara Shelby said, "but Adelaide is such an
innocent. I don't believe she has an inkling of her husband's past, nor what happened, although she pretends to.
That dreadful scandal, you know. Oh—hadn't you heard,
Mrs. Hunter? Well, let me tell you . . ."

Before Clara could say more, the maid came into the
hall and threw me a curious glance. I hastily knocked on
the door, opened it and went in. "You're late!" came a
chorus of voices, and Clara Shelby looked very embarrassed.

How I longed to draw up a chair, lean forward with chin
in hand and say, "Come ladies, don't be shy. You can tell
me; what happened? What scandal?" But of course I did
not dare. I would have shocked them as well as myself.

After that my curiosity about Lillith grew stronger,
flourishing in the dark, secret corners of my mind like a
tree bearing forbidden fruit. I would look at Cage on the
rare occasions he was at home, giving him furtive glances

from under my lashes as we sat at either end of the long dining table or over brandy in the drawing room, trying to get up the courage to say, "Please tell me about Lillith." But I never did. Sometimes we had dinner guests, for Cage, a social animal, liked to be surrounded with people, and he would impulsively bring home business acquaintances, occasionally men he scarcely knew. Their wives would often come, too. One evening a couple named Hayes dined with us, and after the meal when Mrs. Hayes and I left the men to their cigars and brandy and had gone into the drawing room, she said to me, "Well, I see that the Folly is looking as grand as ever."

She was a woman in her early forties with a fresh country complexion and vivid blue eyes.

"You have been here before?" I asked.

"Once—some years ago. That was when the first . . ." She paused, turning a little pink, giving me a quick, embarrassed look. But I nodded reassuringly and graciously, casually, my heart beating fast, supplied:

"The first Mrs. Norwood?"

"Yes, I came to a large ball she and Mr. Norwood gave. It was quite an affair. A hundred people, perhaps more. Two orchestras had been hired. She loved to dance, you know."

"So I've been told," I murmured.

"She had a lovely rose-colored gown, one she ordered especially from Paris. She looked very beautiful, very happy that night. One would never guess . . ." She stopped, and I who had been hanging on her words with a breathless impatience could scarcely contain the urge to shout— *go on, go on!*

". . . under the circumstances it was inevitable," she continued, "sooner or later . . ."

And then Martha came into the room and asked, "Shall I serve the coffee now?", and the subject was not brought up again.

Charles's long awaited letter finally arrived. McCorkle brought it to me one afternoon as I was sitting in the small parlor reading an article in the *Alta Californian*, one of the more reliable San Francisco papers, a story about a colored woman, Mammy Pleasant, who had brought suit against the street car company charging that they had prevented her from riding in their vehicles. I thought it rather bold of the woman and wondered if Martha was following the story, too. It would be just the sort of situation to pique her interest.

When the letter came, however, I tossed the paper aside and then tore the envelope open with shaking, excited fingers. It was a short letter, cold, disappointing.

"My dear Adelaide," Charles wrote. "I was much surprised at your inquiry. I would have surmised that your husband had acquainted you with his domestic circumstances in a truthful manner before he married you. I firmly believe it was his duty to do so. It certainly is not mine, and I have no intention of writing about his former wife and the child, Octavia. I was once told that they were none of my affair, and truer words were never spoken. I do hope you are in good health. Yours ever, Charles."

The paper trembled in my hands. If Charles had slapped me across the face, I would not have felt more rebuked. I thought him hard. He could have refused to tell me—that was his right—but in far kinder words certainly. He was angry, that was plain, and I wondered if he and Cage had quarreled over Cage's marriage to Lillith. Why? "You are making a mistake," he had said to me. If he had believed that, why hadn't he given me some explanation?

I reread the letter again, then folded it and put it back in the envelope. The envelope was dirty, smudged with fingerprints from the many hands which had touched it, McCorkles too, no doubt. But there was something else. I held the envelope up giving it a searching look. It seemed as if the seal had been broken twice, once by me, and once before, the wax rather skillfully resealed.

I rang for McCorkle but no one came, a not unusual occurrence in an understaffed house. Still, it irritated me. I went out the door, crossed the hall, and down the back hall to the kitchen. Martha was there alone. "Where's McCorkle?" I demanded.

"He's gone out. Has he done something?"

"He certainly has. He's opened my mail. He's . . ." Then I suddenly remembered; McCorkle could not read.

Martha was watching me as if she had guessed what I was thinking. No, McCorkle had not opened my letter, *she* had. I was too angry to be intimidated.

"It was you," I said. "You. And you've done this be-fore."

"I don't know what you are talking about, Mrs. Nor-wood," she said smoothly.

It galled me, that voice, those calm, stony eyes. "You have been opening my mail—oh, not all of it, only a letter here and there."

"Why should I do that, Mrs. Norwood?"

"You know the answer better than I." She was trying to fluster me; I had to keep reminding myself that she was a servant, nothing more. "But I can guess that you wish to prevent me from obtaining certain information."

"What information, Mrs. Norwood?"

She had me there, skewered to convention, to my rigid upbringing which considered inquiries concerning illegiti-macy bad form. And because she had gauged me so neatly, my anger rose, flooding my face with red hot indignation.

"You don't like me, do you, Martha?" I said, forcing myself to look straight into her eyes.

"No, Mrs. Norwood," she replied calmly. "No, I can't say that I like you."

"And you don't like Mr. Cage either, do you? You ac-cept his money, his food, his shelter, but you don't like him. Well—answer me!"

"He's Octavia's father . . ."

"Stepfather."

"He's Octavia's father and I would never do a thing against him. But that don't mean I have to like him."

"But why? Why do you stay?"

"For Octavia. I stay for Miss Lillith's daughter, and I'll do my best to see that she grows into a fine young lady and marries well like I promised her mama."

"But you don't relish Mr. Cage."

"No, Mrs. Norwood," she said.

"I think you are very uppity. You don't know your place, and if I had my way I'd send you packing."

Her eyes flickered dangerously. "But you don't have your way, Mrs. Norwood. You don't know nothing 'bout me." Her speech, as it always did in anger, became harsh and faulty in grammar. ". . . so don't go throwing those grand Southern words 'round. Uppity! You want to know why I don't like Mr. Cage? He's a Southerner, that's why, a white man and a Southerner and I have good reason to hate his kind. I am not the black ignorant nigger you think I am. I am a quadroon, but God knows I ain't proud of my white blood. I can tell you that to your face 'cause I don't care what you think. I ain't afraid of you. Yes, I'm a quadroon. My father was a plantation owner's son, a white man. He took my mother and used her and when he got married to a white lady aristocrat he left Mama sitting in a little room in New Orleans—I was four years old, but I remember, I still remember how she cried. She was very pretty, my mama. She had smooth skin like velvet, a light, light color and such a pretty nose." Martha's throat worked and I saw that her hands were clutching the sides of her skirt.

"I don't see what that has to do with me." Her emotional outburst embarrassed me. "I really don't . . ."

"You'll see," she interrupted venomously. "Just listen at me, Mrs. Norwood. Listen to what someone else got to say. My white father didn't leave us much money, and when that was gone my mama took up with another man, a white man, too. He was the first of many, so many I can't remember. I couldn't count if I tried. They came and they went, white men, every one. Some of them beat her— they all treated her like dirt. She was nothing. She was a nigger, no matter how pretty she was, no matter she was freed, they still thought her a piece of property. You look surprised; ain't you had slaves?"

"Yes, but . . ."

"Yes, but they was all happy, ain't that it? They all just loved being owned like cattle, ain't that it?"

I didn't know what to say. I had never thought of our Negroes like that before. I had always taken them for granted. Even during the war I had assumed they were content, that our bitter quarrel with the North had only confused and frightened them.

"Now, just how happy would you be if someone owned you lock, stock and barrel—like a mule or a dog?"

"We never mistreated . . ."

"That ain't the point. But what's the use of arguin'? I'll tell you what happen to me. Do you want to hear?" And when I did not answer she went on. "You don't want to hear, but I'll tell you anyway. I'm tellin' you so's you'll understand a few things 'bout me. My mama died when I was still small, she died and I was taken in by a Yankee minister and his wife—as a servant, mind you, a servant without pay. Just my room and board—and I had to keep my place, but the minister's wife did teach me how to read and write, how to figure and how to speak proper. She liked to show me off as her little heathen." Martha's lips twisted wryly.

"I ran away," she continued, "I couldn't stand her well-meaning, double-faced Christian airs. I came to San Francisco. I worked as cook, washerwoman, scrubwoman, every mean, dirty, low-down job you can think of. Then I met Miss Lillith. She was so beautiful. I had never seen anyone so beautiful. At first I thought she would make me my good fortune. But then I got so fond of her, like a daughter she was to me, the only person who ever treated me as if I was a real human being. When she got married, she brought me here to the Folly, and I saved all my earnings, every penny. I made a couple of smart investments, too. I'd get tips from Mr. Cage's friends; I made money. And . . ." She stopped here and gave me a long look.

"Well, I can't see no harm in telling you now. I'm kinda proud of it. I took my money and gave it to the Underground."

I was shocked. The Underground was a notorious network funded by do-gooder Yankees to induce and assist simpleminded darkies into running away from their owners all over the South.

"Yes—I gave every cent I could to the Underground. I never forgot my own people, never forgot them and if I had had the power, I'd have brought out every single slave."

"But that—that was criminal, they were . . ."

"Property?"

Mr. Benton had once called them chattels, which had infuriated Papa. Mr. Benton said that it was wrong for one human to own another and Papa said he talked like a preacher. I hadn't thought much about it at the time, but now . . .

"Property, yes," Martha said scornfully. "You can't see it any other way, can you? Neither could Mr. Cage. You don't know what pleasure it gave me to sit here in the kitchen with my friends and plan to rescue—yes, we called it rescue—a half dozen more slaves from such and such a place while Mr. Cage sat in the parlor plotting with his cronies to take over California for the Confederate cause." She laughed. "Didn't do too well, did he?" And she laughed again, a cold mirthless laugh.

The laugh angered me. It made me forget all about wanting to see her side of the argument. "You have the gall to tell me this? What makes you think you are so—so invulnerable? What makes you think I cannot dismiss you?"

"You can't. Mr. Cage could, maybe. Why don't you ask him?"

"I most certainly will."

Until then I had been hesitant when speaking to Cage about Martha, all stops and starts, searching for the right, tactful words. Not any longer. Her revelation and my own anger had loosened my tongue. Fortunately, my outrage did not have time to cool down as Cage came home for the noon meal, something he rarely did. The minute I heard his voice in the hall, I hurried down the stairs.

"I want to speak to you in private," I said, as he shrugged out of his coat.

"If it is unpleasant I'd rather not hear until after I've eaten, Adelaide."

"It won't take long," I said. I couldn't wait; a meal under Martha's cold, watching eyes might weaken my resolve.

After Cage had shut the library door behind us, he went immediately to the cabinet and got the whiskey bottle out. "A drink?" he asked.

"No—no thank you. Cage—it's about Martha. She's impertinent, if not brazen, to put it mildly. However, it's more than that." I went on to tell him how she had bragged of her part in the nefarious Underground.

He listened, his lips pursed in a small, soundless whistle. When I had finished, he said, "So that's what the renegade was up to. I wondered why our kitchen was always so full of darkies."

He did not seem in the least ruffled and his reaction annoyed me. "She still has them in—I've seen them come and go. Not only that, but she's insolent, the way she speaks to me."

"She has got a tart tongue. But I'm used to it, Adelaide. And you will be, too, in time." He drained his glass.

"Cage—she used you, she used this house for scheming against you."

"Hmmm," he said, holding his empty glass up to the light. "I suppose you could say that she did."

His attitude continued to baffle me. "But Cage . . ." There was a pleading note in my voice which somehow had slipped in against my will. I wanted to appear determined, strong, insistent, but the interview was not going the way I had planned.

"Adelaide, my dear, Martha is a competent housekeeper, she's the envy of all my friends and acquaintances. Why, if you could hear them complain about slovenly, lazy, devious servants—*and* insolent, too, my God, insolent!—you'd appreciate Martha and forgive her her little peccadillos."

Peccadillos! She undermined all that he stood for and had sneered at him for allowing himself to be hoodwinked. And he called it "peccadillo"! How could he?

"But—but Cage, does having a competent servant mean more to you than harboring an enemy?"

"Adelaide, Adelaide," he said reprovingly, "you do have a flair for dramatics. Enemy, indeed! The war is over, my dear. Long since. We can't go on fighting it for the rest of our lives, like those poor fools in the Tidewater are doing. We're the new age, the new era. The past is the past; why drag it along with us like a heavy ball and chain?"

Was he right? Was I making much ado about something that did not matter when viewed in the larger scheme of things? Was I being petty, narrow-minded, even bigoted, in contrast to his generosity, his capacity to forgive and forget?

"Perhaps if she were anyone else . . . ," I began. If she were anyone else I think I may have been able to sign a truce, to meet her halfway. But she wasn't anyone else; she was Martha. And curiously enough, I suddenly realized that my dislike of her had little to do with the color of her skin. Martha was a coldhearted, embittered woman who made no effort to disguise her antipathy toward me. How could I explain? How could I describe her hatred, my fear of her, to Cage? How could I tell him of the eerie feeling that so often overcame me when I was alone, the feeling that Martha stood somewhere in the shadows watching me?

"Martha is a fixture here," Cage was saying. "Why, the

Folly would not be home without her. Octavia is attached to her, loves her so dearly. Come, sweetheart," he put his arm about me and bent to kiss me lightly on the top of my head. "Learn to get along with her, be patient. All right?" And when I did not answer, he kissed me again, "What do you say, sweet?"

"All right," I agreed, smiling wanly.

But it wasn't all right, and the smile I gave Cage hid the bitter knowledge of defeat. Martha had won another battle.

Chapter 18

OCTAVIA celebrated her sixteenth birthday that winter and we gave a ball in her honor. One hundred guests were invited, all her young friends along with Cage's friends and acquaintances, too. It was a gala affair, written up in the papers as the event of the season. Octavia had a dress especially ordered from Paris, white satin pulled back over a bustle on which wreaths of flowers and cascades of violet lace were sewn. Her lovely figure, the flat abdomen and narrow waist, the swelling bosom, were all outlined daringly. A proud Cage presented her with a real pearl necklace, and I gave her the earbobs to match. She was so happy, so dazzled with the gifts—things she had wanted for ages!—I thought for one moment, from the way she smiled and her eyes sparkled, she would overcome her coolness and kiss me as she had Cage. Instead she said, "Thank you, Adelaide, thank you." Her voice, however, was warm, warmer than it had ever been, and I began to hope that perhaps we might yet become friends.

The ballroom that evening was transformed into a splendid sight, ablaze in lights and thronged with bejeweled, fashionably gowned women and faultlessly attired men. Quantities of champagne were served, and an orchestra played waltz after waltz interspersed now and then with a Virginia reel for the benefit of those Southern guests who still retained their nostalgic memories of home. Jay Cooke came, escorting a Miss Sennell this time, a young thing hardly older than Octavia with a pert nose and saucy eyes. She wore a daringly low-cut dress and a golden, heart-shaped locket which dangled provocatively between her breasts. She smiled a lot.

"Where did you meet her?" I asked as Jay Cooke led me through the glides and dips of the Hunter's Waltz.

"I don't think you would really like to know. In fact, I

am sure you would not. I assure you she is not from one of our 'society' families."

"I see," I said and looked over at her. She was dancing with Cage. "Are you going to marry her?"

"Heavens, no!"

"She's very attractive," I said, watching as Cage suddenly grinned down at her. He was holding her very close.

"She is—and has half a dozen beaux, none, I might add, who are anxious to marry her."

"Why not?"

"I don't really think she is the kind of girl one marries."

"Oh." I looked at her slyly and saw Cage bend his head and lay his cheek against hers for a moment.

A knifelike pain shot through me. The music turned sour, the lights dimmed, the brightness went out of the evening. So pretty and so young.

"If—if you will excuse me, Mr. Cooke?" I said in a muffled, miserable voice, releasing his hand, "but I must see to the refreshments."

"But the dance isn't over," he protested.

"Please . . ."

He led me to the refreshment table. "Adelaide, you mustn't . . ."

"Please." My throat felt thick. "Please. Why don't you go and dance with your lady? She might feel neglected."

I started to help myself to salmon aspic, oysters, salad and rolls, heaping my plate high with food I had no intention of eating. But I had to do something and I did not want to look at the dancers.

Jay was still standing behind me. "Why do we torment ourselves, I wonder?" Jay Cooke said over my shoulder in a low voice. "Why do we always strive for what we can't have?"

"I don't know what you mean," I said coldly.

"I'm speaking of love, Adelaide. A much maligned and misunderstood emotion. Why do people always want to love someone who doesn't love them? Such a waste, don't you agree?"

"Mr. Cooke . . ."

"A waste. All that repressed agony when it would be so much simpler for two people to meet and to fall in love mutually, satisfyingly, happily. But it rarely seems to happen that way. When I look around I sometimes wonder how a man and a woman ever get together on equal terms at all. It seems that one always loves the other much more."

"Mr. Cooke . . ."

"Why do you do it, Adelaide? Why do you punish yourself?"

"Go away—*please* go away."

He went. I heard him go. I didn't want to think of what he said. Those words made me hate him. I didn't want to think of why they hurt, of why I hated him. I loved Cage, and Jay Cooke was trying to destroy that love, he was trying—but I would not let him.

I took my plate and crossed over to one of the alcoves along the side of the ballroom. It was furnished like the others with high chairs, back to back and low rosewood tables. I sank down on the cushion gratefully and began to toy with my food. I had not been there but a few minutes when I suddenly heard a young girl's voice behind me. "Sit here for a moment, Arthur. I'm famished and my feet are killing me."

Arthur said, "Mine, too. What marvelous food, eh?" There was the scrape of cutlery on china.

"It ought to be," the girl said. "Oysters and lobster and all that champagne to wash it down. She's very rich, you know."

"Oh—is she?"

"Yes. Well, you don't have to wonder about that. Have you taken a good look? Plain as a shovel. And Mr. Norwood—such a handsome Lochinvar!"

"They say Octavia's mother was very beautiful."

"Yes, but you know what they say, don't you? Why, I've heard . . ."

The girl's voice stopped abruptly, and I looked up to see a matronly woman in black rustling taffeta balancing a heaped plate and a glass of punch. "Is the chair next to you occupied?" she asked politely.

"No, no it isn't. Won't you sit down?" Despite her heavy bosom, plump solid arms and double chin, she had the face of a girl. I did not remember her. There had been too many new people that night to recall everyone, and thinking she would feel offended if I confessed my ignorance and asked her name, I said nothing.

"Such a beautiful party," she sighed. "I'm so glad we did not miss it. I must be sure to thank the hostess."

So we had not met then. But again shyness held my tongue.

"We came late," she explained, a forkful of aspic poised in her hand, "so I did not get the chance to meet Mrs. Norwood. They say she's rather cold, snobbish, doesn't say much—comes from one of those old Virginia families."

"Oh," I said, turning pink.

"Has gobs of money, not much to look at." She chewed thoughtfully for a moment. "And the daughter—they're giving this bash for. My Lord! What's the world coming to, I wonder? You know," and she lowered her voice in a confidential manner, "she's not legitimate. S'truth! She was born before he and first wife were married. S'truth! He adopted her, made it all legal, said the girl wasn't his—but I wonder—well, it takes all kinds, doesn't it?"

"Yes, doesn't it," I repeated, my voice harsh in my ears. *All kinds.* I got to my feet with an effort. "Excuse me?"

He . . . made it all legal, said the girl wasn't his. Plain as a shovel—married her for her money. Cage, oh Cage!

The crowded ballroom swam before my eyes, crystal chandeliers rainbowed, the dancers swirled. I began to thread my way around it, holding my plate like an offering until a passing waiter took it. The music droned on in my ears, another waltz. They were all the same, the same tempo, the same tune, the same fiddles scraping and squealing and sobbing, the dancers sweeping and dipping and twirling like mechanical toy dolls. And the voices, the shrill laughter. "Plain—plain as a shovel—plainnnnnn." A man's face above a white shirt front and white cravat suddenly obscured my vision. "Nice party, Mrs. Norwood."

"Yes, isn't?" brightly, almost feverishly.

I didn't care, I hated them all. They were gossips, hypocrites, parasites, gorging themselves with food, their mouths dripping venom. "She's rich, haven't you heard, he married her . . . the daughter's a bastard, yes, says it isn't his. . . ."

I despised them. I never wanted to see any of them again. My one desperate wish now was to get away, somewhere far, a place that was dark and cool, where I could lick my wounds and cry in peace. I came to the stairway and somehow stumbled my way down to the second story.

"Adelaide . . . !"

It was Jay Cooke. I did not want to see him. I did not

want to see anyone. I hurried faster, but he caught up with me in the corridor.

"What is it? I saw you leave and thought . . . What is it?"

"Nothing," I said and turned away.

He took hold of my arm. "There's something wrong, I can tell."

"No," I said, keeping my face averted. "There's nothing wrong. Please, let me go. I wanted to tidy my hair, that's all."

"Your hair is all right. You're crying."

"I am not." But the tears were running down my cheeks.

"Take my handkerchief."

I shook my head no. But he pressed it into my hand, and I buried my face in its white folds. He was still holding my arm but with less pressure, and I had the terrible urge to turn and hide my face in his shirtfront, even though I disliked him so. I would have wanted to do the same with the devil himself had he been standing there, so keen was my misery.

"Can't you tell me what it is?" he asked gently.

"I—it's just everything." My voice came out muffled and broken.

"They—the gossips have been at it, have they?"

I nodded.

"I'm surprised at you," he said after a moment. "I'm surprised at your taking on just because a couple of fat geese have been thoughtless enough to gabble. Why—they aren't worth a second thought, much less tears. You ought to know that."

"Well—yes, but . . . ." I looked up at him with smarting eyes and tear-streaked cheeks. "Do you think I'm plain?" I asked like a wistful child.

"Certainly not," he replied without hesitation. "You have a special beauty, different, but beautiful all the same."

I searched his eyes for the familiar mocking gleam. But his look was sober, direct. Nor did he show any sign of pity, something I would have hated as much as his amusement. Still I did not quite believe him.

"You are saying that to be kind."

"Why should I be kind? To you—of all people. You rejected me, if you remember, and I have not forgiven you." He grinned.

I sighed, feeling easier.

"Come now, Adelaide, there must have been something else that was said to upset you so. What is it?"

I bit my lip and frowned. "Mr. Cooke—is it true that Octavia is Cage's daughter?"

"I thought he told you. . . ."

"He told me that he had adopted her. That's all."

"Yes, he adopted her. She is not his daughter, however. Take my word for it."

"But her father . . ." I protested.

"He's dead."

"Clara Shelby says he died when Octavia was ten years old. Please, Mr. Cooke, I want to know—and don't, don't lie. I want to know the truth—not to wonder when people are whispering. Was she—is she illegitimate?"

"Yes," Jay Cooke said.

"Oh," I said. "Poor child." I suddenly recalled how she had come back from Rose Valley with reddened eyes. People were so cruel. "Then her mother was not a widow?"

"No," Jay Cooke said.

"You don't like talking about it."

"I think it's up to Cage to tell you, if he wants you to know."

"That's what Charles wrote." And when Jay Cooke said nothing, I went on. "You must think me terribly petty, terribly mean-minded and shallow, like the other gossips. But I can't help it. I can't help wondering about those years Cage was away, about the first Mrs. Norwood, it's only natural. She was so beautiful and people keep comparing me. . . ."

"If they compare you, you can rest easy, you are at a distinct advantage."

"You are only saying that to pacify me. Why should I be at an advantage? What was she like? What . . . ?"

"Adelaide, you are not going to worm more information from me. Why don't you let it alone? Sometimes it is better to forget the past."

"And you think I shall be hurt if I know."

He made no comment.

"It's all so very mysterious. It makes me wonder all the more."

"Adelaide, please don't wheedle."

I drew in my breath.

"You keep harping on it."

"I'm not harping!" I cried, knowing that I was angry because he had put a name to it. "I'm sorry I said a word to you." I threw his handkerchief at him. "I should have known. No—let go of my arm—let go!"

"As you wish." He withdrew his hand. "If you want to know about your husband's past, ask him. Ask him, why don't you? If he loves you, he'll be honest, make a clean breast of it. A husband should have no secrets from his wife."

"Be quiet!" How unerringly he could find the sensitive mark and sink the shaft in.

"Adelaide . . ."

"I don't want to listen!" I turned and flounced off down the corridor. I could feel his eyes still upon me as I flung open the door of my room.

"And I wouldn't hide in there if I were you," I heard him call. "They'll talk all the more."

I slammed the door shut, too angry to cry. Standing there with my back to the panel, my heart tripping madly, I thought, I don't want to see him again. I shan't return to the ballroom. I shan't. But gradually my anger cooled, and I began to think more sensibly. Jay Cooke had been right in one respect, if no other. If I stayed away, they would all be whispering that I had quarreled with my husband or that I was a bigger snob than they had supposed. "My dear, she ran off in the middle of the party," I could hear the broad-bosomed woman saying. "Why do you suppose she did that?" Bored, someone would answer. "She's a highbrow and bored." But someone else, the young girl, perhaps, who had spoken to Arthur would chime in, "No, I think she was jealous. She is terribly jealous, I hear, and when she saw her husband dancing with that pretty Miss Sennell. . . ."

Jealous. I clenched my fists so tightly the nails dug into the flesh. The sound of my breathing seemed to fill the room. I stood there for another few minutes perhaps, then I went to the dressing table and sat down in front of the mirror. My reflection was there but it might have been that of a stranger. Mechanically I smoothed my hair back, pinning a stray curl into place. I pinched my cheeks to bring a little color into them and bit my lips. Then I got up and went out of the room and back down the long corridor.

When I returned to the ballroom, the same waltz was playing. No one seemed to have noticed my absence. Cage was talking to a group of men at the refreshment table, and Octavia was waltzing with a young, red-headed man. She looked very happy.

It was dawn before the last guest departed. We were both very tired and Cage was drunk. He had sent Gandy to bed hours before so I helped him off with his coat. He sat down heavily on the chair, and I knelt to remove his shoes.

"I enjoy those parties so much, don't you, Adelaide?" he asked, hiccupping loudly.

"Yes," I said, "very much. Octavia was pleased."

"I think so. All this will be hers some day unless you produce an heir."

"I should like nothing better, Cage."

"Good." He yawned loudly. "Good old Adelaide."

The shoe fell from my hands and I started on the other, frowning over the lace, trying to screw up my nerve. "Cage—Cage, I wanted to ask—I wanted to ask—I wondered . . ."

I looked up. He was fast asleep, his head sunk on his chest.

We had a visitor in early March, Ted Neale, my step-grandnephew, grown into a handsome blond lad of eighteen. He had come West, he said, to "better his prospects," having ("to put it bluntly, Aunt Adelaide") none at home. His father, Henry, had sold off a good portion of Beech Arbor in two different lots and on this reduced acreage had decided to concentrate on the breeding of thoroughbreds. "Not much future for me there," Ted added ruefully.

We told him he was welcome to stay at the Folly for as long as he liked. The first night he met Octavia I could tell by the expression on his face and the way his eyes followed her every move that the poor lad was smitten. Octavia, however, treated him with studied coolness, nor did she deviate from her air of irritating remoteness in the days that followed.

"She hardly speaks to me," he complained bitterly one evening when we were alone. "And if I ask her out to the theatre or supper, she says, no. Yet she will go with that Hunter person, a moron by the looks of him."

"She doesn't care for Hunter either," I assured him. "But she must have someone escort her to parties and sociables —and she has known him for some time."

"He's rich, I suppose that's it."

"Yes, he's rich but I don't think she cares so much for his money as for the fact that he's older. She seems to like older men."

"He's going bald," he said morosely.

"And you are so handsome." I chucked him playfully under the chin. "Cheer up—there are other girls."

"Not like her."

As the weeks progressed and his suit continued to meet Octavia's chilly resistance, he grew more and more unhappy. In the meanwhile, however, Cage had introduced Ted to Mr. Ralston who had found employment for him in his Bank of California. Ted seemed to like his work, although I often wondered how he could concentrate on it with Octavia so constantly on his mind. He moped about in the evenings, grumbling about her, never going anywhere. Sometimes late at night I could hear him pacing the floor of his room, and my heart went out to him. I knew only too well how it felt to be so young, so untried, so full of ideals, so vulnerable to hurt and rejection and so much in love with someone who did not care.

Finally he came to Cage and me after supper one evening and told us that he was moving downtown to Klabber's boarding house. "I can't stay under the same roof with Octavia," he said after we pressed him for the reason. "It's too uncomfortable."

He left a vacuum. Though gone at business for most of the day, he had always been home in the evenings, and I missed him, especially when Cage stayed over in the City. No matter how glum his mood, I could always manage to coerce Ted into reminiscing about Beech Arbor, and I had enjoyed those talks as well as his companionship.

After Ted left I began to have a recurring nightmare, a frightening dream of someone secretly watching me in a mist-shrouded forest. In this dream I heard a drum beating like the one which had echoed through the moonlit night when I had first come to the Folly. It was always the same;

SHADOWS OF THE HEART 231

a slow, steady tap at the beginning, and then as the dream progressed, it grew louder and louder and still louder until the sound became a wild throbbing in my brain.

I would wake shivering and clammy with sweat, lying so terribly afraid in the dark, for always these dreams seemed to come when Cage had elected to spend the night in the City. Thank God I did not have them often for they left me exhausted and moody all the next day.

It was at this time, too, that I noticed Octavia went out a good deal alone. She took the buggy (which we had acquired in addition to the carriage) almost every afternoon, returning late for supper, sometimes not until eight or nine o'clock. In the past she had always been in the company of friends who came to fetch her, so I did not think it strange when she said she felt she ought to reciprocate and provide transportation for these same friends. Her excursions, rides in the park, shopping tours, seemed harmless enough, but when Louella Fairfax stopped by one afternoon to inquire whether Octavia was ill, I knew something was wrong.

"I haven't seen her in weeks," Louella said. "And neither have any of the other girls."

Martha, when she heard this, was as stunned as I.

That night when Octavia came home I cornered her. "Your father will be very dismayed to hear that you are going about in the City unaccompanied."

"Tish Carpenter and I have been stopping at her dressmaker's," she said.

"That's not so," I said. "I know for a fact that none of your friends have seen you these past few weeks."

"Who said that? Tish?"

"No, Louella Fairfax."

Her face got very red. "I don't know why she would tell you such a thing."

"Possibly because it's true. What have you been doing?"

And when she remained silent, I continued. "I would prefer not speaking to your father about this."

Again she said nothing.

"You haven't been seeing some boy, someone whom you can't bring to the house, have you?"

"No!" she shouted at me. "No! And you've no right to question me, do you hear? No right!" Bursting into tears she got to her feet and ran out of the dining room.

I went after her. "Octavia—Octavia, please . . ."

She was running up the stairs. I followed, "Octavia, if there is anything . . ."

She reached the landing and began running down the corridor. When she got to her mother's bedroom, she flung the door open, then slammed it shut behind her.

I reached the door a few moments later, certain that she had locked it. But when I turned the knob, it gave easily. I went in. "Octavia . . . ?"

There was no answer. The room was pitch-black. "Octavia . . . ? Please come out, I want to talk to you. I understand."

No answer again. I groped my way blindly to the mantel and felt for the matches. Fumbling with the box, I extracted one and scraped it on the brick hearth. By its flame I found a large candelabra and lit several of the candles. The flickering light threw an eerie, reflective glimmer around the room.

"Octavia?"

I didn't see her. The portieres were closed. She was hiding. "Octavia, please don't be so foolish."

I drew every curtain apart. "Will you come out?" I asked the dim, bending shadows, "Octavia, if we could talk . . ."

I looked beneath the bed, in the wardrobes, in the alcove which held the washstand, behind the curtains again. Octavia was gone. She was not in the room. She had vanished, an act as impossible as it was terrifying.

Chapter 19

I stood in the center of the room, a motionless figure, my white face multiplied in the dimly lit mirrors on either side. The winking candlelight made grotesque shadows across the bed and carpet and upon the walls beyond. I was alone, undeniably alone.

"Octavia . . . ?" The shadows swallowed the sound of my husky voice. "Octavia . . . ?"

Was I losing my mind?

Octavia had come into this room just moments before. I had seen her with my own eyes. I could have sworn it—and yet. . . . I forced myself across the carpet and stared up at the portrait of Lillith.

There was nowhere to hide, nowhere.

The room had but a single door, the one I had come through myself. The only other egress was by way of the windows, two stories above the ground. Where had Octavia disappeared to? Perhaps I had not seen her enter, perhaps I had imagined it, perhaps she had not come into this room at all.

But she had, she had.

My mouth felt dry, and I could hear the sound of my beating heart, the sound of my breath drawing in and out. Nothing else, just that pulse and my heavy breathing.

"Octavia . . . ?" The hoarse whisper was mocked by my stricken image in the silvery mirrors.

Behind me one of the candles sputtered and winked out, and the light became a fraction dimmer. The smell of melting wax and the faint odor of jasmine drifted across the room on a gauzy plume of smoke. Lillith looked out at me with her misty eyes, a small cruel smile curving her red lips. *I know*, she seemed to say, *I know*.

What? What did she know?

She was dead. She could not hurt me. But Octavia was

her daughter, and *she* could. Nonsense, I told myself. But where was she? I turned slowly, fearfully until I had made a full circle. Had she gone up the chimney? Too small. Disappeared, vanished like the smoke which had been there a moment before and was now dissipated. Where? Where?

"Octavia . . . ?" my voice close to panic now.

Suddenly a small bodiless chuckle answered me, and every hair on my head seemed to stand straight up.

"Octavia . . . ?"

Again the chuckle. It had come from behind the wall, from behind one of the mirrors. I stood frozen, encased in ice, my hand pressed to my cold lips. After a long, long moment I brought myself to move and with a wildly beating heart went up to the mirror, trying not to look at my pale face, the frightened, hollowed eyes. I touched the frame, my fingers going over the cupids and the fat, golden apples. One of the apples moved under my touch. I grasped and turned it, and slowly, slowly, the mirror swung inward on creaking hinges. Beyond me yawned a black void.

From somewhere in that blind hole came the sound of faint, receding footsteps. Relief washed over me, leaving me limp. I wasn't mad, I hadn't imagined Octavia's disappearance. She had simply slipped behind a mirrored door into a secret passage. Why the passage was there, exactly what it meant, were questions that would trouble me later, but for now I was curious, and angry, too. Octavia had played a terrifying trick on me, and she was not going to get away with it.

Taking a single lighted candle from the candelabra, I crossed the threshold and entered the passageway. I had a few moments of hesitation, for the candle gave but little light, and the blackness beyond the reach of its feeble beam was absolute. The air had a stuffy odor, too, suffocating like a long, unused cellar.

Swallowing hard, I bunched my skirts in one hand and with the other held the candle high. The passage was narrow and ran past me on either side. About two feet from where I stood I noticed a small wooden hinge and a wooden bolt on the wall at what would be a man's medium height. Going to it, I discovered that the bolt fastened a little door. When I opened it and stood on tiptoe, peering through, I found myself looking into the bedroom I had just left.

A spy hole! Here, in Lillith's bedroom, of all places! Why? What was the purpose of it? I bolted the little door again and began to walk along the passage, my eyes straining to see if I could find other such openings.

I hadn't far to look. They were there at spaced intervals, the same spy holes cleverly cut into the wall. With all the ornately gilded carving, all the pictures, wall hangings and mirrors on the other side, detection would be nigh impossible unless one were acquainted with the presence of the spy holes in the first place. No wonder I had often felt I was being watched. But by whom? If Octavia knew about the passage, then it followed that Martha did, too. Was Cage aware of it? He must be, I thought, he must be. He was proud of the fact that he himself had helped design the Folly, that he himself had overseen the building of it. Under such circumstances how could a secret passage possibly have escaped his notice?

But there was more. As I slowly progressed along the narrow corridor, I came upon a staircase leading down. The steps, I noticed, like the passage floor itself, were not dusty. Someone had lately walked up and down these stairs, not once, but many times, in bare feet perhaps, for I could not recall hearing the sounds of footsteps, though I had heard the creaking of boards and rustling noises which I had attributed to mice. At the bottom of the stairs the passage again ran along the house and here, as above, were the little peephole doors, one for the library and one for the dining room. Neat, clever little doors for snooping.

When I thought of the evenings I had sat in either room, a chill creeping up my back, feeling that hidden eyes were observing me closely, telling myself that it was all my imagination, I grew hot and cold by turns. Someone had been watching me, a live, flesh and blood person and that someone, I strongly suspected, had been Martha.

I followed the passage to the end, finding a small wooden door. It was unlocked. When I opened it, I found myself standing behind a trellis entwined with a tangle of ivy which faced the brick wall of the garden. Anyone who knew about the door and the passage could come and go at will without being seen from the house, since the entrance was so well concealed. The thought that entry to our house could be made in such a secret, sly fashion disturbed me.

I said nothing to Martha, keeping my find to myself until Cage came home. Nor did I have the opportunity to confront Octavia. She had gone out, Martha said. Towards suppertime a boy arrived, carrying a note. It was the same twelve-year-old boy riding the same decrepit old mule Cage always sent with his messages when he planned to spend the night in the City. Of all nights, I thought, my heart sinking, when I needed so much to talk to him.

The table was set for one that evening. "Octavia is staying with the Hunters until tomorrow," Martha said, setting my meal before me.

"She might have had the courtesy to tell me herself."

"She asked me to give you the message."

"I see."

Nothing more was said. If Martha had any inkling I had followed Octavia through the mirrored door into the secret passage, she gave no sign. Octavia herself may have been unaware of it.

"More wine, Mrs. Norwood?"

It was always "Mrs. Norwood," never "Miss Adelaide," a formality which carried a slight sting, but I never had the courage to ask her to address me more familiarly.

"No, thank you, one glass is enough."

The following afternoon I was drawing on my gloves in the hall as I waited for Gandy to bring the carriage around when I heard voices raised in the kitchen. Since the servants never quarreled, at least not audibly, for Martha's tight authority would not permit it, I raised my head in surprise. It was not the servants, but Octavia and Martha who were having words.

"I'll do as I please!" Octavia shouted.

"You lie to me once more and I'll give you the back of my hand. You ain't going to do as you please, hear me? And shut that door, I don't want the whole house listening."

The door slammed shut, but I could hear them still going at it hammer and tongs. I wondered then if Octavia had lied to Martha, if she had really spent the night at the Hunters as she had said. That girl was bound for trouble, deep trouble, and I felt that it was my responsibility to stop her, and I could not do it alone. I needed help.

When Gandy came with the carriage, instead of instructing him to take me to the City of Paris as planned, I asked him to drive me to the Bank of California where Cage now had a small office from which he conducted his business affairs. I never went to see him during hours for he had once criticized Shelby for allowing Clara to disturb him whenever she had the notion. But I felt this was something that could not wait. The secret staircase had been there for a long time, and we could discuss that at our leisure, but not Octavia. It was imperative that she be prevented from committing some indiscretion which might damage her reputation.

Once at the bank I had the doorman announce me to Cage, and a minute later he came out himself, arms extended, a smile on his face.

"What a pleasant surprise, Adelaide!" His genuine pleasure brought a flush of happiness to my cheeks. Oh, why couldn't life be simple, I thought, why did irksome jealousies and little worries have to intrude?

"Cage—I hate to disturb you . . ."

"Not at all. Come in—come into my sanctuary." He took my arm and led me into his little office.

Seated at his desk I said, "It's about Octavia." He listened, his eyes turning grim as I described her erratic hours, the quarrel between her and Martha that morning.

"Do you think she's seeing someone?" he asked when I had finished.

"If so, it is someone she obviously cannot bring to the house."

"Drat! Martha's always been able to control her. I wonder now she can't. Octavia's been spoiled, she's gotten completely out of hand. But I shall soon put a stop to that," he added resolutely. "I'll pack her off to a convent school."

"Isn't she a little old for that?"

"I don't know. But the threat itself might bring her to heel." He tapped his fingers on the desk. I noticed then that he looked very tired; he had lost his healthy color, and there were bruised circles under his eyes.

"You need more rest," I said, stretching out my hand, squeezing his. "You look all done in."

He gave me a wan smile. "When I've made my first

million and am on the way to the second, I'll take a long rest. But you—this isn't very much fun for you, is it?"

"Oh, Cage, I don't mind, not really," I said, basking in his concern, forgetting the long, lonely hours during which I had waited for him. "By the way—did you know there's a secret passage and staircase at the Folly?" I asked lightly, thinking how amusing it was in retrospect.

"What? Passage? Oh, *that!* The passage. Of course. It had completely slipped my mind." He smiled. "It was a whim of mine." And when I gave him a questioning look, he went on, a little embarrassed. "Well, no, not entirely, more than whim perhaps. You see, the Folly was built some years before the war, but even then we sensed it coming, sensed that North and South were drawing up sides. A group of Southerners, myself included, decided to meet secretly for the purpose of making sure that California came in with the Confederacy. Later we were to form the organization known as the Knights of the Golden Circle, but at that time some of the men, for business reasons, did not want to be seen attending what they felt were 'suspect' meetings. So I had the architect put in the passage."

"Oh," I said. "And the peepholes?"

"What peepholes?"

"Didn't you know they were there? There are peepholes looking out into half the bedrooms and the dining room as well as the library."

"Are you sure?" he asked, shocked.

"I saw them yesterday."

"I had no idea," he murmured. "None." His eyes were strangely troubled, not angry as I had expected, but perplexed and troubled.

"I hope you won't think it spiteful or fractious of me, but I have the strong feeling that Martha's been spying on us." I said.

"Martha?" He frowned. "So—that's how . . . ," he broke off.

"That's how what?" I asked when he did not go on.

He balled his hand into a fist and slid it across the desk top, angry now. "She has no right to spy, none at all! I'll—I'll have it out with her—I'll . . ."

"Cage—I have no proof, of course—it's only a feeling, but . . ."

"I wouldn't put it past her, not at all, not at all. Let me handle it, Adelaide. I'll take care of the whole mess, Octavia and Martha both—don't fret about it." He gave me a taut smile, then lifted my hand and kissed it. "Need money?" reaching for his wallet, extracting several large bills with hands that had a slight tremor. "Go out and buy yourself a new gown, a new bonnet. I don't want you to worry your head about any of these domestic matters."

"Cage . . ."

"I'll be home for supper tonight. I promise. There's a dear."

Seated in the carriage as Gandy and I rumbled down the dusty street, I felt somewhat bewildered, if not a little annoyed. I wondered why Cage had said nothing about dismissing Martha. "I'll have it out with her," were his words. Out with her, for spying! Why, anyone else would have sent her away without a moment's hesitation. Was it possible that Cage was afraid of Martha? It seemed so preposterous, and yet why hadn't he vowed to dismiss her? Did Martha have some hold over Cage? What? His housekeeper, his own servant? It was a mystery to me.

I don't know what Cage said to Martha or she to him, but when Octavia was confronted, she created a terrible scene. No sooner had Cage forbidden her to leave the house without one of us accompanying her than she went into hysterics, throwing herself on the floor, screaming that she would kill herself, run away, set fire to the house; commit any number of wild depravities. Cage went very white, and for a few moments I thought he would relent or go to pieces himself. I did not dare interfere; she had hurled insult after insult at me already, accusing me of being a Judas, a tattle and a wicked stepmother all in one breath. I could do nothing but stand by, watching her kick her heels and pound with her fists on the carpet, feeling just as helpless as Cage.

It was Martha who finally took control of the situation. She came striding into the library from the kitchen where she had been listening to Octavia's caterwauling and lifted the struggling girl to her feet. Before Octavia could let out another howl, Martha smacked her hard across the face. Octavia gasped, her mouth fell open, and her hand went to her cheek. Then she began to sob brokenly.

"You are all as mean as the devil," she wept, while Martha stood by. "Mean—*mean!*"

"Who have you been seeing?" Cage demanded.

"I—I'm not seeing any—anyone," she sobbed. "And even if I were—you could torture—kill me and I wouldn't tell. I *hate* you all! Hate you! Hate you!"

Her outrageous behavior shocked me. Never, in my most emotional moments, would I have dared speak to my elders thus. And poor Cage—he looked so distraught and ill.

He tried again to find out whom Octavia had been meeting, but she stubbornly claimed over and over again there was no one.

Finally in desperation he simply left her in the library, going up the stairs to our room. I followed him. "She has got to leave," he said. "I can't see any other way but to send her to school."

After some thought he decided on a school in Marysville, an academy for "select young ladies" run by the Convent of Notre Dame. He did not have the nerve to tell her himself, so he called Martha in the next morning and asked her to do it for him. A few minutes after Martha had gone from our room, we could hear Octavia screaming down the hall, and then she came bursting through the door. She accused Cage of trying to get rid of her, of being a monster, a hypocrite who did not believe in religion but was willing to sacrifice her to the nuns in order to save his own soul. "You don't even go to church at Christmas," she hurled at him.

Pale, with bloodless lips, he shouted at her, "Shut up! I hate scenes, I've had enough, and if you don't shut up . . . !" And he ran from the room. I found him later in the library, an opened brandy bottle and a glass at his elbow as he sat slumped in a chair.

"I don't know why I put up with her, I really don't know," he muttered when I tried to comfort him.

The following week Octavia went off to the school, with the promise that if she behaved she could come home at Easter and stay.

Two days later Cage left also. He and Mr. Ralston were going to Virginia City on a business matter. I had asked, rather shyly, to go along, but Cage had pointed out that it was not a pleasure trip. They would travel as quickly as possible by boat and on horseback, sleeping in whatever accommodations they could find on the way. They would be gone several weeks, perhaps a month.

"Why don't you have Clara Shelby stay with you?" Cage had suggested.

"She's visiting her mother in Stockton," I answered. "No —I don't really need anyone," this with a forced smile. "It's not as if I were a child. I'll manage."

But after Cage had gone, I thought, how? How will I manage? I hated being in the house alone with just the servants and Martha, although Martha, since our trouble over Octavia, had seemed less hostile toward me. Still, she was there, and I never could be too sure that she wasn't watching me from behind the wall, standing in the secret passage, her eyes glued to the peephole. Cage assured me that Martha had sworn she had never spied on anyone, but I found it hard to believe.

The days passed slowly. Somehow I managed to fill them with trivia; I went to the City, to my sewing circle, shopped, had lunch with several women acquaintances, none of whom I really cared for as much as I did Clara. They made me feel uncomfortable; I could not see myself ever confiding in them, even superficially as I had with Clara. Once I asked Ted Neale to come home with me for supper, assuring him that since Octavia was away at school, he would have no embarrassing confrontations. He accepted my invitation, and we had a pleasant, though rather boring evening, for he could talk of nothing except Octavia. God knows I tried to listen sympathetically, but before long I found myself catching my yawns and fluttering my eyelashes to keep my heavy eyes from closing shut. Still, he was a warm, breathing, friendly person, and I asked him to come again. He promised he would, though his promise lacked conviction. Perhaps he was just as bored as I was.

If the days dragged the evenings were much worse. How I hated to see dusk fall, dropping a gray mantle over the world, hated to see the lamps lit and the shadows gathering like conspirators in dark corners. I dreaded the forlorn sound of the ships' horns in the bay on foggy nights, the cotton-wool mist pressing against the windows, creeping in chilly little drafts under the sills. And the silence—that terrible, pervading silence so characteristic of the Folly, a silence permeated by the sound of its many clocks. Sometimes I thought their loud ticking would drive me mad. I would go to bed early, often to lie awake until the wee, small hours, listening to the creaking boards, the whispering behind the walls which sounded like mice or possibly Martha walking softly down the secret passage.

She always served me my supper now.

"Some more wine, Mrs. Norwood?" It was a Saturday night, two weeks since Cage had left.

"No, thank you, this will suffice."

"Is something wrong?" she asked anxiously, the decanter poised in her hand.

I shot her a quick look. Usually she accepted my refusal of a second glass of wine without a word. Why should she suddenly be solicitous?

"No. But I believe I'll finish this glass in the drawing room instead of having brandy. Are there any more of those walnuts?"

"I put a fresh bowl out this morning."

"Thank you, and tell Doreen it was a delicious meal."

"Yes, Mrs. Norwood."

I picked up my wine and went out of the dining room and across the hall to the library, conscious that she was watching me. As soon as I shut the door, I dumped the claret into a potted rubber plant. Truthfully, it had been sour; probably the bottle had been left open in a warm place, but I did not want to argue with her about claret. The fewer words I had with her the better.

I sat down before the low table that held the bowl of walnuts and pulling them close, began to crack and eat some. I had no particular fondness for walnuts, but the sound of their splintering shells helped to dispel the awful clock-ticking quiet, made me feel less lonely somehow. It never occurred to me at the time to wonder that a bowl of walnuts should be able to give me even such small comfort, but for years afterwards I was never able to look at walnuts without a ridiculous feeling of warmth.

I grew drowsy earlier than usual and went up to bed. For once I did not lie awake tossing and turning, but fell into immediate sleep. Presently I began to dream, the same horrifying dream of mist, of eyes watching me from behind shrouded trees while a drum boomed to a primitive, spine-chilling beat. And as in similar nightmares of the past I began to run, but this time instead of running on and on endlessly, I awoke with a start.

Moonlight was streaming in through the half-drawn curtains, throwing strips of silver across the bed and carpeted floor. For a few moments I thought I was still dreaming, for though my eyes were wide open, the sound of the drum beat continued. Tat-tat-tatatat, boom, boom! I heard voices, too, chanting voices.

Rising on one elbow I listened. Tat-tat-tatatat, boom, boom! It wasn't the sound of my heart; it came from outside. I got out of bed, shivering in the chilly darkness. Then, going to the window, I parted the curtains. A fiery glow emanated from beyond the garden wall, the same bright red glow I had seen months ago. Nothing but that glow and the smoke rising in spirals was visible, but I heard the chanting, and I knew that this was not part of a dream but that something eerie, some strange ritual, was taking place.

What?

I drew a cloak about me, hesitated, then shoving my feet into slippers went out into the hall and down the stairs. Here I paused again. A little nugget of common sense told me that I was behaving rashly, that I ought not to intrude upon something that might prove dangerous, but a compulsive curiosity, the need to prove to myself that what I heard was not fancy, the drum beat, the night, the mystery, all of it drew me on.

I went through the side parlor where barred moonlight checkered the floor, out the French doors and across the moon-drenched garden to the gate in the wall. I hesitated once more a moment, my hand on the latch. I could hear the singing more distinctly now, the beating of the drum, though the words of the singers remained unintelligible. *Don't*, that nugget of common sense warned, *don't go. Suppose "they" discover you?* But the drum beat throbbing in my brain drowned reason out. *What is it?* My heart pulsed. *Where? Who?*

I opened the gate and stole through, gliding under the trees until I stopped short, my hand flying to my mouth as the clearing came into view. Too stunned to retreat, I could only stare at the scene before me.

Even now it remains clearly etched in my mind, an

eerie, macabre picture against the backdrop of night, a living frieze from some artist's mad conception of hell—the fire, the plumed smoke and the rock behind it like an altar. On the rock stood a box, and around it dancers were slowly moving, all naked, black men and women swaying and singing, their bodies glistening in the light from the leaping flames. Suddenly a man turned his head and I shrank behind a tree trunk, holding to the rough bark, my knees shaking so badly I could scarcely stand. Had I been seen? What did they do to curiosity-seekers, or to those who had stumbled upon them inadvertently? What did they do to spies? Torture, burn them? I cowered there with eyes squeezed shut, clinging to the tree, trembling with dread, regretting my impulsive decision to leave the safety of my bed, anticipating a steellike grip on my shoulder, the angry cries and shouts of the others as they rushed forward to drag me from my hiding place. But the running footsteps, the gripping hand I feared, never came. The weird singing and chanting went on, and soon I summoned the courage to peep out again.

A woman dressed in a long, blue gown, her hair flowing past her shoulders, was now standing near the box. She had her back to me and as I watched she held up her hand. The dancers stopped suddenly, their arms dropping to their sides. The drum became silent. The woman began to speak in the same monotone I had heard before, in a language as esoteric and obscure as the singing words had been. A tall black man came forward and took the box and placed it on the ground. The woman stepped up on it and continued speaking. The bright flames crackled and snapped, the listeners' sweating faces gleamed with awe and fear as they gazed up at the speaker whose head was still turned from me.

Her words came faster. She stepped down from the box, lifted the lid, and reaching into it brought out a writhing snake, its brown and green diamond-patterned skin rippling in the firelight. A cold sickness gripped my stomach. How horrible! How disgusting! I wanted to leave, I wanted to turn away and go back through the garden, but something hypnotic, something I could not explain held me there, quivering, yet rooted to the spot.

The watchers bowed low to the ground as if in adoration, as if in worship. A murmur rose among them, a pleading, begging, whispering torrent of words. The woman's voice grew louder. She held the serpent high above her head, gave a shout. Then it was taken from her by the tall black man who put it back in the box.

The woman in blue began to dance, her body contorting, imitating the motions of the snake, and as she danced the blue dress slithered down past her shoulders, her hips and her thighs until she stood naked. The others began to dance, too, slowly at first, then faster and faster, their torsos partially obscuring the woman, their hands clapping in rhythm, their feet stamping upon the ground. A flask passed from hand to hand as the drum beat grew more insistent, the dancing wilder. Through a welter of outflung arms and clapping hands I glimpsed flashes of the woman, turning and turning now, still dancing. Suddenly the others parted, and I saw her face clearly for the first time, familiar brown features boldly highlighted by the leaping flames of the fire.

It was Martha.

Chapter 20

I have only the vaguest recollection of how I got back to my bedroom. I dimly remember stumbling through the trees, my handkerchief over my mouth, reaching the gate, going through as the hinges groaned, tripping and nearly falling to my knees in the garden, and then fleeing up and up the long, winding staircase.

When I closed the door behind me, my breath was whistling painfully in my nostrils, my heart hammering so hard it seemed about to burst through my gown and wrapper. Groping for a chair, I sank down, clenching my fists, biting my lips against the giddy, swirling dark. Gradually the sickening feeling began to disappear and my breath came easier. I looked about the room for reassurance, trying to grasp some sort of reality, for already the scene beyond the garden had taken on the aspect of a horrendous dream, a nightmare, a monstrous fantasy.

But the faint red glow still reflected in the windows told me otherwise.

What was it? What had I seen? Black magic, the rites of the devil? No, there had been no burning cross, no mock priest or communion, only the worship of the snake. And then I remembered that I had once read in a journal Charles had brought home how those who practiced voodoo used the snake as a representation of their god, the snake who spoke through the tongue of a high priestess. The article explained that the cult had emigrated from the West Indies to Louisiana and also hinted at something indecent in their rituals, debauchery and goodness knows what else, things that I had not understood. It was unchristian, obscene. Voodoo—and here in our backyard too! Oh, God—I was afraid!

Shivering I drew my wrapper closer. Martha! I recalled now so many things that made sense. I could see why

Martha wielded such power over the servants, why they cringed and did her bidding. I could see why our kitchen always seemed to be full of her friends, darkies who came to her for occult advice, for charms perhaps. I knew now why she had wanted me to drink the wine tonight, why it tasted sour. It had been drugged. How many times before had she done this? How many times before had her followers obeying her command congregated in the dead of night to chant their scabrous songs and beat upon the drum?

Did Cage know? Impossible. If he had known about the voodoo cult, he would have categorically dismissed Martha. Spying he might have condoned—might—but these obscene rites—never. Oh, how I wished he were at home! How I wished this had not come about when he had to be so far away. It would take another week, perhaps two before he returned. In the meantime—what? I rubbed my clammy hands together. What? I could not let Martha know what I had seen. It was too dangerous. I must pretend ignorance, make believe I had slept through it all.

I rose and was removing my wrapper when I suddenly realized I was missing a slipper. A little cold pain clutched at my heart as I lit a candle and searched for it on the floor, going over every inch of carpet from window to bed to door. I could not find it. Be calm, I told myself, don't get upset, it's probably on the stairs. I went out, pausing a moment, listening. Then I moved slowly down the hall, scanning the carpet for a blue slipper. I came to the staircase and began to descend. There was no slipper. Nor could I find it in the entry hall or the side parlor. I had lost it either in the garden when I stumbled or in the small copse of trees beyond the garden wall, but I could not force myself to go out again and search for it.

Through the French window I could still see the rosy glow of the fire, fainter now, and by straining my ears could hear the distant murmur of voices. The very thought of that activity under cover of darkness set me to quaking all over again. No, I could not leave the sheltered security of the house. My only hope was that Martha and the others would be too delirious with drink and ritualistic fervor to notice a slipper lying among the trees, and perhaps I could safely retrieve it in the morning.

But in the morning when I went to search for it, I found nothing. I was returning through the rose garden past the dew-wet hydrangeas when I saw Martha standing in the small herb garden near the kitchen door. She was looking my way.

"Good morning," I said to her as I got closer, my heart tripping like a hammer.

"Good morning, Mrs. Norwood. Out early, aren't you?"

Her eyes met mine, and I knew at once that she had discovered the slipper.

"Yes—I thought I'd take a little stroll before breakfast," I said with forced cheerfulness.

"Nice day for a stroll," she said.

Was she wondering how much I had seen last night, how much I knew? But it hardly mattered. A little would have been enough.

"Will you be eating breakfast soon, Mrs. Norwood?"

I couldn't eat a bite, not a morsel she had touched. "No—I—I've decided to go into town and have breakfast at the Barlett Hotel with—with Ted Neale," I improvised. "He's asked me so many times."

Did the lie fool her? Probably not. What would she do to me? How would she try to prevent me from talking?

"Would you like some coffee before you go out?"

"No, thank you, Martha." Would she poison me? A voodoo high priestess would know all about poisons. Oh, God, I wished I had slept through the night, wished I had never seen the dancing and the snake and the fire. "Have Gandy bring the carriage, please." But no, Gandy was one of *them!* "Oh—Martha," as she turned away, "on second thought I believe I'll take the buggy."

It was a cold morning, bleak as winter, the kind of March morning typical of San Francisco with a gray overcast and a brisk wind that pierced the bone. That I was frightened and scared did not help. I had no idea where I was going, what I would do. My one thought as I took the reins in my gloved hands and clucked at the horse was to get as far away from the Folly as I could.

I need help, I thought, rattling along, needed it badly— from a man, preferably, a man who could face Martha without flinching. But whom to ask? The husbands of the ladies I knew were all strangers except for John Shelby, and he had gone to Virginia City with Cage and Mr. Ralston. Ted Neale was too young. Jay Cooke? The thought made me flinch. I recalled the last words we had together,

the sardonic smile, the sarcastic tone to his voice. Asking
him for assistance would be like eating wormwood. But it
was either Jay Cooke or back to the Folly, back to Martha
and the terrible unspoken knowledge which lay between us.
There was no one else who could help me—no one.

The city streets were more crowded than usual as I
guided the horse toward Jay Cooke's office on Montgom-
ery Street. People on foot, in carriages, on horseback,
hurried by, some jostling and pushing in their haste, all
going in the same direction. It must be Steamer Day, I
thought, remembering that Clara Shelby and I had once
before been caught in a similar crush. Steamer Day, so
called for the twice monthly arrival of steamers from Panama and eagerly awaited by the citizenry of San Francisco,
meant mail and news brought from the East—from home.
It was a day of barter and trade, for the receipt and shipment of goods, a day on which bills were presented and
paid, a half holiday. I hoped as we made our way through
the converging throng that Jay Cooke had not gone down
to the wharves on business of his own.

He had, as it proved, but the clerk said his employer
would be back shortly and had me wait, seating me on a
small sofa in the inner sanctum. It was a simple, but taste-
fully furnished room with a large, highly polished walnut
desk, a captain's chair, several handpainted glass lamps and
the brown velour sofa on which I sat. On the wall were two
woodcuts by Charles Nahl—a highly esteemed local artist.
There was the faint aroma of pipe tobacco in the room,
too. I had never seen Jay smoking a pipe; perhaps he did.
It struck me as I waited, surveying the woodcuts, that I
actually knew very little of Jay Cooke. He was a broker of
some sort, Cage had once told me, but exactly what he did
I had never been interested enough to find out. Our meetings had almost always been so abrasive, my irritation, if
not anger, had gotten in the way of curiosity. I wondered
why he had never married. He claimed I was the only
woman he had ever loved. But men always said that
whether they meant it or not.

Sitting there in that ordered quiet, leaning back on the
cushions, listening to the comforting scratch of the clerk's
pen, my experience of the night suddenly seemed even
more bizarre than ever. How I would explain it to Jay
Cooke without seeming like a hysterical female, I did not

know. But whatever I did, I must try to remain calm, to appear rational, to make my statements seem logical and real.

An hour passed. Halfway through the next, Jay Cooke finally appeared. He was surprised to see me.

"Is something the matter?" he asked with characteristic abruptness.

"Does 'something' have to be the matter in order for me to pay you a call?" I asked, trying to remain self-possessed but barely succeeding. I wanted to lead up to my mission gradually, not blurt out my desperation like a frightened child.

"You've never visited me here—or anywhere else before." He sat on the edge of the desk, his dark eyes surveying me. "Naturally I would think there's something the matter. Your husband hasn't . . . ?"

"Run off?" I queried, trying to keep my voice light. "Sorry to disappoint you. He and Mr. Ralston have gone to Virginia City on business."

"Ah—yes, I remember now. So—you are here." He let out his breath and grinned.

"I was in the neighborhood and thought I'd drop by." The interview, having begun badly, now seemed to be straying from my original intentions.

"A purely social call." His grin widened.

"Why—yes."

"While your husband is away."

The suggestive, mocking tone in his voice dissolved the last shred of my shaky, hard-won composure and heat rose to my cheeks. "Must you always be such an ill-bred—ill-bred . . . !"

"Cad is the word, I believe."

It had been a mistake. A mistake. Why had I come? I might have known that nothing could be gained. The situation was hopeless, impossible. Jay Cooke, a master at clouding the issue, adroit at the subtle and sometimes not-so-subtle jeer, was the last person I should have sought out.

"I'm sorry," I said, my voice shaking. "I'm sorry to have troubled you." I got to my feet.

"Wait . . ." He put his hand on my arm. "There *is* something wrong, Adelaide. I can tell."

"No, there isn't."

"Something's happened."

"No," I repeated, and suddenly the thought of going back to the Folly alone swept over me like a cold, gray fog. In my mind I could see Martha's face, her implacable eyes, the crystal glass of drugged claret at my elbow reflected on the polished oak dining table, the long evening with the clock ticking away.

"What is it?" Jay asked, his voice softened, gentle, bending down as he tried to see my averted face more closely.

Tears rose to my eyes. "N—nothing." The fire, the chanting, the relentless boom of the drum, the box on the altar, the writhing snake . . .

"Oh—Jay," turning to him, shuddering. "Oh, Jay, I'm so afraid."

"My dear child . . ." He drew me into his arms, and I leaned my head against his chest and wept, forgetting that I had hated him only a moment earlier, forgetting his insults and gibes, thinking only that his arms were comforting, that his chest was broad and strong and that my fear was too much for me to bear alone.

He pressed his handkerchief into my hand, and gradually my weeping subsided. I wiped my eyes and he released me. "Sit down, Adelaide, and tell me about it. Whatever's happened must have been pretty awful for you to call me by my Christian name."

"Did I?"

"Come now. It's quite all right. You've certainly known me long enough. Sit—make yourself comfortable."

I sank onto the sofa, clutching the damp handkerchief between my hands. "I—I didn't mean to fall apart—I . . ."

"Please, please, Adelaide, don't apologize. It was I who was at fault. I promise—I shan't bait you again. Tell me."

So I began at the beginning, from the day I walked up the stairs of the Folly to meet Martha's cold eyes. I told him about her insolence, about the secret passage and stairway, about her activities in the Underground and finally about the voodoo orgy I had witnessed the night before. He listened in silence, never interrupting, his dark, sober eyes fastened on mine. When I finished he drew in his breath.

"Voodoo . . . ! Of all things." He shook his head. "But—thinking about it, I guess I shouldn't be surprised. Martha is a woman capable of most anything."

"Cage doesn't know about the voodoo, I'm sure," I said hurriedly. "In the past he's always—well, put up with her. He says she's so efficient, and Octavia is so fond of her, but now. . . ." my voice trailed off.

He contemplated me for a long moment. "I'm sorry, Adelaide, but I don't think this latest will make any difference. Cage won't dismiss her."

"But why? How do you know? What a thing to say!"

"Do you love your husband, my dear?"

"Very much," I said staunchly, meeting him full in the eye.

"I don't know if I have the right to tell you this, but, Adelaide, if I went up there and told Martha to pack her things, she'd only laugh at me because she knows Cage is not going to dismiss her. He's afraid to."

"Afraid? Cage afraid? Why—that's preposterous!" Yet wasn't that what I had at one point dimly suspected myself? "Why should he be afraid of Martha?"

"She's blackmailing him. She has something which she is holding over his head."

"Cage? Something—what? What is it?"

"That I won't reveal. I've said too much already, and you must promise me that you will never repeat it to Cage."

"It's not true, then," I said stubbornly, not wanting to believe him. "If it were true you would tell me."

"No—and don't try to trick me, my dear."

"It can't be too terrible," I said, trying to catch some glimmer of a clue in his blank face. "A bad check? Poker losses? A—a woman?"

"I'll ask Cage then," I threatened. "I'll ask him."

"And tell him that I revealed he was being blackmailed? I can't say that would be a very honorable thing to do, and by you especially who sets such store in 'honor.'"

"You would throw that up to me," I said ruefully. I seemed to be right back where I had started from. Martha would still be at the Folly and everything, the insolence, the spying, the voodoo, the fear, would go on as if nothing had changed. What had Cage done that was so reprehensible? There was nothing I could possibly think of that could create such a situation. Nothing. Jay had been exaggerating. When Cage returned from Virginia City, I would ask him. But in the meantime . . .

"Is Octavia there with you?" Jay asked.

"No—she's at school. I'm alone." And still afraid, I wanted to add, but he must have sensed it for he said:

"I'll go back with you and have a heart-to-heart talk with Martha. She'll listen to me. I'm one of the few men in this city who can talk to her on an open, equal basis."

"You mean she's blackmailing others?"

"Unfortunately, yes."

"Why—that's outrageous! It's—it's illegal, a crime! Blackmail! How does she get away with it? Why doesn't someone turn her in to the authorities?"

"Who? It's the case of belling the cat. Who would dare have his particular rascality exposed? Too many men in this town have dark pasts, my dear, too many have made their money in tricky real estate deals, bogus stock, manipulated markets, what have you. Some have run away from criminal records in the East, forgeries, robberies, even murder. They're not about to make themselves public by accusing Martha."

"And you ask me to believe that a—a servant has been privy to all these unwholesome secrets? Why, Jay . . ."

"That always puzzled me a bit, too. But now that you tell me she is high priestess of a voodoo sect I can see where it would be simple as ABC. Think a minute, Adelaide. Many of the servants in hotels, boardinghouses, at livery stables, eateries, in private homes, brothels, wherever the bigwigs gather, are darkies, blackfolk who look up to Martha, who are in awe of her, who would be glad to curry favor by spying for the high priestess."

"Why does she do it?"

"For money, perhaps for power, but I wouldn't be surprised if it was for simple revenge."

"Yes," I said, thinking of her bitterness against the planters who had owned slaves. "Yes, revenge."

"Can you blame her? Look at it from her standpoint."

"But—she never was a slave."

"Her people were—and for all intents and purpose she might as well have been. Certainly in New Orleans, certainly in San Francisco. Unfortunately the Gold Rushers and the people who followed, many of them Southerners like ourselves, brought their prejudices. We may not be as harsh on them as we are on the Chinese, but we don't allow them to have equal justice in our courts; we make it difficult for them to own property—or even to ride our street cars."

"You speak as if I disliked darkies. I don't, you know that. Why, I loved our Sissie. . . ."

"I'm sure you did. You loved her same as you would a great big motherly dog. No—Adelaide—don't get upset, but if she'd have said to you one day, 'I think I'll sit down and join you for lunch', you would have been mortified to say the least."

"Well—I'll be . . ."

"Ponder on it, Adelaide. And the voodoo, too. The Christian religion hasn't done much more for them—or her—but try to make them passive, accepting."

"To think that you condone . . ."

"I'm not. I'm not condoning voodoo or blackmail— simply trying to explain why someone as tough as Martha would resort to it."

"I find this talk rather strange, especially from you, of all people."

"Yes, isn't it? Sometimes I surprise even myself." He picked up his hat and gloves. "Well, then, shall we go? And on the way I'm going to stop at the bank and ask Ted Neale to stay with you until Cage gets back."

"Ted Neale, but . . ."

"He won't miss his work at the bank, if that's what's worrying you. As long as he comes to the Folly each evening and spends the night. Or would you rather have me?" He grinned.

"I shan't dignify that by an answer," I said stiffly.

"It's all settled," Jay assured me, closing the door. He had suggested I wait in the drawing room while he spoke to Martha, and I sat there in that large, velvet-hung room for an anxious hour, literally on the edge of my chair. "I put the fear of the devil into her."

"It's hard to imagine Martha afraid, even of the devil."

"Well—she is now. I told her that one more nightly caper or disrespectful word to you and I would go straight to Captain Lees of the police department. And I didn't care who among my friends would be hurt. I think she believed me."

"Would you—I mean, go to the police?"

"If it came to it, yes—to protect you—definitely yes," he asserted, looking at me with an intensity I found disturbing. I lowered my eyes, thinking I ought to thank him for his trouble, yet suddenly unable to find the words.

"I'll speak to Cage when he gets back," Jay went on, "although God knows he should have been able to handle this problem long ago."

"He—he doesn't have time to concern himself with household matters," I said, looking up quickly.

"Household matters? Fiddle! He doesn't like to face up to unpleasantness, that's all. He lacks gumption."

"I don't know why you are always putting him in a bad light," I said, annoyed.

"Do I?"

"Yes—you're always finding fault. You're—why you're jealous of him. And don't try to deny it," I added with some heat.

He observed me for a few moments, his eyes narrowed. "Love is so blind," he said with biting irony. "Cage the paragon. Cage, who even if he does wrong is quickly forgiven. He's a gentleman, a Cavalier, dashing and romantic."

"If you are going to get nasty, Jay Cooke, I don't want to hear it." How quickly he could switch from an understanding benefactor to a bullying detractor. It was almost as if he were uncomfortable in the role of a kindly, courteous gentleman.

"Suppose I do, suppose I get nasty, as you put it. What then?" his voice was edged with venom. "Oh—you won't listen. Again. It makes me so angry to see your obtuseness. You're so intelligent, so clever, really, more than you put on—in many ways. But about Cage you are a fool, blind as a bat."

"You're jealous," I repeated, hurt and dumbfounded by his attack. "Pretending to be Cage's friend—but you don't like him. You've never liked him."

"Hogwash! When we were young lads, we were the best of friends. Two fancy-free bucks, gambling, drinking, going out on the town. It was fun. We were grown-up boys and I enjoyed it. But, Adelaide, you can't go on being a grown-up boy all your life. Somewhere, at some point, you have got to become a man."

"A man? How dare you? How dare you imply that of

Cage. . . !" I lashed out at him. Oh, what a fool to think this man could ever remain pleasant for more than five minutes.

"I'm not implying. I'm stating. Cage never got beyond the happy boy stage. Although I must admit he's not always quite that happy, but still he thinks and acts like, well, like Ted Neale, only Ted Neale probably has more sense."

"Why—you—you insufferable . . . ," I spluttered. I wanted to strike out at him, to wipe that jeering look from his face. "I hate you! I don't care what you've done for me. I hate you! You are saying all those horrible things because you envy Cage. You envy his birth, his breeding, his looks, his charm. You are plain jealous—jealous of everything, even, even . . . ," my mind sought blindly for more, "even because he once had such a beautiful wife."

"Lillith?" he asked, raising his brows. "Jealous of Lillith? My dear, she was a whore."

"How—how dare you!" Choking with fury, I picked up a vase and hurled it at him. He ducked and the vase hit the stone mantel, shattering into fragments as it fell to the hearth. For a long time the echo of the tinkling china was the only sound in the room. Jay stood looking at me, his brows still raised.

"Get out," I ordered in a low, tense voice, sinking down on a chair. "Get out—you foul-mouthed creature."

His face suddenly darkened. He moved, not to leave, but to cover the distance between us in three, quick strides. Grasping my arms, he jerked me to my feet, and for one terrible moment I thought he would strike me. But instead he shook my by the shoulders.

"Stop . . . !" I cried, outraged.

"I don't know why I've bothered," he said, the words coming out through clenched teeth.

"Jay—"

". . . bothered, trying to protect you from unpleasantness. Trying to protect you the way everyone else has been doing, ladylike, sheltered, precious Adelaide." The descriptive adjectives were hammered at me like blows of a mallet. "It's high time you knew the truth, and I am going to tell it to you. Yes, Lillith was a whore. I did not call her one out of pique. No—don't try to wriggle free. Listen! Damn you, listen!"

His fingers dug into my arms. I did not want to listen. I, who had yearned to hear all about Lillith for so long, suddenly did not want to hear. I was afraid, afraid of what he would tell me, afraid of him, afraid of the angry glitter in his eyes. I wanted to get away, but he held me fast.

"She worked in Belle Cora's 'boarding house'," he went on resolutely, his eyes fastened on mine. "Do you know what a boarding house is, my dear? A sporting house? Well—yes, then you know something, don't you? Lillith was one of the girls. I was with Cage the first day he saw her. She was sitting in Belle's open carriage—Belle liked her girls to drive about in style, you know—Martha was with her, a proper chaperone, they always liked to pretend they were ladies. Well—she was sitting in the carriage, dressed all in lilac, yards and yards of crinoline skirt, wearing a fetching lilac bonnet and twirling a lilac parasol. She was a picture, I must admit, fresh complexion, dark hair and sparkling eyes. Cage was bowled over. He didn't care who or what she was. He had to have her—and for himself alone. He did not want to share her with other men, those who paid for her services, those who . . ."

"Stop!" I cried. His grip was bruising, hurting me. "You're lying! You're saying horrible, impossible things about Cage. If you think I believe—for one moment . . ."

"Then you tell me what you know about Lillith. What has Cage told you? Who was she? Where did she come from, who were her parents? Family? Well—my dear, what do you know?

Nothing, my confused, frightened brain thought, nothing except that she was beautiful. "A widow," my brother had said, and from Martha, looking at me out of hard, yellow eyes, "The Folly was a fit setting for her." Even Clara, that inveterate gossip, had refused to tell me more, and Cage had never mentioned her name. She had been shrouded in silence; a mystery. I thought of all the times past, those years on the James River when I had wondered, and now here in this house, these recent weeks and months tormenting myself, speculating about the sort of person she had been, while her portrait upstairs smiled secretly behind the curtain, the red lips curved, the violet eyes misted. Lillith with a red rose between white breasts. Lillith, a whore.

"Well?" Jay demanded, "I'm waiting. You haven't answered my question."

The little snips of chatter, the bits of gossip I had caught at odd moments, the sudden, embarrassed silences. The conversations that died when I entered a room. The half-finished sentences, *my dear, didn't you know . . . ?*

"No," I said, "no, I didn't know."

He released me. I swayed for a moment, dizzy, a little sick. But when he put out his hand to steady me, I brushed it violently away.

"You're strong," he said. "Stronger than you think. You'll get over the shock."

I wet my lips. "There is . . . ," pausing, trying again because my voice was high, unnatural, ". . . there is nothing you can say that—that will change my love for Cage."

He smiled, a smile that was cool, scornful. "Still the loyal little wife, I see. And I suppose you are thinking that Cage did the noble thing by our Lillith, a young, pretty woman with an illegitimate child and no protector, no family, no father or brother to stand between her and the cruel world. So he married her when he could have put her up just as well in a small house as his mistress. Married her out of the goodness of his kind, generous heart. Well, you're wrong. He married Lillith because that was the only way he could obtain exclusive rights to her. You see, she had a lover—oh, yes, those girls sometimes do fall in love with a particular customer—she had a lover, a petty gambler, a very rum character by the name of James Royce. He was Octavia's father, but he couldn't or wouldn't marry her, and Lillith, whether out of umbrage or because she thought she yearned for respectability, became Mrs. Cage Norwood."

I sat down. I felt very tired, drained of my anger. I couldn't honestly blame Jay for telling me. I had asked for it, "wheedling," he once called it. And if I hadn't made him so angry, he probably would have remained silent. Still—it did not matter. I was bound to hear it sooner or later from someone.

"Charles and I tried everything to dissuade Cage, even getting him drunk on his wedding day," Jay went on. "But he would have none of it. He quarreled with Charles, and Charles refused to speak to him again."

The letters hardly mentioning Cage, saying nothing, not

answering my questions. The coolness between the two men that had puzzled me so.

"Well—there you have it." Jay fell silent, the blaze gone from his eyes.

Lillith, a whore. "Did—did he, Cage . . . ," I began after a few moments, clearing my throat, "did Cage love her very much?"

Jay did not answer at once. His face was blank, inscrutable. It was a question I should not have asked, but so much had already been said I didn't care.

"What can I say?" Jay finally spoke. "How can one man gauge the true feelings of another? All right, the best I can do is tell you what I think. I think he did love Lillith—as far as Cage could love anyone. Now does that answer your question?"

"Yes," I said in a small voice. What I had hoped for was Jay's avowal that Cage's feelings for Lillith had been a passing whim, a burst of brief passion, nothing more. How could it have been otherwise? A woman like that.

Jay picked up his hat and started for the door.

"Where are you going?" I asked.

"Back to the office. This is Steamer Day and I've been gone from business long enough."

"But—but aren't you going to tell me more? Aren't you going to tell me how—how she died?"

"Ask Cage," he said, throwing me a piercing look. "Ask your precious Cage."

Chapter 21

JAY'S disclosure, though shocking, should have come as a relief. Now, at last, some of the mystery which baffled me had been cleared away. More than that, my feelings of inferiority were no longer necessary. Lillith, as a prostitute, no matter how beautiful, was hardly a woman toward whom I needed to feel competitive. She was beyond the pale, a female who had sold her body in the basest, most blatant manner. It wasn't a question of my snobbery at all, but of pride, pride of ancestry, of breeding, of an upbringing which had indelibly impressed upon me the morality of home and family. I felt that I could never accept the proliferation of sporting houses in San Francisco as a necessary evil as so many ladies of even good society seemed to do. To me they were cesspools, and because Lillith had come from one, I could disregard her, forget she had ever existed.

But strangely enough, this was not the case. Lillith still haunted me, not only because of her beauty, but because Cage had married her. Together they had appeared before a priest or preacher and had exchanged holy vows, had become man and wife. If Jay had told me that Lillith had been his mistress (as Mrs. Walters had been), I would have been shocked, hurt, dismayed, but eventually I would have persuaded myself that I still had the edge. I was Mrs. Cage Norwood.

But *she* had been Mrs. Cage Norwood, too.

It was a fact I could not dispute. What I did doubt, however, was Jay's belief that Cage had married her because of a grand passion which could not be denied. Somehow, in some way, I felt that Cage had been tricked into matrimony. I remembered Martha's words, "I thought she (Lillith) would make me my good fortune." Martha was clever, ambitious. She had latched onto Lillith, seeing in the girl's beauty a way to better herself, to get a toehold on the fringes of polite society where she might pursue to advantage her schemes of blackmail. With Lillith as Mrs. Norwood she need never fear poverty. Even if her nefarious schemes failed, she would always have a roof over her head, good meals and a comfortable berth. Then after Lillith died, Martha concentrated on Octavia. The girl was as beautiful as her mother, and with her the possibilities, too, were infinite. I could see now why Martha had insisted on Octavia's legitimacy, insisted that Cage was her true father. She wanted Octavia to have at least one respectable, well-born parent, one who would attract an advantageous marriage, an offer from an eligible bachelor of good family. I could also understand why she had been so upset with Octavia's behavior, why she had concurred with Cage's decision to send the girl to convent school. Octavia's reputation, at all costs, must be protected.

Martha did not like Cage, she had as much told me that, but he was necessary. And, in a sense, I was, too. Like Cage I came from the kind of blooded stock that created the proper aura at the Folly, an atmosphere of respectability, one which would help Octavia and indirectly Martha also.

So Martha needed us. Knowing this, my fear of her *should* have disappeared. But like my feelings of inferiority toward the dead Lillith, they did not. The very sound of Martha's voice in the front hall would send a shiver up my back, the swish of her long skirts in the dining room set my heart palpitating. I tried to convince myself that there was nothing she could do to harm me, tried but failed. She had always been an enigma, and though she had been frank (up to a point) in revealing her feelings and her former life to me, there was much about her that remained a dark mystery. I did not trust her. She had spied upon me, I was sure, watching me from those little peepholes behind the walls in the secret passage. Why? Why had she watched me in the dining room, in the library and most likely in the bedroom, too? Why? Perhaps she wanted to catch me at some indiscretion in order to blackmail me. Perhaps she needed to feel in the ascendancy, obsessed by a desire to have others obligated to her.

And how was Cage obligated? What secret of his did Martha keep? It seemed unlikely that Lillith's unsavory past was such a closely guarded mystery. What then? A business deal? Perhaps Martha had spied on a meeting in which intricate, sensitive matters of high finance had been discussed, plans that if leaked to competitors would prove disastrous. Perhaps that was why Cage never had business meetings at the house, but always at the Belmont or Union hotels.

It was all conjecture on my part, of course. I did not know, I could not really be sure. I longed for Cage to come home, for this time I was fully determined to overcome my shyness and speak to him, to tell him about Martha, to ask him to share his worries and problems with me. Husbands and wives should have no secrets from one another. Barnabas and I never had.

I saw very little of Martha in the next few days. Ted Neale, as he had promised, came every evening. Neither Jay nor I had told him anything except that I was lonesome and wanted company. It was good to have him there, to feel that he was within easy call should I become frightened again during the night. Lucinda served us our meals. Martha was not well, she said. But Martha, I sensed, was only biding her time. She was not one to take Jay's scolding lying down, and I guessed she was plotting to get back at me. How and when were questions that plagued me through many a daytime hour and dream-haunted night. Catching a fleeting glimpse of her in the garden, in the hall, or passing quickly from the drawing room to the nether parts of the house, showing herself briefly, always out of earshot, I felt we were playing cat and mouse.

I instructed McCorkle to nail up the peepholes, the door in the garden, another door which I discovered behind a portrait in the library, and the gilded apple which opened the entrance from Lillith's bedroom. I thought that coached by Martha, he might pretend to follow my orders, leaving at least one door unsecured. But surprisingly he went about his job thoroughly, hammering away with honest zeal. He was rather shocked, then intrigued to find a hidden passageway at the Folly, conjecturing that it must have been used to smuggle contraband goods into the City. What goods he did not specify, even when I pointed out to him that nothing seemed contraband in San Francisco, since every form of vice, including opium, came freely into port.

"Is that so?" said McCorkle.

"Yes," I assured him. "It wasn't the need to smuggle contraband that put the passageway there. It was a whim of Mr. Cage's, a whim which he no longer finds amusing."

I hoped he would relay this message to Martha and that she would not miss its double meaning.

Two nights after McCorkle had nailed shut the passage I woke suddenly from a deep sleep, my heart beating an inexplicable tattoo, not knowing what had roused me, only that it was something frightening. Frowning, I pushed myself up on one elbow, my eyes straining to penetrate the darkness. The black shape of the wardrobe loomed in one corner, in another a tall chiffonier. Everything else, the dim mirrors, the dressing table, the chairs and the lounge lay in deep, impenetrable shadow. The only light—more of a glimmer—came from the dark patch of mist-clouded window where the curtain had been left half-opened. A profound stillness shrouded the house, a muffled silence that seemed ominous and filled with foreboding. Far, far away a foghorn moaned eerily, and then the silence flowed back once more, swallowing the last echo of the horn.

My hand was reaching for the candle and box of matches I always kept on the bedside table when I heard a scratching behind the very wall along which the secret passageway ran. For a brief instant my breath caught as I listened to the little rasping sounds and then I realized what it was. Mice, I thought, letting out my breath, sinking back on the pillows. Mice. They always seemed a problem at the Folly.

I settled myself more comfortably. I began to think about Cage, picturing him in my mind so clearly, the light hair, the broad, handsome smile, the cleft in his chin. How I wished I could reach out across the miles, put my arms around him, talk to him, snuggle up and kiss him. I wondered what he was doing. Sleeping soundly, no doubt, as only he could do.

Suddenly an ugly, insidious laugh broke into my thoughts, an evil laugh, sending me bolt upright in fright.

"Who is it?" I whispered hoarsely into the dark.

The laugh echoed through the room again, a mindless snicker. It emanated from the far wall, the same wall from which I had heard the mice scratching earlier. The passageway, the hidden passageway which was supposed to have been boarded up! I listened, while holding my breath. The small scratching again, the rustle. Someone was there —who?

And suddenly I knew that it could be no one but Martha. Who else would be standing there now? She must have removed the nails from one of the doors, crept through the secret corridor until she had reached my room. The snickering laugh was meant to frighten me—her way of getting even, her retaliation for revealing the voodoo rites to Jay Cooke.

Trembling with anger now, I lit the candle. No further sounds came from the wall as I put on my slippers and wrapper, determined to have it out with Martha at once. If I were to wait until morning, I might lose the fine white edge of my anger, might even lose my nerve. And I wanted to give her a tongue-lashing, one that would make her think twice before she tried another trick like that again.

The corridor was lit by a single gas jet at the far end. The yellow, blue-eyed flame flickered and danced among the shadows on the mirrored walls. I hurried along the thick carpet and paused before Ted's door. Ought I to call to him, tell him what I had heard, ask him to go with me for support? I tapped lightly upon the door, waited a minute or two and when there was no answer decided there really was no need to rouse him.

Reaching the bottom of the stairs, I went into the library and tilted aside the picture which concealed one of the passageway's secret doors. Still nailed up. Martha must have entered through the garden then. I left the library and made my way down the narrow back hall toward the kitchen, pausing suddenly at the sound of voices—Martha's and a man's. How quickly she must have descended those stairs! And she had a visitor—at this hour! At the thought of her sitting there calmly, having conversation with a stranger (perhaps even discussing how she had frightened me), my blood began to boil all over again.

I pushed through the swinging door. Martha was sitting at the kitchen table in her dressing gown, and Ted Neale— of all people!—was seated opposite her. They both turned and gaped at me.

"Couldn't sleep either, Aunt Adelaide?" Ted asked, rising to his feet.

"No," I said, a little taken aback by the unexpected. "I—I was up."

"I got hungry," Ted said sheepishly, offering me his chair. "I woke up hungry as a wolf. And I came down looking for another piece of that apple pie we had for dinner." There was half a pie and a pot of tea on the table. "And then I went and dropped a jug of milk on the floor. Got poor Martha here out of bed."

"I don't mind," said Martha, more amicable than her usual self. "We got to talking," she went on, standing respectfully behind her chair, "didn't realize the time passed so fast. My, it's past two!" This with a glance at the clock over the stove.

Butter wouldn't melt in her mouth, I thought bitterly. How she did lie.

"How—how long have you been here, Ted?" I asked.

"Long? Why . . ." He scratched his tousled head. "Dunno—an hour, maybe. What would you say, Martha?"

"It was one-fifteen when I came into the kitchen," she answered. "I know—because when I heard that jug crash, I bolted right out of bed and knocked my bedside clock over. I was sure we had burglars."

"One-fifteen?" I asked, a cold hand squeezing my heart. "And you've been here ever since?"

"Yes, Mrs. Norwood," Martha said, eyeing me curiously. "Is there something wrong?"

"I—I don't know," I said, suddenly feeling very weak.

"Sit down, Aunt, sit down," Ted urged anxiously, indicating the chair again. "Some tea maybe, Martha makes very good tea."

"Yes, please . . ." I sat down heavily.

Martha went to the stove and put the kettle on.

"Have a nightmare?" Ted asked solicitously.

"No," I said. "There was—there was someone in. . . ." They were both looking at me. ". . . someone in the passage. Someone laughing."

Martha narrowed her eyes and Ted gazed at me bewildered.

"What passage?" Ted asked.

I told him about it. He whistled softly.

"And you heard someone laughing through the wall?" he asked.

"Yes—it—it couldn't have been more than fifteen minutes ago."

"We were here," Ted said. I knew I could not doubt his word. "We heard nothing. Was it a man or a woman?"

"It—it could have been either, now that I think of it. It was—well—hardly human." I shuddered, remembering.

"Could it have been McCorkle—or Gandy?"

"I don't know," I said.

"I'll go out and have a talk with them," Ted offered grimly. He was wearing a greatcoat over his nightclothes. "Don't you fret now, Aunt Adelaide, we'll get to the bottom of this."

His assertiveness, his manly air would have amused me had the occasion been a different one, but now I smiled wanly, grateful for his help.

After he left, Martha, keeping her back to me, busied herself at the stove. An embarrassed silence filled the room, one that seemed to ring with charges and countercharges. Had she ordered Gandy, or McCorkle, to frighten me with that weird laugh behind the wall? Bribed them, perhaps, made it all seem like a joke? I watched her as she moved with neat, unhurried precision, filling the tea caddy, getting a clean cup and saucer from the cupboard.

"Pie, Mrs. Norwood?" she turned at last, facing me across the room.

"No, thank you."

She eyed me for a few moments. "You should have come to me," she said. "You should have come to me instead of going to Mr. Jay Cooke with that story."

"I don't know what you mean."

"I beg your pardon, Mrs. Norwood, but you do know. You thought you saw something, and you went to Mr. Cooke. And now you are trying to make up another story about a voice behind the wall, someone laughing. You would like to say it is me. But this time you can't prove it. I have a witness. You can't prove the other—either, but it's your word against mine. And you know what that means. A Southern lady against a darkie. You can say anything you like and they'll believe you."

"How dare you speak to me that way when you know it isn't true!" I cried. "Do you deny that you were practicing voodoo? Do you?"

"Of course I deny it. I think you dreamed it like you dreamed tonight."

I was too stunned to speak.

"You dreamed it because you want sympathy. Pardon me for speaking out, but I have to defend myself, you see. You're a lonely lady, so much alone in this big house with nothing to do, so you dream bad dreams and get the gentlemen to fuss around you. Mr. Cage, too. But Mr. Cage is gone a lot. And Mr. Cage, he still thinks of *her.*" Her chin tilted upward. "He can't forget the lady who was his first wife."

"How dare you!" I flared, hurt, angry. "How dare you speak to me in this manner?"

"Yes—I know you will go to Mr. Cooke again. And to Mr. Cage. But what good will it do?"

"Be quiet!" I commanded. "I know all about *her!* I know who and what she was, so you needn't paint her as a lady."

Martha stared at me in astonishment, and then before she could speak, Ted walked into the kitchen.

"I had a time rolling those two codgers out of bed," he said, rubbing the chill out of his hands. He did not seem to notice my perturbed state nor Martha's blank look. "They both swore they never winked open an eye all night, never set foot out-of-doors."

"Of course they would swear," I said, bitterly, convinced now that Martha had put one or both up to playing that hideous trick on me.

"Are you sure?" Ted was asking. "Are you sure it wasn't just a dream, Auntie? A bad nightmare?"

Martha was watching me covertly.

"I'm sure," I said. Either man had plenty of time to board up the door he had used and scoot back to his bed. But what could I do? How could I prove it?

"Thank you—Ted. Thank you."

The only way out of my dilemma, to insure such an incident would not happen again, was to dismiss the entire staff, even the cook. All of them. I would never rid myself of Martha otherwise. But Cage would have to do it. I didn't care what hold Martha had over him. I would *make* him send her away.

A strong, determined resolve—one, however, that was easier to keep in Cage's absence than in his presence.

He returned two days later, in the morning, while I was still upstairs fixing my hair. Hearing the sound of his laughter in the hall below, I ran from the room to the top of the stairs.

"Cage!" I called with delight, leaning over the stairwell.

He smiled up at me and as I met his eyes, the familiar feeling of warm happiness went through me like sweet wine. And when we met on the landing and he took me in his arms, everything else was momentarily forgotten, the fears, the doubts, the shock, Martha, the Folly, everything except that he was at home, that I loved him, that I had missed him, that I never wanted him to go away again.

"We came back late last night," he said, disentangling himself with a small, rueful smile, "but the City was fogged in and we had to put up at a hotel."

Last night. A sudden picture of gray-misted windows and dark shadows flashed through my mind. The insane laugh . . . "Oh, Cage, I wish you had been here. You see . . ."

"Miss me, did you?" his eyes smiled as he chucked me affectionately under the chin.

I wiped the worried frown from my brow and smiled back at him. I couldn't tell him now. I couldn't dump all that unpleasant load on his shoulders, not at the first minute of his homecoming.

"Let me tell you about my trip." He put his arm around my waist and led me down the stairs to the library. "We had the most extraordinary experiences. Virginia City now boasts an opera house, Piper's, it's called. And I can tell you it is a sight to see those bearded, rough-looking miners in their red shirts, sitting there like sinners at Sunday school, listening to Adelina Patti warble Mozart."

"I wish I had been there."

"Oh—my dear, I doubt you would have felt comfortable amidst that uncouth crowd." He went to the cabinet and brought out the whiskey decanter. "And there are no real ladies in the town, they are all—well, you know what I mean."

"Yes," I said, not looking at him. I wondered what he would say if he knew that I knew about Lillith. Would it hurt, make him feel ashamed? I couldn't tell him, I thought. Not about Lillith.

"I'm glad I went," he was saying, pouring himself a whiskey. "I've got a good look at the mine operations, especially at the Yellow Jacket. I think Ralston's mines are running out of silver, and I feel it would be wise to take my money out and invest it in another one. A fellow by the name of Don Sayer approached me with a very interesting proposition." He paused, looking at me with a smile. "But then, Adelaide, I'm afraid I'm boring you."

"No—oh, no. Please, go on please. I want to hear, to know everything."

"You needn't fear I'm not taking good care of your money."

"*Our* money," I corrected. "Our money, Cage."

"Well—our money, then. Adelaide, I am going to make us rich. Have faith, have trust."

"But I do have faith, darling."

"Good." He bolted his whiskey and refilled his glass. "And what have you been doing, pet, while I was gone?"

I hesitated a moment. "Oh—a little of this and that," I said at last. "Nothing much. But, Cage, I wanted to tell you . . ."

"I need a bath badly," he said, wrinkling his nose. "I haven't had a decent bath since I left home. Oh—it feels so good to be back at the Folly—after all those terrible hotels. What were you going to say?"

"Nothing much," I repeated. I would tell him later, after supper perhaps when I could catch him in a mellow mood.

But Cage slept all day and went out again in the evening, late for an appointment, he said, and I did not see him until the following night when he brought Jay Cooke home for supper. I was not happy to see Jay and wondered if he had invited himself.

"I bumped into Ted Neale at the bank today," Jay managed to whisper to me while Cage was busy pouring him a whiskey. "He told me you had some kind of disturbance the other night. Have you spoken to your husband about Martha?"

"No—not yet," I answered coldly.

"As I thought," he murmured.

I sat through the meal on tenterhooks, thinking that Jay would broach the subject of Martha's voodoo rites at any moment. But the two men chatted on, discussing the building of the continental railway, the Central Pacific's race to meet the Union Pacific at Promontory Point. "It will help business here in San Francisco," Cage said, "there's no doubt of that. But what I object to is the Central bringing in all that Chinese labor. They'll be stuck here in San Francisco. They can't be sent back, I'm told. There will be coolies running amok everywhere now."

"Well," Jay said, "I expect they have as much right to run amok as anyone else."

"Are you out of your mind, or are you saying that just to annoy me?" Cage asked.

"Probably both," Jay said and laughed.

When the last plate had been cleared away at the end of the meal, I was loath to excuse myself while the men sat over port and cigars, for I wanted to hear what Jay would say, but so strong was habit, I rose automatically, smiled at the two men standing politely at their chairs, and left.

I went into the library and taking a book from the shelf, sat down with it in my lap, my ears cocked toward the dining room. No sound reached me, not even the murmur of voices, although I had left the library door ajar. I never looked at the book, just sat there, my fingers drumming on the cover. Lucinda put her head in the door and asked if I would like coffee, but I refused.

Presently, because I could bear the loud ticking of the mantel clock no longer, I left the library, lingered for an indecisive moment in the hall, fighting the urge to lean against the dining room door and listen, then went into the drawing room. I waited a long time. At one point I found myself pacing the floor, gnawing at a corner of my handkerchief. I forced myself to sit down and remain calm, but my mind continued to rush from one speculation to the next. What was Jay telling Cage? Everything? Was he talking even now about Lillith, how I had "wheedled" him into revealing her "profession"? What was he saying?

At last the door opened and Jay came in alone.

"I've told him," he said without preamble. "I've told him that you know about Lillith, that you're frightened of Martha and why. He still refuses to dismiss her."

"Where is he?" I asked, peering over Jay's shoulder. "Where is Cage?"

"He's in the dining room on the way to becoming very drunk. He's asked me to give his excuses."

"I—I don't believe you. What have you said to him? He's angry—I know he's angry—I know it. He probably feels that I forced the information from you. He's so ashamed; he didn't want me to know. What did you say— for heaven's sake—what?"

He looked at me, his eyes narrowed and hard. "Is that all you're concerned with—whether he's angry or not? Doesn't it bother you that he hasn't had the courage to explain to you himself the situation here? Can't you see he's weak and spineless?"

"Weak! Spineless! Oh—oh, you are incorrigible! Incorrigible! Why did you come tonight? *I* never invited you."

"But you *did* invite me, remember? Remember when you came to see me, frightened out of your wits and asked me to talk to Martha?"

"Yes—yes, but you're so rude, you make it impossible to have any kind of reasonable discussion, and you're so down on Cage. . . ."

"And now Cage has gone to pieces. The whole thing has overwhelmed him. Too much. He'd like to bury the past in a big, dark hole and shovel it over with ten feet of wet cement. But he realizes now that it can't be done. I advised him to make a clean breast of everything, to confide in you—his wife. But he hasn't the guts. . . ."

"You keep saying that," I broke in angrily. "And I resent it. Has it ever occurred to you that he might have wanted to spare me?"

"Tommyrot! Cage has always tried to shy away from the disagreeable."

"And I suppose you would call the war agreeable? He returned to Virginia from California to join up when he didn't have to. He fought to the very end."

"Yes, he *was* in the war until the very end, I'll concede you that. And to give the man his due, did commendably well. He's not afraid if he's got a gun in his hand and can see his enemy. It's what he can't see that frightens him— it's the feelings of others, the implied reprimand, the banked fires of anger or love. Do you understand? He surrounds himself with people and likes them as long as they don't come too close, as long as they don't speak of uncomfortable, unpleasant things."

"That's not true!" I denied hotly. "He is a warm, loving

person. He's always had close friends. And as for being afraid of people speaking—why, he married Lillith, didn't he? Well, didn't he?"

"I told you why. To him Lillith was a toy, a toy he could not have unless he made her his wife. And people, if they talk—and they do—are not the same people he grew up with. No, he doesn't like to face the unpleasant. Never has and doesn't now, my dear. And so he has asked me to tell you the rest of the story."

"*You?* I'm going to him, I don't believe it. I'm going to him."

"I would not recommend it. You will find him very drunk and probably incoherent by this time. Sit down, Adelaide. Please."

I sat down on the edge of a chair and glared at him.

"Don't be angry. I don't relish this, if that's what you're thinking, don't relish it at all. I like Cage in a way—and if it were not for you, I'd probably like him more."

"If you like Cage so much," I said with asperity, "then why do you say he's spineless, without guts? A fine friend! You're nothing but a . . ."

"Hypocrite," he sighed. "All right, my dear, I see that only a dire cataclysm will wake you from your Sleeping Beauty dream. All right, let us say that he prefers I tell you because what he has to say would be too painful for both of you. Does that make you feel better?"

"No."

"Stubborn, aren't you? Do you want to hear, or shall I take my hat and go?"

I said nothing.

"Adelaide—"

I swallowed the bitter lump in my throat, struggling between anger and the urgent need to know. "All—right," I conceded reluctantly.

He sighed as he sank back into his chair. "Do you mind if I smoke?"

"Go ahead—please."

He lit a cigar, the flame illuminating his smoothly chiseled cut features for a flaring instant. So—he doesn't relish his task, I thought scornfully. The devil himself could not be enjoying it more.

"You've asked me often enough how Lillith died," he

began. "I can tell you now." He paused, frowning for a moment at the tip of his cigar. "My dear—she was murdered."

Murdered! Strange, I should have been shocked but I wasn't. I suppose in the back of my mind I had realized all along that her death could not have been anything but violent. There was too much secrecy surrounding it to indicate a peaceful passing away. And San Francisco was a violent place. It was true the Vigilante Committee had long been disbanded, and outlaws like the Hounds and the Sydney Ducks had either been jailed or deported, but it was a city where men went about armed, where duels were common, and where shootings were reported almost daily, killings which often sacrificed innocent bystanders.

"How did it happen?" I heard myself ask.

"She was shot, killed along with her lover, James Royce, while they lay in each other's arms. Upstairs if you must know, upstairs in Cage's bed."

I felt the blood drain from my face. Upstairs!

This was different, not a woman accidentally shot, not what I had expected. I said nothing. I couldn't have, even if I had found the words. Shot in her lover's arms. It was something that happened to other people, lurid gossip one read about in the scandal sheets. Her lover—Lillith—upstairs—Cage's bed. God!

"Would you like a glass of brandy?" Jay's voice came to me from a long way off.

"What . . . ?"

"You aren't going to faint?"

"No—no . . ."

"I'll get the brandy. You have some in the library, don't you?"

"Yes . . ."

I tried to blank my mind out while he was gone, tried not to think of the gilt-framed mirrors, the sky blue ceiling, the cupids and garlands of roses. Tried not to think of the lovers lying there, the smooth satin bedspread pulled aside, the pillows rumpled. Tried not to think of the dark figure who had held the gun above them, the shot . . .

"Here you are." Jay put the glass in my hand. "Drink it, my dear. You'll feel better."

I swallowed a mouthful and the liquid burned in my

throat, spreading downward with pleasing warmth, but the pictures in my brain kept coming, mad pictures on a carousel.

"Drink some more."

I took another sip and held the glass, looking down at it. Jay did not speak. After a long while I raised my eyes.

"Who—who did it?" I finally ventured to ask.

"No one knows. Of course, Cage was suspected, but several witnesses came forward to testify on his behalf. Martha was one. Naturally a colored woman's word would not stand up too well in court, not the way the law reads here, but John Shelby corroborated Martha's statement. He claimed that Cage had spent the night with him playing cards."

"Claimed?"

"I'm not saying he lied. Don't bristle, please. But Shelby is on Martha's list, not a published secret, by any means; I just happen to know that he owes her for keeping her mouth shut about some indiscretion of his. And Martha could have persuaded Mr. Shelby to back up her story. Martha did not want Cage to hang because of Octavia, you understand."

"Yes, yes, but do you think . . . ?"

"That Cage murdered Lillith and James Royce? No, I don't think so. It was not the sort of thing Cage would do. I told you he is a brave man with a gun in his hand, and he is. He is an incredibly skillful shot, I don't think there is anyone who can beat him at ten paces. He might have called James Royce out for a duel, but I don't think he would have shot a defenseless man in the back, even if the man was in bed with his wife."

I winced and turned my eyes away. Poor Cage, I thought, poor darling. What he must have suffered, what he must have gone through, the horrible scandal and then being accused of murder as well.

"So you see why it would not be prudent to ruffle Martha's feathers too much?" Jay asked. "Why it wouldn't do to dismiss her?"

"Yes, in a way. But must Cage carry that load all the rest of his life? If he didn't do it, and he's been cleared, then there's an end to it."

"There isn't an end to it, Adelaide. Cage was never brought to trial. But now—we've heard only this morning that James Royce's brother, Lawrence, is in the City. He intends to sue Cage for the loss of his brother, he intends to prove that Cage killed him. And so there will be a trial, despite everything."

"No . . ."

"Yes," he nodded, "yes. And Martha must play an important part. I'm afraid, my dear, you will have to accommodate yourself, since I can't see Martha leaving the Folly, at least not for a very long time."

Chapter 22

LAWRENCE Royce's lawyer must have convinced his client that it would be more advantageous to have Cage tried for murder before suit was brought. I suppose he reasoned that if convicted Cage would have a poor defense against a civil charge, and his estate would be held liable after Cage had been found guilty and executed. Whatever his reckoning, Royce's lawyer, Percy Simpson, by claiming new evidence succeeded in having Cage indicted.

The trial was set for the fourteenth of June.

We hired our own lawyer, Gordon Peele, a man of mature years with a mane of snow white hair and a deep baritone voice that would have done credit to any Shakespearean actor, a vocation, in fact, he had once practiced in his youth. He had a reputation for swaying juries and making strong men cry, and though his fee was exorbitant, we were told he was well worth every penny of it. His first act was to have Cage released on bail.

That night Cage apologized for keeping me in the dark, saying that he had hoped I could have been spared.

"I'm not sorry I married Lillith," he said. "It was the only honorable thing to do. But I should have realized that she was ill-suited for—well, for matrimony."

We were in our bedroom finally, having the heart-to-heart talk we should have had months earlier. I was sitting on a chair while he paced the floor. My eyes followed him, back and forth, back and forth. When he said "ill-suited" I thought of Lillith's violet eyes, the black hair, the red rose nestled next to the white skin. Had he loved her, did he love her still?

"She was treacherous, no doubt, but you see she was young. She had never had anything, her mother and father died in a small pox epidemic, and she had to shift for herself when she was scarcely more than a child. I try to think of that when I want to condemn her."

I tried to think of it, too. But it was difficult for me to believe that anyone endowed with the face of an angelic temptress could not make her way in the world with ease, could not have whatever she craved. Beauty opened doors, broke down walls, breached class and group, gave even a harlot entrée into the world of respectable happiness. Beauty was God's gift, bestowed on the very few, the very special. I recalled my own youth, never deprived of food and shelter or even of a caring parent, but lacking the self-assurance that comes to a girl with a pretty face. I had my share of pain in shyness, suffering under the cruel, thoughtless tongues of well-meaning friends, miserable, voiceless, hanging back, longing for a love I could not have, having to make do with second best.

"Royce apparently never gave her up," Cage was saying. He stopped at the bedside table to refill his wine glass from the decanter. "He hounded her behind my back until he had his way. Mind you, Adelaide, I'm not too sure I wouldn't have killed him, there in the bedroom perhaps or later in a duel. God knows—I don't." He ran his hand through his hair.

Did you love her, even after . . . ?

"But I swear to you—I did not commit murder. I swear to it."

Do you love her now?

"I believe you, darling," I said.

"I've no idea who did. None. Nor does Martha. Royce had a wife, I heard, but she was either dead or somewhere back East. So it could not have been a jealous wife. Another woman, perhaps a mistress of Royce's, but that was not the sort of murder a woman commits. A woman would have used poison instead of a Colt. Incidentally the gun itself was never found."

Could I kill out of jealousy? I wondered. Could seeing my husband make love to another woman enrage, blind me to right and wrong, could it infuriate me to the point where shooting him would seem a logical, simple act? No, I thought, no. But if he loved her still?

Cage was saying, ". . . in such cases it's a matter of course to believe the husband is the guilty party." He clinked the bottle against the glass, his face flushed, his hair tousled. "You notice I say 'believe,' not 'suspect'; they thought they had an open and shut case. Even Captain Lees, who has the reputation for being the best detective in the country, was almost certain of my guilt. Well," the corners of his mouth turned down, "I didn't do it. Thank God, I had Shelby, Martha and the servants to back me up. I didn't do it. I was playing cards until four in the morning and slept until five on the Shelby sofa when I left to go home where I found—I found them."

She died in this room, Martha had said.

I wondered how Cage had felt when he opened the door to the bedroom and discovered the lovers locked in their mortal embrace. Had he exclaimed, *Lillith, my love . . . !*

"There were no clues, none at all," Cage said. "No one saw the assailant or heard the shots. The other servants sleep over the stable so it wasn't likely they would hear even if they were awake. As for Martha whose bedroom is beyond the kitchen, she swears she slept through the night and knew nothing until I roused her at five in the morning. Captain Lees believes the murderer knew about the secret staircase and passage and used it that night."

The secret passage built as a whim, built in Cage's bachelor days for meetings of the Golden Knights. Did Lillith laugh about it, did she tease him? Did she love him at all?

"The police must have detained and questioned at least two dozen men," Cage continued, "all of Royce's gambling cronies, the people he owed money or who owed him. But they all seemed able to prove they were nowhere within miles of the Folly. They all had alibis. So the case was shelved. Now—this Lawrence . . . ." He shook his head.

I didn't dream the house would be so full of memories, Cage had said that first night. Had he been remembering Lillith, remembering how she looked sitting in the open carriage, her lovely face shadowed by a twirling, lilac parasol? Was he remembering her now?

"I hate the scandal," Cage said. "It's a sordid mess, a public trial. I hate it for all the vultures it will gather, the newspaper reporters, the crowds of idlers and sensation-seekers. But most of all I hate it for you, my darling."

He gave me such a sad sweet smile it caught my breath, instantly wiping every bitter thought from my mind. Rising impulsively I ran to him, kissing him on the cheek, the mouth. "It's all right, my darling," I said. "Whatever happens, I love you—I always will."

The trial was held in the imposing new City Hall on Kearney Street. When we clattered up to the entrance in our carriage, the crowd had already assembled and we had to fight our way through the crush. Cage had wanted me to stay at home, but I wouldn't hear of it. I knew it would be an ordeal, that facing a multitude of curious eyes would be painful, but I could not let people think I had deserted my husband in his hour of need. Nor did I wear the veil Clara Shelby had suggested. To appear veiled, I told her, would infer I either had something to hide or that I had already—before the fact—gone into mourning.

When we entered the courtroom itself, there was a momentary hush as every head craned in our direction. Cage, taking a firm grip on my arm, led me down the narrow aisle to the seats reserved for Clara and me behind the witness bench. Voices, exclamations, a catcall followed us. "Don't take any notice, if you can," Cage said in my ear, but the excited mouthings of the crowd roared in my ears like a threatening sea.

Cage left me feeling bewildered and anxious in Clara's charge. "My dear," she whispered, "have you ever seen such a mob?" Dressed in an eye-catching blue brocade, silk dress and matching plumed bonnet, in contrast to my own sober gray attire, she gave the impression of secretly enjoying the whole affair. Holding my hand tightly, she squeezed it whenever she recognized anyone she knew. "There's old Mrs. Fairfax, the grandmother," she whispered in my ear. "And I do declare—Mrs. Walters—I wonder that *she* would come—and Jay Cooke! Alone. By the door, Adelaide."

But I kept my eyes riveted straight ahead. In front of me sat the witnesses, John Shelby, Martha, Lucinda, Gandy and the cook and some stranger in a tight-fitting black frock coat. Out of the tail of one eye I could see the reporters gathered at a special table. One of them went over to Cage and said something, and Cage shook his head. He had refused to give interviews to any of the papers, and his lawyer had done the same. Clara said it was a mistake as the news people were printing all sorts of allegations anyway, in fact not only trying Cage in their columns, but finding him guilty as well. However, since neither Cage nor I bothered to read the dailies, we gave little thought to what was written.

The chamber door opened, and we rose as the judge entered wearing his black robes. Judge Simon, a portly man, reputed to have an irascible temper, was a teetotaler, a trait our lawyer deplored. Teetotalers, in his opinion, were apt to be narrow fanatics, and he would have preferred a man who, if not a heavy drinker, could at least bend a convivial elbow now and then.

We sat down; the clerk rapped us to silence and the proceedings began.

Frank Bushe, the prosecutor came forward, nodded to the jury, glowered at Cage, and then launched into his opening speech. A tall, sober-faced man with a waterfall of whiskers running down either cheek and a full black beard masking mouth, chin and cravat, Bushe thundered out the charges against Cage like God sitting on Judgment Day. As I listened, a feeling of dismay and gloom rolled over me. I could see that we were in for a long trial and that the reporters, craning their ears and their eyes, would be given sensational grist for their mills. Moreover, it soon became apparent that our hope for enlisting sympathy for Cage as an injured husband, further injured by an accusation of murder, was indeed a slender one.

Bushe pictured Cage as a renegade, a blackguard, a gambler, a man who frequented houses of ill-repute and no matter how many times our own attorney, Mr. Peele, bounced to his feet shouting, "Objection!" the judge overruled him.

"This man, this so-called gentleman," Mr. Bushe roared, pointing a finger at Cage, "this so-called gentleman took the life of two people, shot them in cold blood. Now I want you to remember we are not trying the morals of the late Mrs. Norwood here, we are not trying the morals of James Royce, what we are trying is a murderer who has walked the streets of San Francisco a free man for the last ten years. Justice, I say, justice must be done. And you gentlemen of the jury, you . . ."

I will say this for our attorney, Mr. Peele, he was not one to be easily cowed, and he responded in kind with alacrity, presenting Cage as a well-intentioned, noble and generous husband, who plucked a "poor, soiled flower" from a den of iniquity, bestowing upon her the honor of his name only to have it besmirched. "But he did not kill her; Mr. Lewis Cage Norwood is not the kind of man to take the law into his own hands, no matter how provoked."

And so it went, day after day, the duel between Peele and Bushe, with every degrading morsel brought out in the open for the public to feast on. The courtroom crowd was obstreperous, loud in their acclaim for Bushe who seemed a favorite of theirs. They wanted a conviction, they wanted to see an aristocrat brought low, they wanted to see him hang. And I am not too sure that the upper crust—"society"—did not secretly feel the same. Cage had committed the supreme transgression. It was not that he had married a lady of light reputation, not that he had allowed himself to be cuckolded or even that he might have committed murder, but that he had been caught, his name and background splashed across the papers, his dirty linen washed in public. This was no honorable duel, no matter decided secretly over pistols, but a bawdy show for the whole world to smirk and laugh at. Not until the famous Sharon-Hill trial later on was the riff-raff so entertained, society so shocked and shamed.

As the trial progressed, the witnesses were called one by one. Martha, I must admit, was the best of the lot. Whereas John Shelby looked self-conscious and often spoke in a mumble, Martha never flinched, never permitted herself to be flustered by Bushe who kept hammering away at her, trying to trip her up. She looked him square in the eye, answering each question in a calm, unruffled and very cold voice. Despite my antipathy toward her, I had to admire, to applaud, almost to like her. Martha's evidence, I felt, would help enormously in turning the tide in Cage's favor.

But when the stranger in the black frock coat got up and went into the box as Bushe's witness, he succeeded in nullifying Martha's testimony completely. His name was Morris Sandborne—occupation, architect. He had designed the Folly.

Both Cage and his attorney had known of his scheduled appearance but had said nothing for fear of causing me undue alarm. I wished they had prepared me, for it was he who revealed the presence of the secret staircase and that it opened out into the bedroom in which Lillith and James Royce were murdered.

"Anyone—*anyone*," Bushe exhorted, "could have used the stairs, and no one, not even the estimable housekeeper, Martha Browne, would have known his identity. John Shelby claims that Mr. Norwood spent the night with him, but does admit—does admit, mind you—that they retired around four in the morning and that Mr. Norwood rose at five to go home. I put it to you, gentlemen, wouldn't it have been a simple matter for the accused, after he had made sure the others in the household were safely asleep, to rise from his sofa bed, slip on his clothes, sneak out of the house and make for the Folly posthaste? Perhaps he suspected his wife's infidelity, perhaps he expected to catch her and her lover *flagrante delicto*. My feeling is that this is precisely what happened. My feeling is that . . ."

"Objection!" Mr. Peele cried, springing to his feet. "We are not here to listen to Mr. Bushe's feelings. He has no proof, no proof other than scurrilous allegations. Conjecture of the lowest kind."

"And what proof do *you* have, Mr. Peele?" Bushe retorted.

Someone among the spectators shouted, "You bloody liar, Mr. Peele!" and another man jumped up and punched him in the nose. The next moment the courtroom erupted in a melee, shouts and curses rang out, fists flew, and ladies screamed, some of them falling into a faint. Clara and I clung to one another while the gavel banged, Mr. Bushe roared, and the crowd fought, pummeled, shrieked and hollered. A contingency of extra police were called in, and they finally quelled the riot.

The judge, beside himself with anger, adjourned court for three days.

It was a gloomy three days for us at the Folly, although Peele assured us we had nothing to worry about, that the evidence was circumstantial and that unless a witness could swear that he had seen Cage at the scene of the crime, no jury would convict him. To our collective horror, however, such a witness was produced when court convened once again. The witness was not some vagrant picked up off the street, but a respectable, side-whiskered gentleman by the name of Howard Soames, who had worked as a guard for Lobb and Company, a downtown firm.

Mr. Soames claimed that on the night in question while walking his dog past the Folly he was almost forced from the road into the ditch by a horseman going "hell-bent-for-leather." The rider dismounted, he testified, opposite the gate and tethered his horse in a small clump of bushes just beyond the ditch. Then he crossed over, ". . . stealthy-like," Mr. Soames said. "But there was a full moon and I got a good look at him."

"And do you see that man now, Mr. Soames?" Mr. Bushe asked, pausing dramatically before he went on. "I want you to be most careful. A man's life is at stake. Careful, now, but do you see that man in this courtroom?"

"Yes," Mr. Soames replied. "He is sitting right over there—the defendant, sir, Mr. Cage Norwood."

Cage turned very white.

Mr. Peele jumped to his feet. "He's a liar!" he shouted. "That man has perjured himself!"

And again pandemonium broke loose in the courtroom, forcing the judge to dismiss until the following morning.

We were very quiet, very glum on the ride home. Neither Mr. Peele nor Cage spoke a word. I felt as if the bottom had dropped out of everything, and the silence of the two men terrified me. What did it mean? Why had this witness suddenly come forward? I longed to speak of it, but Cage sat with his head averted, and Mr. Peele stared straight ahead. Unapproachable. I knew they had much to say but did not want me to hear. Bad, it looked very bad.

At supper Mr. Peele commented, "Of course, he perjured himself."

And I said, "How?"

Mr. Peele merely shrugged his shoulders and would say no more. When the cloth had been cleared and port and cigars brought, I did not rise to leave but sat resolutely in my chair, determined to stay and hear what was said. I had reckoned without Mr. Peele, however.

"Mrs. Norwood?" Mr. Peele rose politely. "If you will."

"I would like to remain," I said.

"I think not," Mr. Peele said. "Please do us the courtesy?"

I looked at Cage, hoping he would countermand what I felt was an order. But he was busy pouring wine and said nothing.

Worse and worse, I thought, walking slowly into the library. Mr. Peele does not want me to hear because he is afraid—afraid of what? Afraid that Cage was not telling him the truth? But I couldn't believe that. I couldn't believe Cage would lie. He was *innocent*, innocent!

And so I sat there in that horrible room, assailed by doubts, my mind whirling in confusion. Had Mr. Soames really seen Cage? No—he was mistaken; it had been someone else, someone else who had galloped up to the Folly "hell-bent-for-leather" and tethered his horse across the road. And yet . . .

Cage had reason to suspect Lillith of adultery, a woman whom marriage did not suit, he had reason to guess she might still be seeing her former lover. Had he gone back to the Folly that night, found her with Royce and killed the two of them? Dear God, even if he had, would a jury convict him? In France he would have been exonerated. In France where they understood "crimes of passion" he would have gotten off scot-free. But this was not France, this was San Francisco where anything could happen, where Cage was being tried before a judge and by a prosecutor, eye-for-eye men, Old Testament to the core.

But how could I presume? How could I condemn my own husband of a crime he swore he did not commit? I must not love him, I thought, I must not if I could feel this way. But—oh!—I *did* love him, despite everything, I loved him now more than ever, if that were possible. I loved him because he was beleaguered, because he was fighting against terrible odds, because he needed me, because he was Cage.

The door opened and Martha came in balancing a tray with the coffee things.

"Are the men ready to join me?" I asked.

Though my relationship with Martha had undergone somewhat of a change during the past few weeks, I still did not trust her completely for I knew she would remain loyal only as long as she found it expedient to do so. I never let myself forget that underneath her pose of a faithful and obedient servant lurked a devious mind and a heart that could be hard as granite. But for the present we were allies, and I knew that because of Octavia she wanted Cage to be exonerated as much as we all did. (Octavia, thank goodness, was still away at school, where we hoped she would remain until the trial was long over.)

"Mr. Cage and Mr. Peele will be along pretty quick," she said. The cups rattled as she set the tray down.

"Martha," I began, "Martha, you heard that man, Soames today. What do you think?"

"I think he's a liar," she said without hesitation. "Just as Mr. Peele called him. That man is a liar and I intend to prove it."

"How?" I asked, interested.

"I have ways," she replied mysteriously.

The trial dragged on. Mr. Soames, recalled to the stand, was cross-examined by our Mr. Peele, who, not wanting to be outdone by Mr. Bushe's theatrics, provided some of his own, pacing back and forth like a caged lion for several minutes, before he turned suddenly and growled at the witness, "And why haven't you come forward sooner, Mr. Soames?"

Mr. Soames, imperturbable, placidly retorted, "I didn't think anything of it at the time. I guessed what I saw was a man in a hurry to get home, although it did seem a bit queer his leaving the horse tethered across the road. But then I'd heard the rich people up at the Folly were apt to do funny things."

A titter of laughter rippled across the courtroom, and the judge, frowning fiercely, rapped for silence.

"My good man," Mr. Peele said, drawing out the words in an icy voice, "when I wish for your opinion, I shall ask for it. You were not brought into this court of law to entertain the mob, or, I might add, to perjure yourself, but to give evidence, the truth, the whole truth, and nothing but the truth, so help you God!" he finished with a resounding bellow.

"Now . . . ," he went on, his finger shaking under Mr. Soames's nose, "*I* want to know, the court wants to know, why it took you not days, not weeks, not months, but *years* to come forward. Please—if you will—we are waiting on your answer."

Mr. Soames drew himself up. "Certainly, Mr. Peele. The fact is I didn't know a murder was committed. You see, I left the next morning for Gold Hill in the Comstock as I wanted a better job and heard they were looking for security guards in the mines. I was on the road the better part of two weeks, so I never saw a newspaper, and by the time I reached Virginia City I guess the news had blown over. I did not know there had been murder at the Folly until day before yesterday when I got off the boat from Sacramento and picked up a copy of the *Alta* with Mr. Norwood's picture on the front page."

"And *then* you remembered? *Suddenly*—out of the blue you remembered walking a dog in the middle of a black— oh, pardon me—moonlit night ten years earlier?"

"Yes, sir. I remembered because I nearly got knocked in the ditch."

"Hmmm. I daresay it wasn't the first time you nearly got knocked in a ditch." Another wave of laughter, another rapid banging of the gavel. "Well, then, Mr. Soames, so out of the goodness of your heart, for the sake of justice, for the love of city and country, you came forward."

"Yes, sir."

There was no shaking him. Earlier Mr. Peele had sent his clerk snooping to see if he could find out something he could use against Mr. Soames. It was true the man had worked as a guard for Lobb and Company, but that business establishment was now defunct, and the exact dates of Mr. Soames's employment were difficult to ascertain; in fact after ten years very little about Mr. Soames could be ascertained. By his own admission instead of working as a guard in the mines, he had decided to go out on his own as an itinerant peddler and "did fairly well, too." As we all knew, a peddler's movements were more difficult to trace than a bumble bee's.

They were back at it again.

"Would a man be walking his dog at four in the morning?" Mr. Peele asked.

"Why yes," Mr. Soames asserted. "I did not get off work at Lobb's until two A.M. when my relief came. You see, my hours were topsy-turvy. I got home, had a bite of supper and then took Fritz for his nightly stroll."

He stuck to his guns, a stolid, unemotional little man dressed very neatly with a high, white, starched collar. Rather like a minor bank clerk, very respectable, rather fearsome in his respectability. Nothing rattled him, nothing until another surprise witness was brought in the next day, this one by our own Mr. Peele.

Erikson was his name; and it was he who brought the prosecutor's house of cards down. He had been a jailer in

Fresno (a city somewhat south and east of San Francisco) and recalled that Mr. Soames had spent three days there in June of 1862, a day before, during and after the murder.

"He went under the name of Greenwood then. Got drunk and was arrested for attacking an officer of the law. He had a record of petty forgery. I brought the records with me, so you can see. Yes, that was the man, that was Mr. Greenwood, as calls himself Soames now."

When Erikson's testimony was backed up by the Fresno sheriff who had arrested Soames and by a local business-man who accused him of forging a bank draft, Soames's composure cracked. He had lied, he said tearfully, but it wasn't his fault.

"I was down and out, poorer than a church mouse," he claimed, great tears of self-pity rolling down his whiskered cheeks, this man who had come close to sending my hus-band to the gallows. "It wasn't my fault when I grabbed at a chance to eat my first decent meal in months and to have some decent clothes and a little extra left over."

"You were paid to testify?" Mr. Peele asked, his voice trembling with outrage and shock. "By whom?"

"I—I don't rightly know. You see it was all done mys-teriously—that is, a note was left for me at the Bella Union bar—the barkeep couldn't remember who brought it, and I was told to go to the Jackson Street wharf after dark if I wanted to make a few dollars for very little work. I went and waited and waited around and finally this woman approached me. The night was foggy and she was veiled so I couldn't tell you what she looked like."

"Short or tall, fat, skinny?" Mr. Peele pressed. "Surely you could see that much."

"Well—I'd say neither tall nor short, and she was wrapped about in a large shawl so I can't say if she was skinny or fat."

"And she gave you instructions?"

"Yes—she told me exactly what to say. I met her again the next night, and she brought me half the money and took me through my paces again. 'Half now', she said, 'half when he gets hung.' "

Later when the court adjourned while the jury deliber-ated, Mr. Peele invited us to his suite of offices across the street. Here, over brandy, he questioned Cage closely as to whom this "mysterious woman" might be.

"I haven't the slightest idea," Cage said, a puzzled frown between his eyes.

"Obviously she was a go-between," Peele said. "Do you have any enemies that would like to see you dead?"

"I have enemies—naturally—in business one usually does," Cage answered. "But I can't think that any of them would take such drastic measures."

"Hmmm. It's possible Lawrence Royce himself hired the witness. He seems like a most vengeful man, anxious to get a conviction. But I doubt we could ever prove it. Nevertheless, we shan't have to worry about Royce for very much longer. I believe the jury's verdict is now a foregone conclusion."

Peele was right. An hour later when the jury came in with a resounding "Not Guilty!" I burst into tears, I couldn't help it; I wept from sheer happiness right there in the courtroom with everyone looking on, cried tears of relief as Cage put his arms around me.

Mr. Peele was jubilant. We thanked him a thousand times, but he said the real thanks went to Martha. It was she who had dug up Mr. Erikson in Fresno. "God alone knows how she did it," he said.

How did she do it? How did she manage to accomplish what Mr. Peele's clerk had failed to do?

"I have friends," was all she would say. "Lots of good friends, here and in Fresno."

Later when I asked if she had any theories as to who committed the murders she said no. But there was something in her face, a brief flicker, the tic of a muscle in her cheek when she uttered that one short word, that gave me the odd suspicion she had more than a theory, that she knew who had fired those fatal shots, perhaps had known from the very beginning.

Chapter 23

I had thought once the trial was behind us and the dark secrets between Cage and myself gone, we would reach a new understanding, a new and stronger intimacy. But such was not the case. Once again he began to absent himself frequently, many nights staying over in town. "On business," he said. He drank a good deal too, and seemed just as reluctant to speak his thoughts as he had been in the past. Once when I was bold enough to ask him what he did that kept him occupied so many evenings a week, he said I wouldn't understand. "I don't want to trouble you with the intricacies of finance, my dear. You see, I've left Ralston and have invested my money in something that promises to bring a far greater return."

"But, Cage, I would like to know, I want to know everything you do, I'm your wife."

"Don't you trust me, Adelaide?" he asked with a chilliness that threw terror into my heart. I didn't want him to be cold to me, ever. I didn't want to quarrel, I didn't want him to think I had regretted for one moment signing my money over to him. I wanted him to love me as I loved him.

"You know that I do, darling," I said, going to him, kissing him on the forehead. It was a brow cool as marble. He did not kiss me back.

"I've made you angry, Cage—darling—I don't know why I said that—I don't—really—it's only because I wanted to share—but I realize it is not proper for a woman to meddle, although I hadn't meant to," the words tumbled out, silly, idiotic.

"Please, Adelaide," he said stiffly, "don't go on. I'm *not* angry. I would appreciate, however, if you exhibited a little more trust and didn't catechize me every time I am forced to spend the evening away from home."

Had I catechized? "Yes, darling," I said, taking his hand, looking into his face. Then after a long moment, "Am I forgiven?"

He gave me a wintry smile.

Octavia came home from the convent the following month ostensibly on a visit. She had grown an inch taller, and the few pounds she had gained rounded her figure out to a new maturity, enhancing her resemblance to the portrait of her dead mother. At sixteen and a half she had become a very beautiful young lady. She was also kinder to me. I think her having been away in a place where her whims and her wishes were not catered to plus the sobering news of her father's trial—which, much to our surprise, she knew all about—had much to do with it.

She had always been aware although hazily, that her mother had not come from a socially prominent family and that she had not died a natural death, but the exact circumstances of Lillith's demise had been kept from her. Cage, and I think Martha, too, had hoped that this latest airing of the scandal would not have reached her in Marysville. But it was vain hope. Gossip travels faster than the wind, it seems, and Octavia heard of the trial through a school chum's aunt who had visited the convent. The news spread throughout the school within minutes of the aunt's disclosure, throwing Octavia into hysteria. She was all for going home at once, but fortunately the Mother Superior, a level-headed woman, managed to calm her down, smoothing over the tale and persuading Octavia to stay on until Easter recess.

Nevertheless, Octavia did not want to return to school. The girls she claimed were snobs, and Cage, declaring he was in no mood to debate the issue, submitted to her desire to stay home. He had always been fond of her, but now his fondness seemed rather absent-minded, as if he were thinking of other matters, and I could tell that Octavia was trying valiantly to conceal her hurt.

If Cage seemed indifferent, Ted Neale was not. Hearing that Octavia had returned to the Folly, he wrote me a note, begging me to put in a kind word for him. "Ask if I may see her, Aunt Adelaide, please. I promise I shan't embarrass her—I shall act very properly, very circumspectly."

Octavia did not show much interest in seeing Ted again, but when no other suitable beaux appeared to escort her to parties or balls, she consented. It was obvious that she was being snubbed by the swains of good family, most likely on the stern advice of their mamas; for I could not imagine a young man in his right mind being able to resist Octavia's beauty despite her dubious background. But they did not send their cards, nor did they call. What invitations Octavia received were from the lesser lights, the *nouveau riche* who were only too delighted to consort with the granddaughter (though adopted) of a Riverknoll Norwood.

If Octavia was pained by the lack of invitations from acceptable, high society callers (of the unacceptable, the drunks and rakes, there were more than one, quickly dismissed by Martha before they got their feet in the door), she gave no sign. She had always been a hard person to read. She could get angry, yes, but not often, and except for that time when she had thrown herself on the library floor refusing to go to convent school, I had never seen her lose control.

Perhaps her aloofness was due to Martha's influence in whose care she had been since birth. Octavia had the same unnerving way of looking directly at you out of impenetrable, blank and very cold eyes. Since that first meeting when she had thrown herself into Cage's arms after his three-year absence, I had not seen her demonstrate open affection toward him, though I believed she was still as fond of him as she was of Martha—or of anybody. Toward me she exhibited a cool politeness. With Ted she was often rude.

Poor boy and so head over heels in love. He confided to me that he wanted to marry her. I wisely kept my counsel, for I knew only too well that if his father had any inkling of the situation, he would come posthaste to San Francisco and quickly fetch Ted home. Tidewater society might be reduced to genteel poverty, working the land with their own bare hands, but their standards, their code, hadn't changed one iota. From Aunt Tildy's letters I learned that though some rumors of Cage's troubles had reached them, they were vague enough to be meaningless. "We hear that Cage is involved in some sort of lawsuit," Aunt Tildy wrote and I did not enlighten her. Nor did I mention Ted's courtship of Octavia, hoping that in time he would grow weary of his vain pursuit. For Ted to bring home a bride whose antecedents were not thoroughly known to the third generation back would prompt an inquiry which might very well reveal the truth, a shocking one closing all doors to him along the Tidewater, to say nothing of his own door at Beech Arbor.

Martha, of course, looked with great favor upon Ted's suit, greeting him with one of her rare smiles whenever he called. She also saw to his comfort. Would he care for a glass of wine while he waited for Octavia? Perhaps he would like to come into the library where there was a fire to ward off the chill. "Octavia was just saying this morning," she would state, "I wonder if Mr. Neale will come by today." Martha would muse repeatedly. She did not exactly fawn on Ted, but her manner came close to it, close enough sometimes to make me cringe inwardly. I had to keep telling myself that I must not be harsh on Martha, that were it not for her, Cage would have been a condemned man and I, a widow.

Overall, however, the situation between Martha and myself was so improved from days gone by I really could not complain. She no longer frightened me. I could relax, be my own mistress without feeling uneasy or timid. I no longer peered into mirrors to find a white face and eyes made enormous by apprehension. The dark nights during which I had lain awake hour after hour in a cold sweat were over. If Martha still practiced voodoo, she did so far removed from the Folly. The bad times were gone, finished. The house, too, had given up its secrets, Lillith's ghost had been laid to rest; the haunting, like the fear, was over now. The Folly and I had finally come to terms.

Or so I optimistically believed. How premature I was, how wrong, for the Folly was far from done with me; my real travail was just beginning.

At the start I thought it was sheer absent-mindedness, an uncharacteristic, hazy forgetfulness that made me misplace objects, confuse the time of day or see things that were not there. I remember very well the first time it happened. It centered around a nonexistent cat. Dogs I love, pet birds I tolerate, but cats I cannot abide; they literally make me ill. It is not that they frighten me, but their presence, something in their fur, perhaps, sets me to sneezing uncontrollably. Sometimes I will even break out in a rash. For that reason I cannot allow one in the house. Fortunately the

Folly's cats were yard and stable creatures, and so we never had any arguments about their appearance inside.

Imagine my consternation, then, to walk into my bedroom one midmorning to find a huge orange tabby curled up on my bed. I immediately rang for Lucinda, and when she did not appear, I pulled the bell rope three times for Gandy. No one came. Although we had since hired two "undermaids" (cronies of Martha's—she refused to work with anyone except whom she could vouch for) my urgent summons remained unanswered. The tabby meanwhile slept on, and I dared not touch it because of the rash. Caught in a flurry of sneezes, my eyes weeping profusely and with my handkerchief pressed over my mouth and nose, I hurried from the room, down the stairs and back hallway to the kitchen.

Martha, Lucinda, and one of the new maids (Cora by name) were at the round table calmly drinking coffee. I was so angry at finding them at their ease I could not speak for several moments.

"What is it, Mrs. Norwood," Martha asked. And when I said nothing, "Is something wrong?"

"Didn't any of you hear me ring?" I asked indignantly, breaking my angry silence.

They looked at one another and then at me. "No, Mrs. Norwood," Martha said. "We heard nothing. When was this?"

"A few minutes ago," I said. "I rang several times, for Lucinda, for Gandy. Surely one of you could have heard and come upstairs."

"There was no ring, m'am." Martha said. She had a particularly mocking way of saying "m'am," though her face betrayed nothing that would pass as disrespect. "I'm sorry."

The others nodded in silent assent.

"Then I daresay the bells are out of order," I said crisply. "However, in the meanwhile I need help. Someone let a cat into the house and I would like to have it removed. At once, if you will."

Cora, a young and very pretty mulatto, rose. "Oh—and Cora." I said, "see that you take the spread up and give it a good airing. I'm very sensitive to cat hair."

I waited for her at the bottom of the staircase.

Five minutes went by, ten and then she called down to

me, "Mrs. Norwood? Are you certain the cat didn't run out when you opened the door? 'Cause he's not here, Mrs. Norwood."

I went up the stairs. "Of course I'm certain. I shut the door purposely so it wouldn't stray off into another part of the house."

"There's no cat," she said. "I can't find him. Here, kitty, kitty," she began to call.

The bedspread was smooth. "Run your hand over it, Cora," I said, "to see if there are any hairs."

She did as she was told, but there was nothing, not a single, short, orange strand to show that the cat had been curled up in my bed.

"Perhaps he's hiding somewhere," I said, looking around.

Cora began to call again, "Here, kitty, here, kitty." But I knew he wasn't there because if he had been I would have been sneezing by now.

"Perhaps he slipped past me without my noticing it," I said after she had searched beneath the bed and behind the wardrobe once more.

We went out into the corridor. "Maybe Miss Octavia has seen him," she suggested, but not before I caught her giving me an odd look.

Octavia was sprawled on the bed, leafing through a fashion journal. She had been there all morning, she said, and never saw or heard a cat.

We did not find it. Moreover, Gandy said that none of the cats at the Folley were orange tabbies. "Some stray, then," I suggested.

How a stray could get into the house, pass unseen up the stairs and enter my room was open for conjecture. But I didn't want to think about it. There was something strange in the cat's appearance, and it secretly gave me the shudders. Had I imagined him? But that was preposterous.

Then there was the business of the library clock. I came in one late afternoon to find that it had stopped. I was alone in the house, I remember, Martha and the servants having gone to a funeral and Ted and Octavia to a tea dance. Cage was in the City. I had never particularly liked the clock, and now that it had ceased to function I had a good excuse to get rid of it. As soon as Gandy came home, I decided, I would have him remove it from the mantel and store it somewhere.

I remained in the library for a half hour or so. It was a chilly day for late June, windy with a gray overcast. From where I sat I could see the trees along the drive bending in the wind. Cage said that June was always a dismal month, something to do with air and sea currents, but that we could look forward to brighter weather in July. The cold had seeped into the room so I put a match to the kindling in the grate and threw in several sticks as the blaze caught. Strangely, the fire seemed without warmth, and I wrapped a shawl about my shoulders. Then I brought a book down from the shelf. The books at the Folly were good ones; volumes of poetry, Shakespearean plays, novels by Trollope, Dickens and Scott, but no one had apparently bothered to read them as the pages were mostly still uncut.

I selected a volume of Shelley. I liked his poems, they were so romantic, but today for some reason I could not concentrate on the printed page. I felt restless, uneasy, almost as if someone were watching me. It dismayed me because I thought I had gotten over those little shivery qualms. The passage was sealed; no one was at home but me. Why should I feel nervous?

Deciding a cup of tea would put me to rights, I went into the kitchen to make myself one. It took a little while as I was not accustomed to the stove, and it was some minutes before I managed to light it. When I finally had brewed a pot, I put it on a tray with a cup and saucer and a few chocolate biscuits I found in the cupboard. Sugar and lemon, too. There, I told myself, I haven't forgotten how to do without servants.

When I got back to the library, the odd feeling that something was wrong hit me almost the moment I opened the door and crossed the threshold. Not wrong, exactly, but different, something was *different*. Then I heard the clock tick in that loud, noisy way it did. It must have started again, I thought in exasperation, sometimes clocks did that. I never understood their vagaries. But when I looked at it, my heart froze in my breast.

The clock had not missed a single minute of time. It had stopped at three; I remembered distinctly seeing the small hand at three, the large one at twelve. Three. And I had come into the room at a quarter past. But now the clock said four-thirty, four-thirty just like the watch I wore pinned to my dress—four-thirty.

I'm imagining it, I thought, I'm imagining. It couldn't be. A clock may start up again on its own but does not move its own hands and adjust to time.

My arms were shaking so badly I thought I would drop the tray. I set it down very carefully, biting my lip. Even if the clock had started up again the moment I left the library, there was still that half hour or so it had remained silent. Where had those minutes gone? Had the clock really stopped, had I sat there reading Shelley or did the words come to me in my head as I slept there on the chair. Was it a dream, was it real?

Or—was I losing my mind?

The clock went on ticking, the pendulum going to and fro, to and fro. The sound seemed to fill my ears, crowding into my skull, my brain. It resounded in the room, echoing from wall to wall just as it had done on an afternoon months and months ago. The cupids above the dial smiled their simpering, mocking smiles, staring at me maliciously from the corners of their eyes, cupids with white faces, pink cheeks and yellow curls. Made of china like the clock, they were inanimate objects, unthinking, lifeless lumps of clay and wire. But all the while, the tick-tock filled the room like a living heart. Four thirty-five, four thirty-six. I wanted to pick up the book, hurl it at the cupids, smash the glass face of the clock that was slowly driving me to the brink—but I was afraid. Afraid of a clock! "Stop!" my mind screamed. I put my hands over my ears. "Stop!" and turning in horror, I fled.

After that I became wary. I avoided the library as much as possible. I had McCorkle remove the clock and store it in the attic, one of those scrimshawed turrets that rose out of the roof of the Folly like an excrescence. And that, I thought, would be the end of it.

Then I began misplacing objects. More than once when I could have sworn I put a book, a vase or my sewing basket in one room, it would turn up in another. The sewing basket especially seemed hard to keep track of. I used it fairly often during that time, on most afternoons when I sat in the small parlor embroidering a linen table-cloth. It was my habit to leave the basket there by my chair when I had finished for the day so that I could easily pick it up again when I returned. The first time I missed the basket I summoned Cora who swore she had seen it there that very morning when she dusted the room. *She* had not moved it. The basket was subsequently found in the drawing room on a small sofa facing the fireplace. I did not recall taking it into the drawing room the previous day, though I might have done so.

That was the odd thing about those little "losses of memory"; they were lapses that were possible, not likely but possible. At one point I thought Martha, the maids, or even Octavia were playing tricks on me. That was the day I could not find my brooch. It had belonged to my mother, not a valuable piece of jewelry but one that I cherished. I kept it in a small ebony box with an inlaid ivory lid, but on that particular afternoon when I reached in to get it, the brooch was not there.

I suspected one of the new maids had filched it, thinking perhaps that because I had earbobs, necklaces, pins and various trinkets more valuable and flashier, I would not miss the rather plain brooch. Both the girls when questioned, however, vehemently denied taking it (Cora breaking into tears), and, of course, I never would have had the nerve to ask Martha, even if I had suspected her. Martha might spy, manipulate and plot; but I doubt she would ever stoop to thievery. She had that kind of tough pride.

And yet when the brooch was found the next day in a sideboard drawer in the dining room (where I could not have possibly put it), I wondered if Martha, out of spitefulness or sheer malignant dislike, was at the bottom of these queer happenings. Perhaps she was trying to reduce me to fear again. But why? Lillith's secret, which she had guarded so jealously, was no longer a secret. Why should she want to punish me? Why should she want revenge? Revenge, I thought—of course! How could I have possibly forgotten the dark night of the voodoo and how I had subsequently put a stop to those evil, midnight revelries. And later, when I overheard Lucinda talking to one of the new maids, I was sure Martha's resentment still rankled. "Martha's losing her hold," Lucinda said. "The darkies are looking to a new high priestess, Mammy Pleasant—they're all flocking to her now."

Martha would not be one to lose face among her people with good grace. Blaming me, she would fume inwardly, planning some way to even the score. And though stealing might be beyond her, revenge was something she held dear as life's blood. I recalled only too well how she had spoken against Cage because he had sided with the Confederacy. And even though she had valued him as a parent for Octavia, she had struck back at him in the best way she knew how by her involvement with the Underground. Her work for that organization had not been altogether altruistic (was Martha ever altogether altruistic?) but had been motivated in part at least by the secret satisfaction of retaliating against Cage, an enemy.

Was I her enemy now?

I didn't know for certain, but I began to watch Martha very closely. It was the old cat and mouse game once more, although who played cat and who played mouse was a moot point. I had to be cautious for she had eyes in the back of her head, and if she once suspected that I was keeping her under surveillance, I would never be able to catch her making a wrong move. To make sure she was not using the secret passageway, I examined the three doors, the one in the garden, the one in the library and the one in Lillith's room, twice a day for signs of their having been tampered with. They remained tightly sealed, not a nail out of place, not a splinter or a flake of paint to be found on the ground, nothing to indicate the doors had been reopened even temporarily.

Perhaps Martha did suspect I was watching her, for a week went by without my having once "misplaced," or lost anything. I began to breathe easier. It was much more comfortable to calculate how to deal with a flesh and blood adversary than with the frightening but ephemeral concept of my own failing mind. Yet I could not go on indefinitely, furtively following her movements. My best hope was that she would soon grow confident again and resume playing her little tricks, enabling me to pounce upon her and snare her red-handed.

Then she and Octavia left for ten days. Octavia had been invited by the Ralstons to a ball at Belmont given in honor of the Japanese ambassador. I think Ted Neale had wangled the invitation, and Martha went along as chaperone. They were to stay on afterwards for a round of picnics and parties. Cage and I had not been invited, because, I suspect, feelings between Ralston and Cage since their break were strained. Cage was miffed, he loved parties, but I did not mind. I still shied away from large, formal affairs; I had never gotten used to them, and with Martha and Octavia gone I could relax for once, be off my guard.

For two days I went about feeling better than I had in a long while. I liked being my own housekeeper, liked going into the kitchen in the early morning, instructing the maids, handing the cook a menu for the evening meal. I liked having Gandy and McCorkle look to me for orders. It gave me a feeling of poise, of authority, of worth, and when Martha came back, I thought I could find a tactful way to have her relinquish some of her duties to me.

And then something happened, an oddly familiar occurrence which plunged me into the depths once more.

One morning, in the parlor while I was embroidering on a tablecloth, I suddenly remembered I had neglected to tell the cook that we would be having guests on Saturday night for supper. I went into the kitchen just as the servants were beginning a late breakfast. I spoke to the cook for a few minutes, not more than five, and then returned to the parlor, to find the ginger-striped cat sleeping in my chair.

If I had seen a ghost, I could not have been more petrified. I stood there, my hand at my throat, staring at it in horror, my heart thumping painfully against my ribs. A tabby, the same one. I blinked and blinked again, hoping it would go away, but it was still there. A cat, I thought, only a cat. But I wouldn't touch it, I couldn't. Backing away, I reached the door, went through, and as I closed it, peeped through the crack to make sure the cat was still there.

I hurried into the kitchen. "Cora," I said, "there's a cat in the small parlor. Please come and remove it."

She rose from the table, wiping her hands on a napkin. Then she followed me down the back hall and across the entry hall to the parlor.

I opened the door. The chair was empty. The cat had vanished.

We began to look for it, high and low, under chairs, behind the portieres, in the cupboard, under the small side table. There weren't as many places to look as there had been in the bedroom when we searched for the same cat weeks earlier so it did not take quite as long. I kept calling, "Kitty, kitty." my voice rising with alarm.

Cora said nothing.

Finally I dismissed her with some feeble, mumbled apology.

After she left I stood in the middle of the room, my thoughts in whirling confusion. I could not blame the appearance and disappearance of the cat on Martha or Octavia, who were miles away, nor on the servants who were all in the kitchen. What had I seen? A hallucination? I was frightened, terribly frightened. And for the first time I began to seriously think that perhaps I *was* losing my mind.

Chapter 24

I longed to talk out my fear with someone, a mature and sensible person who would assure me that I was perfectly sane, someone who would convince me that I was not losing my mind just because I thought I saw a cat in my chair or thought I had left my sewing basket in the parlor and not in the drawing room. It would have been such a relief just to unburden myself, to bring my horrible apprehension out into the open instead of having it secretly gnaw at my vitals day and night. But there was no one.

Clara Shelby, though an understanding friend and one I could count on to listen with sympathy to my troubles, was not, however, one I could trust. Inadvertently, without meaning to, she might drop a word, a thought, a phrase about the state of my mental health, and from there other tongues would pick it up, spreading rumor and gossip like the wild fires which periodically swept San Francisco. I could just hear them, "Why, my dear, didn't you know? Adelaide Norwood—crazy as a bedbug." The whispers and the knowing shakes of the head, the confidential winks. "Yes, unfortunate man, Cage, his first wife—a, well, you know what I mean, and his second, wrong in the head."

No, Clara Shelby would not do, and as for Cage I could not see how it was possible to approach him with such a bizarre problem. He seemed more remote than ever these days. He wore an abstracted, worried air, and my few attempts at drawing him into conversation were met with a grunt or a polite, almost inaudible monosyllable. At supper, when and if he came home in the evening, he often drank more than he ate. One night, after a very long and weighty silence, he told me that business rivals were badgering him to the point where he sometimes feared for his life and that he had hired a man to ride with him.

If I had been less preoccupied with my own trouble, I

would have been shocked and terribly worried as well. It never occurred to me that Cage, a courageous soldier, a man so coolly able with dueling pistols would ever need another man's protection. His situation, or predicament, must have been grave indeed to warrant the hiring of a bodyguard, but at the time I could only think how lovely it would be if I, too, could rid myself of fear by hiring a formidable escort.

I thought of writing Aunt Tildy and indeed started a letter to her. But I could find no words to explain adequately my dreadful anxiety, and what I had already written looked foolish. And so I tore the paper up. It was just as well. There was nothing Aunt Tildy could do, and she was too old and too crippled with rheumatism to make the long trip across the thousands of miles which separated us.

Confiding in Ted Neale was out of the question, and the only other person I knew more than casually in San Francisco was Jay Cooke. I had last seen him at the trial, and not alone since that terrible evening when he had told me about the murders and that Lawrence Royce was trying to have Cage indicted for them. I had so many mixed feelings about Jay. Deep down I knew that if ever I was in desperate trouble, I could come to him and he would help as he had done that day I told him about Martha's voodoo rites. But he could also be nasty and cutting, provoking me to intense dislike, and sometimes I wondered if the help he gave was worth the accompanying barrage of unpleasantness I first had to endure. If I came to him now with my tale of woe he might very well wonder aloud, in his customary, mocking way, how it was that a wife who thought she was going mad would not seek the advice of a husband rather than that of a male friend.

So I said nothing, but kept my secret locked tightly inside me. I walked, I sat, I moved through the days, carefully, like an invalid, afraid to breathe deeply, to talk more than was necessary, my heart beating with dread, anticipating the worst. Again I became fearful of opening a closed door, of entering an empty room. The cat might be there, or a clock stopped, or my sewing basket gone. I gave up embroidery for my hands had begun to tremble. Sometimes I walked in the garden, back and forth along the path, my skirt sweeping the dead leaves and fallen rose petals. Then I would stop suddenly, thinking the servants might see me pacing and speculate. They might even surmise the truth. I couldn't bear that—I couldn't bear their sliding glances, the curious stares, the sound of muted laughter behind the kitchen door.

Octavia and Martha came back from Belmont. Octavia had little to say. "The ball was nice," she commented laconically. "The guests were a bore."

"Even Ted Neale?" I asked.

"Even Ted Neale."

But she went on seeing him, because, as she frankly admitted, there was no one more interesting in the offing, and he did manage to get the choicest invitations.

I thought I would feel better if I became engrossed in "good works," and so volunteered my services at St. Mary's Hospital. I visited the sick, helped to feed, read and write letters for them just as I had done in Richmond during the war. And though the atmosphere was a great deal more palatable than it had been in those bloody, war-torn years, I soon discovered I simply could not cope. I could not concentrate on the tasks at hand. Often I would sit for long minutes at a bedside unable to utter a word. I forgot names, became confused easily and more than once found myself on the verge of weeping for no apparent reason. Still I went doggedly on, telling myself that soon, any time now, it would all go away. The bewilderment, the fear, the numbing depression would vanish. But it didn't go away. And on the day I broke down and sobbed openly when a patient accidentally upset a lunch tray in my lap, I knew I had reached the nadir of my desperation.

I consulted a doctor on Kearney Street, Dr. Johnson, a gaunt man with a domed forehead and hollowed eyes. Physically I was sound, he said. It was just a matter of nerves. He gave me a sedative, told me to take more exercise and involve myself in volunteer work. "Idle hands make idle fancies," he chided, patting my arm.

I remember crying all the way home in the carriage.

The torment went on. Objects inexplicably began to change shape. A cologne bottle I had always remembered as tall and slim suddenly became a squat, cut-glass decanter, a circular vase of crystal blue metamorphosed into a white pear-shaped bowl, and a small china dog which stood on a table in the dining room seemed daily to grow larger and larger. I kept all these little shocks, the signs of a crumbling mind, well-hidden under the tight-lipped, white mask of my face. No one must know, no one must guess my secret. I was so terrified, so ashamed. When I thought Octavia was beginning to look at me in an odd way, I avoided her as much as possible.

Finally one gray, gloomy day when I sat in my room thinking how easy it would be to end my agony by swallowing the entire bottle of sedative pills Dr. Johnson had given me, Cora tapped on the door and announced that Jay Cooke was in the entry hall below, inquiring if I were at home.

"Tell him no," I said. I had no desire to see him.

Cora returned a few minutes later. "Well—what is it?" I asked rather testily.

"Mr. Cooke say he was just passing. He has a letter from your brother he thought you might like to read."

"Why didn't he send it up then?"

"He didn't say why, m'am. He wants to give it to you in person, I guess," she said.

Not even Charles's letter could tempt me from my hiding place. But suddenly I thought—why not Jay, why not try him as a last resort? He was clever, in some matters quite astute, he had wide experience and perhaps had once come upon a case like mine. Of course, I need not tell him it was me who was suffering from such fancies, but—but a friend. Yes, a friend of mine who thought she was going mad.

"I can't see Mr. Cooke now," I said to Cora. I looked a fright, my hair straggling from its pins, my eyes all puffy and red. "Tell him—tell him I'll send a message when it's convenient to call.'"

The more I thought about Jay, the more I began to hope. I felt I had so little to lose. Even if he should jeer at my "friend" there would be some comfort in simply speaking out, in hearing myself utter the words which had lain like a frightening weight on my heart. But I wanted to talk to him alone, not here in the intimidating atmosphere of the Folly, and I thought if we could meet for lunch in a public place, I might be able to converse more freely. But first I must ask Cage for permission. It seems strange to me now, how in the light of my panic I still clung to the proprieties—a married woman did not meet with another man, bachelor or married, in public or private, without her husband's consent.

Cage said "Of course, you can have lunch with Jay," when I told him Jay had received a letter from Charles and wanted to share it with me. "It will do you good to get out, you're looking a little pale these days."

So he *had* noticed.

"The St. Francis has a nice restaurant," he suggested. "Why don't you lunch there?"

"Yes—yes, the St. Francis—I'll write Jay and let him know."

He met me in the large, plushly furnished foyer. "Adelaide . . . !" he exclaimed, taking my hand, smiling, his dark eyes sharp as they scanned my face.

"It was good of you to come, Jay," I said.

The hotel lobby was crowded with porters rushing hither and yon, travelers arriving and departing, crying children clinging to distraught mothers, men standing about in knots talking and shouting to one another above the general hubbub.

"I can't hear myself think," Jay said, taking my arm. "And I daresay the restaurant is no quieter. Why don't we go down the street to Gobey's and try some of his boiled terrapin?"

"Well—I don't know . . . ," I said, looking around.

"It will be perfectly all right, I assure you. We need not take a private room but can sit in an alcove in full view of prying eyes and tattling tongues."

"If you think it's a place for ladies . . ."

"Certainly. In fact Gobey calls his place 'Ladies and Gents Oyster Parlor.' "

It had sawdust on the floor and red tablecloths, but they were clean and the place was much quieter, if not as elegant as the St. Francis.

We had the terrapin and oysters on the half-shell and little clams in some kind of marvelous cream sauce. Everything was delicious, but I found that my appetite had shrunk so I could do no more than take a few bites of the dishes set before me. Jay, who ate heartily, made no comment. I was grateful for his silence. I wanted time to muster my thoughts and words. I had gone through a

variety of approaches and speeches in my head that morning, discarding one and latching onto another, wondering if
I should say this, or that, wondering if he would ask my
friend's name, wondering—until my head had begun to
spin.

"Aren't you going to ask me about the letter?" Jay asked
suddenly, putting down his fork and reaching for his glass
of wine.

A faint blush warmed my cheeks. "I did not want to
interrupt your meal, Jay," I said. I had forgotten all about
Charles's letter. My own problem had grown so enormous
as to blot out everything else. "May I read it now?"

It was a long letter, descriptive, full of details of Charles's
business ventures (he was in pipe fittings now), but the
main news was that his wife had borne him a son. They
had named it Ward after Papa. A son, I thought, and he
hadn't written me, his sister. Was he still so angry?

"I'm sure you will be getting your own letter any day,"
Jay said, reading me as only he could. "Mine just came a
little sooner."

"Yes, I'm sure." I folded the letter carefully and gave it
back to him. Charles and I were once such good friends.
How could a brother and sister drift apart so? I had no
other family, but Charles. Yet I had chosen Cage as my
husband, as my family, and though that choice was the
cause of our differences, I still had no regrets.

"Would you like some fruit? Brandy?" Jay asked.

"No, thank you, Jay. The meal was excellent."

"Yes, wasn't it?" He signalled a waiter. "Charles seems
to be doing fairly well."

"I'm glad. I'll write and congratulate him.'

The waiter came and cleared the table. Jay ordered a
brandy.

"You may smoke if you like," I said. I knew he enjoyed
his cigar at the end of a meal.

"How sweet you've become, Adelaide," Jay said after he
had requested the waiter to bring a box of his best cigars.

"I've always been amiable," I said, smiling brightly.
"You've just never noticed."

"Perhaps."

The waiter returned with the brandy and cigars. Jay
made his selection, dismissed the waiter, and leaning back
in his chair touched a long match to the cigar. He watched

me through a curl of smoke, but said nothing. I looked down at my hands folded primly in my lap and suddenly wished I had ordered brandy, too. It might have given me courage, or at the least, something to stare at, to hold.

"What is it, Adelaide?" Jay asked after the silence between us had reached an awkward stage. "There's something on your mind. Out with it."

"Well," I said and cleared my throat. "Well—I thought I might ask your advice about a friend of mine. I won't tell you who—she has entrusted me not to mention her name. It's—it's a delicate matter, but I can't seem to help her and I thought you might."

"You flatter me, Adelaide, but I'll do my best. What is this—this delicate matter?"

I found the gleam in his eyes and the tone of his voice as he pronounced "delicate" disconcerting.

"It's not what you think," I said blushing.

He raised his brows. "And what am I thinking?"

"Oh—do behave, Jay," I said in desperation.

Immediately the gleam vanished and his face became sober. "I'm sorry. You are upset, aren't you? This friend means a great deal to you?"

"Yes. She—she is very close. And Jay—she thinks she is losing her mind." I hadn't meant to blurt it out that way, but perhaps it was for the best. It would make further explanation easier.

"Tell me," he said.

I began with the cat and went on from there to describe how the sewing basket would appear and disappear. I told him about the changing shapes, the feeling of confusion, the fear, the depression, the weeping.

"Is this a married lady?" Jay asked when I had finished.

"Yes—yes, she is."

"And she hasn't told her husband?"

"Why—no, she hasn't wanted to worry him." The questioning look remained in his eyes so I added, "But she's seen a doctor and he could do nothing for her."

He leaned back in his chair and studied the end of his cigar for a moment. "How old would you say she was?"

"Oh—not thirty yet."

"Then she isn't going through the change of life?"

I felt my cheeks go red once more. "No. No, she isn't, and please don't tell me she needs exercise."

He knocked the ash from his cigar and taking a long pull from it, threw his head back to blow smoke rings into the air. "Could that friend possibly be you, Adelaide?" he asked casually.

"Oh—no! No!"

He leaned forward and with intensity, "It *is* you, isn't it?"

"Jay . . . ." I bit my lip as the hot tears rose to my eyes.

"I thought as much."

I began searching blindly in my bag for a handkerchief. Why did he have to be so brazenly honest, why couldn't he allow me the comfort of pretense?

"Don't cry," he said in a low voice. "I know my bluntness is rude, but it's much better to be honest with one another instead of you and I tilting in a fog."

I shook my lowered head. "I'm so ashamed," I whispered.

"You needn't be, Adelaide. Don't—don't cry. Here, have a sip of my brandy."

"No—please," biting my lip. "I'm sorry I've embarrassed you. I hate making a fool of myself in public."

"I don't give a damn about the public!" he said in a low, angry voice. "You ought to know that. I simply don't like to see you this unhappy. And it's so unnecessary. There's a solution to your problem, I'm sure. If we examine it, we're bound to find some very logical explanation to what you firmly believe are distortions of your mind. Perhaps Octavia's been playing games with you."

"I—I . . ." Sniffling, I blew my nose, then tried again. "I—I thought so, too. I thought it was Martha rather than Octavia—but you see they went to Belmont for a week, and those things went right on happening. And I—I couldn't help but think . . ."

"How absurd, Adelaide, how ridiculous! You are the most unlikely candidate in the world for going mad—or even balmy. I have never known a woman who was so sane, so sensible, so practical. Your passion for Cage is your only aberration."

"But why—why should I feel this way?"

"I think what has occurred is quite simple. The cat might have well been a stray. Cats can slip in and out of doors in the twinkling of an eye, so I wouldn't worry about the cat. But *you* did and as a consequence got yourself into such a state—brooding over it that great, gloomy house, you began to imagine all sorts of weird things. The mind is very powerful, Adelaide. Once you set it on a course it acts like a runaway steam engine charging along a track, gathering speed as it races toward disaster."

"And you think that is the basis of this horrible fear? That I am making up these things because I have the notion I might be going—going mad?"

"Very probably, Adelaide. Why don't you try ignoring these 'things' for a while?"

"I did try, Jay. I did. But . . ."

"But not hard enough. Give it a concerted effort, hmmm? Really, Adelaide, I am sure it will work."

He looked so strong, sounded so positive, so certain, I could not help but think he was right. If I used firm determination, if I refused to let panic get a hold, if I convinced myself that it was perfectly natural to be forgetful, I might eventually rid myself of the hallucinations which were plaguing me. I might, I just might.

"You are looking better already," he said, squeezing my hand. "What did I tell you?"

He lifted his brandy glass, and for an instant his eyes registered surprise as they focused at something over my shoulder.

Some instinct warned me not to turn my head and look. But I did, I did.

Cage was coming out of one of the private rooms, and he had Mrs. Walters on his arm.

He saw us at once. There was no time for retreat. The momentary stunned look on his face was followed by a bright smile, and leaving Mrs. Walters behind, he began to thread his way through the tables toward us.

Fanny Walters—and a private room.

I don't know what kept me upright, what kept me sitting there straight as a ramrod. My fear of going mad seemed miniscule, petty compared to what I felt now. It was as though some powerful force had dealt me a sudden blow just below the heart and everything inside was crumpling with pain. I wanted to lie down, to howl, to cry out that it hurt so badly. But I went on sitting there, my face wiped clean of expression.

"My dear—Adelaide!" Cage said, taking my cold, rigid

hand, bending over, putting it to his lips. "What a pleasant surprise!"

The St. Francis has a nice restaurant, he had said.

"Yes, isn't it?" I heard myself reply tonelessly.

The St. Francis, conveniently removed from Gobey's on Sutter Street.

"And Jay!" pumping his hand. "Haven't seen you in a donkey's age. How are you?"

"Never better," Jay said.

"So you two decided to try Gobey's," Cage beamed. "Wonderful food."

"Yes, isn't it," I said.

The St. Francis, while he had planned to take *her* here. To a private room.

"Mrs. Walters had some business to consult me about," Cage said, "and we decided to do it over lunch."

"Yes, how nice," I said, my lips stretching over the words like stiff rubber. *You wouldn't understand financial intricacies*, he had told *me*. But Mrs. Walters apparently did.

"Mrs. Walters said to say hello," Cage continued. "She had to hurry on. Well, Adelaide, I must be getting back myself. See you later, darling. Jay."

There was a long silence. I did not look at Jay. Cutlery rattled, there was the clink of china, a man laughed, a deep baritone, rollicking laugh. I stared at the wall beyond Jay's head.

"I'll say this much for Cage," Jay remarked, breaking the silence between us. "Cage has elegant *sang froid*. Not many men could carry off such an embarrassing moment so coolly."

I said nothing. I wished I was drunk—now—I wished I were dead.

"At least," Jay went on, "he wasn't caught in a more compromising situation."

My throat worked but I could not speak.

"Adelaide . . ." Suddenly looking contrite, he put his hand out and touched my arm. "I am sorry this had to happen."

"Has he—is he . . . ?" I could not go on. All those nights he said he had to stay in town because of "business," the nights I had sat alone or with a truculent Octavia at a long table in the vast dining room, the nights I had lain awake waiting to hear his key in the lock, his step on the stair.

"She doesn't mean anything to him, really. She's—why she's just another woman."

A black pit seemed to yawn before me. "There—there are others?"

"My dear, surely you must have realized when you married Cage how difficult it would be for a man like him to remain faithful?"

"No!" I cried. There must be some mistake. It was perfectly innocent. He and Mrs. Walters were discussing business, they had engaged a private room because they did not want to be overheard. Not Cage. He was faithful, he was honorable. "No!" But all those lonely nights came rushing back, flooding my mind with doubt, with clawing jealousy.

"I'm sorry," Jay repeated. He did not argue, did not name names or mock me for denying it. He knew. Everyone knew. And the wife was always the last . . .

"How long . . . ?" I wet my lips, "how long has this been going on?"

"Not very," he said.

Oh, God, I thought, not very. We hadn't been married a year. Had I palled on him so quickly then, or had he never been that enamored of me, never found me adequate? Some wives did not care if their husbands slept with other women, wives who looked upon the physical side of marriage as distasteful, wives who did not want more children. But those wives did not mind. I minded, I minded very much. I could not bear the thought of another woman lying in Cage's arms, of another woman kissing, caressing him, of Cage making love to her. It hurt. It hurt terribly.

"Adelaide, my dear, I hate to see you this miserable. You don't have to put up with it, you know. Leave him, my dear. Don't torture yourself. Leave him, he doesn't deserve someone like you."

The secret staircase a whim, Mrs. Walters seated next to him at our dinner party, her enormous blue eyes looking up at him, full of suggestive allure. Women had always found Cage attractive; they flocked around him wherever he went. But he didn't have to accept their offered favors, he didn't have to have affairs. He didn't have to encourage them, take them to private dining rooms. . . ."

"Adelaide, he has given you more than sufficient grounds for a separation."

"What—what? Separation? Oh, no, Jay, no." And let Mrs. Walters have him? I couldn't, I couldn't leave him, never see him again, I couldn't let him go. Jay did not understand. I loved Cage. It hurt, but I loved him. Despite everything, through pain and disappointment and shock, I still loved him. "I—I wouldn't dream of such a thing."

And I knew then I would never confront Cage with what Jay had told me, knew I would forgive him and go on loving him no matter what, knew I would go on believing that some day, in some way, it would all work out.

Chapter 25

CAGE apologized that evening. Not that he confessed to infidelity—the word never passed his lips—but I'm sure he sensed my feelings of hurt and betrayal, and he sought to make amends.

"I would not want to cause you a single moment's pain or embarrassment, not for the world," he vowed, looking into my eyes, his own deep with concern. "And from here on in I promise you if I have any business matters to discuss with a female, no matter if she is ninety, I shall do so at the bank or in my office."

"It *was* a little bit of a shock, you see. . . ."

"My dear, of course it was." He took my hand and caressed it. "And I can't blame you for thinking the worst. Believe me, Adelaide, darling, it shall never happen again. I promise you."

He was very sweet to me. He had brought flowers and a beautiful garnet necklace with garnet earrings to match. Very expensive. And he had kissed me so tenderly, not once but dozens of times. Later upstairs he made love to me, and when he fell asleep with his arms clasped about me, I nuzzled my head under his chin, sighing happily. I felt secure again, wanted. I had won him back. Cage was my husband; I loved him, that was the most important thing in my life. How fortunate I had not made a scene, how fortunate I had not taken Jay's suggestion and demanded a separation. Separation! The thought made me shudder.

Cage came home every night for supper now. The bodyguard who usually rode with him had been dismissed and McCorkle had taken his place. "Couldn't be trusted," he said of the guard. Cage wore a pistol under his coat when he went about in the City; his enemies, he said, were dangerous men. He tried to explain his new venture, mining stock in a company that was going to make us millions by a new process for extracting silver from the ore, but though I listened intently, my eyes glued to his face, I hardly heard a word. He was so handsome; I would sit at the dining table devouring his face, taking in the cleft in his chin, the charming dimple on the right side of his mouth, the gray blue eyes, the light hair, the aristocratic poise of his head.

Octavia seemed happier, too, now that she saw her stepfather more often. He teased her about Ted Neale, but she only laughed at him. "Ted's as comfortable as an old shoe. He's not really a beau."

"*He* thinks he is," Cage said. "And I'd watch myself. Old shoes have a way of becoming indispensable."

"Oh—pooh!" Octavia said, leaning over and kissing him on the cheek.

I was not jealous of their fond bantering. I was happy to see them together, to have Cage at the Folly every night, an affectionate father, an affectionate husband. When Octavia did not go out with Ted, we three would sit in the drawing room, Octavia playing the piano, Cage singing, and I with my sewing on my lap. (I was still having the old trouble with the shifting sewing basket, but I ignored it.) We made such a pretty domestic scene. I would sit there thinking how lovely it would be to have a daughter of my own, or a son. Either one, or both, would surely have Cage's light hair, his eyes, his sculptured nose, and the girl would be a belle, so beautiful. . . .

"You're dreaming again," Cage would laugh, and I would smile at him, my heart in my eyes.

It lasted all of two and a half weeks, that happy domesticity, that feeling of being a family, the comfortable, safe, secure feeling of hearth and home. Then Cage began to stay out again, one night, two, three times a week. Business, he said. I did not question him. Inside, my heart writhed in pain, but I never said a word. He looked pale when I saw him; he began to drink heavily again. And his eyes rarely met mine.

Quickly, very quickly I slid back to the old pattern, the anxieties, the fears. Octavia kept to herself, Martha and I rarely spoke. I was alone, so utterly alone, and I had not the energy to go anywhere, to visit, or simply to ride into the City for an afternoon of shopping. Objects began to change shape again, to disappear and reappear. I heard noises at night, strange noises, the babbling of a voice, the playing of a harmonica. Where the sounds came from I did not know. Were they in my head? Jay said I must make the effort to ignore my fancies. But it was all very well for him to speak, he did not have to live at the Folly, he did not have to feel the walls closing in on him as I did. He did not have to spend the long hours alone, to pause before a door, too terrified to open it. He did not have to come into the drawing room and see that the glass lamp had been replaced by a china one, nor confront the maids who vehemently denied touching either. He had never been afraid in his life. He thought it was merely a matter of self-control. Was it possible that I had once agreed with him?

Autumn arrived, each bright, hard blue and golden day shorter than the one before. The nights were getting longer. How I dreaded those nights and the gas-lit corridors upstairs, the mirrors reflecting flickering light and the dark, empty rooms where the sound of the wind could be heard moaning under the eaves. How I hated the rustle of the dried leaves tumbling before a breeze on the garden walk, the swish of Gandy's broom as he swept in an everlasting attempt to clear them away.

One afternoon Clara Shelby came to call.

"Where have you been?" she asked, unpinning her hat. She smelled of lavender and the fresh out-of-doors. I was glad to see her. "My dear, have you been ill?"

"No, not exactly," I replied. "I just haven't been feeling up to par lately."

"You aren't starting a baby?" she asked, her sharp eyes going over my figure.

"No—no, I'm quite sure not. Would you like some tea?"

"Please."

I rang for Cora. Clara removed her gloves. "How is Cage? I haven't seen much of him either."

"Oh—he's busy, very busy," I said cautiously. She might tell me things I would rather not hear, bits of gossip, rumors that he had been seen with Mrs. Walters, painful little snippets of talk that might send me into a torrent of weeping. Why had I been so happy to see her? I wished suddenly she had not come.

"We are having a White Elephant sale," Clara said. "To raise money for the hospital, you know. And I thought perhaps you could help."

"I would love to," I said. Why had I offered tea? It would only prolong her visit. "But—I'm sorry, I don't think I'm up to it."

"Well—I won't press you. You've grown awfully thin, strung up, too. Nerves, I bet. Hmmm . . . have you seen a doctor?"

"Yes, Dr. Johnson. He thought the same. He gave me a sedative."

"Oh, they give sedatives for everything these days. It's supposed to be a cure-all. Sedatives and rest. Since we don't see you I presume that you are getting plenty of rest?"

"Oh—yes, yes, plenty of rest." Here it comes, I thought, cringing inwardly, any moment now.

"The ladies miss you. It's a pity you can't help out, but if you can't perhaps you have something you could donate? Something you have grown tired of, and that someone else might like to buy."

I thought at once of the cupid clock. "Yes—as a matter of fact I have a clock, quite valuable I'm told. It's up in the storeroom."

Cora came in. "Tea, Cora, please, and some of those little sandwiches Doreen does so well. And oh, Cora—no, never mind." I decided suddenly to fetch the clock myself. It would take up some of the time and thus give Clara less chance to talk about Cage.

"It won't be but a few minutes," I said to Clara when Cora had left. "The clock's upstairs. Do you mind?"

"Certainly not. Anything for the cause."

I hurried up the stairs, got the bunch of keys from a drawer, keys which I rarely used, and went out and down the corridor to a small staircase. Ascending, I reached the third story. I had been up there only once before with Martha to pick out some extra chairs when we had given our ball. The third floor was a sham. It was nothing more than a long, bare corridor with uncarpeted floors and curtainless windows that looked out through fretted gingerbread carvings. The turrets were spaced at intervals. I came to the first and after trying several keys found the right one. The room, conical in shape with a ceiling that came to a point, was empty. Dust had sifted in from the high windows and the air vent, along with brown, crumpled leaves and a bird feather or two. The next turret was more as I remembered, full of old furniture, bed springs, a commode, dusty pitchers, cracked mirrors, blackened lamps and chipped china what-nots. I saw the clock sitting on a shelf above two trunks. Pulling a rickety chair over, I climbed up and got the clock down. Then I looked around for something else I might donate. Perhaps a lamp or two could be cleaned up, one had leaded glass, another had hand-painted roses, and there was a large painting, a seascape the ladies could probably sell.

I was examining the picture more closely when the door behind me suddenly whined on its hinges. I turned just in time to see it softly click shut. I stood for a moment looking at the door rather stupidly, and then I heard a sound which brought my heart leaping to my mouth.

The metallic sound of a key turning in the lock.

I ran to the door. "Who's there?" I called. "Who's there? Is it you, Cora? Lucinda?" And when there was no answer, "Octavia?" But Octavia was not home, she had gone out with Martha to do some shopping.

I rattled the knob. "Who is it? Let me out! Let me out at once! Gandy, is it you?"

I stopped to listen. There was no sound on the other side. None. I turned and twisted the knob, shaking the door again. It was locked. But how could it be? How could a key turn itself and lock me in? I should not have left that bunch of keys hanging from the open door, I should not have come up here, but told Cora to fetch the clock. Oh—what a fool! And now I was locked in.

Don't panic, I told myself, don't panic. Clara will miss you after a bit and send someone up. But it was impossible to remain calm because I knew the key could not have turned and locked the door unless a hand had guided it. And there had been no one there, I had heard no breathing, no footsteps, nothing. Just that click of the turning key. Dear God . . . !

But no—no, I mustn't think of it, I mustn't. It would be so easy to go clean out of my mind, shut up here in this cone-shaped room full of dead relics and discarded scraps with the wind soughing eerily through the air vent at the top. Almost like a human voice, a ghostly, human voice. I thought of Lillith then and what Martha had said that first day, "Gandy swears he's seen her." Strange that Lillith should come to mind now when I hadn't thought of her in so long, when I had been sure the trial had finally laid her memory to rest. But she seemed to be here, now, in this room. These trunks, were they hers? Those lamps, had she put a match to them once in years past, when the gloom had gathered in the drawing room, a match flaring in the darkness, lighting up the violet eyes? Her eyes seemed to be looking at me now from behind that torn feather bed, from over the rim of that wardrobe, in the dark, cobwebbed corners, there, beyond . . .

But no, I mustn't think of it. I mustn't.

I began to pace the small narrow space, back and forth like a caged animal. Why did no one come? I went to the door again, rattled the knob, pounded on the panel. "Hello! I'm here! Here! Can anyone hear me? Please . . . !" I sank to my knees. Perhaps I could work the key back. I found a hairpin, but my hands were shaking so badly it took a minute or two before I was able to poke it through the keyhole. There, there—almost. The key kept slipping out of the hairpin's pincerlike grasp. My hands were sweating, and I had to stop to wipe them on my skirt. Then I tried again. Almost . . . Suddenly the key ring on the other side fell with a tinkle and hit the floor with a soft, brassy clash.

I leaned my head against the door, fighting tears, but they came anyway, slowly trickling down my cheeks. A small sob clogged my throat. Better to cry than to go mad. But the room was growing darker, the tiny arrowed glints of sunlight that had slanted down through the high windows when I had first entered the turret had disappeared. Soon it would be evening and then night. Night meant blackness, a void of nothingness, and the shapes around me might start to change, might come to life, moving closer and closer all around me forming a ring, closer and closer. And the wind would increase, mourning, moaning, keening. And I would still be here because Clara would have forgotten all about me, because Cage was in the City, and the servants did not care. It might be morning, perhaps another day before anyone would think to look in the turret, and when they did come, they would find a raving maniac, a wild-eyed madwoman.

I sprang up and began to pound on the door again, screaming hoarsely, "Help, help!" pounding with my fists, kicking with my feet, yelling, shouting, driven by a horror beyond reason.

Suddenly, abruptly, without warning the door swung open, and I fell through, stumbling, clutching the empty air for support, dropping with a cracking thud to my knees. I leaned on my hands, my head hanging forward, panting, the breath whistling noisily in my ears. I was too dazed to wonder how the locked door had opened so suddenly, too overcome with relief to do anything but try and catch my breath. I remained there on my knees breathing in and out, and gradually my heart began to beat less painfully. I pushed the fallen hair from my eyes, tucking it behind my ears. And then the door behind me clicked softly shut, an insidious sound, one that sent a flash of panic through me once more.

I leapt to my feet. Looking neither to the left or right I fled down the corridor, found the stairs, stumbled to the bottom, and without pausing continued to flee along the carpeted passage. I saw a man's back suddenly loom ahead of me. I must have made some feeble cry, though I was not aware of it. The man turned. It was Cage. The last thing I remember was the look of surprise on his face.

I was put to bed and Dr. Johnson summoned. He arrived within the hour, slightly out of breath, his cheeks flushed as if he had been running. He was much dismayed to learn I had fainted, clucking and scolding at me, asking if I had been taking the pills he had prescribed. When I said no and tried to explain what had happened, he waved my words aside, saying, "Nonsense, it's nerves, I tell you." He gave me another bottle of pills and strict instructions to remain in bed.

When he left, Cage came in to see me. He looked uncomfortable, uneasy, sitting on the edge of his chair, running his hands through his hair. "I hate to see you this way," he said, and I realized this was the first time I had taken to my bed with an indisposition since our marriage. Cage did not like sickness, his own or in others. He liked everyone to be hale and hearty.

"I'll be all right," I assured him. "It was just—just such an ordeal and I . . ."

"What ordeal?" he interrupted. "What are you talking about?"

"Oh—hasn't Dr. Johnson told you? I was locked in the turret—the attic upstairs."

"Locked in the turret?"

"Yes, I went up to get a clock for Clara's White Elephant sale. Didn't she mention it?"

"She did mention something about a clock, but I had no idea you had gone up to the attic. I came home at four-thirty and found her in the drawing room. She was drinking tea. I had only been there five minutes when she said she couldn't wait and left."

"But, Cage, didn't you think it odd that I should leave my guest like that and not reappear?"

"As matter of fact, I had too much on my mind to think of anything, especially something that seemed unimportant at the time."

He was annoyed, and for once I did not try to placate him. Unimportant! I thought of the musty smell, the keening wind, the dark shapes leaning down toward me in that small space, the suffocating, trapped feeling, the rising hysteria.

"Someone locked me in," I said, swallowing hard. "The door closed and the key turned."

He looked incredulous. "I can't imagine—how did you get out then?"

I knew he would ask that, so I was prepared. "Who—whoever it was—came back and unlocked the door."

"But why should anyone want to do such a crazy thing?"

"I don't know," I said in a small voice which came dangerously close to breaking. I didn't know. It seemed so senseless. I didn't know if anybody had done anything. It might have been my mind playing tricks on me again, my imagination running into wild, improbable fancy. Perhaps the door had never been locked. Perhaps the wind had closed it and I thought. . . .

But I couldn't tell that to Cage.

"I'll talk to the servants," he said, getting to his feet. He leaned over and gave me a cool kiss. "Take care, darling. If you need anything, ring for Martha. I won't disturb you anymore tonight."

But I wanted to be disturbed. I wanted him to come to

me, to put his arms around me, to tell me that there was nothing to fear, that he would take care of me, that everything would be all right.

I was sitting in the little parlor downstairs when I heard the dull echo of the knocker hammering on the front door. Footsteps followed shortly and the sound of the door opening. A male voice said, "Tell Mrs. Norwood that I am here, please."

It was Jay. Three days had gone by since my horrible experience in the attic. I was feeling stronger physically, but my mental state left much to be desired. Cage had not returned to our bed. He said that I would get well quicker if I slept alone. I wanted to tell him that exactly the opposite was true, that I needed him, but I could not find the words. I felt hurt, rejected, and in between frightened, frightened that our marriage was failing, frightened that I might have another episode—God knew what!—and this time be unlucky enough to remain unhinged.

I did not want to see Jay. It would be like the time at Gobey's when he told me to "make an effort." I did not need anyone to jolly me up. I did not want anyone—except Cage.

Martha opened the door. "Mr. Cooke is here," she announced.

"Tell him . . ."

But he was already looming over her shoulder. "Thank you, Martha."

She hesitated a moment, but he smiled charmingly at her and she left. He quietly closed the door behind her.

"I'm not up to visitors," I said irritably.

"I know you're not. That's why I'm here. I saw Cage and he said you were under the weather. What is it? The same problem?"

"I don't know why . . ."

"Is it?" he asked, his voice not as brusque as usual, but oddly gentle.

When I made no answer he came and sat beside me on the sofa. "You can tell me," he said, taking my hand. I looked into his dark eyes and found their steady gaze comforting. I don't know why. Perhaps it had something to do with his appearance of solid strength, his wide shoulders, the way his muscles bulged firmly under the smooth fit of his coat, his dark face which now registered sympathy.

"Jay . . . ," my voice faltered, my resistance melting under his kindly look.

"It's all right, all right," he soothed.

"You see . . ." My throat worked as sudden tears burned my eyes. "You see—I don't know whether it's my mind or whether something really happened. It's been so hard—so hard—to think—to know what to do. . . ."

"Start at the beginning, my dear."

I clasped my hands tightly, fighting for control. Then, slowly, pausing every now and again to get a firmer grip on my voice, I told him about Clara's visit, how I had gone up to the third story and found myself locked in the turret room. When I had finished, he said:

"The servants?"

"They deny coming upstairs at all. Martha and Octavia were not here. They did not get home until six. Clara, I understand, left at four thirty-five, five minutes after Cage arrived."

"What time did you go up to the attic?"

"Oh—about four-ten, four-fifteen, perhaps."

"So Cage was in the house while you were looking for the clock."

"Yes, but he didn't know."

Jay continued to look at me, his head cocked slightly to one side. "Didn't he?"

"What, what are you trying to tell me?" I asked. "You can't mean . . . ! But you can't! That is utterly ridiculous! Cage would never . . ."

"I didn't say it, Adelaide." He let go of my hand and got to his feet.

"I don't like you even hinting at it, Jay."

He went over to the mantel and stood gazing at the portrait above it, a small child holding an apple. "Has your husband told you where he's spent a good many of his nights these past two weeks?" he asked.

My cheeks flamed. "If you've come here to repeat gossip, dirty gossip . . ."

"Adelaide, Adelaide," he turned, facing me, a reproving look on his face. "I would never bring this up if I were not worried about you. Cage is seeing that Walters woman again, surely that can't be a surprise to you?"

"Yes!" I lied heatedly. "Yes, it is a surprise. Because it isn't true!"

He shrugged. "Very well. Have it your way. But that isn't all. He's lost quite a bit of money—some venture that fell through. And he's gambling again."

"Well—what of it?" A tight band had formed around my heart. Gambling. I didn't care about the gambling, if only Fanny Walters did not exist. "Why should it concern you?"

"I take it, it's your money he's gambling with. Your money he's losing."

"What of it?" I repeated irritably. "Is it any of your business?"

"Cage is not my business, but you are. Look here," he said, coming back to the sofa, "I don't want to see you hurt, and I mean hurt literally. There's something else you might as well know. Mrs. Walters is divorcing her husband. Aside from being a trollop, she is also a wealthy woman. She owns several of the plushier bordellos in the City and, I understand, is coining money."

"I fail to see . . ."

"She might have ambitions, Adelaide. She might have ambitions of becoming Mrs. Cage Norwood."

"Why that's—that's insane!"

"Is it? I know you are going to say that Cage is already married. But think, Adelaide, anything can happen to a wife. Anything. A wife that is going mad might even conceivably kill herself. A wife that is . . ."

"Stop!" I sprang to my feet. "I'm not the one who is going mad—you are! Of all the fantastic, mean, insinuating—I knew I didn't want to see you! I knew it! Get out. Go!" And when he made no move, "Well—what are you waiting for?"

He shrugged. "All right, I'm going. If you need me . . ."

"Get out!"

I stood there rigid until I heard the outer door slam shut. Then overcome with misery, I sank down on the sofa and burying my head in my hands, wept.

Cage and I were at breakfast the next morning when Martha brought me a note which had just been delivered by hand. "It's from Clara Shelby," I said to Cage. "She's giving a luncheon next Wednesday. 'Please do come'," I read aloud, " 'I know it's late notice but I thought it a pity not to have some kind of get-together before the White Elephant sale'."

I had sent the clock and several other items over to Clara's, again expressing my regrets that I was unable to assist at the sale itself.

"Are you going?" Cage asked.

"No—I don't believe I will. I don't feel up to it."

"I think you ought to go," he said. "It will do you good to get out."

"But . . ."

"It will put the bloom in your cheeks to talk to someone other than me for a change. Besides, Clara will be very disappointed. Why don't you write and tell her you will come?"

I was so pleased he had finally accepted Clara as my friend, so pleased to hear him taking an interest in my little social affairs, something he rarely if ever did, that I said, "Yes, I believe I will," before I even realized it.

"Good. I can't spare McCorkle, but perhaps Gandy can drive you."

"I'll take the buggy," I said. "I don't mind driving alone. Gandy is always so upset when he's called away from his chores. And Clara lives so close."

However, when Wednesday arrived—all too soon—I awoke wondering why I had ever let myself be talked into accepting. I felt depressed, moody, and the prospect of having to get dressed and go out, of having to sit through a heavy noon meal, chatting of inconsequentials to a group of women I did not care about, loomed like a dark and oppressive cloud. I was tempted to forgo the luncheon, tempted to send my regrets, but Cage was home and it might be awkward. He had come home late the night before, very late, and not very sober, and so had overslept in the morning.

"I saw Shelby last evening," he said as I sat before the mirror combing out my hair, "and he tells me Clara has given him strict orders not to show his face today until seven in the evening. She's invited quite a gaggle of women, and, of course, is looking forward to having you."

"How kind," I murmured. "But I was thinking . . ."

"You haven't changed your mind?"

"No," I said quickly. "No, I haven't."

I chose the dark green moire with the ivory braiding. The colors were not flattering to my present pallor, but once I had the dress on I did not feel like changing.

"Very fetching," Cage said.

"Thank you."

I put some rouge on my cheeks, hoping to give my face a healthier look. But the effect was garish, unreal, and I wiped it off.

When I was ready, neither McCorkle nor Gandy could be found to bring the buggy from the stable to the front door. Cage went out to do it himself.

A few minutes later he came clattering up the steps where I was waiting. He kissed me goodbye as he handed me into the buggy. "Have a good time, dear," he said. I remember the smile on his face and the wind ruffling his hair and the way he looked waving to me as he stood there.

As the horse trotted down the drive, going through the gates and turning left at the street, my heart filled with a strange misgiving. It was as if I were being dragged to some unwilling fate, a black and perilous doom. A heaviness hung on my shoulders, a dark cloud over my head. It's just a mood, I told myself, trying to shake it, a temporary state that will soon pass. But when we reached the crest of the hill the feeling deepened, flooding me with a terrible irrepressible foreboding. I had a desperate urge to turn the buggy around and go back. But what would I say to Cage? I could think of nothing that would sound sensible, and he would only be displeased with me. So I went on.

We started down the hill, and again the strong, overpowering feeling came over me that something was wrong. Unable to stem the rising panic, I shouted, "Whoa!" pulling on the reins.

And to my horrified astonishment the reins tore free from the bridle and dangled ineffectually in my hands.

For one jolting moment I could not utter a sound. And then I was screaming, "Whoa! Whoa . . . !" But the horse, free of restraint and catching the fright in my voice, jerked forward into a gallop. "Whoa . . . !" Downward he thundered, his ears flat to his head, pebbles and dust flying under his hooves. The buggy bounced and swayed, throwing me from side to side. I managed to grab the edge of the door, holding to it. "Stop!" I screamed, and the wind took my voice and flung it into the whiplike gale as the landscape reeled past. "Whoa!" but the horse went faster, panicked now by the clattering buggy hard on its heels, faster and faster. I was going to die, here, now, any moment, crashing into oblivion. "Whoa . . . !"

The door flew open, I saw Fanny Walters's pretty face, I saw Cage smiling, and then I remembered no more.

Chapter 26

IT was night. A lighted lamp, heavily shaded, stood on the table by my bedside and next to it sat Octavia reading a book. I stared at Octavia in disbelief. She had never before entered my bedroom and for her to be sitting there calmly perusing a book was so fantastic I at once came to the conclusion that I was dreaming. I must have sighed or made some sound, for she looked up.

"Aunt Adelaide . . . !" she exclaimed in a very undreamlike manner. "You're awake. Papa will want to know." She put the book down and got to her feet.

"I'm thirsty," I whispered, wondering at the strange hoarseness of my voice. I seemed to be wrapped in pain, every muscle and nerve ached from my toes to the top of my scalp.

"Yes—yes, of course." She disappeared for a moment, and I heard the chink of china, the soft gurgle of water.

"Here—I'll help you," she said, leaning down, putting her arm about my neck. She smelled of lemon verbena, a clean, fresh scent. God—! How my head ached. The water was cool, delicious to my parched throat.

"Papa will be so glad you've come to," she said. "And Dr. Johnson. He said you were lucky. You only broke an arm when you could have—well! It could have been a great deal worse."

"Worse?" Octavia's uncustomary kindness, the pain, the thirst. I stared at her. "Worse—? Oh—!"

"Don't you remember, Aunt Adelaide?"

"Yes," I whispered, closing my eyes, trying to blot out the sudden memory of that wild, terrifying ride, the runaway horse and the swaying buggy, the tumble through space.

327

"Papa said I'm to call him the minute you open your eyes."

"No—please." I put my hand out and plucked at her skirt. "No, not now, please."

"And Martha . . ."

"I don't want to see anyone." She looked down at me, biting her lip. "No one, Octavia—thank you, thank you for waiting, but I would like to be alone now—for a while."

"There's a bell—here—just in case."

"Yes—thank you."

She left, giving me one last puzzled, backward glance. The lamp flickered as the door closed. I shifted my head on the pillows, acutely conscious now of my bandaged arm in a sling around my neck. It seemed on fire with pain. I wondered if Dr. Johnson had left me any pain pills, but I did not want to ring the little bell. I needed to be alone. I wanted time to think. Moving my head again to a cooler place on the pillow, I closed my eyes and let my mind drift.

I had come very close to being killed. Very close. Had it been an accident? Cage had brought the buggy around. Hadn't he noticed the loose reins? "He's lost a lot of money," Jay had said. "He's gambling again." Supposing he . . .

But, no, how could I entertain such a thought—even for an instant? Cage loved me! He did!

But in the cold clarity of my mind I knew that he did not. He had never said he loved me. There it was—a fact, indisputable, hard, but true. He had never said he loved me. Never. Not when he married me, not when he brought me to the Folly, not even when I lay in his arms in his bed. He did not love me. Jay Cooke had intimated that Cage was incapable of loving any woman. I did not know. Perhaps he loved Fanny Walters, perhaps he wanted her. "She has ambitions," Jay had said.

I squeezed my eyes tighter against the light. It was too painful to contemplate. I won't think, I told myself. I'll think about it later when I feel better. But I *had* to think about it *now*. I could not keep Cage away indefinitely.

Suppose I was wrong?

Granted Cage did not love me, granted he had married me for my money. But did that mean he was deliberately trying to get rid of me? Wasn't that a little far-fetched? A little bizarre?

I thought of the secret passageway and the clock in the library, the cupid clock that had finally gone to the White Elephant sale. I remembered the afternoon it had stopped and started again, remembered my horror and the cold creeping numbness in my limbs as I stared at it in disbelief. The secret passage looked into the library. The door to it had been nailed shut, but how was I to know for certain there were not other doors, doors only the builder —or the owner—of the house would be aware of? How simple it would be to slip in and out, how perfectly simple to move the hands of a clock, to bring my sewing basket from the little parlor to the drawing room, to change one lamp for another.

But Cage went to the City every morning, I told myself.

Yet he might manage to return unseen just often enough to play his little game and then allow my terrified mind to do the rest for him. But—somehow—Cage in the role of slinking, devious, malicious trickster did not ring true. Who then? Martha? But I had already gone through that. Unless she could have traveled witchlike by broomstick from Belmont during the week when several of these occurrences had taken place, I could hardly lay the blame on her.

I thought of Cage again. Why had he hired a bodyguard, spreading word around that his "enemies" were out to get him? Was it insurance, a kind of guarantee that should anything happen to me he could say I had been mistaken for him? But that, too, seemed incredible. And what of my entrapment in the attic—was that incredible, too? I recalled only too vividly the surprise on Cage's face when he turned to me in the corridor as I fled toward him in horror.

And the runaway buggy? He had given me the reins, smiled, kissed me, told me to have a good time.

Ah—no—no.

Where was my mind taking me? I must not go on this way. I loved Cage, I loved him. How could I be thinking all these horrible thoughts?

Because they were true. My face hurt, a pulse throbbed in my temple. I had to face the truth, the facts. I had to decide, I had to make up my mind what to do. To go on living

at the Folly was to court inevitable disaster. Fortunately I
had come through this latest episode alive, my mental fac-
ulties intact, but God alone knew what would happen the
next time. Did I value my life, my sanity? Was it worth
giving up my marriage for safety's sake, this marriage that
I had gone into with such wild hopes, such buoyant happiness? Could I face the shame of failure, the wagging
tongues, the knowing looks, the little asides like, "she
couldn't keep him, that's why he strayed?" For I would
never disclose my real reason for leaving Cage. They would
think. . . . But did I really care? The worst part, the
horrible, miserable part was that I would never see Cage
again. But if it were a matter of life and death, then what?
What did I want to do?

I could go back to Virginia. I could stop with Henry, his
family and Aunt Tildy at Beech Arbor. I wouldn't say
anything to anyone about a permanent stay, just that I had
come for a visit, one that would go on and on indefinitely.
After a while Cage could get a divorce on grounds of
desertion.

A divorce. More final than a separation.

How smug Jay Cooke would feel. How righteous. "I told
you so," he would say. The thought made me wince. But—
what difference would it make if I were to win, only to die
or spend the rest of my life behind the bars of an asylum?

I was going through all the arguments once again when
a sudden tap on the door made me start. A muffled voice
said, "Adelaide?" I closed my eyes and pretended to be
asleep.

I heard the door open and softly shut, the tread of a
heavy step. Someone was standing over me. It was Cage—I
could tell by the aroma of tobacco and whiskey. I kept my
eyes tightly shut, but oh—what an effort it cost me! What
an effort to keep breathing normally, what an effort to keep
my heart at a quiet pace, my arms and legs still. For I
was terrified. What would he do? What did he want? I felt
his shadow on my eyelids, felt him bending over me, peering into my face. Dear God, I thought, in another moment
I will scream. *He is going to kill me, he is going to kill me
and no one will know. He killed Lillith and now he is
going to kill me.*

I felt his hand on the pillow under my head, and the
hairs on the back of my neck literally stood on end as a

cold chill scrambled up my spine. Would it do any good to open my eyes, to cry, to plead, to beg for my life? He was lifting me, his arm supporting my neck, lifting the pillow. Did he plan to smother me? Did I want to look into the eyes of my murderer? Oh, Cage . . . !

He lowered my head, and I felt the cool pillow under me. He stood for a moment longer, then the dark shadow on my eyelids grew darker and I knew that he had turned the lamp out. I held my breath, waiting, waiting. Presently I heard his step as he crossed the floor, heard the door open and shut, and at last I was able to let out my breath.

I lay there for a long time staring up into the dark, my eyes brimming with tears, bitter tears, overflowing, spilling down my cheeks. Had Cage really meant to kill me, then changed his mind; had Cage, a fastidious man, shrunk from outright murder with his bare hands? I did not know. What I did know was that I could not go on this way. The torture, the waiting, the fear were worse than death itself. Tomorrow, I decided, I would write to Aunt Tildy.

The next morning shortly after I had sent Martha away with the untouched breakfast tray because the sight of food made me nauseous, Dr. Johnson came to look in on me. He was happy to see I had regained consciousness without loss of memory, dismayed that I was not eating anything.

"You must do everything you can to keep up your strength," he said. "You will be eating for two now."

I said, "What?"

"My dear, didn't you guess? Why, you are in the family way."

I stared at him. "No," I said, "no."

"Indeed, you are, Mrs. Norwood. I'd say about three months."

"How could that be?" I had put down the disruption of normal bodily functions to my nervous and distraught state. But to be pregnant . . . ?

"A question I cannot answer in light of your accident," the doctor said. "It is close to a miracle that your fall did not cause a miscarriage. I can't explain it myself. But they say they found you on a soft patch of sand, which probably cushioned the impact. Yes, my dear, bruises and cuts and that broken arm, but you kept the child."

Kept the child. A miracle. I was so stunned it took

several moments for the news to register, and even then I could not believe it. Impossible. A child? Tears sprang to my eyes. I had wanted a baby for so long, for so many years, even when I was married to Barnabas. But now . . . ?

"Are you sure?" I asked. It was too late for children, too late.

"Of course, I'm sure. And I've already informed your husband. You don't mind, I hope. He's overjoyed, delighted. His first child, he said."

Cage! Was he happy, or was it just a pose? A pose, I decided. It might make it harder to remove me, a woman in the family way. Or would it be easier?

"I didn't think he wanted children," I murmured.

"Of course, he does. All men want children."

"Do they?" I asked.

"You're acting very strange, I must say," Dr. Johnson clucked disapprovingly at me.

"Perhaps—perhaps it's because I am suddenly homesick. I miss what little family I have back in Virginia. My aunt —cousins. I thought of taking a trip."

"Out of the question!" he exclaimed. "Entirely out of the question. Do you want to lose that child for certain? Kill it? I've just finished explaining to you how narrowly you escaped having a miscarriage, a trip of any sort—well, I won't answer for the consequences."

"But I can travel a good part of the way by rail now. They haven't quite finished the transcontinental railway, but most of the line is ready for use."

"I see I haven't made myself plain, Mrs. Norwood," he said with controlled irritation. "If you insist on embarking on any sort of journey, large or small, in any sort of conveyance, you will lose the child. It is as simple as that. I don't know what's got into your head. I certainly don't. I should think you would want to be home with your husband at a time like this." He paused, observing me for a moment or two. "There's nothing wrong, I hope. Nothing between you and Mr. Norwood, is there?"

"Oh, no—no, not at all."

How could I tell him, I think my husband is trying to kill me, drive me mad? In the light of past complaints he would think I was already mad. He would put me away somewhere, in an institution perhaps, take my baby from me. Did I want that?

No, I thought. And suddenly I realized what the baby meant to me. Suddenly—I wanted it. I wanted it desperately enough to endure anything, fear, discomfort, pain, even entrapment in this gloomy, ghost-ridden house.

"Well—then?" Dr. Johnson asked, waiting for an explanation of my strange behavior.

"Of course, you are right," I said, giving him a small smile. "Perfectly right. I shan't go. It was stupid of me even to consider it."

"That's a good girl," Dr. Johnson said, patting my arm. "Your husband has been waiting all this time very patiently outside. He's told me he's anxious to see you."

"Oh, not yet! I—I'm not ready. Couldn't he come later, perhaps?" I pleaded, flustered.

Dr. Johnson looked at me sternly. "My dear, he's already seen you with your face black and blue. No reason to put him off."

"Still . . ." I wasn't worried about my face, though I realized I must look a sight. I was worried about confronting Cage. What would I say? Could I pretend everything was as it should be?

But I had no time to think about it. Dr. Johnson rose from his chair and went to the door. "You can come in, now," he said.

Cage looked very contrite, embarrassed, yet in an odd way excited, almost happy.

"Adelaide . . . !" he exclaimed, striding past the doctor, his arms outstretched. "Adelaide, my darling!" He leaned over and kissed me on the forehead, on the cheeks, on the lips. "You have no idea . . ." He sat down on the edge of the bed, taking my hands, kissing each finger in turn. "My darling, my sweet—if you only knew how worried I've been. I must have paced a deep path in the carpet. Ever since—my God! when I think of it! And all my fault, my fault. I should never have let you go off in the buggy alone, never, never. I've dismissed both McCorkle and Gandy for negligence—but I still take the blame."

He brushed the hair from my forehead and kissed me again, such a tender, sweet gesture it brought a lump to my throat. If only he meant it, if only . . .

"Cage . . ."

"Hush, sweet." He put his fingers to my lips. "I don't want to be forgiven. It was my fault and when I found out that you—that we—oh, Adelaide." There was a suspicious glitter in his eye. A tear? Was he sorry, really?

"I'm going to turn over a new leaf, so help me God. Home every night, cold sober. I promise—Adelaide, I swear it." He laid a warm hand on either side of my face. "I'll make it up to you—I swear."

Had I heard those words before? Did they seem to have a familiar ring? Ah—but no one in the whole wide world could deliver them with such utter conviction as Cage.

"Cage, I thought . . ."

"I know you did, my darling, and quite rightly. Yes, I've been neglecting you. But that's all in the past. There is no one more precious to me than you. And the child to come —a boy, I hope." He grinned like a boy himself, a grin that melted my heart. Oh, why did he have to be so handsome, why had God given *him* such charm and *me* such gullibility?

"I shall take good care of you, darling," he promised earnestly. "Very good care."

Did I believe him? Did I dare? Did I have a choice? If only he would say those three words, *"I love you,"* the words that would make everything all right again. I longed for them the way a thirsty traveler in the desert longs for a sip of water. I searched his face, my lips trembling, but when he spoke he said:

"I want you to follow Dr. Johnson's instructions to the letter. I want you to have everything you need, anything you crave. We are going to have a beautiful boy. Don't you agree, darling?"

"Yes, Cage," I said. "Yes, I'm sure we will."

Again he was kind, so kind I began to think seriously I had imagined all those horrible things about him, imagined he had wanted to be rid of me so that he could marry Fanny Walters. After all, it was Jay who had put the idea into my head, wasn't it? I was wary at first, but when the weeks went by and Cage still came home regularly each night for supper bringing little gifts, trinkets, flowers and perfume, when he continued to have but a single glass of wine with his meal and a small glass of brandy afterwards, when he went on being attentive, my doubts began to disappear. And when nothing untoward happened, when no fearful "losses of memory" occurred, then those doubts vanished altogether.

Martha's attitude remained impassive, noncommittal. She said she was glad for the baby, made all the appropriate sounds, but I felt she couldn't have cared less. Her concern, her main interest at the Folly was still Octavia.

Octavia herself reacted strangely. She was old enough to know about such things as babies and so I told her, thinking that she was also old enough not to be jealous. But she seemed to be, and I supposed it was because she felt that our child would completely disinherit her. When I explained that Cage had set aside a substantial sum for her use alone, she still appeared unconvinced. She spoke to me now with thinly veiled resentment, just as she had done when I first came to the Folly. One day when I questioned her again about it, she said it was my imagination. "I don't resent you," she said.

But I knew it was a lie. Ted Neale still squired her about. Poor Ted, making little headway, kind, dogged, knowing he was being used, but just as enamored of the beautiful Octavia, just as faithful.

I saw Jay only once during that time. It was before I had begun to "show" and could still go about in public. My arm had healed, and the bruises had vanished from my face, so I went down to the City of Paris to buy some baby dresses. Coming out of the door, I ran into Jay on the sidewalk. He took my arm and drew me aside.

"Hello, Adelaide—it's been so long. I heard about the accident. You're all right now? I must say you look wonderful, blooming."

"Thank you."

"I assume things are going well?"

"Yes—very well."

"Ah—I had hoped—if you will forgive me—I had hoped otherwise," taking my hand, kissing it in a mock, gallant gesture.

"Well—you're wrong," I replied shortly, but there was such an impish gleam in his eyes I couldn't remain cross with him. "I hate to blast your hopes," I added, giving him a small smile.

He still held my hand, but oddly enough I did not make any move to withdraw it. There was always something

electric, something vital about Jay, and in my present condition I could feel it more keenly than ever. Why that
should be, I could not explain unless he had simply caught
me in one of my benign moments. Buying things for the
baby and preparing for it in any way always gave me a
feeling of well-being.

"Well, now, I wonder what could be putting such roses
in your cheeks?" He leaned closer.

Ought I to tell? No, of course not. One did not discuss
such intimate matters in public, much less with a man, any
man no matter how close to the family he might be. It was
improper (Aunt Tildy thought it scandalous) for a pregnant woman to admit she was expecting; only her dearest
women friends and her doctor should know. Even Cage
referred to my pregnancy as my "delicate condition."

"By golly, they are natural roses, too," Jay was saying,
peering into my face. "Cage must be doing well by you
after all."

The dark, mocking look in his eyes left no question as to
what he meant.

Shocked and angry I jerked my hand from his grasp.
"You have no right to speak to me in that fashion!"

"Why not? You and I have had a long acquaintance.
You've not kept secrets from me before. You've . . ."

"Oh—you're impossible! Impossible! I've never known
such a—such a . . ."

"A cad," he sighed. "I wish for once you could find
something more—shall we say—original?"

I turned my back on him and strode to the carriage.
"Goodbye!" he called. "I hope it is a boy."

My cheeks flamed but I did not look around.

Once my figure reached the ungainly stage I did not
venture outside the cloistered walls of the Folly. It would
not have been seemly. So I remained at home, knitting,
embroidering and reading, slowly making my way through
all of Shakespeare's plays. We had no visitors. Even Clara
Shelby stopped paying calls. Ted Neale when he came to
fetch Octavia was shown directly into the drawing room,
so I never got to talk to him. But I did not mind, not as
long as Cage came home every night. And he did. He
seemed preoccupied, though, and I suspected that he was
drinking again, surreptitiously, for he went on making a

show of having a single glass of wine and one of brandy at supper. Again, I thought that worry over business matters had brought what had become almost a perpetual frown between his eyes, and I went so far as to question him one day.

"There's nothing to be concerned about, Adelaide," he said. "A few problems, but I am well able to solve them." It was something unpleasant, I could tell, and he did not want to talk about it. Sometimes as he sat in the small parlor with me when the mist pressed against the windows and the ships' horns moaned on a foggy evening in the bay, I would look up from my sewing and catch an odd listening look in his eyes, a look very close to fear.

But why and of whom should Cage be afraid? I told myself it is my imagination, Cage is afraid of nothing.

As for my own fears, my little traumas and anxieties, they had disappeared completely, and as the days wore on I seemed to withdraw more and more from the world into a pleasant, warm cocoon. My thoughts were quiet ones. I would often imagine myself at Green Springs. It was a fanciful pastime I never tired of. In my mind's eye I could see the curtains fluttering at the long windows on a summer's day, the dark row of oaks that led down to the river, the gray river itself and the ships gliding silently by. I would see the hedges of hawthorn in bloom, the mock orange and the clovered lawns, even imagine the scent of freshly mowed grass as heady as strong perfume. I wished I were home, home before the war, the way it used to be, but it was only a dreamy nostalgia, no pain or urgency.

Life went on around me, and gradually I took less and less notice. Cage's white harried face barely intruded. The servants were like shadows, even Martha seemed so far away I walked every day in the yard, weather permitting. How clear, how different objects looked to me now. It was as if I had been given another pair of eyes. I became keenly alive to color, to shape and texture. Each leaf in the garden stood out in varying shades of green, yellow or brown; the curl of a dying petal on a spent rose seemed as strange and as wonderful as an unfolding bud. I felt serene, content, more so than I had been in years.

And then one afternoon my serenity received a jolt. I was sitting in the garden wrapped in my cloak, for the weather had turned quite cold, when looking up I saw

Octavia watching me from an upstairs window. I was too far away to catch the expression on her face, but from the hasty way she withdrew, I suspected she had been observing me without wanting to be seen. Why, I had no idea. Except for that brief period after my accident, she had never taken the trouble to become friendly, never completely shed her indifference toward me. Perhaps I had imagined that quick movement, perhaps she had been passing a window and merely happened to have looked out.

Nevertheless, I began to take more notice of her. And to my surprise I found that whenever I was in the same room with her she kept her eyes on me. At dinner I would look up to meet her level, violet gaze so many times it could not possibly have been coincidence. She never said anything, just stared. And, too, she would turn up suddenly at odd times, on the stair, at a door, in the corridor, and once I came upon her just as she was leaving my room.

I was too stunned, I remember, to say anything. It was she who spoke. "Oh, Aunt Adelaide, I wanted to borrow a hat pin, mine seemed to have all disappeared."

"You might have asked," I said.

"Yes—I know, but you weren't anywhere around. Ted's downstairs—and he's in such a hurry. . . ."

"I see. And did you find it?"

"Find . . . ? Oh, the pin. Well, no. I didn't."

"Come in, then."

The papers on my desk had been mussed and the bottles on my bureau shifted, not too obviously but enough for me to realize Octavia had been going through my things. I was furious. "You have the gall—the nerve to . . ." I swallowed. "I certainly would not feel free to search your room, no matter how much I needed a hat pin."

She blushed. "I'm sorry—very sorry," she mumbled.

I said nothing but looked at her, and she met my eyes defiantly. After a moment I spoke in a hard, controlled voice. "Just what was it you were looking for? And don't tell me it was a hat pin."

She bit her lip but kept silent.

"Perhaps I ought to check the contents of my jewel box."

Her flush deepened, but the defiant look did not leave her eyes. "I have jewels of my own," she said. "I have my mother's. Why should I need yours?"

"Why—indeed. Then what were you looking for?" I opened a drawer where the papers had been riffled through. "Are you going to tell me or do I have to force it out of you?"

"Force what out of me?" she asked with an infuriating, innocent air.

My first impulse was to box her ears. The impudent chit! But I wasn't about to sink to a free-for-all, certainly not in my condition.

I turned on my heel, went to the door, locked it, and put the key in my pocket. Then I came back and sat down on a chair. "You might as well have a seat, too," I said, "because you are not leaving this room until you tell me just what it was you wanted here."

There was a flicker of surprise in her eyes.

"You see," I said, smoothing the folds of my dress over my burgeoning stomach. "I am not quite the same person I was when I first came to the Folly. I am not afraid of you, Octavia, I'm not afraid of Martha either—of anyone."

It had passed through my mind that Martha, for devious reasons of her own, had sent Octavia on her mission of spying, of searching. If so I meant to nip it in the bud at once. I was not going to go through another long round with Martha. I felt strong, very strong. I was about to produce a son and heir for Cage—why not?

"Are you going to tell me?"

She did not sit down, but some of the dare, the hostile challenge, had gone from her eyes.

"I could have your father force it out of you. Perhaps he might keep you in—or send you back to the convent."

"No . . . !"

"Hmmmm. What is it then? Are you trying to discover if I have any secret love letters?"

"Yes," she said.

I smiled. "Really now, that isn't much better than the hat pin, is it?"

"It's not funny. I'm trying to find my mother's murderer."

"In my desk, my bureau?" I asked incredulously.

"I'm looking for correspondence. I'm looking for a clue . . ." She bit her lip.

I stared at her. "Do I understand correctly, my dear? You suspect *me* of murdering your mother?"

"Yes."

I had never thought of Octavia as particularly bright, assuming she had ordinary average intelligence, now I wondered if she actually had that much.

"Your mother died, my dear," I said in as reasonable a voice as I could muster, "years ago when I was still living in Virginia."

"But you could have hired an agent," she said. "You could have sent money, paid someone to have her killed."

I tried to digest that. "I *paid* an agent to have your mother murdered? But why?"

"Because you were in love with Papa, because . . ." Her face got very red. ". . . because you wanted him."

That was a little easier to swallow since it held a morsel of fact. Yes, I had been in love with Cage, but the rest of the idea was so ridiculous as to be almost laughable. Almost, not quite. "How long have you harbored this notion?"

"I really didn't think much about it until last week when . . ." She paused.

"When what?" I waited. "Did Martha put this notion into your head?"

"No, she didn't. Don't look at me like that, I tell you she didn't."

I let that pass though I had my doubts. "And so your theory is that I hired a man to kill your mother so that I could marry Papa. My dear Octavia, hadn't anyone told you that I already had a husband at the time?"

I could see that this came as a bit of a shock. Her brows drew together, and she hesitated before she spoke. "Well—no—but . . . " She looked me straight in the eye. The old challenging I-dare-you-look. "But I don't see how that mattered."

God keep me! I thought, wanting to shake her until the teeth rattled in her head. The ninny! "My husband died in the war," I said, struggling hard to keep a hold on my temper. "I was—was quite fond of him. We were happy. I would have died rather than harm a hair on his head."

She said nothing, just stood there, staring at me, her eyes enormous.

"I never corresponded with your father during the years he lived here in San Francisco." I pointed out.

"You corresponded with your brother Charles. He was in San Francisco."

But the sting had gone out of her voice, and I noted with surprise that she was on the verge of tears.

"That's true, and I have no doubt that you read the two letters he has written me since I've been here."

She was silent. Her eyes grew larger, and a tear clung to one of her lashes. She struggled with the tear, biting her lip, her misery, her unhappiness becoming more and more acute. I could not go on feeling angry with her. She was so young, so vulnerable and already had lived through enough scandal and virulent gossip to break a far older person. Her mother, a prostitute, had been murdered in the arms of her lover. There was no way to soften those ugly, uncompromising facts. The trial had laid them bare. How could I fault her for at least wanting to know the name of her mother's murderer? How could I fault her for grasping at even the most far-fetched of theories?

"What did those letters tell you?" I asked, my voice softening.

"Nothing," she said. The tear began to trickle slowly down her face, but she made no move to brush it away.

"Octavia. . ."

Another tear.

"Child—child . . ." Those silent tears had reached me in a way nothing else could. "Child, I swear by the baby I carry I had nothing whatsoever to do with your mother's death."

Still another tear. She swallowed. She tried to speak but no words came.

"Do you believe me, dear?"

Her throat worked and the tears were brimming now. I got up from my chair and impulsively held out my arms. She ran into them with a choked sob.

I had a long talk with Martha the next morning. She vehemently denied she had in any way implied or suggested I might have conspired to have Lillith killed.

"I never speak to her about her mother anymore. She knows that I won't. After the trial I told her, forget it, it's done, finished," Martha asserted.

"Octavia is a very unhappy child."

"Yes—unhappy, when she's got no call to be," she said with a trace of bitterness. "She lives in this beautiful house, never had to work a day in her life, never had to go hungry, never had to sell her body for a bite to eat. I don't think she's got a right to be unhappy."

She sat for a few moments, reflecting, the corners of her mouth turned down. She looked old, tired. There were lines on her face, deep grooves between her eyes that had not been there before. I wondered how old she was, if she had aged so in the last few months because of her rumored rivalry with Mammy Pleasant. It seemed strange to me then, looking at her, at the weariness stamped on her proud face, that I had ever been frightened of her.

"I told her," Martha began again, "I told her so many times she would only come to grief if she kept on looking for the man who killed her mother."

I started at that. "A man killed her mother?"

She gave me a blank look.

"Martha—do you know who killed her?"

"Seems you asked me that before."

"But—you never answered my question. Do you know?"

She sighed, a heart-heavy sigh. "Yes, I know. He's a dangerous man. But the Devil himself couldn't force me to speak his name."

"But—you must, you must . . . !"

"I must—nothing," she said with the old spirit, her mouth clamping shut. I knew that mousetrap look.

Was it Cage? I wanted to ask. But I knew she would never tell me.

Chapter 27

M Y son was born towards evening on June 18, 1868. We named him Lewis Cage, Lewis Cage Norwood II. He was a beautiful child; I couldn't get over how beautiful he was, a child of mine hatched, it seemed, from the ugly duckling. His limbs were perfectly formed, his little chin and darling nose, his eyes, his mouth, all put together so flawlessly.

Cage agreed he had never seen a prettier, more handsome baby. Watching him lean over the sleeping infant, the look of foolish joy on his face, I wondered how I could have ever entertained the notion of leaving Cage. Had I once been afraid of him, of the house, of Martha, had I once been afraid of losing my mind, my life? It all seemed so vague, so long ago, like something that had happened to a character in a novel or a play, not something that had happened to Adelaide Norwood at all.

During the weeks and months that followed I lived in a state of euphoria, a kind of never-never land. We had a marvelous christening party for little Cage and subsequently gave a dinner and a musical evening. Now that Cage was established as a respectable *pater familias,* society forgave his former transgression and showered us with invitations. I seemed to have lost my shyness; I laughed a lot; people said I was a changed woman. Jay Cooke said so, too. He had come to the christening, of course—we had invited over a hundred people—and I saw him again one evening when Cage and I, the Shelbys and Hunters went to the theatre. We had a box, I remember, at Macguire's Opera House, and the famous Adah Isaacs Menken had come from New Orleans to perform. All of society was there in full glittering array, the men in their black, formal evening clothes, the ladies in long silk skirts, their ears and throats asparkle with jewels. "The Carriage Set," as Clara remarked behind her fan. Her hair was done in the latest mode with long, "follow-me-lad" curls over one shoulder. It was she who espied Jay Cooke in the audience on the ground floor before the curtain went up for the first act, and she waved to him with her fan.

"They tell me," she said, leaning back in her chair, "that he is really getting serious about the Porter girl. She's the McCullough heiress, you know, very pretty, too."

For some strange reason—since I certainly was not in love with Jay—this news gave me a queer pang. "Well," I said rather tartly, "he is certainly old enough to settle down."

"Yes," she said absently, her eye roving the ringed tiers of boxes, "he is, isn't he?"

He came to our box during the first intermission. He knew everyone; there was a flurry of greetings. "Well, Mrs. Norwood—Adelaide—," Jay said to me, smiling into my eyes. "I must say motherhood has transformed you."

"Oh?" I said rather archly, waiting for the barb I felt was sure to come.

"Yes, I think you have flowered. A late bloomer is the term, I believe. But then I always knew that given half the chance you would."

"Really."

"Don't become a coquette," he said, lowering his voice. "It doesn't suit your style."

I knew it, I thought, I knew it! The man couldn't bear to give a compliment without following it up with some little shaft to spoil it.

"When I want your advice on how to conduct myself," I said sweetly, "I shall ask for it." And I turned abruptly away from him to engage Mr. Hunter in conversation.

The baby thrived. We had hired a nurse for him, a Mrs. Yardley, a nice, wholesome, buxom type from the country, but she and Martha were at loggerheads, and I sensed trouble in that direction. But, I thought: Why anticipate unpleasantness? Perhaps the situation will smooth itself out in time.

Octavia, too, should have been a source of concern. It was not that we were still contending; in fact, ever since that episode in my bedroom, our relationship had improved. But she seemed changed. Always noncommittal, indifferent, almost phlegmatic, she now seemed extraordinarily happy, smiling to herself, humming tunes under her breath, often just staring dreamily into space. She claimed that by joining a singing club (called the Swallows) she had found a hobby at last which engrossed her, that meeting new people had given her a fresh lease on life. Yet there was something in her eyes which betrayed that claim, something, some secret that pleased her very much. It niggled at my conscience. I would look at her, think about it, shrug, push the uneasy feeling to the back of my mind. I wanted my life to go on running smoothly. I wanted to go on living in my never-never land with the baby, with Cage, with a cozy domesticity, ignoring disturbing ripples and treacherous undercurrents. I wanted to go on blindly overlooking the hints and signs that all was not well.

For a long time I even refused to notice Cage was beginning to drink once more, that again he was frequently absent from the supper table, and lastly, disastrously, I tried to close my eyes to the fact that our financial situation had changed, that unpaid bills were piling up, and we were slowly but inexorably sliding into debt.

I should have been forewarned when Cage, who loved to throw parties and lavish sit-down suppers, told me that we would have to cut back drastically on our entertaining. "A small monetary pinch," he explained with a wan smile. "Nothing to worry about—we'll just have to tighten our belts for a short time only."

I did not mind. We had plenty of money—or so it seemed. I let the nurse go as a gesture of economy but we kept the other servants (McCorkle and Gandy, too, both of whom had been long since rehired), kept the barouche, the landau and the buggy and the four sleek horses housed in the stable.

Martha continued to do the household accounts, dealing with the tradesmen and paying them (or not paying them, according to how often Cage gave her the money). In the past I had resented Martha's position but now with my time divided between little Cage and various social obligations, I was too busy to give her more than a passing thought. And I would have gone on in this fashion, oblivious to all but my own routine, had not Octavia come to me one afternoon, angry and upset.

"Martha says I am to stop going to my club," she said, her cheeks flushed and her eyes blazing.

"Club? Oh, you mean the Swallows," I said. "Now why should she object?"

"She says I'm away from home too much."

"I can't see any harm in singing several times a week with a group of young ladies and gentlemen." We were in my bedroom, and I was playing with the baby, slowly twirling a crystal pendant over his crib.

"I want you to speak to Martha," Octavia said.

"You know my word doesn't carry much weight with Martha. Why don't you ask your father?"

"He told me he was too busy, he said I should talk to you."

I sighed. "Very well, I'll see what I can do."

"When?" she asked impatiently. "I am expected at the Opera House in an hour. And Martha says I can't have the buggy, that if I want to go I'll have to walk."

I tucked the pendant back into the neck of my gown and rose from my chair. "Really—Octavia—couldn't you. . . ? All right, I'll see what she has to say now."

I rang for Martha, and in a few minutes I could hear her coming up the stairs. "She'll tell you all sorts of things," Octavia said quickly, in a rush, "all kinds of things that aren't true. She wants me to stay home and just go out with Ted Neale. My God—Ted Neale! He . . ."

Martha knocked and came into the room. Her face darkened when she saw Octavia. They both began to talk at once:

"So—you've come here behind my back!"

"I can go where I please, you have no . . ."

"Be quiet! You spoiled . . ."

I tried to speak but they ignored me, their voices growing louder and angrier until they were shouting at one another. I stood by, feeling sick and resentful. I hated quarreling. I had become like Cage in that matter; I wanted everything and everyone around me to be pleasant and agreeable. I was thinking I would take the baby and leave them to their argument when they both stopped for breath.

"Wait . . . !" I cautioned before they could commence their battle of wills again. "Wait! Let me have a word. I can't put up with this sort of thing. Octavia, perhaps you had better let Martha and me discuss this alone."

"No—not without me," she said sullenly. "If I'm not here, I can't defend myself."

"All right, stay, but I have trouble making myself heard when you insist on shouting."

"I'll—I'll keep quiet," Octavia promised.

Martha said, "She's got a tongue on her, that girl. I don't know where she got it, her mama was always so sweet. And she can't tell a thing straight. Mrs. Norwood, she ain't been going to practice. Now—you hush up, Octavia! Just you hush up! I know for a fact because I sent Gandy down to the Opera House yesterday."

"Spying on me," Octavia said scornfully, "you've been spying on me."

"Not yet, I wasn't. I should have, but Gandy went down to take you your cape. It started to rain yesterday afternoon—remember?—and you'd gone without a proper wrap, if you please, so I sent Gandy with the cape, and you weren't there. None of them young people had seen you for weeks."

"They're wrong," she asserted. "I don't know why they should have told Gandy that. As for yesterday I needed stockings and a petticoat, so I went into the City to do some shopping. What's so terrible about that? And furthermore I don't see why every movement of mine has to be watched."

Martha stared at her, her narrowed eyes hard as stones. "Because you lie," she said between her teeth. "You lie—like a hussy. You know that? You've been seeing that man, haven't you?"

"Who? Who? What man?" Octavia demanded.

"I don't know his name because you won't tell me. But it's the same man you saw before—before your Papa sent you to Marysville."

"I never . . . ! It's not true!"

"It *is* true. And I'll have it out of you, if it's the last thing I do. Is he married? Is he? Is he a married man, is that why he won't come calling like a decent gentleman, or is he some low-down scoundrel, some rotten, no-good . . ."

"No—!" The cry was torn from Octavia. She stared at us, her eyes wide, her hand at her mouth, and then she broke into a fit of sobbing.

"What did I say?" Martha exclaimed angrily, her fists clenched at her sides. "Didn't I say right? I should have known. The scum of the earth . . ."

"He isn't—I love him!" Octavia wept. "I love him! I've never loved anyone in my whole life as I love him. He's everything to me. Oh, God—can't you understand?"

That age-old cry torn from the heart—can't you understand? How well I knew it. The seemingly blind indifference of others to one's deepest needs, to one's anguish and despair. I remembered myself as a girl, weeping for love and wishing that I had someone who "understood." How could I help but feel Octavia's pain?

I went to her and put my arms around her shaking shoulders. "There, there, my dear," I soothed. "We shall work it out somehow. If—if your young man is at all suitable, if he loves you, couldn't he come to the Folly— meet your father, do the right thing?"

"He—he says he will," she said, turning her tear-stained face up at me. "But he says Papa will not like him because he—he's older than I."

"Older? How much older?"

"He—he's thirty-five."

"Well . . . ," I said after a moment, "that is a bit old for you, but still that's no reason why he shouldn't introduce himself. How did you meet him, my dear?"

"I met him through a friend at a—at a tea dance."

Martha, who had been breathing heavily while she listened to Octavia, suddenly exclaimed, "You didn't! You didn't meet him through no friend, at no tea dance. Else I would have known, we would have seen him here at the house. He picked you up on the street, that's what he did, you—you whore . . . !" She stepped forward, her hand lifted to strike Octavia, but Octavia sprang nimbly aside.

"*Don't* call me names, Martha—don't you dare!" she challenged with brimming eyes.

They faced each other in tense silence. Little Cage Lewis began to gurgle and croon.

"Who is this man?" I asked quietly.

"His name is Barry Holden," Octavia answered.

"Holden?" Martha looked at me.

"The name is unfamiliar," I said.

"He *is* a gentleman," Octavia insisted. "He dresses beautifully and lives in the best suite at the St. Francis. And he has never tried—never gone beyond the proprieties. He—he wants to marry me. And I love him," she added on a tremulous note.

"I'm sure you do, my dear," I said, "but you know that marriage is out of the question unless he presents himself to your father—and your father approves, of course."

"Oh—Papa's bound to like him," she said, brightening. "Barry is so—so likeable. And he's prosperous, well able to take care of me."

Martha pressed her lips together. "I've never heard of him. What does this Barry Holden do?"

"He's in finance," she said.

"What's he look like?"

"Handsome, oh, Martha, so handsome. He has dark auburn hair and brown eyes. He's not as tall as Ted Neale, but he has broad shoulders, a very manly figure, distinguished. If you could only see him I know you would find him a perfect catch for me."

Martha said nothing.

I said, "If he feels diffident or shy about calling on your father, Octavia, I'll have Cage write Mr. Holden a note and invite him to the house. In the meanwhile, however, I think it would be wise if you did not see him."

She was stunned. "Not see him . . . !" she wailed. "Oh—no! He—he's waiting for me—now."

"If he loves you," I said, "he won't mind waiting."

"But *I* will. Aunt Adelaide . . ."

"I'm sorry."

Her face dropped. "Oh—!" she exclaimed, her cheeks flushing with anger. "How could you? How could you? You are cruel, cruel! Monsters, both of you!" she flung at us.

"Octavia . . ."

"Cruel!" And wheeling about she dashed from the room.

The sound of the slamming door startled the baby and he began to cry. I picked him up. Martha said, "Mr. Cage don't care about Octavia. He don't care what happens to her anymore."

"That's not true," I said, holding little Lewis Cage close, soothing him. "You know how fond of her he's always been."

"Always, but now he's got a son . . ."

"Oh, Martha, please," I chided, but inside I felt a little

chill. God alone knew what went on in her mind. If she should take a notion to dislike the baby—what would she do? Did she still practice voodoo? I wondered. Perhaps— but I mustn't think of it. She would not dare harm the baby.

"I'm not going to wait for Mr. Cage," she said. "Tomorrow, I'm going to see that person, Barry Holden, I'm going to see what kind of a man he is."

"Yes," I agreed. "Perhaps you should."

Cage, when told about Barry Holden, said the name was unfamiliar to him also. "And I know just about everyone of importance who is dealing in real estate, stocks or banking," he added. "The little minx—I don't like this. And she's too old to send back to the convent. I ought to marry her off to some nice young man. What about Ted Neale?"

"She is not in love with Ted Neale, I'm afraid she finds him scarcely tolerable."

"I see—well, she's still young."

"She's seventeen and she seems determined to marry Barry Holden—that is, if he asks her."

"I'll write to the man. He's staying at the St. Francis, you say? First thing in the morning, I'll send him a note. Remind me."

But in the morning Cage was in a tearing hurry to be off—he was late for an appointment. "I'll write later today," he said, giving me a quick, absent peck on the cheek.

Octavia trailed down for a tardy breakfast, a morose look on her face. She had nothing to say, and I was too busy going over the luncheon menu with Martha to take the time to coax her into conversation. It was my day to have the ladies of the sewing circle, and I wanted everything to be just right. Fruit-cup, consomme, sole, fresh peas, salad and pecan pie. "And coffee, plenty of coffee," I reminded Martha.

Octavia said she did not plan to make an appearance, to sit with "that bunch of hens." A little stung, I told her that her sour face would not be welcome.

"If that's the way you feel—well!" She pushed back her chair, threw down her napkin and slammed out of the room. A moment later we heard her ascending the stairs.

"I don't like the way she acts," Martha said, shaking her head. "I don't trust that girl. After I serve your ladies I

want to go have a look at that Barry Holden. Cora and
Lucinda can clear away."

"Yes, yes, of course, do go."

The meal itself was a success, the ladies exclaiming de-
lightfully over the fish course, especially, the sole done up
in a fanciful sauce with a grapelike eye staring out at us.
For the rest it turned out to be a rather long afternoon. I
had never quite gotten the hang of small talk or gossip, and
Clara Shelby would go on forever about the Turner boy
who gambled and who kept an actress, a topic which I
found of little interest. Nor did Mrs. Fairfax's long account
of her sister's latest ailment capture my attention. In short
—I was bored, so it was with a sigh of relief that I saw the
last lady out at about five in the afternoon.

I went up immediately to little Cage who had been in the
care of Cora for most of the day. She had just changed
him, and he looked so fresh and pretty and smelled so good
I squeezed him until he yelped. After Cora left I fed him
and then rocked him until he fell asleep.

Fog was rolling in from the sea when I rose to draw the
curtains. I watched for a few moments as long fingers of
white mist drifted across the wall, obscuring the flower
beds and the walk. I shivered, a cozy little shiver, and
pulled the curtains shut. Then I eased my feet out of my
shoes and laid down on the bed for a short nap. The house
at this hour was always very quiet—today, it seemed, more
so than ever. The servants were also resting before beginning the evening meal, Martha had not yet returned, and
Octavia was still licking her wounds in her lair.

I closed my eyes and waited for the slow drowsiness of
sleep to take over. Suddenly a slight clicking sound jarred
me wide awake. A board, I thought, or the baby moving in
his crib. Sighing I turned over on my side, letting thoughts
and pictures float idly in my head once more—Clara
Shelby's new, peacock blue dress, Mrs. Fairfax's lorgnette
catching a ray of sunlight, and Mrs. Turner's rings, winking
and blinking. My head was becoming fuzzier and fuzzier
when the click came again louder this time, sharper.

I sat up.

It had grown darker; there were deep shadows in the
room now, and the small lamp I had lit on the table near
the window gave but a feeble light. Suddenly, sitting there,
I felt cold, a strange chilliness, the same goosefleshed sen-

sation I had felt so long ago when I had imagined (or had I?) someone was watching me. But there was no one, no one except me and the sleeping child. Besides, I chided myself, I am past all that, past the irrational fear, the starts, the cold, clammy hands, the sudden dampness sprouting on my forehead. I am past that. I have become quite the placid housewife, the tranquil mother.

The click did not come again.

And yet my heart went on beating, fluttering like a frightened bird's wings. The hairs along the back of my neck seemed to rise, moment by moment. Why? Why? It was all so ridiculous! I got up and went to the window, pushing the curtains aside. Nothing could be seen now but thick rolls of cottony fog and the hazy outline of a tree. Night was falling fast. The clock said a quarter to six. Shouldn't the servants be stirring? I asked myself. Where was Martha? Where was everybody?

I went to the door and opened it, peering out. The gas lamps had not yet been lit, and the long corridor lay in a pool of darkness. Suddenly I heard another faint sound, different than the click, and cocking my head, I strained to listen. A muffled groan reached my ears. I was out of the room and at the head of the stairs in a moment. Looking over the rail, I saw a familiar, dark-clad figure lying on the floor at the bottom.

"Martha . . . ?" I called. "Martha!"

I was answered by another groan.

I flew down the stairs. She was lying on her back, one arm outflung, her neck at a queer angle, her eyes closed. "What happened?" I cried, kneeling beside her. She was hurt, badly.

Her eyelids fluttered, then opened. Her lips moved, and I could see that she was trying desperately to talk, to tell me something.

"Don't," I said. "Don't tax yourself. I'll have Gandy fetch the doctor."

"Holden," she whispered. "Holden—an evil man. He—he. . ." She closed her eyes again.

"Lucinda!" I called. "Lucinda!"

"Don't," Martha said in a broken voice. Her hand inched to mine, and she took hold of my wrist in a painful, nail-pinching grasp. "You must stop—must stop her—

Octavia. He is—he is the Devil. He pushed. . ." She winced and her throat moved convulsively as she swallowed.

"He pushed you—where—how? Who? Barry Holden?" I was distraught and mad with fear.

"He pushed—the stairs . . ."

"What stairs? What stairs? Not here—what do you mean?"

She mumbled something, delirious with pain.

"Lucinda!" I shouted.

"I'm here, m'am," she cried, running into the hall. "Oh —my God!"

"Don't gawk, send Gandy for Dr. Johnson. Hurry, you fool, hurry!"

"Martha, I'm going to get you some brandy." She still had hold of my wrist and I tried to pry her fingers loose. But she held on with a strength that amazed me.

"No—not brandy—Octavia—stop her. I promised her mama," her tongue moved over her dry lips, "I promised her mama—so much like my mama, she was, soft and pretty and helpless. . ." Two tears rolled down her cheeks. "I—I said—I said I'd care for her, Octavia—and you've *got* to, you've got to stop her—now!" Her breath was coming in gasps.

"I'll have Gandy move you first."

"No—Miss Adelaide, no." She had never called me Miss Adelaide, always the more formal Mrs. Norwood, and her sudden assumption of my Christian name drove my fear to the brink of panic. ". . . stop Octavia—please, Miss Adelaide—I never—I never meant you any harm—and now you must . . . stop her."

I ran into the drawing room and whipped the fringed shawl from the piano. Dashing out, I quickly covered Martha, then went up the stairs as fast as my pounding heart would allow.

I knocked on Octavia's door and without waiting for an answer opened it and went in. The room lay in darkness. "Octavia. . . ?" Silence. Groping about, I felt my way to a table and with blind fingers found a match. The light flared as I lifted the chimney of a lamp and lighted it. Octavia was not in the room. I looked all around. The little minx, I thought, sneaking out. I was turning to go when I saw the note pinned to the pillow of her bed.

It was short. "Dear Papa," it said, "by the time you receive this I shall be Mrs. Barry Holden. Please forgive me, Papa, but I love him, and he loves me and we did not want to wait. Octavia."

Chapter 28

MARTHA was dead before the doctor arrived, dead without having spoken another word.

"She must have fallen down the stairs," Dr. Johnson noted.

"Yes," I said, "yes."

An accident. The stairs winding round and round, Martha ascending them in that quick, stiff gait of hers, tripping, falling.

"She must have gone up and down those stairs hundreds of times," I murmured.

How strange that she was dead. I felt a curious void, curious because I had never really liked her, curious because there had been long stretches when I actually hated and feared her. Even toward the last when it seemed she had mellowed somewhat, I did not feel entirely comfortable in her presence. And yet I admired her inflexible, touchy pride, her championship of Octavia, her loyalty to Cage when he needed her—and that, at the end, she had called me Miss Adelaide.

She was dead. Killed by a fall.

"I never understood her," I said. A woman, not a darkie, but a woman in limbo, not belonging, cold, scrambling for a place, a haven. Had she really been that fond of Lillith? "She was the first person who treated me decent," she said. "So like my own mama. . ." Her own mama, her own life. I could see now where she had depths I had not thought to probe. I was sorry I hadn't tried. Depths. Someone had once called Martha a "puzzle." Who had it been? I couldn't remember.

"Sad—sad," Dr. Johnson nodded dolorously.

We were sitting in the little parlor, Dr. Johnson and I, waiting for Cage whom Gandy had been sent to fetch.

Poor Cage. Two shocks awaited him; Martha's untimely death and Octavia's sudden elopement.

"I must have been asleep when Martha came in," I said, breaking a short silence.

"You'd be surprised how many people maim and kill themselves by a simple, accidental fall," Dr. Johnson observed.

How had she missed her footing? I tried to picture her falling, her arms thrashing about wildly as she sought to grasp the rail to stop herself, the bumping, the painful roll as she tumbled to the parquet floor at the bottom. How long had she lain there before I found her? How long in pain had she moaned, waiting for someone? I had come too late. The doctor said she would have died in any case, but I had been too late. "An evil man," she had said, struggling to tell me more. "He pushed . . ."

Had Barry Holden pushed her down the stairs? Here at the Folly? But, of course, that was impossible. Her broken mind had made her delirious. She was saying things out of context, things that had little relevance. "He pushed . . ."

Had it been an accident?

I shivered. The fog pressed against the windows. Dr. Johnson sat with his chin sunk on his chest, his eyes closed. Beyond the kitchen in Martha's room her corpse lay, awaiting funeral arrangements. She had no next of kin that we knew about. Would her friends, the people she had helped through the years with money and jobs, to escape from slavery, give her a decent burial? Would they have some sort of voodoo rite?

I shivered again. How long it was taking Cage! Gandy who had been told not to come home without him had been gone for over an hour now, almost two. I tried not to question why Gandy might be having a hard time locating Cage. I tried not to think of a lot of things, Martha lying dead, Octavia's empty room, the fog, the accidents, the feeling of dread that kept stabbing at my heart.

But it was no use.

Something was wrong, dreadfully wrong. Accidents. I thought of the time I had been locked in the attic, how I blamed Cage for it, how I later had convinced myself he was innocent. Had it been an "accident"? Had the runaway buggy been an "accident"? What at the Folly was "accident" and what was not? Sitting there in the silence with the dark, mist-haunted night clamped tightly down over the turreted rooftop, I felt there was a grand design to the strange events, both past and present at the Folly, that some diabolical web was slowly weaving about us all, that it had not yet finished spinning and criss-crossing its threads, that there was much more to come, as the web grew tighter and tighter. It was a feeling that denied rational thought, a strong intuition omnipresent and morbid. The house had somehow been ill-fated from the start, it was not meant for happiness, but for tragedy and death.

The sensation of doom was so strong I rose to my feet and without waking the doctor went upstairs to look in on little Cage. He was sleeping, with a cherubic look to his fat, pink cheeks. I was bending over the crib when I heard the front door slam. Cage! I tucked the covers hastily about the baby's chin, planted a soft kiss on his eyelids and hurried from the room.

Cage looked ghastly, bruised eyes in a chalk white face. "How did this happen?" he asked as I came down the stairs.

"She fell—that is what we assumed since no one saw her," I answered. In his distraction he had forgotten his hat, and his hair was rumpled by the wind. "And Octavia —I don't know. I was here all afternoon with the ladies. She might have slipped out when we were busy in the drawing room. It would have been easy."

"No one drove her in the carriage? Gandy? Martha?"

"No, Martha took off alone in the buggy—she went to see Barry Holden, that is what's so odd . . ."

"What's odd?" he asked sharply.

"I don't exactly know," I said slowly. Octavia. Could Octavia have pushed Martha?—meeting her on the stairs, arguing with her, knocking her out of the way, then running down to Barry Holden who was waiting for her outside? Could Martha's last words have meant, "*she* pushed me," instead of "he"?

"I need a drink," Cage said, brushing past me. "A large drink."

I followed him, thinking no, not Octavia. She couldn't be that coldhearted, that ruthless.

"Dr. Johnson is still here," I said. "Asleep in the parlor."

"He is?" Cage's hand shook as he splashed whiskey untidily into his glass.

"Yes—he arrived too late. She—Martha was already dead."

Cage took a long pull at his glass, and the color began to creep back into his face. "I suppose he has to make out some sort of report for accidental death," he said.

"Yes."

"Terrible." He shook his head. "Terrible business."

There was a small silence. Then I asked, "What do you think we ought to do about Octavia? Go to the police?"

"The police?" He looked shocked. "Good Lord, no. I've had more than enough of the police. I'll hire a private detective. Eggard—good man, he's done work for me before. If anyone can find Octavia and that scoundrel she absconded with, Eggard can."

But Eggard had little luck.

Ten days later he made his report to us in the library. An unsmiling man of thirty with a sallow, pockmarked skin and a large handlebar moustache, he stood with his back to the fireplace while he read from a dog-eared notebook, giving us a step-by-step account of his search. It seems he had checked every hotel, every boarding house, every saloon, inn and private club in the City and the environs beyond. He had haunted the rail depot and the boat docks and the carriage stands without success. No one had seen a man escorting a young girl of Octavia's description. Not a clue could be found. The couple seemed to have vanished into thin air. Cage instructed Eggard to keep looking.

Three weeks went by, and then one afternoon a small Chinese boy dressed in a long gown and felt slippers knocked at the front door. He told Lucinda he wanted to see Martha, refusing to go round to the back service entrance, refusing to state his business. I heard him and Lucinda arguing as I sat in the little parlor and came out to see what the trouble was.

"You—Martha Browne?" he asked. His English, though heavily accented, was intelligible.

When I told him I was the lady of the house and that Martha was dead, he gaped up at me. "I have letter for her," he said, holding up a smudged piece of paper. "But I don't suppose to give it to no one but her."

"That's all right, I'll take it," and when he thrust the

paper behind his back, I added quickly, "I'll pay you a dollar for bringing it." He waited until Lucinda got the dollar and placed it into his grimy hand before he relinquished the note. Then he turned and fled.

"Wait . . . !" I cried. But he ran on down the drive without stopping.

The letter was from Octavia.

Dear Martha:

I hope with all my heart this reaches you. You were so right, dear Martha, how can you ever forgive me? How can I forgive myself? I have made a terrible mistake—he is a demon! He is—but I can't describe him, I can't find the words. He will not let me go. He says I am to be part of his revenge. What revenge? You see—he is a madman. Mad! Oh, what have I done? I cannot ask Papa to come here for Barry has threatened to kill him if he does. So *you* must, Martha dear, *you must!* I cannot tell you exactly where I am, though I think it is in Little China. The woman who comes with my food (Barry is out a good deal) is Chinese, and what I can see from the window is a large store front with Chinese lettering—oh, and it has three huge Chinese lanterns hanging over it, red, green and blue. Please come, Martha. *You must.* He keeps me prisoner and I'm so afraid—he says he will kill me. For God's sake, Martha, please—help me!

Octavia.

I reread the letter, trying to decide what to do. The sensible course of action would have been to instruct Gandy to find Cage or Eggard and go at once to Little China. But Gandy was laid up with a stiff back, McCorkle, of course, was with Cage, and Octavia's letter charged with such desperate urgency brooked no delay. I decided to go to Octavia on my own. I told Lucinda I would return shortly (looking back, I can see with amazement that I really believed I would), and throwing a cloak about me, went out. It was eleven o'clock by then, a cool, misty morning with a stiff wind blowing up from the bay. I got the buggy harnessed without Gandy's help, double checking the reins to make sure they would not give this time. I had a general idea of where to find Little China—a section in the vicinity of Kearny and Grant Avenues where the Chinese huddled together in their shops, cigar factories, restaurants, and tenements—having gone there once with Clara on one of her shopping tours. It wasn't a large place, I remembered vaguely, and Octavia had given me a fairly good description of the store.

But as I bowled down the hill, hanging tightly to the reins, I began to have misgivings. Was it wise to go alone? Octavia had written that Barry Holden was out a good deal, but what if he should be there? Would he try to harm us both? He wouldn't dare, I thought, and thought again. He had dared to elope with Octavia, daughter (or stepdaughter) of a socially prominent man who had the influence if not wealth to pursue him, why should he stop at harming Octavia or me? "He is a devil," Martha had said, and Martha had not been afraid of anyone.

Should I inform Cage? I would have to find him first and he was not always at his office, and Octavia had warned in the letter that Barry Holden meant to kill Cage. Why? A madman, she had called him. He sounded violent. His hatred for Cage was a mystery, and on second thought I realized I could not risk involving Cage. And I hadn't the foggiest notion where to find Eggard.

But what a fool, I thought, to go alone and unarmed.

We were crossing Market Street when I suddenly remembered Jay. I did not stop to analyze or even remark on the curious fact that whenever I found myself in a dilemma Jay came to mind. I only decided instantly, on the spur of the moment, that he would be just the person to extricate Octavia from this thorny situation. He would not refuse me. Whatever else Jay might be, insulting, mannerless, crude, even hateful, he never had been unwilling to help if he could.

Yes, I would ask Jay Cooke. I did not want to go to the police. I agreed with Cage that we had had enough of the police at the Folly, more than enough as far as Octavia was concerned. I had no wish to create a public scandal, for she had not said in her letter whether Barry Holden had married her. If the gossips got wind of her running off with a man, then she would be branded harlot for the rest of her life. She was too young for that, and she did not really deserve it. Love had made her act blindly. I knew only too well how that could be.

Much to my dismay, however, Jay Cooke was not at his place of business. "Is he at home?" I asked the clerk.

"No, m'am. He's gone across the bay to Oakland. I don't know when to expect him back. Late tonight, probably not until tomorrow morning."

I stood there, biting my lip. Could I wait? Could *Octavia* afford to wait? What if, at this very moment, she was in distress, in danger? What if she tried to escape and he killed her?

"Would you care to leave a message?" the clerk asked.

"I don't know."

I questioned myself, does Octavia mean this much to me? and immediately I felt ashamed. She was young, she was in trouble, she had not harmed anyone. Her letter addressed to Martha proved beyond a doubt that she did not even know of her "accident," let alone have any part in it.

Again I debated whether I should attempt to find Cage. Meanwhile, time was steadily passing, it was one, half past one, soon it would be two o'clock. How terrible I would feel, if in procrastinating, I reached the place Octavia had described only to find her harmed or gone.

"Have you paper and pen?" I asked the clerk.

He brought them and I wrote a hasty note, telling Jay what had happened, describing the store front, the three lanterns as Octavia had, asking him to come in case he should return sooner than expected.

Then I went out and got in the buggy, my jaw set, determined not to be afraid, determined to have the upper hand with Barry Holden. Perhaps Octavia had exaggerated, perhaps this Barry creature was bluffing and only needed a firm command, a threat of punishment, a few stern "my dear sirs," and he would let Octavia go.

Heartened by my little stint of whistling in the dark, I clucked up the horse and we started off.

Little China was more crowded, its streets much narrower than I had remembered. The moment I entered it, I found myself in another world, the City left miles behind. Even the air smelled differently; exotic, pungent, rancid and sweet, as if the far-flung, mysterious Orient had come together here in compressed essence among the crooked alleys and lanes. The sidewalks were congested with foot traffic, little old women hobbling along, their black pantaloons peeping out from beneath black gowns, old men gathered in knots, wearing loose jackets and skull caps, their long queues hanging down behind. I saw younger women shuffling along on bound feet, herding slant-eyed, solemn-faced children before them. Chinese vegetable vendors dressed in blue cotton blouses and trousers and broad inverted hats, padded along on soft slippers, threading through the crowds as they carried flexible poles over their shoulders, poles slung on either end with huge baskets overflowing with fresh greens and colorful fruit. I saw Chinese fishermen at the curbs, displaying their silvery, slithery catches and the peddlers trotting along, their wares packed in cases tied up with great squares of yellow silk. Everywhere along the thronged streets commerce buzzed with the pulsating rhythm of the busy market place. Yet I detected a hidden, sullen resentment. Two men in loose jackets and skull caps stopped to stare at me, while another took his time getting out of the horse's way. They did not like me, this woman in fashionable dress driving a buggy alone, and if I hadn't been on my way to Octavia, I would have turned the horse about and gone back. But somewhere in this maze of cheap shops, odorous restaurants, factories, gambling and opium dens—and God knew what else— Octavia was being held a captive, and I could not abandon her.

So I went on, the horse and buggy slowly pressing through the jammed streets, past shop after shop, some of them no more than small cubicles with narrow doorways. And though I kept looking sharply to the left and right, I could not find the store front Octavia had described.

Presently I came to a corner and on impulse turned the horse into another narrower byway, a dusty alley lined by weatherbeaten frame buildings with small ramshackle, overhanging balconies. Here the street was virtually deserted, withdrawn, immersed in silence over which hovered an aura of shuttered secrecy. I was wondering if the street led to a dead end when I saw a man emerging from a doorway, the entrance to a large store, its high elongated window hung with three lanterns, blue, green and yellow. *That* must be it, I thought. I stopped the buggy and sat contemplating the strange, black calligraphy inscribed on the lanterns.

Octavia had said she could see the store from her window, which meant she would be across the street. I turned my head and looked. A shop and above it blank, featureless windows, the curtains drawn shut.

As I sat observing the dilapidated building, a young Chinese woman carrying a small child came along. She stopped at the side of the buggy and stared up at me, a thin girl with a pockmarked face. "Hello," I said. She jiggled the child and continued to stare.

"Do you know if there's a young girl living in that house across the street?" I asked. "White skin—dark hair?"

The woman said something I could not understand. The child gazed thoughtfully at me out of black, almond eyes.

I looked up at the windows again and thought for one wild moment of calling out to Octavia. But long habit held my tongue. One did not shout like a fishwife from a public thoroughfare. I tied the horse to a convenient post and crossed the narrow, dusty roadway. Shielding my eyes against the light, I peered in through the shop's grimy window, and a string of desiccated fish stared back at me. Beyond the fish there were tables and chairs. A cafe, but I could see no activity, no customers, cook or waiters.

A rickety staircase stood to the side of the shop, and gathering my skirts in one hand, I began to ascend it. The steps swayed under my weight, once or twice rather widely, sending my heart into my mouth. When I reached the landing, I opened a door and found myself in a small, dim hallway flanked by several doors. The reek of fish, mingled with the faint odor of sandalwood, permeated the confined air. I was wondering which door to knock on when I heard a name spoken in a muffled voice.

"Martha . . . ?"

It was Octavia! "Octavia . . . ?"

"Yes—yes," the muted assent came, broken by a sob. "Who is it?"

"Aunt Adelaide, dear, where are you?

"Here—over here."

I went to the far door and turned the knob. The door, of course, was locked—what a fool not to expect that it would be! "Thank God, you're here," I heard Octavia say.

"My dear—are you all right?"

"Yes—yes. Couldn't Martha come?"

"No, dear, she's—she's not well." Better to give her the bad news later—now was hardly the time. "How am I to let you out?"

"I think he leaves the key on a ledge above the door." Her voice sounded as if she were very far away. "Look. And if it isn't there you will have to get the landlord—although I think . . ."

"Wait!" I exclaimed as my fingers moving along the dirty ledge closed on the key. "I've got it!"

I unlocked the door with a trembling hand and went in.

Dust-moted, baffled sunlight seeping in through a gap in the curtains revealed a sparsely furnished room, a bed, a commode, a chest and a chair. Octavia was seated on the chair and not until my eyes became accustomed to the shadowed light did I realize that she was tied to it.

"Octavia . . . !" I ran to her.

Tears were streaming down her face. I kissed her and a sob shook her as she leaned her cheek against mine. "Thank God—! Thank God, you came!"

I unbound her arms which had been pinned around the back of the chair in painful, awkward position, then I untied her ankles. She had been gagged, too, but had managed to work it loose. It hung now about her neck, and I undid that, too.

"What kind of beast did this to you?" I said angrily, trying to massage the warmth back into her cold, numb arms.

"I don't know, I don't know. Oh, Aunt Adelaide, what a goose I've been. When Martha and you and Papa . . . ," her voice broke.

"Don't cry, darling, there, there. We'll have you out of here in no time."

"The minute—the minute," she said tearfully, "the minute the preacher pronounced us man and wife he turned on me." I saw now that she was wearing a ring. "How could a man who one minute said he loved you more than life hate you so desperately the next? Oh Aunt Adelaide—I've ruined everything, everything . . ."

"There, there—can you walk?"

"My feet—I can't feel them."

I knelt down and began to rub her ankles.

"He says he wants vengeance," Octavia said in a low

voice. "I don't know what he means, but he only laughs when I ask him. A monster."

"Give me the other foot, dear." She extended it. "How did you manage to get the note out?"

"The woman who brought my food—I bribed her with a gold brooch. Barry didn't miss it. Oh—Aunt Adelaide . . ."

Suddenly the door behind us creaked loudly. I paused, my hands on Octavia's foot. Her eyes got enormous as she stared fixedly over my shoulder. Neither of us spoke, neither of us moved. It was as if we had both been stricken dumb, frozen into startled silence, I, on my knees, she sitting on the chair. It was so quiet I could hear our breathing.

The door creaked again and my heart went rocketing into my mouth. Then silence again. We waited and waited. The air fairly hummed with our tenseness as we sat there, ears, eyes straining, waiting through time that stretched from minutes to hours to centuries.

Suddenly down below in the shop a man began to speak, a faraway voice talking rapidly in a language I did not understand. Then he stopped and the awful quiet fell around us once more like a black curtain. I wet my lips. Octavia could not take her frightened eyes from the door.

The silence went on.

After what seemed like another age, the hinges scraped again. Still on my knees, I turned. The door was slightly ajar. "Who is it?" I wanted to cry, but couldn't. I was afraid of the answer. Who else could it be but Barry Holden? It was his stealthy way of tormenting us. Octavia gave a small, almost inaudible groan and slipping from the chair to the floor put her arms about me.

"He'll kill me," she whispered. "He'll kill us both." I could feel her heart through her gown beating crazily.

We sat huddled together. Charred cooking smells began to fill the room. Downstairs the Chinese were fixing their afternoon meal. Should I shout, call to them? But they would not come; they were foreigners. We had put them outside the pale, forbade them the justice of our courts, underpaid them, destroyed their property, even killed them with impunity, why should they risk coming to the aid of two Anglo-Saxon women?

All this may have gone through my head, I don't remember. The fact was I was too congealed in cold fear to think or feel rationally. The charred smell had raked a memory, one that I had long since pushed to the bottom of my mind, the memory of a day years ago, when I had stood on the edge of a field gazing at the smoking embers of the Hayley house, the day I felt the hairs on the back of my neck rise because I *knew* that someone was watching me, someone with cold, inhuman eyes.

And now something horrible was about to happen and I could not move a muscle to stop it. We went on waiting, arms entwined, staring, staring at the door. It was the waiting that pained us most, the anticipation of the dread unknown.

Octavia whimpered and buried her head on my shoulder. Why didn't he come in? Why didn't he get it over with? If he was going to shoot us why didn't he show himself, gun in hand? *Anything* was better than this screaming silence.

I don't know how long we sat there, the two of us. The door had not moved in all that time, no sound came from the dark, odorous hall beyond. Had he gone? I was just beginning to wonder when I heard quick, heavy steps on the stair. Someone was coming up. Octavia lifted her head. I drew in my breath. And the next moment the door was flung open and Jay Cooke stood there. He was hatless, his cravat awry, his dark hair falling over his eyes.

"Adelaide! Are you all right?"

I hadn't the strength to speak, not even to exclaim, but I did give him a weak, trembling smile.

Chapter 29

ALL the way back to the Folly as we clattered along the streets in Jay's buggy, Octavia remained stiff-lipped and silent. But when we reached home and Cora inadvertently revealed that Martha had died, Octavia became hysterical. She wept, laughed and screamed in such an alarming manner Jay was forced to strike her before we could get her under control. Cora and I put a sobbing Octavia to bed, and afterwards I sent Gandy to fetch Cage and Dr. Johnson.

Jay and I waited in the little parlor. I had eaten nothing since breakfast, but I wasn't hungry. I was drained, so numb with fatigue I could have fallen asleep sitting up.

"Let me get you something," Jay said. "You look dreadful. A glass of brandy, something."

"No, I don't want brandy. I don't want anything. Have some yourself, if you like."

He was silent for a few moments. "You were a fool to go there alone, you know," he said finally, his voice edged with anger.

"Yes, I know," I agreed, hoping we could avoid an argument.

His eyes flashed at me.

"You're upset with me," I said. "And I haven't thanked you properly, either, but it goes without saying . . ."

"I don't want your thanks," he said shortly. "I would like for you to start using your head, especially when there is danger of your losing it. Didn't it once occur to you, my dear numbskull, that you might have been walking into a trap?"

"A trap? You mean Octavia would have deliberately . . . ?"

"Not deliberately, but she might have written that letter under duress."

367

"It was addressed to Martha, not me."

"But *you* went, and Cage, if he were here, might have done the same. By the way—why didn't he go?"

"Because he didn't know," I said wearily. "I didn't tell him. The letter said Barry Holden would kill him."

"And so you protected him by going yourself. Oh, you *are* a fool, a much bigger fool than even I imagined. I wonder how he will feel when he finds out he's been shielded from harm by a woman's skirts."

That stung me. "Why must you twist everything so?" I said bitterly. "Of course, he'll be put out with me. But what's done is done."

"You didn't go to him," he mused, "but you came to me for help. Do you think Cage will like that?"

"He'll scold, but he won't make a scene, if that's what you are driving at. Cage doesn't make scenes or think the worst, like you."

"He doesn't? He doesn't imagine that you'll become too friendly with another man? Bed him, perhaps?"

"You're crude," I said, disgusted.

"He's not the jealous type, is he? But where you're concerned, my dear, why should he be? You are so blindly infatuated . . ."

"I love him!"

"Ah—yes. Love. And he loves you."

I said nothing.

"He loves you so much he doesn't care if it's me you come to when things get really nasty."

"Oh—shut up!" I clapped my hands over my ears. "I'm sorry I ever asked you for anything, sorry I left you that note. Furthermore, I promise I shall never do it again. Oh, I know I've said it before, but this time I mean it!" I rose to leave.

"Adelaide . . ." He was on his feet, barring the way, the mocking look wiped from his face. "No—don't go, please. I'm sorry. It's wrong of me to keep baiting you. Please wait."

"I'm tired, Jay, and . . ."

"Please. I apologize—sincerely, abjectly. I *am* a cad. I admit it. I always succeed in making you angry—God knows why—when it is the last thing I really want to do. Perhaps it is because I am angry at myself, angry because I am just as infatuated with you as you are with Cage. And it's so hopeless."

I stood there, staring at his shirt front, not knowing what to say. He sounded sincere. Did he mean it?

"If I had any sense," he went on, "I would have nothing to do with you, go away from here, never see you again. I have even thought of getting married." He gave a short, mirthless laugh.

I looked up at him quickly.

"Would you mind?"

"Of course not, I'd wish you well," I said, my eyes sliding away from his dark, serious gaze.

"Would you?" He took my hands, holding them tightly. "When I think of how you looked when I found you an hour ago. Sitting there on the floor—so frightened, your face so white . . ."

I thought of it, too. I had wanted to forget, to wipe that terror from my tired mind, but now it all came back like the sudden sweep of a cold, drowning tide, the door creaking open, the awful stillness, the charred odor, the tense waiting. I forgot about my anger towards Jay as the memory of that chilling fear clutched at my heart and an involuntary shudder shook my body.

Jay drew me into his arms, and I was dimly aware of the need to resist, but the feeling of numb terror was so vivid in my mind I had not the will to push him away. His arms, hard, muscular and strong, were like a sanctuary enfolding me with a vital toughness, a solid, tender, protective warmth. I had been through so much horror I needed that secure feeling. I wanted to feel safe and not afraid. I wanted to be held by someone who was robust, powerful enough to keep the dark shadows at bay.

"Adelaide," he whispered in my hair. "Adelaide." He tilted my chin back; his eyes were black as night. Then his lips were on mine, soft at first, kissing me lightly, then harder, more insistent, passionate, hungry.

"No," I heard myself moan even as I felt the heat flood my neck and face, a melting of will, of thought, a terrible, delicious weakness that made my knees buckle.

"You like it," he said, raising his head. "You like it. Admit it! Admit you've never been kissed this way before. That old man you married the first time, then Cage . . ."

At the mention of Cage's name, my mind suddenly cleared and I drew back, straining at his arms.

"Let me go!" I cried, pushing at his chest.

But he held me in tightly. "Admit it!" His eyes blazed and his mouth came down on mine again.

I struck him, I hit him with every ounce of indignation and outrage I possessed.

He released me and stepped back, his hand going to his jaw. He was breathing heavily.

"I could kill you!" I exclaimed. "Of all the dirty, sneaking—have you no shame?"

"No," he said, "not when it comes to you."

"If you touch me again, I'll scream. I'll scream so loud . . ."

But he didn't touch me and I didn't scream for just at that moment we heard the rumble of wheels in the drive. Both Cage and Dr. Johnson had arrived at the same time.

We were sitting in the parlor again, and Jay was arguing with Cage.

"I can't go to the police," Cage said. "Don't you realize that it will only make matters worse? Don't you understand what Octavia has already been through, that further scandal would destroy her? She's a very frightened girl right now, she says her only wish is to forget Barry Holden as quickly as possible. 'I never want to see him or hear his name again, Papa', is what she keeps telling me over and over."

"But why let him go scot-free?" Jay argued. "He held Octavia against her will, threatened to kill her *and* you. He sounds like a very dangerous man. I strongly advise you to lodge a complaint."

Cage sighed. "What good would it do? He's her husband and under the law he has a right to hold his wife—willing or not."

"But he hasn't the right to keep her under duress while he promises to do away with her and his father-in-law."

They continued to debate until Cage relented. "All right. Whatever you say. I'll go to police headquarters in the morning. But I have to leave for Sacramento in the afternoon. I have an important appointment I simply can't put off."

"You institute a warrant for arrest," Jay said, "and I promise I'll follow it up."

I privately thought Barry Holden was too slippery a character for the police to catch. If Eggard, the detective, whose sole task it had been to search, could not find him, how could they? But surprisingly, they did apprehend Holden and only two days after Cage had signed the complaint. Cage was still in Sacramento at the time, but Jay, informed of Barry Holden's arrest, went down to headquarters as he had promised. Later he came to the Folly and told me what had transpired.

"They let him go," he said in disgust. "The man claimed he never laid a hand on Octavia. 'My wife,' he said, bland as you please, 'has a taste for theatrics.' "

"Why, that isn't true!" I denied emphatically. "I found her bound to a chair, her arms and legs tied, frightened out of her wits."

"*He* claims that Octavia staged the entire 'imprisonment'."

"He's a liar," I stated flatly.

"I wouldn't be surprised. He's a very smooth, urbane sort of man. Not at all what I expected."

"You know him? Of him?"

"Of him, only slightly. But I found out something very interesting about your Barry Holden today. I discovered that he, under several different names, has been systematically stripping Cage of everything he owns. Nothing the law can catch him for, mind you, but he has very cleverly manipulated stock, enticed Cage into questionable deals whereby Cage has lost and he has won."

"But how is that possible?" I exclaimed, shocked.

"Cage is gullible. Furthermore I am sure Cage has no inkling that Barry Holden has used other men to wield his trickery, that behind a front he has adroitly managed Cage's downward slide. The Folly, you may as well know, is also mortgaged to Barry. The ruffian even had the audacity to boast of it."

"I don't understand," I said, baffled, frightened. "Why has he done this? Why?"

"For some reason he has an abiding hatred for Cage. I can't guess why. And he remains mum on the subject. I surmised he married Octavia to get back at Cage. He didn't deny it when I accused him, never said a word, only smiled, the most dreadful frozen smile I've ever seen on a man."

I tried to picture him, this faceless creature with a frozen smile. "And Cage doesn't know him?"

"Has never seen or met him. Quite frankly, neither had I until yesterday. Very few people know Barry Holden. He prefers to work, I take it, behind the scenes."

Cage arrived home the next afternoon. When I confronted him with what Jay had told me about Holden's financial maneuverings, he broke down and confessed that he had gone to Sacramento in a last desperate effort to raise money. Even Octavia's "marriage portion" was gone.

"I don't know how it happened, Adelaide." He shook his head. "I had such plans, such wonderful plans, but somehow, in some way they all seemed to come to nothing. To think that Barry Holden was behind it all." He ran his hand through his hair. "I don't understand."

It was night. We were in our bedroom, I was sitting at the dressing table, Cage was standing at the window with a glass of whiskey in his hand. He looked harried, unkempt, miserable.

"Is there nothing that can be done?" I wanted to help him, I would have done anything, anything to wipe that unhappy look from his face.

"I must appeal directly to Barry Holden, it's my only hope."

"Do you think he might listen? Jay says . . ."

"What does Jay know?" he interrupted. "Of course, Holden will listen. It will benefit him if I can raise the capital to pay what I owe. After all, he is a business man, and he'd rather have the money than the Folly."

What money? I wanted to ask, when everyone has turned down your request for a loan. But I said nothing, thinking it wiser to keep silent.

"I must approach Holden diplomatically, of course, without anger, calmly." Cage stared down at his glass. "No mention of his being my son-in-law—I don't want to bring Octavia into this."

"But she told me that he threatened to kill you."

"Oh, yes—that. More than likely it was a statement made in the heat of an argument. Octavia, I've no doubt, did the same, claimed that *I* would kill *him* if he didn't behave toward her properly. I don't set much store by such bluster."

"You've set store by similar threats."

There was a puzzled expression in his eyes as he looked at me over the rim of his glass.

"You even went as far as to hire a bodyguard," I reminded him.

"Yes—but *that* was different. I had good reason to be wary, my dear. I didn't want to worry you, but I had been receiving a series of very menacing letters, too many to be ignored. In the financial world one makes enemies, and some of the men I've dealt with are little better than hooligans."

"And not Mr. Holden? He's not a hooligan?"

"I don't know. He's never threatened me directly, not that I know of. I'm willing to give him the benefit of the doubt, so much so that I plan to invite him here for dinner."

I stared at him. "Here—at the Folly! But Cage, you must be mad!"

"Not at all, my darling. I don't even think a hooligan would dare kill his host at his own dinner table."

"He had Octavia tied to a chair—he . . ."

"I didn't say I condoned his behavior. My God, what kind of a scoundrel do you take me for? No, I don't intend to overlook his reprehensible treatment of Octavia, but I'll get to *that* after we come to some financial agreement."

Octavia, understandably, was furious. How could Cage do this to her? How could he humiliate and shame her, treat her as though she were the one at fault? How could he receive such a vicious animal into his home?

Cage tried to reason with her. "The Folly's at stake, pet. My home—yours. And don't speak to me of honor, please. The Folly *is* our honor—without it we shall be homeless, unable to hold our heads up in society, anywhere. Once we have the house secured then I will make every attempt to get an annulment of your marriage, if that's what you wish, a separation, a divorce, whatever. You need not fear that I, or anyone, will force you to live with him against your will."

"I should hope not," she said indignantly. "And you can be sure I shall avoid him like the plague."

Octavia must have had some second thoughts, however,

for a few days later, much to my astonishment, she expressed a wish to be present when her husband came to dinner.

"But why?" I asked.

"I don't choose for him to think I've gone into hiding, quaking with fear on his account," she answered, adding, "You needn't worry. I shall behave, act very demurely as if nothing at all had happened."

But there was something in her eye I didn't quite trust, a kind of grimness which worried me.

It was to be a small dinner, the only outsider invited, aside from Barry Holden, was Jay Cooke. The cook had become somewhat lax following Martha's death, but as Cage kept telling me, the food did not matter as much as the quality of the wine and spirits. That was also a problem since our wine bill had reached astronomical proportions, and it took some coaxing to extend our credit. But I managed to reach a tolerable solution in both instances, assuring us of a decent, if not gourmet, meal accompanied by the appropriate libations.

The evening arrived chilly but windless and clear. By seven we were all assembled in the drawing room, waiting (not without some anxiety) for Barry Holden. He was late. Cage paced the floor like a penned-up lynx. I could see what an effort it was for him not to have more than the one glass of spirits he had allowed himself. He wanted to have a level head, he said, but sweat beaded his brow and his restless tension had spread to the rest of us. Octavia sat next to me, her hands clasped in a white-knuckled grip, her large eyes fixed, her mouth set. Every sound made her start. I tried to relax, sipping sherry, making innocuous small talk to which no one replied. Even Jay was unusually silent. He sat smoking a cigar, his head thrown back carelessly on the chair cushions, his eyes squinting through the smoke. I had some more sherry. Inside I had begun to tremble.

At seven-thirty there were sounds of wheels in the drive, and a minute later Gandy announced Barry Holden. Cage stood where he was. "Show him in," he said in a controlled voice.

The door opened and he came in, an auburn-haired

man, just as Octavia had said. And the next moment I was rising to my feet in amazement.

I stared at him; our eyes met. Incredible!

"Why—it's Bernard West, isn't it?" I exclaimed. "The Union soldier." The hair was darker, but the hazel eyes, the arched nose and the strong chin were the same, the same as those of the man whose wound I had bandaged, how long, how many years ago? "But—but you've changed your name!"

"So I have," he replied, bowing. "But I am that soldier, m'am."

There was a small, tense silence. Cage gazed at me, a puzzled look in his eyes.

"It was during the war," I explained hastily, still rather stunned. "At Beech Arbor—when they—the bluecoats brought in their wounded soldiers."

"Fortunately for me," our guest said, then turning to Cage, "At last we meet, sir. And Mr. Jay Cooke . . . ," a slight bow in his direction, "I believe I've already had the pleasure—at the police station, was it? Yes, of course. And my charming wife," this time a sweeping, low bend with his hand over his white frilled shirt front. "My lovely, charming wife."

She glowered at him, but did not speak.

Cage, clearly more baffled than ever said, "Have you and I met before?"

"Indeed, but it was an aeon ago. Ah, yes, we have met." He smiled, and I could see what Jay Cooke had meant. It *was* a terrible, glittering smile. "We have met."

The words were freighted with hidden meaning. Why? What was it all about, the names, Bernard West—Barry Holden?

"I don't seem to be able to recall," Cage said.

"Then I shall gladly refresh your memory, but first I think it would be mannerly if you offered me a drink."

"Of course, forgive me. Whiskey? Brandy?"

"Whiskey will be fine."

Bernard West—Barry Holden. But why, why, *why?* I remembered now how even as he had lain helpless and feverish at Beech Arbor I had thought him strange, a cold man yet one with an inner, driving force. He had denied that he was a Virginian, a denial that had rung false. He was masquerading then, as he was now. Why? Who was he?

"Excellent," Bernard West alias Holden said, sipping his whiskey. "You have good taste, Mr. Norwood, but then you always did."

"Thank you," Cage said, pouring himself that second drink. I could see from the slight tremor in his hand that he was making a heroic effort to get hold of himself and I wanted to go to him, take his arm, tell him that everything would be all right. But, of course, I couldn't, even if I had been sure of myself. Instead I remained seated there on the sofa next to Octavia, the sherry glass sweating in my hand, held by a growing dread.

Jay Cooke, who had not as yet spoken, suddenly said, "Mr. Holden—or Mr. West, whichever you prefer—you are speaking in riddles. Why don't you come out with it, instead of shrouding yourself in all this dramatic mystery?"

A small, frigid smile quirked Mr. Holden's lips. "It shan't be a mystery for long. I've looked forward to this night for so many years, you cannot imagine how many, Mr. Cooke."

"No," Jay said laconically. "I cannot imagine."

There was a small silence while Barry Holden seated himself on a chair. "I know why you've invited me to your home, to dinner, to be in the bosom, so to speak, of your charming family, Mr. Norwood, but I will tell you now that it is a futile gesture. There is no appeal, none whatsoever. I fully intend to foreclose."

"But," Cage began, "you haven't heard . . ."

"Heard what? You do not have a dollar you can call your own. Your credit has been overextended as it is. I do not know of a single soul who would lend you the price of a meal."

"If you would give me time . . ."

"Time for what?"

"Mr. Cooke has promised . . ."

"Mr. Cooke, indeed. I happen to know that Mr. Cooke has the bulk of his money tied up in a shipment from the Far East—which shan't reach port for at least another three months. I can't wait that long. No—I am not as patient as I once was. I've run out of patience, in fact, and I mean to have the Folly." He paused, smiling his horrible smile. "I mean to have it if only to burn it to the ground—with my dear wife, Octavia," a nod in her direction, "in it, if that can be arranged."

"You can't mean it," Cage said, horrified.

"Oh, but I *do* mean it. I have meant it for a long, long time, haven't I just told you? Yes, it has been my aim to destroy you, Mr. Lewis Cage Norwood. However—since your wife once saved my life I will spare hers, and her child's—out of generosity, out of respect, but I fear the poor mite will be left penniless."

"You are mad!" Cage exploded. "Insane! I see no purpose in this—this . . . !"

"No, I don't think you do. But the answer is simple." He leaned forward. "Revenge, Mr. Norwood!" His eyes were like burning embers. I had never seen such a diabolical look on a human face. "Revenge!"

"Revenge for what?" Cage demanded.

"Revenge. Simple revenge. I want you to try and remember, Mr. Lewis Cage Norwood. I want you to go back in your mind—back to Virginia, to the James River. Seventeen years, more or less. Seventeen. To Corinne Hayley—does that name ring a bell?"

Cage stared at him, clearly mystified, his face gone blank.

But I remembered. How could Cage have forgotten? The woman with the dark auburn hair and the bold eyes, Corinne Hayley, the woman over whom Cage had fought a duel. I remembered the foggy morning, the trees dripping with mist, the sun clearing the horizon, the pistols, the sound of shots. . . .

"Corinne Hayley," our guest went on, his voice like the steel edge of a knife. "Her husband's name was Noah. And you murdered him. You shot him in Baker's Wood."

The feeling of dread, the feeling that someone was watching me under the trees, the sun on red hair, the young man who cried, "I'll get you back some day!"

"Baker's Wood—Baker's Wood," Cage murmured. "Ah yes!" his face lighting up. "I recall now. A duel. Of course. Why yes, I did shoot Noah Hayley—but it was done in a fair fight with witnesses. He could have killed me as easily as I killed him."

"No! You're wrong! Unfairly, I say! You fired before the count was through. You cheated!"

Cage went rigid and the next instant he was springing to his feet. "Why you . . . !" He lunged at Holden, but Jay quickly thrust himself between the two men. "You—you scoundrel!" Cage shouted, trying to get past Jay's shoulder. "I've done many things in my life, but never, *never* that! How dare you call me a cheat!"

"Settle down," Jay commanded, grasping Cage's flailing fists. "We are not going to get anywhere this way. Come on, Cage—there's a good fellow—not in front of the ladies. Here—let me fill your glass."

Cage, glaring at Holden, sank back in his chair, high color staining his cheeks. Our guest watched him quietly without speaking. When Jay brought Cage another whiskey, he drank, then carefully setting his glass down, still visibly shaken, asked, "Just who in blazes *are* you?"

"Haven't you guessed? I am Bart Hayley, Noah's oldest son."

"Bart . . . ? But I thought the Hayleys—all of them . . ."

"Died in the fire? No—God, Fate, whatever, spared me. You see that evening I had gone to an uncle's house to ask him for help with the spring planting. I stayed the night and so missed the fire. The charred body they found in the ashes and thought mine belonged to a young man my own age, a runaway slave." His lips twisted ironically. "It should have been laughable, you see, a slave, a black mistaken for a white. Perhaps that was why I fought for the Union, to atone for his death. But I lived. I lived and prospered." Again his eyes were fired with venom, with hate. "I always had the feeling my mother started that fire herself, in effect, committed suicide. She was ruined, you see, more ruined, Mr. Norwood, than you could ever be."

"It was a duel fought fairly," Cage repeated stubbornly.

But Bart Hayley was not listening. He went on talking, his face set in hard lines. "I was seventeen at the time. Seventeen, a boy who became a man all in one morning. Seventeen—and I resolved to kill you, Mr. Norwood."

"After all this time . . . ?"

"Yes, after all this time," Bart Hayley said bitterly. "I followed you. I was poor, without money, but I followed you. You went to New Orleans—and I, working my way on a boat, was soon there, too."

New Orleans. And the years in my mind fell away. I

remembered the high hopes with which I had disembarked on the muddy, crowded wharf, the rain, Cage's rooms, my youthful confession, his embarrassment, and waiting alone in the chair and the door slowly creaking open behind me, and then—then the sudden shot. . . .

"That shot!" I cried. "You shot at me!"

Bart Hayley inclined his head. "Pardon, a thousand pardons. Young, hasty, I did not take the time to look too closely. I couldn't see, I thought—but it doesn't matter now, does it? I never wanted to harm you, Mrs. Norwood. I tried to make things impossible here at the Folly so that you would leave, so that you would go back home out of harm's way."

"Impossible?" I heard myself say in a stilted voice. "Impossible?"

"I hoped you would leave, Mrs. Norwood," he repeated in a tone that for him sounded apologetic. "Any other woman in your place would have been long gone."

Impossible. "You mean—you mean *you* moved things around, the cat, the sewing basket . . . ?"

"Yes. But I did not reckon on your stubborn spirit."

"Spirit!" Jay Cooke exclaimed. "Oh, my God. Do you realize what you put this poor woman through? I could wring your neck!"

And Cage, coming forward in his chair, demanded, "What's this? What's this about?"

"Wait—both of you, please," I begged. "I want to hear. I *must* hear. Mr. H—Hayley, if it was you, as you say, how did you manage it? How did you smuggle a cat into the house, change one object for another? And the turret— it was you who locked me in?" It was such a relief to know finally that my mind had not been playing tricks, that what had seemed frightening fantasy was actually real, that I forgot my anger.

"Yes," he answered. "I managed that little game of hide-and-seek through a fortuitous piece of information. The architect of the Folly, one Morris Sandborne—you remember him, Mr. Norwood? Ah yes, of course—well, Mr. Sandborne committed an indiscretion to which I happened to be privy. For my silence he let me look at the plans, *his* set of plans, for this house. Seems that, aside from the commissioned secret staircase and passageway, he had made several of his own. He said he did it to test some structural theory of his, and saw no harm in it. I myself thought the man was a little eccentric, if not mad; nevertheless, this house is honeycombed with passages and secret doorways known only to him."

Passageways! I understood now. I understood why even after the doors had been boarded up I still had the feeling of being watched wherever I went, wherever I sat, eyes following me up the stairs, down the long, mirrored hall, clicks and squeaks behind the walls once attributed to mice but which was actually Bart Hayley prowling the hidden corridors.

"I could come and go as I pleased," he was boasting. "I had access to this house from the very start."

Cage stared at him, a look of disbelief, of shock on his face. "By God—then it was *you* who killed Lillith!"

Octavia, sitting next to me, started, stifling a gasp.

"Yes," our guest calmly admitted. "I shot your first wife and her lover."

"You . . . !" Octavia whispered, choking on the word. I put my hand on her arm to restrain her.

Bart Hayley ignored her and went on, "You see, Mr. Norwood, I had mistaken the man for you. I shot them in error—one which I regretted until I had time to think it over. It came to me that even if it had been you, what a merciful death—too merciful. After that I decided to be more cautious and more exquisite in my revenge. Business deals that went wrong, large sums lost in rigged card games, anonymous letters, a stray bullet wide of its mark."

I remembered Cage's air of preoccupation, his white face, the bodyguard. "Enemies," he said, not knowing who they were.

"I've made mistakes, admittedly," Hayley continued. "Again, if you will forgive me, Mrs. Norwood—the buggy, I had no idea you would be using it that day—and then long before that, somebody by the name of Sands, I believe."

"Horton!" Cage exclaimed. "You killed Horton. By God, you are a heartless, bloody murderer."

"Not heartless," Hayley said. "I felt rather badly about it. I'm not like some, I don't relish killing innocent men." He drained his glass.

We watched him as one watches a poisonous snake.

"I came back to San Francisco after the war, as you did, Mr. Norwood," he said. "I became rich. I made a lot of money—it's easy to do in this city, if you have a mind for it, but I never lost sight of my main purpose in life. I wanted you to suffer, Mr. Norwood, suffer for a long, long time. I tell you it was the only thing I lived for. When they brought you to trial, I had a few bad moments, but you were acquitted—they left you to me."

Octavia, unable to contain herself, shouted, "You killed her! You killed my mother! You used the secret stairway—that is why Martha never saw you!"

"I think she did, but I couldn't be sure. I warned her though, yes, I warned her. I told her that if she ever implicated me I would twist her neck like the roosters they used for their black rites."

Martha knew, Martha had seen, but Martha, warned, had been afraid. No other person had been able to instill that kind of fear in her. She had good reason to be afraid of Barry Holden–Bart Hayley, very good reason.

"You—you pushed her down the stairs," I said, my voice cracked with revulsion. "You killed that woman . . ."

"Yes. She gave me no choice. When I took her precious Octavia, she threatened to tell all. Now—how could I allow that?"

Jay, who had been calmly smoking a cigar through all this, suddenly leaned forward, crushing the cigar out in the humidor. "If I may make an observation, Mr. Hayley," he said, "you are a man with a great deal of brashness. What makes you think that we will ignore your various confessions and not go to the police with them? There are four witnesses here, four against yourself."

"Very well," Bart Hayley answered. "Four people. You will go to the police, and what will they see? Octavia, my disgruntled wife, Mr. and Mrs. Norwood, three of the four who have good cause to spread calumny against me, three people who have good reason to falsely accuse me—think what they will gain if I am hung—the Folly, its mortgage canceled. And the fourth of these witnesses? You. A dear friend who will tell any lie to help the family. More than that, you don't for a minute think I would put myself in a dangerous position without first making sure I was covered? I have at least a half dozen witnesses who will swear on God's Holy Bible that I was in Sacramento on the day the first Mrs. Norwood and her lover were killed. So go to the police—half of them, I might add, are in my pay."

No one spoke. The man's overweening self-assurance was monstrous, appalling. We sat there, staring at him, Cage, glass in hand, Octavia glowering, Jay fingering his dead cigar.

"For revenge," I said scornfully, breaking the silence. "For revenge on Octavia, too? An innocent girl."

"Yes, Octavia," he said in a harsh voice. "What is she to me? I lost mother, father, a sister and brother—for a rich man's fancy, his whim, a seduction he could not even remember. Well—Octavia was *my* whim. I did not have to marry her—don't start so, Octavia, you would have given yourself to me, you smitten fool—but I thought it would add an extra twist to be son-in-law to a whore—dead though she is—and legally related to one of the best families in Virginia at the same time."

His smile was a mockery, a grimace, a horrible masquerade. The man was a fanatic, insane, to be driven for so many years, driven by a burning passion based on the mistaken judgment of a seventeen-year-old blinded by grief at his father's death.

"So . . . ," Cage let out his breath. "So you have your revenge. When you foreclose on the Folly, you will have completely ruined me."

"That was my intention."

"Was?"

"I have since—this very evening, as a matter of fact, thought of a better idea. I propose a duel. Don't look surprised, yes, a duel, now, tonight. Winner take all—the Folly, everything."

"Tonight?" Cage said in surprise.

And I, "You can't be serious!"

"I am never anything but serious, Mrs. Norwood."

"But—it's dark," I protested, "black, you can't see."

"There is a ballroom upstairs, is there not, Mr. Norwood?"

"Yes," Cage answered.

Horrified I cried out, "No! You cannot! He is—my husband—Cage is . . ."

"Too much drink has made his hand unsteady, has it?"

Bart Hayley interposed with a sneer. "All the better for me. Do you refuse, Mr. Norwood?"

"Certainly not! A gentleman never refuses a challenge."

"Cage . . . !"

"Hush, Adelaide, the man wants a duel, he shall have one. Name your weapons, Mr. Hayley!"

A change seemed to have come over Cage. For a moment or two he had appeared to be rather frightened, like the rest of us, but now his shoulders were squared. Here was something tangible he could fight, a known adversary. The vague, the elusive, the shadowy threats he might have feared, but not this, the obvious, a flesh and blood foe. Cage's figure had thickened, the waist was no longer slim, and his face had lost its healthy bronze, but he was still the most handsome, the most gallant man I had ever known.

"Pistols," Bart Hayley said.

When Jay left to fetch them, Cage said, "Adelaide, you and Octavia are to remain here."

"Oh, Cage—no," I pleaded. "No—I cannot. You ask me to do something that is impossible."

"A duel is no place for women."

"I'm your wife—this is—no! no!" I shook my head. To sit and wait, not knowing. "How can you ask me such a thing? Please, Cage—please . . ."

Octavia, her face white as chalk, begged, "Papa . . ."

Jay came back into the room, and Cage said: "The women insist on being present. It is against my better judgment—what do you say?"

I looked at Jay imploringly.

"If they wish," he said after a long pause. "I see no harm in it."

"Oh—thank you, Jay."

"There's something else we must settle before we proceed," Jay said. "Mr. Hayley, I think it would be wise if we had written assurance that should you—ah, lose, the mortgage will automatically be cancelled."

"Certainly," Hayley said.

Jay brought pen and paper from the library, and Bart Hayley wrote a short note, placing his seal upon it when he had finished.

Octavia and I rose and went out into the hall. The men followed. We ascended the stairs in silence.

The ballroom, smelling musty, was black as pitch. Jay

Cooke lit the gas jets, one by one, lit each separate light on the huge glass chandeliers, the wall lamps and then put a match to the candles in the candelabra which stood on the dais where the orchestra played. The huge, deserted, dusty room looked strange under the bright blaze of light. The gilt chairs, the little sofas and tables huddled like white strange shapes beneath the shroudlike covers.

"Are you sure you want this?" Jay Cooke asked Bart Hayley. "No seconds, no doctor? It's quite irregular."

"It's what I want," Bart Hayley said grimly.

Octavia and I uncovered two chairs and sat down. Jay Cooke brought out a small table and put the pistol case on it. When he opened the lid he exclaimed, "One's gone!"

"Let me see," said Cage. "Yes—right. I can't imagine where. I haven't used them in years. The case wasn't locked. I didn't think anyone would steal them." He looked at Bart Hayley.

"Why should I take one of your pistols when I can buy two dozen with the loose change I carry in my trousers?" He rattled the coins in his pocket. "Well, do you have an extra pair handy? If not, we can have Mr. Cooke ride into the City."

"I have an extra pair," Cage said. "In the drawing room desk."

"I'll get them," Jay offered.

Bart Hayley sat down at the other end of the room. Octavia glowered at him but said nothing. "Cage," I said, rising to my feet, taking his arm, "won't you reconsider this insane—this madness? Please—for my sake, for little Cage's?"

He gave me a sad smile. "No, I cannot." He patted my hand. "Come here—I want to tell you something." He led me away from Octavia to the far window. The curtain was drawn, but I knew that night outside would be dark, cold as a tomb, a night without stars or moon. I had this terrible dread in my heart. "Cage—you mustn't."

"It's too late for that, darling," he said. "I want you to forgive me, forgive me for every wrong I have done you."

"No, Cage, I won't listen. I won't!" He wanted to confess. Confessions were for the dying, and I did not want him to die.

"Adelaide—please—don't make it even more difficult for me. But—no tears, my darling. I love you, Adelaide, my

sweet, I love you. There I've said it! Something I've wanted
to say for a long time."

He loved me! He went on speaking but his words fell
without meaning on my ears. He loved me! How I had
yearned for those three words, those words that had spelled
the difference between happiness and despair, in New Orleans, in Richmond, on my wedding night. He loved me.
Yet—all I felt now was this dread, not happiness, not joy,
but a terrible foreboding of tragedy.

"Cage—for . . ."

"Hush!" He bent and kissed me on the lips. I clung to
him, not wanting to let him go, holding him tightly. But he
pried my arms loose from around his neck. "Here's Jay."

I was sitting beside Octavia again. The men were back to
back; I saw them through a haze of tears. It had all happened once before, all of it, the fear gripping my stomach,
the dry mouth, the heart thumping in my ears, the desire
but the inability to look away. Cage risking his life on the
click of a hammer. *Stop them!* my mind screamed, *oh, stop
them!*

They were pacing out their ten strides. It was a large
room, a ballroom with glittering rainbow chandeliers, a
room made for dancing, for waltzes and whispered flirta-
tions, for music and gaiety, not for death. I gripped Octavia's arm, but she shook me off with a sound low in her
throat.

They had stopped, and turning, faced each other across
the wide, dusty floor. Jay Cooke began to count in a loud,
clear voice, "One—two—three . . ."

Suddenly a shot rang out, shattering the silence, crashing, rebounding, echoing from wall to wall, shivering the
glass in the chandeliers. An acrid smell pervaded the air,
and peering through a pall of smoke I saw Bart Hayley,
gun in hand, register a look of triumphant surprise. And
then he collapsed abruptly, falling to the floor with a loud,
dull thud.

"My God!" Cage cried. But he was not looking at Bart,
he was staring at Octavia. She had a gun, still aimed at
where Bart had stood only a moment before, a long-bar-
relled dueling pistol. "God! God! What have you done?"

Cage rushed over to where Hayley lay. He knelt down. I
saw Bart Hayley, even from where I sat, I saw so plainly an
image I will carry to my dying day. I saw his gun hand lift

and knew in that one instant between the drawing in and the exhaling of a single breath, in that one tiny fraction of time, that this was what it had all meant, this was the plan, the Folly's design, Fate's web, God's will.

I screamed just as Hayley's gun went off.

Chapter 30

CAGE died instantly. Bart Hayley, alias Bernard West, alias Barry Holden, died a few minutes later.

I remained very calm. I did not scream or cry out or weep. I was too numb to do anything but rise from where I had been kneeling by Cage's side, marveling at how steady my legs were, how quietly my heart was beating.

"We'll say they shot each other in the duel," Jay's voice came to me from a long way off. "We must protect Octavia —there's nothing that can bring back the dead."

"Yes," I said. "Yes."

Someone was sitting on the floor sobbing quietly. It was Octavia. She had killed Hayley and her stepfather, too, yes, she had killed Cage just as surely as if she had put that bullet through his heart with the gun she had stolen from the case. But I wasn't angry. I felt nothing.

"I didn't mean it," she wept. "I didn't mean that Papa should die. I—I planned to kill Barry at dinner, I should have done it in the drawing room—but—but I couldn't, I couldn't."

Jay drew her to her feet. "Now, sweetheart, get hold of yourself. You're going to tell the police when they come that you heard two shots and that the men killed one another. Do you understand? Not a word about a third gun, do you understand?"

She nodded mutely, her cheeks wet with tears.

I saw Jay take the gun from Cage's limp hand, replacing it with the one Octavia had used.

Then suddenly the room seemed filled with people, though it was only Cora, Gandy and McCorkle. Cora led a still weeping Octavia away. I did not cry. Why, I didn't know. Not a tear, not even moist eyes. Jay's hand was under my arm. "You look like death," he said. "Come and sit down."

"I don't want to sit down," I said in a cold, mechanical voice. "I'll drop right here where I stand, but I won't sit down."

If only I could feel pain, if only it would hurt, if only I had something inside me instead of this terrible void.

"You can't stand here," Jay said. "Come, I'll take you to your room. Adelaide . . ."

"Don't touch me!" I suddenly shouted, the words exploding. "Don't touch me!" The ceiling was falling, the walls caving in, the floor opening, an abyss beneath my feet. "Murderers! You are all murderers!"

And then I was sobbing and screaming and laughing, laughing so hard because the pain was killing me. I saw Jay's hand go up, felt the sting of his blow—and then, nothing.

It was all behind me now. The questioning by the police, the funeral, the calls made by sympathetic friends and acquaintances, oh, those interminable, painful calls. Sitting in the drawing room hour after hour. "My dear, I am so sorry, so sorry, so sorry." "And he was so young." "Poor little Lewis Cage." "My dear, what will you *do?*"

Why did people keep asking me what I would do, when all I wanted was to be left in peace, to go upstairs and suffer my grief in privacy, in silence?

But now they were gone. The shades were drawn morning, noon and night. I did not want it otherwise. I did not want to know about time. Octavia had left to stay with the Shelbys and only the servants, little Lewis Cage and myself remained at the Folly. I spent the long days sitting in the little parlor staring at a piece of unfinished embroidery in my lap, listening to the sound of the wind in the trees outside.

One afternoon Jay came. "I have talked to the people in the bank," he said. "The note Hayley left is not valid."

"Not valid?" I asked dismayed. "But how could that be?"

"No witnesses—disinterested witnesses, they claim. And since Hayley left no heirs, the Folly now is the bank's property. However, they are not in a hurry to foreclose and will let you stay on until you can make other plans."

"Other plans?" I repeated, my back suddenly up. "I have

no other plans. I want to live here at the Folly. I want this always to be my home."

"But Adelaide, my dear, that's morbid. You've never liked the house. You have friends here in San Francisco who have offered their hospitality to you time and time again. You can't stay here and brood. And some day you might want to marry again."

"Marry!" I said scornfully.

"I know it's too soon to think, to speak of it. But . . ."

"I shall never marry again." I looked down at my hands, the thick gold band Cage had placed there almost three years earlier. I remembered my ecstatic smile as he lifted my veil to kiss me. Cage—oh, Cage! "I want to stay at the Folly," I said, my voice catching. "This is Cage's home and mine. You see—you see . . . ," trying to swallow the lump in my throat, "you see, I realized just before he died how unfair I had been to him. He loved me, Jay. He said so that night, he loved me and I had mistrusted him. I can't leave. It would be like a betrayal. I can't leave the Folly. It's all I have of him."

He was silent for some moments. He looked at me, at the wall beyond, at me again. He got up and walked to the window, drew the curtains apart and stared out into the garden. When he finally spoke it was with a low, even voice, devoid of emotion. "I don't want to quarrel with you, Adelaide, not at a time like this. But you speak of love so often, I sometimes wonder if you really know what it is." He turned. "You say you loved Cage, you still do. But is it a woman's love—or is it still that little girl's blinded by what she thought was a dashing Cavalier on a purebred steed?"

"If you are going to disparage Cage . . ."

He held up his hand. "I am not disparaging Cage—I never have. I am merely stating facts. And I do not think he himself ever really tried to hide the kind of man he was from you, either. You just did not want to see—surely *that* was not his fault. You once asked me if he loved Lillith and I told you, yes, as much as he could love anyone. Think about that, Adelaide."

"I am not Lillith," I said, growing annoyed. "I do not see how you can compare the two of us."

He sighed heavily. "You missed my point. But then—

you have always been a marvel at self-deception." He came
and stood over me, his dark eyes meditative as they
scanned my face. "You know that I have loved you for a
long time, not a boy's love, but a man's. You know that I
would give anything to have you—that there were times in
the past when I could have killed Cage myself because—
well, no matter." He drew a deep breath. "I want to marry
you—no, don't shrink away. I know it is too soon. I should
have waited, done the proper thing; one does not propose
to a widow with the husband's body hardly cold in the
grave. But I *am* proposing. Think on it. That's all I ask.
Think."

"It's no use, Jay. I told you, and I meant it, I shall never
marry again."

"Oh, yes, you will. You are too passionate a woman not
to have a man in your bed."

"Why . . . !"

"Not that you are aware of it. It would be too ill-bred,
too vulgar for you to acknowledge it even to yourself. Prim
and proper, a face you deliberately put on. But I *know*."
His eyes flashed. "I can see it in your eyes when you get
angry, I can feel all that wonderful, sensuous storm building up, barely held back. . . ."

"No!" I cried, frightened, angry. "No!"

"Yes, yes and yes." He leaned down and pulled me to
my feet.

"If you do not let me go, I'll scream. . . ."

But his mouth was on mine, the breath stopped in my
throat, his passionate kiss turning my knees to water, sending a wild thrill through my veins. I did not struggle; I
could not think, my mind, my will had deserted me. His
cordlike arms crushed me closer, and suddenly I realized
that he was trembling, too.

I broke away, and when he tried to draw me back, I hit
him.

"My God!" he exclaimed, "you perverse bitch!"

"Get out!" I screamed, my face flaming, shocked, bewildered, angry. "Get out! This is the last time I'll say it. Get
out!"

He stared at me for a long time without moving, breathing heavily, his eyes flashing. "All right," he said at last, his
fists clenched tightly at his sides. "No more. I'm finished.
I'll go. And you—stay here then—alone—here with young

Lewis—stay in this mausoleum, this tomb. I promise I shan't ever bother you again."

A moment later I heard the outer door slam.

It rained a great deal that winter, almost incessantly. People visited me less and less and finally not at all. I did not miss them. I nursed my loneliness, my seclusion, wore my pain like a hair shirt. I saw only the servants, now reduced to two, Lucinda and Gandy, and sometimes days would pass without my exchanging more than a few words even with them. There was little Cage, of course, who grew and grew. He slept, ate, smiled, waved his chubby arms and gurgled pleasantly when I smiled back. But for him I think I should have gone quietly mad.

Then one afternoon Octavia and Ted Neale rang the bell. They were like a breath of spring—young and fresh, rosy-cheeked and happy. I knew before they told me that Octavia had come around—they were in love.

"We are going to be married," Ted said, grinning down at a radiant Octavia.

"My dears—congratulations!" I said, pleased.

Octavia kissed me. "Oh, what a fool I've been, Aunt Adelaide!" she exclaimed, her eyes brimming. "What a fool not to know that . . ." She embraced me again, held me for a long time.

"Only one thing," she said, releasing me, looking solemn. "About Papa . . ."

"Oh, my dear, hush! I won't have you thinking that! I'm sure now Bart Hayley meant to kill him at that duel. So you needn't go on feeling guilty. It isn't deserved."

"Aunt Adelaide . . ." She kissed me once more.

She's different, I thought, not the same. She's changed, she's grown. She isn't a child any longer. And the thought made me feel curiously uneasy as if I had forgotten something, misplaced an important object, a concept, an idea.

They stayed for tea. It had been so long since I had had anyone to pour tea for that I had almost forgotten how. It felt good though, good to talk, to have someone besides myself sitting in the heavily draped drawing room.

"We have been talking about the wedding, planned for June, a small one—just a few friends," Ted Neale said. Octavia did not want to be married from the Folly. She considered it bad luck, and though I didn't like the term "bad luck," secretly I could hardly blame her. Weddings were happy affairs; they should have no reminders of tragedy. They were to be married at the Shelbys with a reception to be held afterwards.

"How kind of Clara," I said, for, of course, Cage had left so little money I could not have afforded to give Octavia even the simplest of weddings.

"Yes, Aunt Adelaide," Ted agreed. "You do have good friends. Jay Cooke especially. What a grand gesture that was, his picking up the mortgage on the Folly so that you can go on living here."

"What?" I asked sharply. "What did you say?"

"The mortgage, Aunt Adelaide. Jay—good Lord!" He put his hand over his mouth. "Did I speak out of turn? Perhaps you weren't supposed to know—oh, my. . . ." He seemed truly distressed.

"Please, it's all right, Ted. I'm glad you told me."

When they had gone I sat for a long time in the shadowed drawing room lost in thought. I was remembering—recalling that time long ago when Jay had taken me to Aunt Tildy's from New Orleans, and how his jeering had caused me to become angry rather than self-pitying. I remembered the times I had come to him for help rather than speak to Cage, how it had always seemed easier to talk about my deepest troubles with Jay. I remembered his touch, his kiss—I did not want to remember, but I did. He loved me, he said, like a man.

And I thought of Cage, for the first time in all the years I had known him, I thought of him as he was, not as part of me, not as my dream lover, my husband, but as he really was. And the picture was not pretty. He drank, he womanized, he gambled, and he lied. Perhaps he could not help it—that was Cage. What had Jay said? "I do not think he ever really tried to hide the kind of man he was—but you didn't want to see."

Yes, I had not wanted to see. But I did now. This last, this recent gesture of Jay's, this quietly paying the mortgage on the Folly (and how dense of me not to guess when the bank failed to foreclose), had shown how unselfish love could be. A grown man's love. And I had been willing to throw it away, for what? A false memory. A wish to spend the rest of my life in a house steeped in blight. A mausoleum, Jay had called it. A tomb, a grave. Did I really want to be counted as one of the living dead?

I got up from my chair and went out into the hall. How quiet it was, how somber, how gloomy. I started up the stairs, those mirrored, shadowed stairs, slowly at first, then faster and faster until I was running, climbing two steps at a time, breathless, but laughing, laughing at last.

That night I wrote a long letter to Jay.

It has been two years since that afternoon in the drawing room when everything seemed to come together, the pattern of my life, the depth of my self-deception revealed as clearly as the stones in a crystal stream. One year and three months since I have been Mrs. Jay Cooke. A year and three months since I have known for the first time the real meaning of happiness, of love, of a good marriage. Soon little Lewis Cage shall have a new brother or sister. I think he will like that for he is a generous child, a loving one. Jay bought us a house in South Park, a section situated at the bottom of the hill from my former home, a charming English-style residence with white shutters and a fretted iron picket fence. If I lean out of an upstairs window and crane my neck, I can just see the chimneys of the Folly peeping above the tree tops.

It stands empty now—no one has lived there since the day I walked away from it with Lewis Cage in my arms—a ghost-haunted place with broken windows and overgrown vines clambering over the weather-stained sills. Yet despite the ravages of time and the havoc of wind, rain and sun, it remains grandly flamboyant, garishly proud, a fitting monument to a man, to a love that died with my coming of age—Cage's Folly—and mine.

Laurie McBain

*Once in her life, every woman must
leave her sheltered world and . . .*

Chance The Winds of Fortune

**Continuing *The Glorious Saga* Begun in
*MOONSTRUCK MADNESS***

Fortune smiled on Dante Leighton, titled lord turned
pirate. Sailing before the Sea Dragon's towering masts,
he plundered hearts and cargos from the Carolinas to
Trinidad's turquoise lagoons. But one treasure always
eluded him. . . . Until, a world away, at the English country
estate of Lucien and Sabrina Dominick, a series of
dazzling intrigues results in the abduction of their
golden-haired daughter, Rhea. . . . And now, in a
gathering wave of turbulent emotion, the fates of Rhea
and Dante converge unforgettably—in a quest for
sunken Spanish treasure . . . and a love worth
a thousand fortunes!

AVON   75796/$2.95   CW 7-80